Y0-BZJ-666

Next Year's Promise

After a wild ride...

Slade gave her a careful once-over before he spoke. "I should've known that a well-bred, city woman like you wouldn't let loose. Won't let things come as they do. Can't handle a rut in the road, a creekbed, or—"

"W*hat* else?" Anne fumed.

He leaned over and gently pushed aside windblown strands of hair from her cheek.

"Getting your face dirty."

Counting from ten backwards, Anne wiped her mouth with the back of her hand. Her bones nearly pulverized, she was supposed to have enjoyed the experience. If that weren't fun enough, Slade's cryptic remarks would finish the job.

"First, you're wrong. And I don't get what any of that has to do with your recklessness." She snatched her sunglasses from her pocket and wiped the dust off them with her shirttail.

Slade stood and pulled her to her feet. The gleam in his eyes set her to wishing for something she shouldn't.

"Reckless? Hell, this is what I call reckless," he said and moved his face toward hers.

What They Are Saying About
Next Year's Promise

"Plots and subplots enhance this romance, while virtual characters deal with true problems. The beauty of the Aussie Outback draws a pictorial of the dusty, hot summer. The symbolism of the dry, fiery bush and the seductive dialect tempt the reader to travel deep into this well researched romance." 4½ Stars

—Nancy B. Leake
Affaire de Coeur
Sept./Oct., 2001

"NEXT YEAR'S PROMISE fulfills its promise of action, suspense, and... love. This year's must read."

—Betty Jo Schuler
Author of Winning Chance
Wordbeams.com

"I enjoyed reading about my country through such a spirited heroine's eyes."

—Lisa Annis
Sydney, Australia

"Slade McGregor surprises and enchants as he tussles with ambitious Anne Kingsley in the most captivating way. Don't miss NEXT YEAR'S PROMISE."

—Gail Fuller
Hamilton, Ontario, Canada

Wings

Next Year's Promise

by

Karen Hudgins

A Wings ePress, Inc.

Contemporary Romance

Wings ePress, Inc.

Edited by: Lorraine Stephens
Copy Edited by: Cindy Vallar
Senior Editor: Pat Casey
Managing Editor: Kate Strong
Executive Editor: Lorraine Stephens
Cover Artist: Crystal Laver

All rights reserved

Names, characters and incidents depicted in this book are products of the author's imagination or are used fictitiously. Any resemblance to actual events, locales, organizations, or persons, living or dead, is entirely coincidental and beyond the intent of the author or the publisher.

No part of this book may be reproduced or transmitted in any form or by any means, electronic or mechanical, including photocopying, recording, or by any information storage and retrieval system, without permission in writing from the publisher.

Wings ePress Books
http://www.wings-press.com

Copyright © 2001 by Karen Hudgins
ISBN 1-59088-985-1

Published In the United States Of America

November 2001

Wings ePress Inc.
403 Wallace Court
Richmond, KY 40475

Dedication

For George, my husband, who kept the faith.

Acknowledgements

Some friends deserve my grateful appreciation for answering questions, referring me to resources, and understanding what it means to write a book. Lisa Annis, in Sydney—thanks for your enthusiastic support and help with research, and introducing me to Bronwyn Turner, who shared first-hand knowledge of sheep station life at Briarleigh. Also for research assistance, my thanks go to Fiona Simpson, who feeds kangaroos over her back fence in West Kempsey. Kim Shepherd helped with the Attunga region, and Lindsay Irons and Kathryn Wenham baked fresh damper for us on a fall afternoon in St. Louis. Steve Plagens provided facts on the ad game. Special thanks go to Gail Fuller and Betty Jo Schuler for critiquing and being such good pals along the way.

One

Anne Kingsley drove by more sheep than she could ever count on a sleepless night. Thousands grazed and roamed the dirty blonde pastures of the Red Gum Station. They appeared to be contented, perfect really. Unlike her, the woolies *belonged* here in the Australian bush country.

Sighing, she brushed red grit from her white shirt. The last part of the four-wheeler trip had proved the roughest. Almost more than she could handle. But after she'd arrived at the main house, the housekeeper served her tea that went down smoothly. She smiled. At least, she found one familiar comfort.

Alone now in the McGregors' living room, Anne gazed up at an Aboriginal painting above the fireplace mantel. Creamy strokes mingled with dots and swishes of brown, pale green and yellow ocher.

More than art, it seemed to be a visual puzzle. She stepped closer, yet the subject of the portrait stayed hidden. Curious, she lingered for a moment, then turned away with her briefcase in-hand. Sinking onto the edge of the big easy chair opposite the television, she pulled her cell phone from her pocket and rang the office.

"Greene and Associates Advertising," garbled through.

"Hi, Jack."

1

"Kingsley? Tell me you made it."

"In one piece, but the fan belt went out on the Land Cruiser. I had to wait in Attunga for a new one." She massaged her left temple with her fingers. "Nice enough people, and I ate a meat pie for breakfast, but can you imagine wanting to live out here? I mean, this feels so removed."

Jack chuckled. "Buck up, city girl. You're on assignment. How's it going with the McGregors?"

"I've not met either of them yet. The housekeeper said she's not sure when Slade or his grandfather will be back."

Anne turned to the window and glimpsed the last few hundred yards of the road that led her into the heart of the sheep station. The dirt lay empty, baking in the February sun.

"She also said that 'Slade runs by his own clock.'"

"That's no surprise. It's a whole different way of life out there."

"Mmm hmm, sure is." She fidgeted. Hesitant about leaving Sydney, she still knew this area would provide perfect backdrops for the commercials she would be shooting in the next few weeks. "I'll call for the crew when McGregor and his grandfather sign the release," she said, hearing a shuffle of papers from Jack's end.

"Better be soon. The home office called. Greene wants you back in Westport by the end of March."

Anne pinched the phone. "Please say you're joking."

"You know I'm not, and he—"

"But I'm contracted to be in Sydney until July."

"Yes, and things have changed. Fast. Jean Linden Products is going to promote a new cosmetic line, and they want you leading creative on the project. So congratulations."

Anne exhaled. This chance would be fantastic, but she didn't want to go back home yet. She needed time to regroup, and the change of scenery had already helped.

2

"Jack, I don't know. I'm not ready—"

"Look," he said, softening his tone. "You had a tough time last year. Just hang in there with us."

"What else can I do?"

He paused and then added, "You know what retaining this account means. For all of us, if you get my drift."

How couldn't I? she wondered. JLP, skin care division of a mega-corporation, ranked number one on the agency's client list. When it emerged as a major sponsor of the Sydney 2000 Olympic Games, Greene & Associates immediately set up a field office to better serve the firm in its advertising needs.

Jack went on. "You'll soon be our best creative project person. You're gaining experience and putting quality stuff out to build yourself a name. Now you've been handed a golden JLP apple. Eat it wisely."

She responded with gratitude. Her colleague of three years possessed an uncanny feel for the business, and she respected his judgement.

"So don't disappoint us. And try to understand where I'm coming from when I say don't let your personal life get in the way. You're free now, Anne. Play your cards right. Greene's watching and he hates being wrong."

Anne's mind reeled. What Jack meant was that if she didn't come home with the bacon on this project, it'd be her job. Could even cost her a career. Pride, anger, and fear competed for expression. She should be happy, but for now the prospect of returning to Westport left her cold.

She closed her eyes and hoped to sort everything out later. With her thumb and forefinger she worried her bare ring finger. Why couldn't certain things in life just go away? Like the slightly indented skin beneath her touch.

"Of course," she heard herself agree, reopening her eyes. "Anything for our client. I'll be in touch soon."

"Now you're talking. Let's knock 'em dead and Greene on his ass."

She said goodbye and put the phone away. The clock in the hallway ticked as she sipped more tea and gazed at her surroundings.

This room, comfortable and quite lived in, was more than a place. It was another person's life. Obviously, someone who was very different from her. A man lived here with his work around-the-clock, or at least it seemed that way. Except for the raising of smelly ewes, she understood this kind of dedication.

Two tawny leather couches claimed space at right angles to the sandstone hearth. Reading glasses sat unfolded atop a clipboard with tally sheets beside a half-rolled-up blueprint. Outdated wool industry trade journals and mail littered the coffee table.

She pushed herself up from the chair and gazed expectantly at the arched doorway that led into the room. Seeing no one, she turned away and began to pace. Until last Christmas, she'd unveiled creative production plans in swank corporate conference rooms.

Thus, a sheepskin, like the one slung over the back of another deep-cushioned chair, had been absent. So were the Wolf Blass Cabernet Sauvignon bottles poking through lattice work in an alcove on her left.

She tried to get a grip. Jack's news had excited and unsettled her. Quick footsteps approached from behind and made her start.

"You need some tucker, Miss, and a refill on that tea?"

Rose, the matronly housekeeper, carried a tray of refreshments to a dark wood trestle table along the wall.

"Thanks," Anne said, "but please don't make a fuss."

Fresh-bread aroma ambushed her while the silver-haired woman quickly laid out the food. "And why not?" She turned around and her pale violet eyes twinkled. "We don't see lady visitors from the city very often. Mostly sundowners or half-lit jackeroos wanting work come knocking at our door. Come, have a seat."

Anne, watching the woman note her gold earrings and red nail polish, said, "Well, not to be unkind, but this place is pretty far off the beaten track."

"Yes 'tis. That's one of the beauties of our rangeland. And after a while, living out here grows on a person. You become part of everything. And when this all becomes part of you," she said, tapping her fingers over her heart, "then you've become true-blue, and you'll never want to leave."

The woman spoke with such conviction that Anne regarded her for a moment. "I suppose it could, but my business won't keep me here that long. Actually, I'll be in Australia much less than I thought."

Rose humphed, as she freshened Anne's tea. "Indeed, I thought so too when I arrived twenty-three years ago. Came down from Brisbane to take care of Slade while his parents went on holiday to the UK. There's where his mum got very ill and died."

"Oh my, I'm sorry to hear that."

"What a time." Rose rubbed her finger over a button on her cotton print dress. "A year later Slade's father left for Perth to work for the railroad. Now Jim and Slade own the Red Gum and they're the bosses."

"I see. Well, they owe you a lot. For staying on, I mean."

"Some might not have thought so, but it worked out suitably." The housekeeper sliced a large, round baked good in generous chunks. "Will you have some damper and ginger marmalade?"

Anne liked the gentle woman and tried a piece. Busy as she must be, she seemed lonely. Much like herself, if she dared to think about it.

Rose whispered, "Now Slade would put my head on a shearing board if he heard me saying this, but don't be surprised if he acts perturbed. He still gets moody and goes out to be alone. I suppose it happens when he thinks back too much."

Anne stopped chewing. Problems always cropped up during film shoots. She was generally prepared to handle them, but dealing with a hostile property owner could get plenty sticky.

"Moody?"

"Yes. A fine man, he is. Except he's not been himself since his wife died last year. Oh, he's much better now, but he still spends time out at Hannah's hut, or doing work that's meant for the crews. Anything to keep busy, I suppose." She sighed. "'Tis a pity to watch a strong man like him dry up and forget his dreams."

Anne understood losing a loved one more than she cared to think about right now, but said, "Maybe he just needs more time."

Rose nodded. "That and someone to care for." Her voice faded as six chimes pealed from the clock. "Oh, dear. Excuse me. Our head stockman will be in to pick up supplies for tomorrow." She unfolded a napkin over the damper. "If you need something, I'll be in the kitchen. Make yourself at home, Miss."

"Thank you," Anne called after her and put away her smile. Her aching body still vibrated from the long, bone-rattling ride. Her eyes burned from dryness and strain, and her boots had grown tighter as the day wore on.

Until now, filming commercials in Sydney had kept her in her element—near the water—like Westport and Mystic Seaport. She understood the water and kindred spirits who followed its rhythms or respected its mysteries. She'd often taken sail herself.

Growing restless, she looked out the window again that framed nothing but land, land, and more land. The orange sun had dropped behind rolling ridges. Surely, Slade McGregor would come home tonight. Even loners had to eat.

"Then again, maybe not." Shaking her head, she noticed a map case that had been left in the center of the long table. She gave in to her insatiable curiosity and pulled the cylinder toward herself. The cap popped off easily, and she withdrew the contents of the case. Her palms now supported a roll of thick, yellowed bark paper. Cinched in the middle with raffia, the document *felt* important.

Slowly, she unrolled the piece of work and placed her briefcase on one edge and a pewter sheep paperweight on the other in order to keep it flat.

"How beautiful," she murmured, examining the detailed cartography. Aboriginal border designs and quality workmanship resembled that on the painting on the wall behind her. Original and impeccable, it added a wonderful artistic touch to a very practical document.

Standing up, she leaned over and rested her elbows on the table. She could identify some of the locations featured in the aerial photographs that she'd brought along of the Red Gum Station. Winding routes to the sites reached far and wide.

Enthralled, Anne marveled about what some people in the world called their "backyard."

~ * ~

Slade McGregor ambled into his living room and halted at the view. A woman was leaning over the trestle table and inspecting his property map. So here's the guest, he grumbled inwardly. A curious, meddling one at that.

He removed his bush hat and gazed at her long khaki-chino clad legs. Tempting, they disappeared into new, expensive boots. A baggy blue shirt hid her rump and her hair waved onto her shoulders. An uncomfortable twist stirred in him.

He conceded that she added certain vibrancy to the room, but she was still an unwanted visitor. He waited a moment, then tossed his hat onto the table where it skidded across the burled wood and careened into her forearm. She jumped like a scared rabbit.

"Find what you're looking for?" he asked smoothly.

Anne whirled around to face him and struggled to keep her balance. "It's magnificent, but I was… "

Fueling his chagrin, he found her parted lips appealing, and she seemed near his own age of twenty-eight. The mug she held in her hand wobbled and dipped, causing its contents to slop over the brim, soar and splash onto the middle of his property map. With disbelief he watched black liquid race across the North Paddock near Mount Kamilaroi.

Slade stiffened, fighting his urge to usher her out the front door. But it was too late for that. The sun was about to go down and even he wouldn't put a Yankee sheila out loose at night.

"I'm Slade McGregor."

Wide-eyed and seemingly vulnerable, she stammered, "Hello. I'm Anne. Anne... Kingsley." In spite of himself, he took stock of her again. Any woman who made it out here on her own must be super determined or else have a few roos loose in her top paddock. He reckoned he didn't need either.

"You've made yourself at home," he noted aloud. Whether this filming venture was a good thing or not for the station, outsiders brought trouble. Too often he'd been called to find their sorry butts in the fog, winch their stuck vehicles out of mud, or return their forgotten belongings.

"A little. Your housekeeper is very kind."

"Yes, Rose is good at what she does."

"And she cares."

He nodded affably, but gritted his teeth. This intruder noticed things. More than ever, he wasn't of a mind to put up with one. He needed to keep things in control, uncomplicated. Just do what he did best. Take care of the sheep, get the wool to market, let all the bad dust settle, and finish the wool scouring plant. Simple. But he didn't fool himself by expecting renewed inner peace. That would evade him forever.

As he strode forward, Anne moved her feet slightly apart to steady herself. Sable brown and large, her well-spaced eyes now held his. Exploring their warmth and intelligence, he soon bumped into an impenetrable wall. He wanted to scale it, but retreated instead. Slowly, on his own terms.

"That was an original map," he said tersely.

"I'm so sorry." Anne straightened the mug. Her voice, soft and durable like brushed fleece, touched him deep inside. A strange mix of feelings put him on further edge.

He untied the red bandanna from around his neck. Before he could say 'lambing season' the woman snatched the cloth from him and began to dab up the mess.

"Please, let me help." Sincere regret shone in her eyes, and he held onto it until his skepticism barged in. He spied her briefcase—a symbol of independence, inflated ego, and little time for family? Maybe, but the tapestried flowers looked homey, more traditional and old-fashioned than she appeared.

He narrowed his eyes. Hell. Sure as a mob of sheep followed the bellwether, she'd want something more than what she'd come here for. As far as he knew it was some kind of a woman's code to take more than she gives.

He forced a smile, but something about her seemed familiar. Possibly her voice? Her hair? He couldn't be certain, but he *knew* he'd never looked into her eyes. Those he would've remembered.

"It's... It's only a map," he said, his conscience taking over. After all, he did throw her off guard. "But an important one. A partnership gift from my grandfather."

"If it's any help, my employer's insurance will cover the value," she said, handling the paper with care.

He moved next to her. The Boronia perfume she wore took him by surprise. These wildflowers bobbed in March's autumn wind along Rainbow Canyon. Taking another whiff, he flung away the memory and glanced back at the damaged map.

"Another can be made, if necessary," he said. With an authoritative flick of his wrist, he yanked the chain on the overhead lamp for better light.

~ * ~

Anne watched Slade as amber rays coasted down over his sun-streaked hair and his strong-planed jaw that needed a shave. Offsetting a straight nose and mouth, his chin held a slight cleft. His eyes sparkled blue and clear, but remained unreadable.

Sleeves rolled up and dusty, his plaid shirt hugged broad shoulders. He slid his hands, tanned and ringless, along his blue-jeaned thighs, then went to work repositioning the map.

Despite the dryness in her throat, she collected her wits and handed him a business card she withdrew from her pocket.

"I appreciate your accommodating my visit on such short notice," she said.

"Nice, but your gratitude is misplaced." His Aussie accent flattered his firm words. "You're here because my grandfather invited your agency to come out to film."

"Okay. That's true." A believer in teamwork, she regretted hearing this. "Nevertheless, the makers of SunMate Sunscreen will be very pleased. And so will my boss."

He gave her card a quick glance and put it in his pocket.

"You're a long way from home, Anne Kingsley."

"Yes, I am. About fifteen time zones worth. You see, we've opened a temporary field office in Sydney."

He was looking at her, not staring, merely surveying. Embarrassment warmed her cheeks. What were those intelligent eyes seeing, or wanting to see? Returning his inquiring gaze, she drew back for a moment, sensing sorrow and a fierce restlessness in him.

"Advertising?" he asked abruptly. "The art of persuasion."

She blinked. "I beg your pardon?"

He crossed his arms and cocked his head to one side.

"That's the nature of your work, isn't it? Persuading people to buy things."

Anne flashed a quick smile about his assessment. She'd often run into curiosity or cynicism about her livelihood.

"There's a lot more to it than that. We help build business futures. Our clients get quality from us, not idle billing hours. And they gain first-rate TV spots. Nothing is second-best."

He hooked his thumbs through his jean loops. Although his slow half-smile was probably natural for him, it taunted her. Giving this man one inch would be a huge, dangerous mistake. Or, worse yet, if she let her imagination go one more round, it'd be all over. Surly as he was, Slade McGregor was still sexier than he had a right.

"Do you realize," she added, struggling to keep on course, "that most of your possessions are advertised in one medium or another?"

He glanced around. "I reckon that's fair dinkum."

She'd learned this Aussie expression meant "true" from her little Aussie dictionary and went on. "Advertising is a big business, Mr. McGregor. It informs people, entertains, and sells many things, like... *wool* sweaters."

A faint smile tripped across his mouth.

"Name's Slade."

She watched his eyes ramble over her as she moved around the table. The soft white cotton jersey under her open chambray shirt replaced her customary business attire. She sat down across from where he stood.

"Okay... Slade. Now can we get to work?"

"It's your show."

The locks on her case sprang open under her touch. She pulled out a large manila envelope and two sets of assorted photographs and laid them in neat stacks.

She looked up at her host. His facial expression changed to apathy while he went to the sideboard and opened a decanter. Prying her eyes off him proved more than difficult.

"Would you like a brandy?" he asked.

"None for me, thank you." She quickly pulled out a notepad and pen.

"Not one to mix business and pleasure?"

Her heart thumped. Unknowingly, he'd touched a nerve.

"Actually, I'm not. And I still have some tea."

Splashing the liquor into a snifter, he asked, "Just a question, but are you always in such a hurry, Ms. Kinglsey?"

"It must seem that way to you. But we operate on deadlines. My crew and I will cause you as little inconvenience as possible. We'll do our jobs and leave in about three weeks."

"Now there's a plan."

She winced. More than moody, this man was downright difficult. Trying to take his manner in stride, she arranged a dozen of the color photographs into a grid that formed an at-a-glance composite of his sheep station.

"These are the aerial shots we took last Thursday."

Cocking an eyebrow, Slade returned to the table and dragged out the chair next to her and sat down. His body warmth filtered through her sleeve, making her skin tingle.

"I remember the day well," he said and viewed the layout. "The plane buzzed our North Paddock. Then we had a helluva time mustering our ewes. Noise makes merinos contrary."

Anne frowned. Sometimes conducting business on location caused unexpected problems. Surely even he, living in this God-forsaken outback field, encountered those. But she turned on her diplomacy, short-lived as it was.

"Okay, I apologize on behalf of our firm. The service we contracted does fly at legal cruising altitude."

"If I'd been consulted before you ever—"

"Perhaps you should discuss that with your grandfather."

"It's been tossed about."

"Oh? Did he tell you that he granted verbal permission for the aerial survey—"

"I heard."

"—which is also appreciated, because the process is expensive. This way reduces ground travel and saves time."

"And time is money?"

"My, you catch on quick," she replied.

"In my business, more wool—"

"Means profit."

Giving her another appraising glance, he popped a piece of damper into his mouth and washed it down with brandy.

"You catch on quick, too, Anne. Faster than a gust-fed bush fire. Cheers."

The lamplight blazed between them, and although he'd paid her a compliment his facial expression still branded her foreign. She tried to ignore that and tapped the envelope with her fingertips.

"Since you and your grandfather are co-owners, the three of us need to discuss the conditions of this release agreement. Is he available to meet with us now?"

Slade dismissed her question with a shrug.

"What are those?"

Anne stewed over his arrogance and pushed the second stack toward him. "These are tight shots. The photographer zoomed in if he spotted something interesting."

"Interesting?"

"Well, yes. Useful. Topographic features that make exceptional settings where we could film. We were lucky. There are three such backdrops on your property. A different one can be used for each segment in the series."

For the first time Slade looked involved with what she was explaining. As he plucked the top one from the pile, she saw deep affection for the land rise in his eyes. The tight lines in his face relaxed, heightening his handsomeness.

The first photograph he held showed the ruddy creek that ox-bowed and disappeared under the crowns of giant red gum trees.

"This location," she said and touched the corner of the photograph with her gold pen, "gives a full range of textures and color. Viewers will feel as if they're paddling up that creek. Appeals to adventure-seeking individuals." Sliding into her world, she relaxed a bit. "They make up seventy-four percent of the market."

Slade nodded. "This is Mossman Creek. Floods mostly in winter, but it surprises us sometimes. By the eighteen eighties its gold was mined out."

Next, he viewed an open pasture with sun-bleached fence posts that leaned this way and that over rolling hills and eventually disappeared by a dry lake.

"A long shot of the country," Anne said. "Here we can zoom into the dramatization with our models."

"My grandfather and some musterers strung that seven-wire fence on the North Paddock. He practically lived outside, and he never used sunscreen."

"He doesn't worry about his skin?"

Slade threw his head back and laughed. "He doesn't worry about much of anything anymore, except Da-Wa's cooking. And we wear hats and long sleeves or dusters."

Anne smiled as he reached for the last photograph. Holding it in his hands, he scanned the glossy surface and zeroed in on its details. What was left of his humor faded. He rubbed the corner of the shot with his forefinger.

A rugged, deep ravine dominated this image. The gorge, surrounded by stratified ridges a half billion years old that probably first served as sea-floor sediment, held tall growing ferns, a waterfall, and colorful parrots. The place was called Rainbow Canyon. That much she knew.

"This is where I most want to film the end of the series," Anne said. "It'll be utterly perfect."

An immediate storm crossed Slade's face, stealing her reverie. He looked away and tossed aside the photograph. Finally turning toward her, he laid his troubled gaze upon her.

"Sorry, you can forget this area."

Stunned, Anne said, "But let me explain. The Canyon gives the best qualities needed. It's nearly impossible to find them— especially of this quality—in one spot. A unique, exotic and rugged piece of Australia. All here."

The glint in his eyes softened, and she sensed he liked her reasoning. However, he raised his palms.

"Not to disappoint you, but Rainbow Canyon is not an option." His voice carried unshakable finality. "And never will be."

Two

Anne tried to understand. "May I ask why not?"

Slade thought for a long moment and drew his forefinger over the map. "Only way to get to Rainbow Canyon is through Nourombie. That's a rugged, narrow passage that begins at Kissing Turtles and ends at the edge of the gorge."

She shrugged. "Oh, if that's all it is, there's no problem. My Land Cruiser—"

"Nourombie is restricted."

"Restricted? How can that be? Isn't it on your land?"

He nodded. "Legally, yes. But not originally, nor was it the Crown's. The Aborigines believe land isn't owned, only managed. They would like to claim native title for Nourombie to be able to manage it exclusively, but can't since the site is on private property. To help, my grandfather and I set up a gentlemen's agreement with them, really more of a gift. Now only Bilwan male initiates set foot into the passage, unless decided otherwise by the elders."

Anne shook her head in disbelief.

"Not even you can enter?"

"Nope. Not my sheep and dogs—or female visitors." He narrowed his right eye. "Interfering would be a mistake. Many

Bilwan people work for the Red Gum and have for a long time. We depend on them as much as they do on us."

She smothered a groan. Somebody missed a big detail, a very critical one. She couldn't access the canyon. Her heart sinking, she caught Slade's hard look.

"What's so special about Nourombie?"

"Part of it's a sacred dreaming site."

Anne pursed her mouth. She was skunked. From the air no one could have known the place was sacred. Sacred carried reverence and responsibility. Like a marriage blessed in heaven, worthy of respect and devotion and fulfilling. The way her life could have been back in Westport if she was still married to Lou.

"So you do understand now? It's not an option," Slade repeated. "Pick another place."

Any other time Anne would have dropped the matter. Although she admired Slade for honoring the culture's wishes, for some reason, she couldn't let this go. More than ever, her instinct ruled. If there was a way around this, she'd have to ferret it out. She ignored her conscience for a second and risked appearing insensitive.

"Anywhere else would be settling for second best. That won't work for me, I'm sorry."

While Slade scoured her with his eyes, her thoughts zoomed ahead to the project plan. Finishing the final episode of "SunMates for Life" starring super-model Susan Sornja and ex-football player Chase Gordon in that canyon assured the series commercial an undeniable edge.

Yet, the fact remained that Anne had leaped out of her citified league into unfamiliar back-country territory and she just might walk away empty-handed.

Slade's voice sliced through her thoughts. "Does 'no' mean something else in Connecticut?"

She lifted the corners of her mouth into an instant sweet smile. A solution popped into her mind, and she widened the smile, making it genuine.

"Look, why don't we ask? All I want to do is cross it to get to Rainbow Canyon, which isn't sacred. I promise not to take pictures, litter, or dig for gold."

He squared his shoulders and Anne upped the ante.

"We're prepared to make it financially worthwhile."

"Does it look like I need your money?" Slade smirked and downed the last of his brandy.

"I meant for the Bilwan people."

He pointed at the map. "Money doesn't fix everything."

Making one last stab at it, she pleaded. "Listen, Rainbow is critical to what we're doing for our client. What we'll offer will certainly reflect this, believe me, and we won't divulge the name of our shooting location if that's necessary."

Slade fell stone silent.

Looking into his reticent eyes, she laid down her pen with a flourish. His obstinance over the matter utterly amazed and challenged her. He knew these people, and the least he could do was give it a shot. So why wouldn't he?

She probed deeper through the layers of blue in his irises. His manner indicated that much more was at stake. Had he given her a real reason, or thrown a big smokescreen?

Her impression of Slade now jumbled into a distorted array. An enigma, indeed, he put forth a laid-back image. But she sensed an unsettling undertow threading through him. Her well-trained eye easily stripped away facades. Studying art, one always started with the foundation to understand what showed on the outside. Many things hung on a skeleton, and that's where one could find personality and truth.

Her skepticism rose. Slade's answer about Nourombie came almost too quickly to believe, and her industry thrived on reaching agreements all the time against the worst of odds.

She wished Slade's grandfather, Jim, was here. After all, he and Jack had made the preliminary arrangements for this project. Certainly the senior owner knew about this problem and could fix it.

She rose and glanced out the window. Dull sienna rays silhouetted the scalloped horizon. Even the sunset looked different, wild. Jumping at her to be committed to film.

"You'll have to excuse me," she said and scooped up the photographs, figuring it was useless to continue the discussion for now. "Can you and your grandfather meet me in the morning?"

Slade's hair still shone like streaked gold under the lamplight as he pushed himself off the chair. His frown disappeared.

"Suit yourself. I'm also interested in seeing him," he said resolutely. "He's overseeing a scratch muster. You can ride along with me early in the morning. Meet me on the veranda at seven, if you want to go along, Mrs. Kingsley."

"Anne," she reminded him. "And I'm not married anymore."

A niggling knot tightened in her chest as he gazed at her ring finger. She scrambled to change the subject.

"Scratch muster? What's that?"

A slow smile lit his face.

"Finding strays. Don't dress up. The weather's supposed to turn dirty."

Aware or not, Slade mercilessly taunted her curiosity and tested her patience. Nearing her limit, she willed her thoughts back to her mission: obtain the customary release—which wasn't a usual part of her job—call the director and crew and finish filming, then get back to Sydney and the world she knew.

"Tea will be ready soon," he added, stretching.

Anne's stomach churned from hunger and nerves. She'd found out that "tea" meant dinner, which seemed upside-down like everything else had just turned. She decided to make do with the bottled apple juice, amaretto biscotti, and cheese she'd carried with her. Rest would soothe her nerves.

"I think I'll do breakfast, thank you, and I really am sorry about your map." She gathered her belongings and caught up with him in the hallway. Her thoughts mistakenly slipped into words. "At least the stain didn't cover the route to Rainbow Canyon."

Slade stopped and slowly turned around. He rested his hands on his hips. His warning look reduced her to damn near precocious child status.

"Don't be a fool, or count on me for being one."

Her pulse soared. A mere fifteen inches separated their noses. His male sensuality stirred her, and his ire fueled her own. What kind of businesswoman did he take her for?

"Advice noted," she said. "I'll bring the rest of my things from the car."

Slade nodded and stalked farther down the hall, opened a door and shut it behind him, leaving her completely puzzled. One moment the grazier exuded warmth and compassion. The next, he blew colder than a coastal winter wind.

Somehow, she'd stepped into a dangerous, unfamiliar game. In her work, she engaged in reasonable games, but disliked playing them since no one escaped politics. So later on, while she bathed crusty, red dust from her skin, the irony of the whole situation struck her: *Games.* She'd barreled all the way out here to film commercials to be aired during the most famous of games—the Olympics. Her employer depended upon her to win the gold, so to speak. If she missed this chance, she may as well forget the JLP opportunity or building a career. There was no second place in the ad game at Greene & Associates.

Trying to relax, she sighed and slid deeper into the rose-scented, bubbly water—one comfort she could never give up.

~ * ~

Early next morning Anne waited for Slade on the veranda. She'd slept fitfully and had come out after eating a rather good breakfast prepared by Slade's Chinese cook, Da-Wa. Listening to the colorful parrots' chatter, she breathed in the already-too-warm air. Holding the leather handle of her attaché case, she opened her senses to roam over the unfamiliar surroundings. What ancient secrets lay buried under the grasses, swirled in river water, or roamed over the loose tarn shed by Mount Kamilaroi that loomed off hazily in the distance?

The changing light, filtered by mist rising from the creek, dappled the gum trees and scrubby wattle. Beyond the fence of weathered pickets stood her leased Cruiser. Its hunter green paint peeked through splotches of red-brown mud.

But the air smelled fresh and she could half believe the housekeeper's sentiment about loving the place. Love grew from respect, and this strange and beautiful country demanded it. Adoration for a place could only happen after learning the reasons why it was the way it was.

This rolling land had its own character and a heart needing to be understood, similar to the hearts of men and women.

She rechecked her watch. Seven o'clock had passed thirty-five minutes ago.

"Is it just me, or does he have no concept of time?"

She turned around, and as she reached the front door, a loud noise sputtered from around the corner of the house. In seconds the abrasive source burst into full view.

Motorcycle, man, and dog zoomed hell-bent-for-leather past the end of the porch. Through the billowy dust she recognized Slade's sun-streaked hair and smooth hat.

Like a stallion, Slade throttled up and charged in a full circle, negotiated a figure-eight around two trees, hesitated, then made a bee-line for the porch. He seemed different this morning. Ready-to-roll and dashingly handsome.

An unspeakable thrill curled her insides. Surely, he was going out of his way to display his riding prowess. But she held little regard for a show-off. She struggled to keep her personal and professional opinions separate. Slade was her host, and she needed his help.

She smiled warily. For a second she feared he'd roar right up the steps, run over her and her trusty briefcase, wiping out her and her project.

She peered over the frames of her sunglasses at his face while his mouth lifted a trifle at the corners. An element of frolic, or satisfaction over scaring the wits out of her? Taking on the challenge, she planted her feet firmly on the porch and tightened her fingers around the handle of her case.

The gleam in his eyes told her he wouldn't hit her. Nevertheless, her next breath lodged in her throat. Something magnificent about him attracted her. But high seas flags flapped in her mind. Yielding to temptation would be so dangerous and possibly destructive.

Anne lifted her chin as the wheels spun parallel to the bottom step and he skidded to a halt. Dust spewed up the steps and showered her pant legs and boots. Glaring, she coughed and shifted her sunglasses to the top of her head.

Slade threw out a leg for balance, dismounted the faded red Triumph, and clunked his boot heel against the kickstand.

"Down, Dusty." The black and white Border collie relaxed his eagle-claw grip and dropped to the ground from his perch of carpet slung over the gas tank. Tail wagging, the dog bounded up to her. She smiled into his bright eyes.

Slade reached the top step and nodded.

"Good morning," she said as evenly as possible.

"G'day. Looks like the new plugs work." He hooked his thumb over his shoulder toward the bike.

Anne's stomach fluttered. Apparently, a simple mechanical test prompted his little show of skill. Disappointment tinged her ego.

"Hmm, hmm," she murmured. "Do you think your grandfather is close by so we can meet?"

Slade pulled off his gloves, stuffed them into his back pockets, and then leaned against the railing. He gestured toward her briefcase and frowned. "We'll find him, but you'll have to leave that here."

She shot him a surprised glance. "Where I go, it goes." Her briefcase served as her lifeline. Everything she needed was in there. She tightened her grip.

"Have it your way," he relented and shrugged. Although the iron roof overhead did a fine job of providing shade, he squinted. "Have you ever been on a bike?"

She swallowed. "Never. Riding isn't something I'd like."

His eyes glinted and despite the uneasiness rising in her, logic interceded. She should meet him on his ground.

"Really? Come with me." He pushed his hat farther back on his head, and the two of them left the porch. Beside the bike Slade lifted the flap of a skin pouch that was Jury-rigged to the back fender. He removed a length of rope and two faded red bandannas and halved the hemp with a pocketknife.

"Shouldn't we take my car?" she suggested.

"Not where we're going."

Dusty ran circles around them.

"And your dog rides, too?"

"Yep. We cover a lot of ground. May I?" He pulled the case from her hand. "Now turn around."

She faced the porch, but kept a cautious eye on him over her shoulder while he fashioned the rope into a sling and slipped it around her case, then lifted the assembly onto her back.

He said close to her left ear, "This ought to do."

The warmth of his breath sped to her nape and rested like a cloud. But the weight of the case hung like a daypack she'd used long ago at Wellesley. He looped the ropes, now padded with bandannas, over her shoulders and tied off the loose ends.

"Well, I'm not so sure that it will," she replied.

"Trust me."

Anne stiffened. He had no idea what a tall order that was. He raised her arms a bit and pulled her closer to him. His leatherwood scent, the early breeze, and his sure smile worked some kind of magic on her. For a crazy moment, she imagined herself settling into the warmth and security of his arms.

"You're ready," he said, admiring his handiwork.

She looked down. The rope, finished off with a lopsided bow, encircled her waist and the briefcase stayed put. He walked around and slapped dust off the sorry excuse for a passenger seat before giving a quick spiel about working with the front rider, leaning into turns, and other safety tips.

Braver, she put her hand on his shoulder for balance and straddled the seat behind him. He gave a short whistle for Dusty and changed gears. The rumble of the motor rivaled the one in her heart and signaled they'd passed the point of no return.

He maneuvered the bike past the front gate and onto the dirt road. Her inner thighs hugged the outside of his, and the bottoms of her feet pressed against the inner soles of her boots. Anything to make her feel more grounded.

Slade glanced at her in the broken mirror, then opened up the throttle. She dared to look at his world whizzing by over the breadth of his shoulders. He seemed a large man, even out here in country that minimized mountains, and he steered the bike with ease, oblivious to her concerns.

Air whooshed through her hair and pried her cares away. Something sensual hit her about all this from every direction.

When the road changed, Slade downshifted and relaxed his legs. They pressed against hers. Inappropriate, she knew, but very inviting. Motor noise and wind prevented holding a conversation of any sort. Just as well. She would only tell him she wanted off when she caught her breath. This was too precarious, too—exciting.

"Hold on," rushed past her ears.

A muddy creek zoomed into view ahead. She retightened her grip around Slade's waist. Downhill they sped right into the narrow rock-forded creek and slowed up only when the tires hit bottom. Coffee-colored water split and splashed up over them. Her feet jarred loose from the pillion pedals. The bike dug into the soft earth and fishtailed up the low bank.

Slade lifted his head and roared with laughter.

The man was in his element, but she was losing her wits.

"Stop! Stop right now," she cried, smacking her palm against his shoulder. Business deal or not, she wasn't going to risk her personal safety, or put up with being the butt-end of a joke.

He pulled up past a stand of trees. Beaming, he made a half-twist toward her.

"Bonzer ride, eh?"

Anne scowled. There wasn't anything terrific about it. If her knees weren't shaking, she'd haul herself off the seat and deck him.

"You certainly do enjoy yourself!" she rasped, putting her weight on her right foot and dragging her left over the seat. She sank onto the ground and seethed up through the sunlight at Slade McGregor. Was he trying to scare her away?

His smile disappeared, and he shut off the motor. Dusty licked her whitened knuckles as Slade kneeled by her side.

"I should've known better," he said, helping her slip out of the shoulder ropes. Uncapping a canteen, he poured water into a cup for her.

"Yes, you should have," she snapped. "Wait. Known what better?"

He gave her a careful once-over before he spoke. "That a well-bred, city woman like you wouldn't let loose. Won't let things come as they do. Can't handle a rut in the road, a creekbed, or—"

"What else?" she fumed.

He leaned over and gently pushed aside windblown strands of hair from her cheek.

"Getting your face dirty."

Counting from ten backwards, Anne wiped her mouth with the back of her hand. Her bones nearly pulverized, she was supposed to have enjoyed the experience. If that weren't fun enough, Slade's cryptic remarks would finish the job.

"First, you're wrong. And I don't get what any of that has to do with your recklessness." She snatched her sunglasses from her pocket and wiped the dust off them with her shirttail.

Slade stood and pulled her to her feet. The look in his eyes set her heart to wishing for something she shouldn't.

"Reckless? Hell, this is what I call reckless," he said and moved his face toward hers.

Three

Anne flinched as Slade cradled her head with his right palm and wrapped his left arm around her. In an impulsive swoop he covered her lips with his. Her heart raced and her sunglasses toppled to the ground.

He set her senses afire, making her skin tingle. Deepening his imploring kiss, he dissolved her desire to run. For some reason, this stranger made her feel safe amidst the darkest danger she could encounter, a matter of the heart.

She fed on his frank longing—until she needed air. Earthly air. Not the thin, ethereal vapor where her consciousness had suddenly jettisoned her. A whimper escaped her throat as he released her and pulled his mouth away from hers.

"Now *that* was reckless," he said huskily.

His breath on her face carried the same effect as CPR, yet she didn't want to come back. She hadn't reciprocated and now it was too late. Speechless, she opened her eyes and looked up at him in time to catch a hint of surprise mixed with the passion in his eyes. Blast him! Without warning, he'd pulled her across the boundary that separated professionalism and personal pleasures.

In spite of his devilish move, her heart foretold, *the man's an angel*. But she didn't believe it. Slade McGregor translated into trouble. Unpredictable, he was the kind of man with whom she'd promised herself never to tangle. Too dark, too dangerous for her to handle on a good day, let alone while a sign over her heart still read CLOSED FOR REPAIRS.

Now she struggled with shame that her conscience served up. She was on company time, for heaven's sake. But *he* stepped way out of professionally acceptable bounds by kissing her.

Slade watched Anne's face stir from the effect of his confounded desire to kiss away her cheekiness. He was as far from reckless as the Red Gum was to the Southern Cross. But how could she know that? Confusion drummed in his head, loud and strong, and checked his confidence.

Sure, he made his point, but once his lips touched hers he went much further. A sorry state, but a small part of him no longer wanted to scare her off. Her loneliness seeped through his own and sparked a bright light like the sun warming the old game trail into Rainbow Canyon.

He released her, stepped back, and ran a thumb along his stubbled jaw. Getting closer to Anne Kingsley invited problems. Her determination, curiosity, and natural beauty formed the combination of attributes he appreciated in a woman. But she was clearly another ambush sent to him by Fate.

Getting close to her would complicate his life. If for no other reason, her curiosity would make him face certain matters. So far, he'd done a great job of burying them in a dark field of the past.

Managing the Red Gum now filled his days. He returned to the main house more. But he still often took care of matters from Hannah's hut, a convenient outstation away from the house. Here, as his wife read by the fire, he had worked on the plans for building a state-of-the-art wool scouring plant in New South Wales.

Slade shook away the memory and smiled warily when his captive finally opened her eyes. The breeze on his chest, where he'd felt her breasts nestle between the panels of his vest, cooled him. He knew her heart raced, too. Every beat resonated in his soul. So enticing, she was. He closed his eyes to rid her from his sight. Instead of the taste of her vanishing, the magic of her kiss echoed through him.

Looking past him, Anne gasped. One by one, Aboriginal men streamed from between waist-high brush onto the road and formed a half-circle around her and Slade. She'd met indigenous people, but this was unexpected. Dressed in loose, dusty pants and faded print shirts, they still appeared a bit intense.

"I'll handle this," Slade said.

Relief broke through her. "Good. I'd hate to make trouble by doing something... reckless."

She returned his admonishing glance and stepped closer to him as a broad-faced bushman with coal-black eyes, a crop of thick hair, and heavy build approached them.

Slade nodded. "G'day, Rudy. On your way back in?"

"Soon, boss. We need to forge another set of iron pegs." He pulled a rusted spike from his pocket.

Anne kept close to her host. Back and forth the conversation flew in English and a few guttural phrases. Slade gestured toward her. She now faced a collective curious stare. Much head nodding followed and Slade pulled her closer.

"Anne, this is Rudy Nara. He's my head stockman."

"How nice to meet you."

Rudy stepped forward and shook her hand. He was self-assured and at ease. His firm handshake impressed her most.

"My pleasure," he said in the deepest baritone voice she'd ever heard. The contrast between his ragged appearance and his social presence struck her.

"Your artwork is beautiful."

Pride brightened the man's eyes.

"You know my work?"

"Yes, I saw some of it back at the house," she said tentatively.

"I learned from my father and his."

Anne relaxed into a business state of mind. "It's excellent. As a matter of fact, a friend of mine and her husband own a small gallery in Santa Fe. Perhaps, she—"

Slade cut her off and addressed Rudy. "We've some matters to settle with my grandfather. Have you seen him?"

He shook his head, then asked his men. A tall, thin crewman responded and Rudy translated his answer.

"Your grandfather rode up to Tailem Flat yesterday. He scratch mustered until sunset."

Anne gazed at Slade, half expecting him to nod, but a frown wrinkled his forehead.

"We'll catch up with him," he said. "And I need you and some others over at Kissing Turtles next week. The fence is near down and those wethers will string right into Nourombie without it."

"Yes, we need to prepare. Our first ceremony," the Bilwan said, "is in a couple of weeks. Many people will come, but they'll not disturb the sheep."

Standing between the two men, Anne sensed their friendship and mutual respect. Feeling like a fifth wheel, she jammed her fingers into her back pockets and gazed at her boots.

"Holy heck," she cried. "What's *that*?"

A sand-colored reptile stretched its neck and hissed up at her, then skittered between her boots and disappeared into the brush behind her.

"Bearded dragon," Slade and Rudy chorused and went on with their discussion.

Her hair prickled on the nape of her neck. She liked most things in nature, she just didn't like surprises. She was a thorough planner, an anticipator.

"It's heading for the creek, I reckon," Slade added. "Dry weather's taking its toll." He nodded toward the nearby ridge. "But we should get some rain out of that." Gray-bottomed clouds drifted over deep-cut peaks.

"Later today," Rudy agreed.

"We've got to go and make some saves before it moves in. By the way, you'll be seeing Anne with a film crew about the place for the next few weeks."

Rudy stared at his boss, then a grin broke free across his face. "Mr. Jim informed me. She's making the Red Gum famous?"

"Not really," Anne said, smiling. "We're making sunscreen commercials to be aired on television during the Olympics. At least, after we find Mr. McGregor and if we can agree on the sites I've selected. One of the areas is Rainbow Canyon." She leveled her sights on Rudy. Testing the waters, so to speak.

Slade interjected, "She knows about our agreement."

Seemingly satisfied, Rudy nodded and gazed at Slade. He picked up her sunglasses, handed them to her and tossed her a rather knowing smile. Her cheeks warmed. She suspected the whole band of men had seen Slade lay his maverick kiss on her.

"My nephew runs many hours," Rudy said. "After he makes it through the trials, he'll compete in the Olympic finals just before the Games."

"I wish him good luck."

Slade tagged her elbow and said to Rudy, "He'll place. The bloke is good. Let's get moving, Anne."

She followed him to the bike, while Rudy walked back to the others and Dusty chased a dragonfly.

"Oh, another thing," Slade called to the stockman. "I want you to draw another map for me."

Twenty minutes later Anne decided that if she rode over another stone ford or into a gully, she'd never sit again. Yet, leaning against Slade's back grew more pleasant with every mile. His hard torso warmed her bosom. Her fear eventually subsided and her confidence grew over his expert handling of the power beneath them.

He cruised to a stop. The dog jumped down, sniffed some scrub, and bounded ahead.

"Whew," she chimed. "How long have you been riding?" She dragged herself off the back of the small seat and took a few steps. Wobbly took on a whole new meaning.

"Since I was twelve." Slade shut off the motor, dismounted, and handed her the water bottle. They were surrounded by thick brush that covered rough ground. "We'll cut through this and climb up top of those rocks."

She threw her head back and let the water slide down her throat. Warm or not, it tasted good.

"Not on these legs."

He gazed at her legs long enough to make her feel self-conscious.

"I reckon you'll make it," he said. "Knowing my grandfather, he's detoured at least three times since yesterday. Hard to figure. Some days won't go by without him being in the middle of things. Others he walks about, even out on the bitumen road. We can spot his ute from up there."

"Ute?"

"Utility truck."

"Good. Like I said, time is—"

"Money. I remember."

She winced as they took off. Her briefcase again resnugged on her back, she pressed through waist-high brush.

"Not so fast," she said, running her tongue over her bottom lip. "We have something to discuss. Why'd you do that back there?"

Slade had already put some distance between them. "This is going to be a tight squeeze." He pointed ahead at a jagged split between large boulders. "But we'll get through."

She caught up to him.

"It was totally inappropriate, and—"

"You're complaining?"

"—entirely unprofessional."

"Looked like you enjoyed it," he grunted over his shoulder. He edged between bushy wattle that scraped his jeans. "But you're right."

"Darn right, I'm right," she said, dodging a tree branch.

"Next time, if the mood strikes me, I'll do it after hours."

Anne nearly slipped and he retraced his steps to help her. Still, the man possessed an unparalled ego. Another good reason to keep her distance.

"You don't know when to quit, do you?" she asked and jerked her hand away.

"Only when it's over," he smiled wryly. "Until she's ready to go again."

Anne gave him an icy glare.

He straightened his mouth. "Some would agree with you about quitting."

"Yeah, and you can count me in the lot."

His kiss had carried the mark of practice. The slope steepened as they approached the timeworn granite outcroppings. She stopped for a moment to catch her breath.

He slowed his pace. "Think as you will, but I can assure you, I'm not a free-wheeling bloke. Not at all."

His sudden seriousness threw her off guard, but his mouth stirred a desire in her to uncover his secrets. Hiking, she pursed her lips. She felt as though she'd known this stranger forever and had walked this ground before with him. Perhaps, his openness generated that impression, she couldn't be sure.

She now felt as if she were on some kind of surreal vacation. But this wasn't a holiday, nor was Slade her tour guide. Business brought her to the Red Gum. So she hoped they'd find Jim McGregor without delays. Although she'd worked enough film projects that suffered them, she hated waiting. Inclement weather could mess up schedules, but for the most part complications were predictable. Expert committees hammered out action plans and strategies, in spite of industry competition, hurricanes, or strikes.

This time, however, the problem couldn't be chalked up to an act of God. A mortal man potentially stood in the way of progress and might cause major career problems. He'd already dragged her into a personal, unguarded realm and resurrected feelings she'd put away.

Either Slade was the most stubborn man on Earth, or just what she needed. Her mind worked as their bodies squeezed side-by-side between the tall rocks encrusted with grey-green lichen.

His question, "What are you stewing about?" broke through her reverie. "You look unhappy."

She took a few more steps and the attaché case grated against the rock surface behind her.

"I'm thinking about my schedule, your grandfather, and the office in Sydney." Tiring, she exited the narrow passageway directly after him and found herself atop a rocky lookout.

"You don't like what you do?" he probed.

"What do you mean? I like it just fine."

"Uh-huh."

Together, they gazed below in silence. As the breeze played across them, the rough tussocked valley stretched out below into a beautiful vista. Mobs of super-fine Merino sheep blanketed the fenced-off hills, flats, and dotted gullies. She'd never seen so many sheep in one area, or a place where they seemed to be most at home. All ready to be captured on film.

Jackeroos whistled off in the distance, and their dogs cast wide and rounded up the sheep from one side. It appeared as though the men were letting the mob think it had escaped, but the sheep strung up the far slope where the musterers wanted them.

"Some of the finest."

Her curiosity piqued. "How many? Ten thousand? Fifteen?"

"A handful," he answered. "When they're good as they are, that's all we need."

Anne rolled her eyes.

Slade grinned. "I mean the men. Those are the best, some of my father's friends. The Red Gum is lucky to contract them when needed."

She bit her bottom lip, knowing she was out of her league.

"Your father's friends?"

Slade quieted. "You'll not meet him. He lives in Perth. He didn't appreciate this." He swept his arm in a wide arc. "It never spoke to him like it does to my grandfather and me. My father had a chance to leave and took it." He pointed to a ribbon of far-off railroad tracks that trickled out of the foothills. "He used to build model trains out of wood when he was a kid. I still have some of them."

"Hmm. My father used to build ships inside bottles."

Slade added, "He moved into bigger scale, investing in private cars he personally designed. Once he rode the Golden

Arrow to Perth for a railroaders' fair and never came back. Last we heard, he'd connected up with my mother's family."

"That's hard for me to imagine. My dad and I were very close." She paused, remembering the good times. "So did your mother's family raise sheep?"

"Nope. Her family raises oysters."

"For pearls?"

He nodded. "Off the West Coast. Broome."

"They're lovely, but sapphires are my favorite."

He seemed to note that, then pointed to a large mob of sheep and said, "In another two weeks those shorn jumbucks—"

"Excuse me?"

Slade placed his booted foot on top of a rock and gripped his knee with his gloved hand. Did he enjoy sharing his world with her? Or did he laugh inside at her ignorance of things out here and stroke his ego at her expense? She knew little of his lifestyle and the jargon of his business.

"They're wethers, or desexed male sheep."

The way he offered the definition didn't make her feel naive. The grazier, long secure in his element, lured her farther out of her world and into his. But she couldn't stay this time. She'd made that kind of trip before for her ex-husband, only to be left behind.

She frowned. "You mean, you…"

"We practice humane controlled growth and use some artificial insemination. We're mainly in the super-fine wool business, but raise some sheep for mutton, too."

She suddenly remembered her mission and focused on Slade. He possessed an unadorned, fresh image. He'd sizzle on camera.

"So you want a lot of new lambs?" she asked.

"Usually. A good season means a substantial wool clip and surplus sheep to sell. We try to start winter with a sizable head tally and hope for a low death rate so we can build the mob from year to year. Then we muster and shear. This is business at its best."

Anne stepped back. The soft magic playing in his voice transformed into that of a shrewd businessman. She watched the workers. They ranged from boys in their early teens to hardened men in their sixties who made mustering look effortless. They walked or rode with an assortment of dogs that dipped into a sea of fleece and popped up again like toast.

"Who are those boys?" she asked.

"Helpers. Those young men who know who they are and what they want. They've graduated from garden work, saved and bought a dog, and are working hard 'til they can get their university schooling and buy a spread of their own."

"I see." She wished she understood even more. Not only to satisfy her curiosity, but it would payoff big-time on the television screen. Her work had earned the reputation of blending fact with universal appeal and heart.

She'd been the Greene & Associates staff member who introduced the idea for the SunMate Sunscreen commercials to be done in series form. A cute story about two adventurers trying to outdo each other and fall in love along the way. The idea came to her while she launched her family's sailboat into the wind and choppy waves off the Westport coast.

That was early one morning after her husband of a year had called and said he'd have to spend another two days in Atlanta. The project idea gained approval and "SunMates for Life" had caught on big. One way or another, the romantic series would draw to a close in Rainbow Canyon. She just knew it, and an idea flashed into her mind. Slade McGregor could have a non-speaking part in the commercial. If she could persuade him. But first, she needed the general release.

"Damn, there's no sign of him," Slade grumped. "Let's go search for stragglers. Then we'll stop and eat lunch at the hut. He could turn up there later."

On the way back squeezing through the crevice again, Anne said, "I thought you people used radios."

"I do, but he doesn't."

Two hours later Anne helped free a trapped, injured lamb from a prickly bush. She tried to sink her fingers into its soft fleece. The more the animal wriggled, the deeper the thorns dug in, trapping him for sure death. Her eyes misted in sympathy.

Slade said, "Sometimes lambs get separated from their mothers. When the mob moves on, the little ones are left."

He pulled a small notebook and pencil out of his vest pocket and jotted a stroke on a new page, then picked up the lamb and held the animal in one arm. Its eyes rolled and legs flung out, then settled.

"Pull that knife out of my belt sheath."

"Sure."

"Now cut off a few short lengths of rope from the bike bag and meet me up by that tree." He tilted his head toward the top of a short, steep incline. "Where there's one stray, there's most likely another. Might need to hold them with a lead."

~ * ~

Slade left Anne to her chore, set the lamb down in a small clearing, and disappeared over the rocky crest of a hill. Trekking down its shadowed far side, he stopped for a moment and listened. The wind had picked up and the clouds hung half way down Mount Kamilaroi about twenty kilometers away. Across another stretch of bush country rose Kissing Turtles, rocks that resembled two land turtles about to touch noses. Beyond this lay Nourombie that curbed Rainbow Canyon.

Beside him, Dusty visually tracked movement from wherever it came. His keen eyes didn't miss the shake of a leaf or his ears the break of a twig. A faint bleat rose from a cluster of bushes down the hill to their right. In an instant, Dusty shot off down into the gully.

Slade started down the steep grade to free yet another straggler. Halfway down he glanced back at the top of the hill. Anne hadn't appeared yet and his bootheels dug into the red crumbly earth. He slid the last few meters on his haunches.

Dusty met him by a lamb. Weakened and wedged between two jagged rocks, it lifted its head.

"Got yourself in trouble, eh?" Slade kneeled down and began to ease the lamb up. Dusty, pacing behind him, growled once. Then again, louder.

"Hold on, boy, almost free now." Slade glanced over his shoulder, seeing the dog's ruff raised stiff.

A chill rattled Slade's spine. Deep-throated snorts issued fair warning from behind him. Slade released the lamb and turned around on his hands and knees. Thirty yards away a menacing stout black, wild pig lowered its ugly snout and charged.

"Hold," he commanded Dusty. Yet the collie zigzagged between him and the nastiest of the swine family.

"NO!" Slade scrambled to his feet. Dusty tore by and the boar turned on a dime, grazing the dog's shoulder with its short tusk. The collie yelped as blood jagged across his shoulder, but he circled anyway and nipped at the pig's legs from behind.

Living up to a reputation for maliciousness, the feral pig drew closer to Slade. Its small eyes trained on him. Slade shouted and quickly sidestepped behind a knee-high boulder. The pig shortened the distance while the lamb, wobbling on its feet, stepped out and bleated.

The pig lunged.

"Back off, lardo," Slade bellowed and heard his own blood pumping through his ears. Dusty tried to thwart the wild animal, but only irritated it more. Damn! This was no time to be caught without his truck, gun or knife.

Four

Anne cut the last of the ropes, hiked up the short hill, and stopped beneath the tall river gum tree. As she gazed upward, martins caught insects on the wing, and brightly colored parrots, scrambled one over the other, chattered and flit about. A kingfisher landed on a curved branch while a stiff breeze ruffled through long, narrow leaves. This unexpected gentleness gave her pause—until Slade's voice rose, close and sharp.

Something about a fat, bastard pig?

She turned toward the direction from where the commotion came, but could see nothing. The urgency in his voice and Dusty's growls and barks summoned her own instincts. She heard another yelp.

"Slade?"

When no reply came she dropped the ropes and ran the short distance down to the motorcycle and grabbed the knife she'd left on the seat. She also took along her personal, trusty brand of help from her briefcase and scrambled uphill. Breathless, she crossed the grass-splotched crest and looked below.

Slade, waving his hat, paced behind a pile of small boulders. He shouted and pitched rocks over the head of a small, teetering lamb. But at what, she couldn't see.

Dusty ran back and forth like a shuttle cock on a wool weaver's loom, dipping up and down. Every nerve and sense she had went on immediate alert. The air even seemed to crackle around her. She kept moving downhill while the noises of man and dog ricocheted off the stone walls of the narrow gully.

Making the last turn, she gasped. Slade, Dusty, and a frail-looking lamb were trapped. In a flash of hoary black, a feral pig charged at its prey, keeping them all at bay.

Her stomach pitched. She knew she was out of her element. Yet, compelled to help, she trekked closer to the fray. If nothing else, she could create a diversion. Seconds could make a difference.

"Hold on!" she cried, as pea-sized gravel skittered from beneath the soles of her boots. "I'm coming down."

Slade jerked his head up, raising his hand for her to stop.

"No you don't, Anne. Stay there."

The pig charged again, goring the frail, young creature over the rocks.

Retaliating, Dusty sank his teeth in the grunting pig's back leg. With one ferocious kick the pig loosened him and the Border collie tumbled backward and yelped again. Slade bolted over the rounded limestone, now holding a thick club of wood across his middle with both hands.

Anne's heart raced. Her knees weakened and the gravel and dust caused her feet to slip from out under her. Down she thunked, covering the rest of the distance on her blue-jeaned seat.

She skidded to a sprawling halt. Open-legged, only a few feet away from Slade, she lifted her head and gazed up. He did a double take. Dread chased away any chance for mirth, and his mouth formed an unyielding line.

No birds or trickling water could be heard, only the most menacing of squeals. As she got up, the pig stared at her and twitched its ears.

"You got my knife?" Slade barked.

She rejoiced. "Yes." She held up her hand, but it was empty. "Oh, shoot, no. I must have dropped it up there."

"Great," he muttered. "Come over here. Slowly."

She began to take his advice. "I've got a plan," she said, sure she was losing her mind from fear.

"Stop!"

She riveted her eyes on the wild pig that now charged by her toward Slade. He dodged it and slammed the wood club against its shoulder as the pig ripped his pants on his right thigh. Luckily, no blood spurted from the wound.

Anne's heart thumped so loudly she could hardly think She pulled together every ounce of her courage and will against the wildness that took hold.

"Over here," she called. "I'm ready for you, you vile, wicked piece of—!"

Slade shouted, "Dammit! Get behind me!"

She lifted her chin and advanced a few steps, and the bush porcine took her bait. "Good. Come and get it." She leaned over and changed her weight from foot to foot as if receiving a serve on the court in the Tennis Club of Westport.

Snorting, the boar charged.

Only a couple of feet from its ugly, hairy face, Anne gripped the canister she'd clipped to her waistband. She pressed the button, releasing super-mace vapor into the pig's face, clouding its small cunning eyes and sloppy snout.

In a one-on-one dance with danger, Anne sidestepped the sure-footed attacker. Thanking her lucky stars, she sped toward Slade, dropping her trusty can of mace in the dirt. The pig ducked its thick head and charged off-course into the brush.

Triumphant, she turned and smiled at Slade. He wrapped his arm around her waist and hoisted her over his shoulder like a bale of fresh woolclip.

"Put me down," she shrieked. His strong shoulders and neck supported her, but uncomfortably. Things began to spin.

"Quiet," he demanded. He whistled and Dusty hobbled over to them. Slade then strode, his gait under full control, away from the pig. He set Anne down unceremoniously on a large tussock of grass. Shaking and seething, she glanced back over her shoulder. The animal charged back to where they'd stood, and opening its mouth, snatched up the canister.

Slade said, "That'll keep him busy."

A loud pop and hiss went off followed by a gut-wrenching squeal. The pig had punctured the can, causing it to explode. Silence followed.

Anne's insides rumbled, but she could now breathe. Her diversion plan had worked. Her voice shook. "I tried to get down here as fast as I could, and you're welcome."

"Are *you* all right?"

She took stock of herself.

"Yes, but look, Dusty's hurt."

Wimpering, the collie limped toward them. Slade brushed past her and dropped to his knees beside his dog.

"Hold on, fella," he coaxed as the last of the sun went in overhead behind low, dark clouds. Unbuttoning his shirt, he removed it. He used the soft cotton to blot away blood from the dog's shoulder and ignored the scratch that bled from his own forearm.

"Is it bad?" Anne asked, reaching his side. The dog's pain reflected in his eyes and in his owner's.

"We need to clean this out," Slade said. "He might need a couple of stitches."

"I've got some Listerine and a sewing kit."

Slade looked at her. His expression changed from wondrous to relief to almost comical.

She told him, "The stuff's in my briefcase."

"Ah, yes." He gathered up his dog in his arms and began to trek back up the hill, Anne at his side.

"Like I said, where I go—"

"It goes."

Feeling a need to explain, she added, "I didn't know quite what to expect, so I packed all kinds of things."

"Do you realize you almost ended up maimed, even dead?"

She held her tongue. This was a fact with which she couldn't argue. He stroked Dusty's ears, looked away, then back again at her. The blue of his eyes stormed into gray.

"I want you to know that your being here concerns me. You don't know this country."

Making their way back up the hill, she protested, "I know trouble when I see it. And I just helped you get out of it."

"Maybe, but you acted on impulse."

Anne steamed. "*Impulse?*" This was a word that had hardly ever turned up in others' descriptions of her. She looked into his eyes. "What's wrong? You can't accept help from an outsider?"

No response came, which annoyed her even more. "That's it, isn't it? Well, I've heard about you guys living out here. Laid-back and resourceful kings of your castles. But how the hell do you know *what* I'm thinking?"

He frowned. "Impulsiveness doesn't fit out here. I reckon I'll need to stay close to you. I aim to keep the Red Gum... accident-free." A strange hitch dropped his voice, and they hiked down toward Slade's Triumph.

"I can assure you that your guardianship isn't necessary," she huffed. "I'll be working. Very busy. Besides, you don't understand. Nothing happens on the set without prior approval from the director. He decides who can be there."

Slade slung her a reproachful glance.

"I'm aware that it's your land," she said, "but part of it'll be our set—for a while, anyway."

"Only with our permission, love. And you don't have it yet."

Resentment charged through her. She didn't like the emphasis he put on the word "love," or the control his share of ownership of the sheep station afforded him. Although she'd have to respect that, she half believed that he enjoyed having her right where he wanted her. In limbo and dependent on him.

His mouth twisted. "It's beginning to rain. My dog needs tending."

"So do you. You've got a scratch." She reached over and touched his forearm.

Their eyes met. Again, out of the blue, his mysterious magnetism melted her resolve. She wondered if he sensed anything pulsing from her, since he didn't seem to miss much.

He pulled back. The breeze ruffled his hair making him look even more rugged and handsome. From out of nowhere newfound strength rippled through her, and the pain in her bottom began to ease. Less than fifteen minutes of riding brought them to a mob of sheep. Slade stopped only long enough for Anne to release the one lamb they'd saved, then gunned it for shelter.

~ * ~

Hannah's hut, tucked in a stand of trees and flowering shrubs, sheltered them from the rain that had let loose about a half-hour ago. The place reeked of history. Rough, flat stones of local vintage were laid laterally and formed the one-story walls that supported a pitched slate roof.

The narrow overhang didn't quite qualify for being a porch roof, but two weather-beaten chairs rested outside the front door. She glanced at the chimney that clung to the short side of the small cottage.

Soggy grass met the first of the two log front steps. Tiny windows, coated with dust, flanked either side of the low-framed door that creaked when Slade shoved it open.

A few minutes later, Anne stood with Slade by the wooden table where Dusty now laid on his side. The rainwater had washed away most of the blood that had matted his coat.

"I've got him," Slade said, supporting the dog's head. "Go ahead and pour some of that mouthwash of yours over the cut. That's good. More over here. Good."

She caught the run-off with one of the faded, thin yellow towels Slade brought from the other room.

"Think this'll be enough?" she asked, praying not to have to sew up the dog's flesh.

"The wound's not as deep as it looks," he said, half to her, half to the dog. "You'll be like new soon, mate."

Slade then opened a small box with an unmarked jar of homemade tea salve, a roll of gauze, and adhesive tape. After fashioning a loose bandage over the wound, he cradled Dusty and tucked him into a wool blanket near the hearth of the deep fireplace. Returning to the table, he reached for another towel from the back of a ladder chair. He swiped the water off his face and ran his fingers through half-dry hair. The downpour had cooled everything off outside and sent shoots of mist through the still open door.

Anne regarded him for a moment. "You're good for each other. You and Dusty."

"We're a team. No one makes it out here by themselves."

"I can believe that." She sat down on a bench and draped a towel around her neck. "I never had a dog for a pet."

"He's well-trained."

"He would've died for you today. He's that loyal."

"Never gave him reason not to be."

Her heart pinged. Is that what happened? Had she given Lou reason to be disloyal? Her cold, wet jeans hugged her hips and legs. She bent over to pull her muddied boots off, but they wouldn't budge.

Slade walked over. "Want a hand?"

By now the worry had left his eyes. She nodded as he lifted one of her feet, and gave a hefty yank first on one boot loop, then the other. She pulled off her socks and nestled her toes into another towel she'd dropped to the old plank floor. Her skin goosebumped, and her soaked underwear began to drive her crazy sticking to her like it was.

Slade's hair fell loosely over his forehead. His t-shirt molded to his pectorals. On one hand, he seemed somewhat at a loss. Then again, contented and at home in the middle of nowhere with few amenities. Looking around, she found no traces of a woman's touch. But the place was being lived in, or worked in.

Her curiosity piqued. Although she'd learned otherwise, he gave every indication that he lived life somewhat as a loner.

"May I ask you a personal question?"

"Sure, but—"

"What happened to your wife? Rose had mentioned you'd lost her."

His motions slowed as he opened the door to an old corner hutch. As he rifled through the assorted supplies on the top shelf, she could nearly feel his mind hum.

"What Rose said is true. Last year ...my wife..." he said, without facing her. "Here, give me a hand with these."

Anne stood and walked to him. "I didn't mean to pry."

"Yes, I know." He passed her several large tins that she carried to the table. Some blue enameled plates came next and a couple of chipped mugs. Overhead, the rain pummeled the roof and filled the quiet.

"You'll find a clean shirt and workpants on the hook in there," he said, gesturing into an adjoining room lined with bunks. "Not much to look at, but they're dry."

She crossed to the table, trying to shrug off the tiredness that overwhelmed her muscles. The concern on Slade's face appeared to be genuine.

"I accept your offer—on two conditions," she said. Now the tables were turned. She could tell he struggled with yielding to his own curiosity.

"And what might those be?"

She picked up the Listerine bottle. "First, you let me fix up your arm."

"It'll keep."

"No, it'll fester. I'm not a Flying Doctor, but I can help with that."

He approached her, picked up the salve and handed it to her.

"Thank you," she said, ignoring his pained expression.

"For what?"

She took his hand in hers.

"For being a man of reason. For a change."

"Hold the psychology and just do it."

His presence chased away the chill in her palm that lingered from riding in the wind and rain. Under her care, his strong and capable fingers soon relaxed. Touching his skin like this seemed as natural as could be. Like the two of them were old friends. The fresh memory of his lips locked on hers rekindled her senses.

Feisty and fertile, her imagination took over from where the reality of that earth-shaking moment left off. In her mind his fingers suddenly proved to be capable in the most intimate of ways. But with gentleness and respect for her needs. A hungry heat danced over her breasts and rushed to the lower part of her body.

Meanwhile, she turned his hand over and exposed the wound on the inside of his lower arm and began to wash it with the antiseptic. His mellow voice startled her.

"You must like nursing."

Embarrassment for certain rosied her cheeks. She avoided his eyes and packed away her wildest dreams. Catching her in the act of reading his map was one thing, but this kind of intrusion was another matter. These were private fantasies!

"Nursing? Not me, a little first-aid is all." She poured the rest of the runny, gold liquid over his torn skin.

"Maybe, but you're humming."

She stole a quick breath.

"You must be mistaken. I don't hum."

With quicker motions she applied the salve and picked up the roll of gauze. She removed the pink ribbon that kept it neat and tidy and began to wrap his arm with the bandage.

"Let me finish it for you," he said.

"Oops, is it too tight?"

"The wrap job is fine. I meant the song." Slade pursed his lips and began to whistle. Pitched perfectly, "Music of the Night" from *Phantom of the Opera* filled the small room. To her wonder, he whistled further into the operatic piece.

She squinted at him. "You're a man full of surprises, Slade McGregor. You know Andrew Lloyd Webber's music."

"And you know about Flying Doctors."

Mutual silence rose between them. Sitting here in a place that only God and Slade really knew where, Anne treasured her memory of *Phantom*. While little else around her was, the familiar music grounded her.

She returned his steady gaze. In all fairness, she realized how much she'd infiltrated his niche in the world, which she knew made him nervous. He'd already said as much with having to keep an eye on her while she worked. Yes, it was his space, but for a while it would also be hers.

Slade picked up the ribbon. "My grandmother was a nurse."

Anne found that unsurprising. The way he freed and carried lambs to safety went beyond saving them for their wool. His attention to Dusty was heartfelt. How he cared for the Bilwan's sacred places also said something honorable about Slade.

"That's how my grandfather met her," he went on. "She was an American serving at the U.S. Army General Hospital in Melbourne during World War II."

Anne knitted her eyebrows. "An American? From where?"

"A town in Texas called Weatherford."

"No kidding. And she stayed *here*?"

He tucked the ribbon into his pocket. "She liked *here,* and my grandfather can be very persuasive. Besides, he loved her."

She checked her watch. "I'm looking forward to meeting him. Soon, I hope." Oh, how she wished to get on with business.

"I reckon so."

"It must have taken great courage and strength for your grandmother to make a good life out of this country back then."

"Some are cut out for it, and some not," he said. "My grandfather bought the Red Gum from a friend who was dying from mortar wounds. This hut was the original homestead. My grandmother, Hannah, and my grandfather lived here until they built the main house in 1953. They had my father later in life."

Anne glanced out the window and gave thought to what was left of her own family and that wasn't much. Except for her mother, everyone was gone, or as good as gone. She had no siblings, either.

"You know, it's raining hard. Do you really think he'll show up."

"Depends. This is the only outstation from here to Rainbow Canyon." He moved toward her. "You're shivering. Why don't you get out of those wet clothes?"

"Not yet."

"You drive a tough bargain. All right, you mentioned two conditions before you took me up on my offer," he said. "Now what's the second?"

She could now think of a whole lot of second conditions, but spending a week or so in the Canyon to film remained as overall Number One. Her intuition told her to tread lightly and hold out for Slade's grandfather. She quashed her original thought and tipped her head at the jar of Kraft Vegemite.

"You don't serve me any of that. You probably grew up on it like I did on peanut butter."

Slade chuckled. "Dusty and I won't mind a bit. I'll come up with something else unless you keep roo steaks and a barbie stowed away in that portable cupboard of yours."

She walked over to the old, but comfortable couch and picked up her briefcase.

"Fresh out. Only a couple of apples and some amaretto biscotti."

"All goes with tea."

She nodded.

"Then dig your tucker out, love."

While Slade prepared part of the meal in the main room of the cottage, Anne excused herself and changed. She adjusted the rope belt that cinched the borrowed tan cotton pants and rolled up the legs. The oversized rust-colored shirt she'd changed into flapped about her chest and the long tails dropped to her knees. It even looked too big for Slade. The soft wool socks she found stuffed in the pants' pockets pleased her most.

Finished changing, she stared at herself in a piece of a mirror that hung tilted on the wooden wall of the Spartan bunkroom. Her hair dried into an unkempt nettle, not a trace of make-up to color her eyelids or cheeks or lips, but her eyes seemed to shine clearer, eager, perhaps less burdened. The crease between her eyebrows had shallowed.

She couldn't decide whether she looked better than ever in this *au naturale* state, or was a complete disaster. She opened her briefcase and pulled out her cell phone. It was after three o'clock now and she wanted to touch base with Jack. The phone speared her eardrum with a high pitch. She tried the number again and got the same result.

Closing the useless instrument, she tossed it onto the dresser. She knew he'd be waiting to hear from her. So far, he was unaware of the hitch about filming in the Canyon.

If only Slade's grandfather would arrive. At a minimum, the three of them could open discussions. Since they were stuck out here in the bush, no interruptions would deter the progress of reaching an agreement. Thunder cracked overhead, and Slade's call spurred her back to the living room.

He'd lit the kerosene lamp that hung over the table. A short-wave radio crackled from the bench near the front door. A fire now heated a billy pot hanging from a bar supported by two iron y-braces that stood in the deep, arched fireplace.

Although the place looked more homey and cheerful, Slade's mouth was set. She took the place he'd laid out for her.

"You don't like the weather, just stick around for a day," he quipped as he poured tea into the old mugs. He'd changed shirts and toweled his hair.

"I can't get through to my office. Must be some storm."

"Worst in a while. Mossman Creek's probably overflowed its banks and taken out part of the North Paddock road."

Her eyes traveled to an old map tacked on the wall as she hungrily bit into her apple slices. She suddenly remembered the photographs of Mossman Creek, one of her choice filming spots. Its beauty was astounding. Then it hit her.

"You mean like mud and torn up trees?"

Slade took his place opposite her.

"And lost sheep."

"Oh, dear."

He sighed a long one. "Mossman can turn into a river quicker than a gun ringer can shear ten sheep. Might be weeks before the water rechannels where it belongs."

She couldn't fully understand the problems this meant for him, but she picked up the regret in his voice.

"This is bad news for both of us," he said pointedly.

She caught his drift. "So it messes up my production plans—big time." She took a sip of the tea and resumed, competing with the rain on the roof. Things were falling more out of place instead of into place.

"I'm supposed to go back to Westport in a month. This storm damage leaves two viable places to film. And you're trying to pull one of them—which just happens to be the best place. I've three episodes to film. Maybe it's good I can't get through to Jack right now, because—"

"You're quitting?"

She focused on him. "No." She released his gaze, nibbled at her biscotti and reached for the honey tin.

Slade dunked his pastry and bit into it.

"Here's a personal question for you. Why don't you want to go back home?"

Her guard shot up. "What do you mean?"

"Your face damn near fell a meter when you said Westport."

Shifting her gaze to the fire, she said, "New England is my home, but this Australia trip came at a good time."

Five

Slade shifted positions in his chair and wondered what was going through her mind. She surprised him by sharing, "My parents made a small fortune with a department store, but it later took a dive. My dad then accepted an offer from a local firm to buy the land for a hotel. He cleared his debts and spent a lot of time with his brother who owned a failing custom sailboat building yard near Mystic Seaport. Wasn't long until they were in business together, and things turned around."

"Good for them. Starting over is hard."

"They had a can-do spirit and a few contacts to get them going." She shook her head and smiled. "They acted like they had their whole lives ahead of them."

Slade sat quietly watching her as she spoke. If only she knew how endearing and comical she looked. Tendrils of her hair bounced as she raised and lowered her chin. At the moment, he actually found her charming. She looked like a different woman than the one he'd found yesterday looking through things in his living room. Today she seemed softer, easier going, likable.

The large shirt he'd loaned her eased away from her neck and slid off her shoulder. She caught it and repositioned the faded cloth. The sparkle in her eyes dimmed, and she lifted one leg and tucked it under the other.

"I don't know why I'm telling you these things. I don't share this stuff with people from my business life."

"Not a bad idea," he agreed, hoping she would anyway. He found her appealingly different. Aside from a natural sexiness, she'd already touched the part of him that needed to give and protect. It'd been building since he'd first seen her. His desire for a woman was never before so fast or intense.

He still didn't know how, but there was definitely something familiar about her. He listened for clues.

"A customer, who lived in the Hamptons, wanted to speed up his order so he could participate in a Fourth of July regatta. My uncle had found some parts from a new supplier and finished the project." She tore away a loose thread from the shirttail. "You see, he and my dad stood by the quality of their work. Before releasing the boat to the skipper, they took it out for a half day for a shakedown cruise."

She hesitated and frowned. He leaned forward. Maybe letting her go on wasn't such a good idea. He should have curbed his curiosity. Damn, he couldn't figure himself out. He'd been jarred off-track ever since he'd laid eyes on her yesterday.

"A fog came up, and they called to shore not long before they collided with a freighter." She had worked the thread into a tiny curl. "You know I love the water," she murmured, "but sometimes I loathe every drop. A day later the Coast Guard found wreckage from the new boat and my father's hat."

Slade let out a low whistle. He wasn't very good with words at times. He set his tea mug down and watched her take in a deep breath before she went on.

"Thank heavens my aunt had died before my uncle and didn't have to go through that. Except my mother did. Even before the accident, she was a fragile, gentle sort. My father was a good provider and protector. Losing him killed her in a way."

"You must miss him."

"Often.

"Your mum's better?"

"She suffers from an early onset of Alzheimers. She was found wandering along the New England Highway unable to remember her name. At times she knows who she is or me, but mostly she doesn't. She's in a good hospice, and I visited her before I came here. All I do now is wait for a call."

Slade refilled her tea. "Go on, please." This was the first time she'd taken him into her confidence.

"I had finished my first semester at college when I was notified about her failing condition. After graduating, I started working for Greene and Associates. I then married one of our clients. We'd met in Boston at a business promotion." Her voice carried regret. "That's a whole other story."

Slade drew his thumb along his jaw and thought this woman had experienced strife that he could have never dreamed up. He understood heartache, from inside out. He lived with loss and knew how to bury the past, never to dredge up the pain again. He owned a well of it, buried deeply inside.

"I should've stopped you."

"Hey, it was my choice." She smiled, unfolded her legs, stretched her arms, and stood.

"And I listened," he said as an uneasiness rose in his chest. Too much, he liked her personal side too much.

"I'll wash these dishes," she said, removing the plates.

Slade got up and walked over to her. "No, you won't. If you don't mind me saying it, you look tired."

Whatever he said, it was either the wrong thing, or she'd had more than enough to handle today. Her eyes fired to copper. "I do mind, Slade. If you could help me find a way to film in the Canyon, I'd be too busy to tell you my life story."

Her flare-up thinned his patience.

"I can't figure you out," he said, raising his voice over a sudden new downpour on the roof. "But what I can tell you is that we best stay put until morning."

"You must be joking," she exclaimed. "Stay out here all night. Alone. With you?"

"Why not? I don't bite."

She didn't answer and her expression darkened. He couldn't stand it when a woman cried or sulked. Either of these classic female behaviors triggered unmentionable emotions in him. The worst was vulnerability.

"I'm going to radio Rose," he said. "My grandfather might have gone back to the house. If you have questions for him, you'll have to stand in line behind me."

Anne turned to face him.

"That's where you seem to want everyone."

Slade unlatched the microphone and shrugged.

"If you want to go, then go. But don't expect me to come after you when you get lost or sick." He meant it, too. He could concede that he'd fall into moods from time to time, but she was becoming a royal, contrary pain in the butt.

As the radio emitted static, the front door of the hut plowed open. He jerked his head toward the movement. A large man, wearing a drizabone coat that hooded his head and face, bustled in followed by a gust of wet wind.

Slade said with full relief, "Hiya, Grandad."

"G'day. What the hell's going on in here? I could hear voices down past the grape arbor."

Slade moved out of the way as the newcomer walked by him and pulled a small carton from under his coat and set down a small Esky on the table.

"We have company," Slade announced pointedly. "How'd you make it up this far? I figured the north road washed out."

"It did. Right in front of me, so I backtracked over Morgan's Hill and beat bush here."

Slade grinned as the elderly man gazed at Anne from under the hood. She pulled the shirt more tightly around herself. He seemed pleased with what he saw.

"Welcome to the Red Gum."

Her response flowed. "Thank you, it's good to be here."

"Has my grandson shown you his manners? If not, no worries. He gets off his bike every now and then, and I don't mean that rattle-trap sitting outside."

Anne smiled as Slade wiped the grin off his face. She moved toward the two of them.

"He's been a... perfect gentleman."

"Hah!" McGregor scoffed. "I know what that means."

Slade protested, "Now just a—"

"I'm glad to finally meet you, Mr. McGregor. Thank you for your invitation to the agency for us to film here. I'm ready to start as soon as possible."

McGregor noted, "Well, look at that. My old shirt looks better on you than it ever did on me. Wore that when Slade was born. Hannah must have kept it. She was sentimental that way."

Slade cringed with embarrassment.

"We got wet." He nodded at the clothing hanging over the back of two chairs by the fire.

"So I see." The elderly man, still hooded, moved to the hearth and put out his hands to capture some warmth. He turned toward the injured dog.

"Hey, Dusty, you laid up, boy?"

"He ran into trouble with a pig. We barely made it here on the bike in the mud."

Anne nodded vigorously.

"What took you out there, mate?"

"Looking for you, and we scratched some."

"How many d'ya find?"

"Two, but lost one to the pig."

McGregor humphed. "So what'd you need me for? You're mostly running the place now."

Anne spoke up. "Would you like some tea?"

"Love some." McGregor flicked water drops away from the edge of the hood. "Here you be. Brought in some of Da-Wa's tucker in case you need it."

Slade thanked him then lowered his voice to a near whisper.

"Look, we've got to talk. Alone, Grandad."

"Sorry, it'll have to wait," he boomed. "I'm staying only a minute. Rudy and I are moving a small mob of ewes higher up from Mossman. The lightening is letting up. He's meeting me down at the fork."

Anne handed the mug to Slade, and he handed it to his grandfather who slugged down the strong, warm tea.

"Now, what's up, Anne? Guess this weather will hold you up for a while? We don't usually get rain like this. It's been a queer year."

She smiled. "It could, but another problem has come around. One of the places I'd chosen to film in is Rainbow Canyon."

As the words left her mouth, Slade caught the sidelong glance his grandfather tossed him.

"That right?" his grandfather asked her.

Slade nodded stoically and leaned against a support post and crossed his arms.

"And I'm told that the only way to access that Canyon is to go through a strip of land called Nourombie. And the problem is that the area is restricted."

Slade could feel his grandfather's eyes staring at him from beneath the shadows of the soaked hood that he kept pulled down.

"Go on," McGregor said.

"But I have a feeling that with your help, perhaps the Bilwan people will let my crew cross it. I met Rudy this morning, and he seems a reasonable enough man. Perhaps, he would be willing to personally oversee our short trip. My agency will make it worth the Bilwan's while. Frankly, it's all I have to offer. Slade, however, feels that our—"

"I can state my own position," Slade interrupted.

"'Course you can," McGregor piped, "but isn't it nice hearing her talk all smooth and polished like that?"

Slade bristled while Anne stepped closer. "He indicated that a financial offer would be of little value to the Bilwan. In addition, when you invited our agency to film, we never expected to run into such a hitch. Rainbow Canyon is perfect for what I need. And since it's necessary to have signatures from both of you on our release form, it was imperative that we open this issue up for discussion and arrive at an amenable solution. We're prepared to go to work as soon as the rain lets up."

"I understand your situation," McGregor spoke with thought and finished his tea. "Has he also explained that we have a longstanding agreement with the Bilwan people?"

Anne lowered her eyes, and Slade felt her disappointment flash across the room. She was getting nowhere. On one hand he felt triumphant, on the other regret hit him.

"Yes, and that many of them work for you. I certainly don't mean to cause trouble or be sacrilegious. If only there was another way into—"

"Well, there isn't," Slade dropped in the middle of her verbal wish. "Isn't that right, Grandad?"

Slade's grandfather shot him a disquieting stare, then turned to Anne. His head bowed and his manner was sincere.

"I can't sign your release. Not yet, anyway, but I'll be back at the house tomorrow. It's time for a family conference, Slade.

You can keep my shirt for as long as you need it, Anne, and don't worry. There're answers for everything." He set the empty mug on the windowsill and turned and said almost inaudibly, "It's a pleasure seeing you again."

Anne tilted her head in surprise, trying to see his face.

McGregor turned away and took his leave, pulling the heavy door behind him.

"Now what do you suppose that was all about?" she asked.

Suspicious, Slade narrowed his eyes and stepped toward her. "Which part?"

"I'm stumped." She tugged at the tails of the shirt. "I don't believe I know your grandfather."

Slade figured otherwise. His grandfather didn't fling himself or words around to impress anyone.

He searched her puzzled face. "He's a man of mystery sometimes. He and Rudy are thick as thieves."

She lowered her hands by her sides.

"Aren't you concerned about him going out in this weather?"

Slade put another log on the fire, then resituated himself on the wood-framed couch and lifted his stockinged feet up on the bench that doubled as a coffee table.

"Worried? He knows every hectare of this place better than Rudy, who's an expert cartographer. My grandfather's too smart to get into trouble. Only when it's something he feels strongly about, do I have to reign him in. And that's not easy, riding herd on my own grandfather like he was my kid."

He recalled the most recent incident. It was about a month ago in Sydney. That confounded fight, to be exact. His grandfather was so dedicated to keeping the Superfine MerinoWoolgrowers Association pure, he got himself into a billy of hot water.

Slade grimaced about the check he'd written to help cover the damages related to his grandfather's passion for keeping things the way they were. But this was a private family matter. He couldn't think of any reason to put his grandfather down in front of a stranger.

"I suppose so," Anne agreed. "Look, since we're stuck here until morning I'm going to get some work done. If Mossman's out of the picture—if you'll pardon that pun—there's a lot of reworking to do. At least that can be ready by the time I call Jack and the crew gets here. And I'll take another look at the photos. Your grandfather's right. There is an answer for everything. Maybe one will click."

Slade lowered his eyelids. "Make yourself at home."

~ * ~

Anne padded from the main room and returned with her briefcase. She set it down on a cleared side of the table and carried the mugs and flatware to a chipped enameled sink with a wooden drainboard.

She peered out the rain-spattered windowpane and through the water curtain that rippled from the roof overhang on the back of the cottage. The terrain rose beyond the hut and she saw the willow tree that stood in the corner of a grassy yard that had been leveled somewhat. Willows grew near water, but she saw no creek. Perhaps, an underground spring watered its roots during the dry season.

By sheer coincidence, a silver-leafed willow also drooped in the backyard of her condo in Westport. Seeing this one here and now released mixed feelings through her, as did anything that reminded her of home anymore.

At one moment, she longed for the good times spent at The Mooring during Friday happy hour with her friends, or picking up fresh cod from Alice's on Saturday mornings.

Now she felt displaced, unattached. On the up side, she basked in reasonable freedom to visit, live, or settle wherever she pleased. No longer did she have to account for her actions to Lou, who had made her life hell not so long ago.

Her memory traveled back. A woman's tormented voice again spoke in her mind. *"Hello? Is Lou with you? Please, don't lie. I know he is."*

Anne held onto the edge of the sink and shook off the haunting memory. Like clockwork, the dull pain reappeared behind her breastbone. She gripped the red pump handle and pushed it up and down. Water dribbled out of the skinny-necked tap and she gazed back out at the tree.

Anger and disgust reseeded in her soul. Would it always be like this? Encountering hurtful memories that took her breath away? For the most part, counseling had helped her regroup during the divorce and made her feel better and less a fool.

She'd come to realize that her best friends were the down-to-earth common sense she possessed and her healthy imagination. Although these qualities made strange bedfellows, she needed them both. She could draw either one out and use it at will. On the job, or in her personal affairs.

Images flew into her mind's eye, and she invited the chance to daydream—anything to neutralize the torment in the woman's voice, to even the score, to punish Lou for what he'd done.

An unpleasant, yet justifiable, countenance crowded her conscience. Outside the window of Hannah's hut, the willow tossed and bent. In her mind she conjured up that Lou was about to be hung from its highest branch. When the deed was over, Anne closed her moistened eyes and her pain disappeared.

Meanwhile, Slade's snore rattled from behind her. She turned away from the sink and stepped past the warm pool of firelight that encircled the table. Reaching the couch, she looked down at the handsome sleeping farmer.

She amazed herself. Of all the men with whom she'd be doing business. A grazier. After witnessing that rude and out-of-control band of woolgrowers who had made complete fools out of themselves in the lobby of her office building the night of her agency's Olympic sponsor dinner, she vowed to avoid them at all costs. She never counted on eating her words, 'remind me never to do business with sheep ranchers.'

She'd caught hell later from Jack for saying that, although she could see his point. But how was she to know that a reporter stood behind her eavesdropping with a microphone?

Slade shifted his arms and turned his head.

A believer of the saying about how when God closes a door, He opens a window, Anne rested her palms on the sheepskin against which Slade rested. She could feel the warmth of his shoulders rising to meet her fingers. Brimming with masculinity, he slumbered. She suddenly wished that things were different. But she wasn't about to get burned again.

Still she could *look* all she wanted. She wasn't dead, for Heaven's sake. She'd just placed herself off-limits.

Unaware of how long she stood and watched his chest rise and fall, she shifted her weight from one foot to the other. A new kind of peace took her by surprise.

She tiptoed away, resettled herself at the table, and snapped open her briefcase. She pulled out files, a yellow pad, and a set of contact sheets with all the photos she and Slade had gone over the night before. A half-hour passed into one.

By now early night had fallen and shadows replaced shafts of daylight. She'd turned up the lamp earlier and was quite comfortable. The proofs were scattered in front of her. Using a small magnifying glass, she enlarged each shot. She scrutinized them for unique detail and looked for a new angle. Something she may have missed. Rainbow Canyon still outranked all the possibilities. This included the small extension that veed off to the right on the McGregor side of the Canyon.

She rubbed her eyes and ran her fingers through her hair. If she couldn't get Slade's grandfather to help her, she and the agency were up against it. Jack had mentioned that the owner of the property across the Canyon, Neville Crane, behaved like a 'little bastard king.' His answer was a flat out, "No," when he'd been called. "Don't want nobody on my land. Period."

It seemed strange to her, actually, how not long after that ruckus in the lobby, that Jack let her know she had been invited to the Red Gum. He'd tried earlier in the year to land this spot, but was refused. She could never account for people's change of heart. She just knew that when it happened, good usually followed. So why question the luck?

She stretched out the kinks in her legs and ambled over to the wall where the old map hung. Yellowed and unadorned, the wrinkled paper revealed another view of the Red Gum. Pencilled notes were jotted here and there amongst the dotted footpaths.

"Lost 73 head. T.J. Boyd, Winter, 1924," she read softly to herself. "Storm took roof off woolshed. March 24, 1945. Skits O'Healey." She read on and collected the tales of the land and station crew over the decades. A tough life.

One of the dotted paths led between Kissing Turtles into Nourombie and forked as it approached the Canyon's edge. The left side continued on, the other abruptly stopped. Another note caught her eye: "Caroline McGregor—"

"Anne?" Slade's hand on her shoulder nearly sent her through the open-beamed ceiling.

She whirled around and flung at him, "Jeez. How long have you been standing here?"

"About as long as you were watching me over at the couch."

She arched her left eyebrow.

"You were asleep."

"Not quite. I smelled your perfume."

Anne lifted her wrist and whiffed her skin. Boronia was the name of the fragrance that she had bought at a perfumery in the historic Rocks area of Sydney. Sure enough, a trace of the fragrance still lingered.

"Did it make you have sweet dreams?" she asked lightly and returned to the table.

He followed and opened the Esky. Pulling out two Tooheys, he popped the lids.

"Quite the contrary."

"Oh? Why?"

He avoided her gaze. "It's after five. Quittin' time in the big city. Want a tinnie?"

She sat down and lifted her feet to the end of the table. Unprofessional, she knew, but now she cared little. If there was any remnant of her boardroom appearance, its presence was purely coincidental.

"I guess I do," she said, taking the beer.

"You want a glass?"

"Please." She soon threw her head back, sipped, and wiped her lips with the back of her hand.

Slade grinned and picked out a sandwich wrapped in a waxed paper bag. She hadn't seen waxed paper in years.

"Want one of these?"

"Sure. As long as it's not wallaby."

"Not that good. It's ham, cheese, lettuce, and mayonnaise on Da-Wa's seven grain bread."

She slid him a quick smile. He tossed her a sandwich, and she unfolded the paper. The bread was outstanding. Slade broke their companionable silence. A ready-to-pounce look gleamed in his eyes.

"You know what I like about you?" he asked abruptly.

Anne stopped mid-bite. She used to dislike it when people tried to figure her out, but eventually learned to let them think as they may since most of the time they were wrong.

"You don't mind taking chances," he judged.

Anne squirmed. Nothing could be further from the truth. The urge to set him straight niggled her. Also, for some reason, this time it mattered what someone thought. That bothered her.

"Maybe, but everyone has their limits. There are some things I'd never risk."

She knew her stance made an impact, but she wasn't sure what he was driving at.

"You mean risk... again? Or that you've never chanced them and never will?"

Anne finished her bite and sighed.

"Both."

"You know what I don't like about you?" he pressed.

"What's that?" She lifted her chin and let the beer bubble down her throat.

"You're not afraid to take chances."

Anne laughed and wiped a spray of foam from the side of her mouth. Both sides of the game coin were the same—kind of. He started this tryst, now she'd finish it.

"Okay. Equal time, here."

"Who said anything about equal time?"

"Somehow that remark doesn't surprise me."

He smirked and polished off the last of his sandwich.

"Okay, here it is." She lowered her legs and leaned forward. Thinking, she laid her palms face down on the wood.

"You know what I like about you?"

He waited more patiently than she expected. Eager interest dared to show in his eyes. Her mind jumped from one possibility to another. One answer she could give would be his eyes. They were so clear, yet mysterious. Except a better idea struck her. The love and respect for his land she'd seen shining in them.

She tapped her finger against her chin. Nah, something else. It should be his incredible physique! That would win hands-down. She let her eyes coast over his handsome face and broad shoulders. No doubt any healthy woman in her right mind would put that at the top of the list.

She opened her mouth, but snapped her lips shut. Foolish woman. Telling him that would be like presenting a conductor with a gift from his orchestra—a new baton. Sure enough he'd want to show what he could do with it.

Brain fog hit her, maybe it was from the alcohol. He was still waiting. "Okay. You have heart," bolted from her mouth. "And a body that won't quit."

Six

Heat burst in Anne's cheeks. Surely she'd gone too far, too fast. Candor like this was reserved for people she'd come to know over time. Eyeing him with uncertainty, she nibbled her bottom lip.

He didn't laugh as she half hoped he would. Instead, his jaw muscles worked as he lifted his hands and covered her own with his. Warmth radiated from his eyes. Enough to make her world stop for a few precious minutes.

"And what don't you like about me?"

Anne's throat clutched.

"Go ahead, mate," he coaxed.

"Mate?"

"Friend." He leaned back and folded his arms. The curious glint in his eyes melted her, but she kept a serious face.

"Hmm," she thought aloud. She supposed Slade's arrogance still vied with obstinance for first place. Moreover, he could swing from raw irritation to skepticism to compassion. His unpredictability made doing business tough and could certainly toy with a woman's heart.

These aside, her senses handed her a more immediate answer. For them it seemed an easy chore. She hesitated and looked squarely into his tempting eyes. This certainly was a time for living dangerously.

"I guess I'd have to say... your body."

Slade lifted a corner of his mouth and stared. His eyes narrowed under his wisp of dark eyelashes. Cocking his head to one side, he lowered his voice into a wounded tone.

"And what's wrong with my body?"

Anne swallowed. It constantly tempted her, for one thing. She suffered a new wave of regret. She couldn't seem to shut up. Something about him drew her out, exposed her.

Now he looked as if he were choking back a bevy of emotions. Was Slade for real? Maybe she was wrong about his toughness. She played the same hand he did and now he looked like a wounded puppy. Only the fire crackled.

"Game's over," she decided.

In a sudden cough, Slade burst out laughing and slapped his knee with his hand. "Had you going, eh?"

Anne raised her chin. "No fair goading the contestants," she said evenly. "You lose by default."

"No, I concede," he said and shrugged. "I never lose."

That she believed. She bantered with him a bit more, and fell into a companionable silence until a serious expression hardened his features. He suddenly looked over at her and said, "I take back my answer."

"Oh? Which one?" Disappointment pinged in her heart.

"What I like about you most is your honesty. Any other woman would have said something like 'your ability to handle yourself in a crisis.' But your answer took guts."

His praise wrapped her ego in silk, but she needed to set him straight.

"Most women *are* strong, Slade."

He looked away for a moment, then reached over and slid his thumb along her chin causing her skin to tingle. She had little stamina remaining from her whirlwind day, and the sudden rush from his tenderness left her giddy.

She gazed up into his face. She couldn't understand him. He seemed so complex, more capricious than the weather, more steadfast than Ayres Rock. A disturbing idea hit her. Troubling enough that it challenged her own confidence about dealing with difficult people. What if Slade McGregor was more than she could handle, even in the course of business?

Her pulse fluttered. His effect on her surprised her even more. Her curiosity sharpened. She wondered what it would be like to have him kiss her again. A real kiss, unlike the cavalier one he'd stolen earlier in the day.

As fast as this outrageous yearning surfaced, it winked out. Her energy was spent and she must have looked like it.

"Dusty needs out," he said, standing. "Then I'll get you settled. You need some rest."

Cloaked in fresh rain, he soon returned. He poured dog food from a sack into a pottery bowl and freshened the water. The sound of crunching with intermittent lapping filled the room.

"You can sleep up in the loft." He pointed toward a wooden ladder that led to a second level that overlooked the main room. "I'll stay here on the couch. We'll leave early and head back to the house."

Twenty minutes later, new logs on the fire sped warmth up to the loft. She plumped worn pillows and spread out a coverlet that had a faded floral print of pink and blue and yellow wildflowers strewn across the fabric. She yawned and sank onto the edge of the bed to pull off the socks Slade had loaned her. The bed springs groaned from beneath the soft mattress.

Undressing, she slipped into a white cotton sleeping shirt Slade had also found in the bunkroom. Since the hem dropped below her knees and the shoulder seams hung way down her upper arms, she had little doubt whose shirt she was about to sleep in. Slade's grandfather's. *How ironic,* she thought. She wore the old clothing of an elderly man who held one of the keys to her completing her project.

Whether Jim would agree to help her get to Rainbow Canyon remained unknown, but she hoped so. She reasoned that if he were dead set against working out any agreement, he'd have said so tonight. But he didn't. So only tomorrow would tell what he had on his mind. She laid her clothes next to her rain-soaked briefcase on a wooden steamer trunk at the end of the bed.

Her hair brushed, she walked to the rail and looked down into the small cozy living room. Slade had turned down the lamp over the table and stripped to his jeans. She swallowed a solid lump. The sight of his bare chest, broad, strong and matted lightly with hair, ignited a torch in her fiercer than any Olympic flame carried to ignite the cauldron.

"Sleep well," he said, flashing her a smile. "And thanks."

His smooth voice resonated through her. Somehow his Aussie accent seemed less foreign. Slade wanted to show her some gratitude. Had he realized that she didn't overreact or make decisions on impulse? Did he understand that although creativity played a big part of her life, she wasn't foolhardy. Surely, he must have reconsidered and formed a new conclusion.

She pushed aside a strand of hair and asked, "For what?"

He held up his bandaged arm.

"Your good nursing job." He winked and whistled the first few bars of "Music of the Night," settled on the couch, and closed his eyes.

Anne stole another glance at him. *The sleeping devil,* she thought and moved away from the rail and tucked herself into the antique bed. The day's events raced around in her head as she began to relax. Instead of falling asleep, she picked up the song where Slade had stopped and hummed to the rain that tap-danced on the roof above her head.

~ * ~

Startled, Anne opened her sleepy eyes. "What on earth?"

Drops of water hit her on the cheek. She turned over and another splat in the middle of her forehead. The bed springs squeaked as she sat up and peered at the open beams through the dark. The tip of her nose caught the next drop, and she pushed back the covers.

"My luck," she groaned, swinging her legs over the edge of the bed.

She gazed toward the loft railing beyond her feet. A faint glow radiated from below. Robeless, she stood and moved to the end of the bed where she picked up Slade's grandfather's shirt from the arced trunk and slipped it back on. Padding to the ladder, she climbed down.

"You're up early," Slade said, sitting on the couch with his legs outstretched on the bench. Contents of the saddlebag from his motorcycle were piled around him.

"The roof's leaking." She reached for the floor with her bare feet.

Removing reading glasses, he slid a pencil stub behind his ear and trained his eyes on her. He'd put on a clean shirt, but had left it unbuttoned. Her presence seemed to disturb him. He set the glasses on the bench, but they fell to the floor as he stood.

"Hannah's isn't what it used to be."

Anne walked over to the couch as he thudded up the ladder with a bucket he'd pulled off a nail by the sink. Overhead, the iron legs scraped the floor as he pushed the bed toward the rail.

"Neither am I," she quipped.

She lifted her hands and ran her fingers up and down the back of her neck and spied an old clock on a side table. Four a.m. Too early to think, eat, or capture dawn's light. Groggy, she stretched as the first raps of the unwelcome water fell into the metal bucket upstairs.

Slade lumbered back down the ladder and came around to the front of the couch where she now stood.

"That'll keep for a while. Besides, the rain's let up."

"Could've fooled me."

She shook waterdrops from her hair. Oh, how she must have looked to him: tousled, the white cotton peeping from beneath the loose overshirt, and barefoot. He, on the other hand, looked rested and awake.

"I apologize for the inconvenience," he said and cleared his throat. "I heard another radio report. Fifteen kilometers on the other side of the Canyon didn't get a drop. They're crying for rain over there. Had three fires already this summer. Not a week will pass before it's hot and bone dry here again. True to bush form."

He picked up a poker and stirred through the burning wood, releasing tiny sparks and new flames. Their glow gilded the bandage on his forearm. Dusty stretched and ambled over to them.

"He's better," she said with relief as he thumped his tail against her leg.

"He's tough. Want some tea?" He picked up the poker and tapped the billy pot that hung over the embers.

She shook her head."You know I could really use a cappuccino and a hot pack."

"Are you hurting?"

"Sore muscles mostly." She lifted one shoulder, then the other. Her legs felt like pegs. No way she wanted to even think about another road trip on that bike with Slade.

"Hold on a sec." Slade crossed the room to the hutch and produced a jar of instant Folger's coffee. "Had an American hunter come through who left this."

He turned up the lamp. The sight of the red label on the jar perked her up.

"Almost perfect," she said, counting her blessings.

She transferred Slade's belongings to the floor and sat down on the couch. Her thoughts strayed. A tale-telling, busy day bore down on her, but she laughed to herself. What was happening to her? By now, sore or not, she'd have already checked off items on her list of things to do and started on tomorrow's. Somehow all this rustic, back-country life sapped the living anxiety out of a body. This was not good. Although she liked what she did for a living, she thrived on the pressured pace. Keeping her nose to the grindstone kept her alive and happy.

Slade rounded the bench with two large blue enamel mugs in his hand and tipped the billy pot to release some water into each. He turned to her and handed her one of the mugs.

"White or black?" he asked.

"Black, please."

The twinkle in his eyes brightened as she took the mug from him. She sipped and tried to relax against the cushions. Her nerve endings picked up a sharp, tight pain that ran from her right shoulder to her neck. The ache stabbed enough to give anyone a start.

"You *are* hurting," Slade said. He walked behind the couch and set his mug on the wood floor. "You need to relax your mind and a rub down will help."

"Thanks, but I'll be—"

He laid his hands, warmed from the mug, on her shoulders and began to knead the tensed muscle.

"—okay," she finished.

His fingers worked in toward her neck. "Wouldn't want you to leave the Red Gum twisted up and harried. It wouldn't be good for our five-star reputation."

Anne sighed. For certain, he could be trying. His fingers played magic on her muscles. The ache began to lighten. So did her head.

He leaned over her right shoulder while he worked. It was obvious he took his brand of nursing seriously. The warmth of his face radiated next to her cheek. She felt hot and mellow as if she'd drunk half a gallon of wine in the last two minutes.

"You know, we learned a lot from my grandmother Hannah."

She sucked in a breath and struggled to get a grip. Reality slipped away, but unlike the manner in which her imagination often took her. No, this was real, all right. And hot.

"Yeah? What?"

"How to never throw anything away. Like this old shirt."

Anne barely heard the end of his last sentence as he pulled the rust-colored shirt away from her shoulder. Now only the thin white sleep shirt separated her skin from his. She could hardly bear another deep, pain-relieving, penetrating swirl of motion from his lanolin-softened palms, without melting into desire.

He leaned in closer and she found herself wanting him to.

She said, "You keep this up and Management might not expect what I put on the service survey card."

"Nothing shocks me," he whispered near her ear. His breath feathering her lobe gave her goosebumps. The masseuse she'd visited could learn heaps from this man.

Even her toes relaxed. He drew back for a moment, as if making a decision. But the power of the moment proved stronger than any reservations he held about going on.

His cheek met hers, but she dared not turn her face toward him. That would be opening Pandora's box. The end, or the beginning? Of what, she could only guess.

Now Slade McGregor's judgment proved wrong. She wasn't the risk-taker he'd thought. Too much depended upon her ability to maintain professionalism. A lot of money was wrapped up in the project she'd come out here to accomplish. Corporate plans, careers—including her own—stood on the line. Jack's advice, *Don't let your personal life interfere* rushed back to her.

She tried to stiffen and pull away, but couldn't. Slade's hands laid claim to her shoulders. He switched pressure from one side to the other, in a steady, mesmerizing rhythm.

One side, then the other. Taunting her. Making sure she understood how much she affected him. Enthralling her in perfectly delightful anguish. She closed her eyes and let her head fall back. Her nipples peaked. A hungry titillation sprang between her thighs.

Anne murmured his name, but Slade didn't reply. She moistened her lips and repeated the name she'd either wished she'd never heard, or the one she'd been waiting for all of her life.

Slade? In a hazy mush, she realized her lips hadn't moved. Only in her mind had she spoken his name. His lips brushed against her right cheek, then her left, then retreated to the back of her neck. When he said, "Annie," his voice cloaked her in well-being.

But where could this lead them? She *had* to stop him before he went one move further. She had to protect them both from certain disaster and embarrassing consequences.

He'd released the shirt from her other shoulder, and she felt the collar work its way down between her spine and the couch cushion. She was sure she could hear light, sweet flutes.

Opening her eyes would be too much to bear. Too dangerous. Once open, they could run right smack into his. With the way she felt, she'd never want to climb out of the blue of them.

"Feeling good?" he whispered.

She nodded, weakened from comfort and discomfort. Her head tilted toward the left as his hand slid over the neckline of the thin cotton. The other quickly followed suit.

His palms cruised along her throat. Dropping sweet fire along the way, his fingers reached her collarbone and played along those ridges between her breasts.

She trembled. Her only recourse was to shrink further from his seduction into the cushion. Her chin raised, as if levitated by his magic, and her lips parted. His male scent surrounded her. She was deliciously doomed.

The truth was that an aspect of her life did depend on Slade, although she wouldn't admit to any such thing, and doubted he would either.

"Then this should make you feel better."

He eased his fingers down her sternum, taking the direct road that led to her breasts. Her nipples needed attention, heightening the hunger in her groin.

Bravely, cautiously, she opened her eyes a slit. She nearly gasped. The sight of his hands draped over her from behind like this, massaging—first gently, then firmly—and her skin under the nearly transparent cotton teased her senses while his fingers headed to one of her most erogenous zones.

The very thought made her more giddy than she ever believed she could be without going into a dead faint. She wasn't the fainting kind, but shut her eyelids anyway.

Adrenaline bubbled through her now. He relaxed his fingers and stroked the soft skin at the top of her breasts. Closer, then he retreated. Closer.

Her mouth awaited Slade's lips. Restless, hungry, demanding. Wasn't he ever going to *kiss* her? In a swift move, her body took over as her mind exploded into fantasy.

Arching back, she lifted her arms and encircled his neck with them. She pulled him over farther as she struggled upward and captured his mouth with her own.

Unwittingly, she'd opened the gates to Nirvana. Slade took over from here. With relentless power, his lips bathed hers in wet tenderness, then crushed them as his tongue searched, and dove into her. She squirmed, and he pulled back for a mere instant only to retrace the new path he'd cleared, fanning desire in her.

Her heart forgot its next beat, and normal breathing became a thing of the past. Any twitches of muscle pain she had had vanished into thin air. Like her spirit, the aches were carried away to a magical place by an earth-bound angel.

Awake, she whimpered when he released her mouth.

"We can make better best," he murmured, letting his fingers slide. Ever so lightly, he grazed the tips of her nipples. She was going to die in desire.

She slowly reopened her eyes and gazed up into his face from beneath her moist lashes. His irises burned with excitement. Such a change from the skepticism she'd once read in them. Hearing his voice say her name anchored her.

"Are you up to it?" he asked.

"I'm up to it," she said, gritting her teeth every time his fingers passed over her starving breasts.

Unfettered, genuine joy spread over his face as he nuzzled his soft stubble against her cheek, which raised another whole set of images in her mind. Still locked into her aura, he maneuvered his hands away from her nipples and cupped her breasts, squeezing their fullness.

"But I can't," she whispered as he stretched over her. She wrapped her fingers around his arms. Flexed for passion and giving endless pleasure, his muscles rippled hard.

In another few seconds there would be no turning back. She was a woman. He was a man. The natural chemistry between them jetted. The classic simple equation for trouble stared her in the face, and paying the consequences would certainly come later. If only it were another time and place. Lord knew she'd gone long without attention of this sort, and this man was different. He tempted her soul to discover his. Most capable of carrying her into the maze of pure passion. Far past any other point of feeling she'd gone before.

"I'm sorry, I can't," Anne repeated, fighting every inch of her body for control. She suspected her words skidded over his head and ended up somewhere in the loft.

"You mean you won't," he said, almost releasing her.

"Yes, that, and I mean I shouldn't. Don't you think we've gone far enough?" she rasped, trying to gather her shattered wits. "We're over the top here."

He smiled knowingly. "I reckon that's a good place to start." He pressed his lips to her forehead.

She lowered her chin and let her arms drop. Her skin thrummed so badly he probably could feel it.

"No, Slade. I didn't come all the way out here to play house. I've a job to do."

He arched a brow and withdrew his arms. He took a moment as if he were rebuilding his tower of blocks that had tumbled over in the last half-hour. The sudden chill in his voice sluiced over her like cold water.

"Then you better get to it."

She sat up and pulled the shirt up over her shoulders.

"I've hurt you."

He stood and walked around the couch and faced her.

"No you haven't. I'd have to care first."

Stunned beyond words, Anne pushed herself to her feet. She had hurt him. And he retaliated equally with harsh words. He stepped back. The dying embers of the fire glowed in the dark and reflected in his eyes.

"Best to roll out of here as soon after breakfast as possible," he said dully, then turned and strode toward the bunkroom.

"Wait. You know I can't 'get to it' until the agreement is signed. Only then can I call for the crew."

Turning around, he ran his fingers through his hair.

"Tell you what. When we get back to the house, go ahead and get your people out here. You've got one other place you wanted to use, so start with it. I'll show you a place far better than the Canyon. It even has a cave."

Crossing her arms, Anne gave the suggestion some thought. The man had the look of a boy worried about being discovered with his hand in the cookie jar. Furthermore, he seemed so sure that women were untruthful, yet she sensed he took a few detours from the road of honesty himself. She supposed he had a pretty drastic reason to hold out like this about the Canyon. One that went beyond crossing through a native people's land.

"Okay, does it have a waterfall?" she asked.

"Like a veil."

"Parrots?"

"Plenty and lorikeets."

"Pristine light in the morning?"

Slade raised a resolute eyebrow and he said, "Yes."

"Perfect, a cave," she said, frustration mounting. "Who'd wear sunscreen in a cave?"

Slade struggled for a moment. "I know you need to do a job. The area is quite spectacular. You'll see."

She sighed and turned away from him. "But it's not *best*."

His voice steeped with finality. "Annie, I don't want you filming in my Canyon and it seems you can't respect that."

"I could if I understood why." She wanted at least to hear the truth. From him, no one else. But he owed her nothing. "And I've never seen such a beautiful place."

He closed the distance between them and turned her around.

"You've got no choice. And before you ask—because you've got that curious light sprouting in your eyes—why I make certain decisions is my business."

Now he had her. But not for long. There was always more than one way to skin a cat, or shoot a scene.

Seven

The tedious ride back to the main house took forever to Anne. Steering around puddles, Slade gazed back at her. *Another test?* she wondered as they slid to-and-fro past kangaroos that bounded alongside the so-called road.

After ending his display of affection with his sour remark about not caring, whatever he thought about her became unimportant. He'd cast his spell over her soul for the last time. From here on out, everything would be strictly business.

"What's up?" he yelled over his shoulder.

"I'm thinking."

"About?"

"Things."

He slowed the Triumph and slid to a stop.

She pulled her cell phone from her pocket.

"You're angry," he said.

Ignoring him, she actually got a dial tone and punched in the office number, but it was busy. Her watch read 10:23 a.m.

"How long will it be until we get back?"

He pushed his hat further back on his head.

"Okay," Slade began. "For what it's worth, I apologize."

She remarked lightly, "Worth is relative. I don't remember that ridge being so close to the house."

"I read you wrong."

"Yes, you did." She followed the topography with her eyes as it cut into deep vees, then eased downward to meet the woods. "Isn't it odd how you can be looking right at something and not really see it?"

In spite of how she knew people's actions outweighed their words, his callousness had ripped through her. She'd been turned on, then off like tapwater.

After she'd recovered her wits and got him to stop luring her into certain trouble, he'd created distance between them. Very quickly, too. Perhaps, she'd ventured too close to what he feared most. Rejection. Or was it that he came to his senses as quickly as she and realized he'd opened doors he shouldn't have? Fear made people do irrational things. So did loneliness.

Whatever, her own feelings undermined her logic. On the one hand, she barely knew him. On the other, it seemed like she always had. Such a strange position.

Unlike putting together a production plan, everything seemed so uncertain. Except for one aspect. He showed no qualms about igniting her passion, or showing his. To his credit, he'd intended to finish what he'd started—a quality she greatly admired in a man.

Whatever it was that quashed his hunger for tenderness, she'd bet her Handycam Pro that it had something to do with Rainbow Canyon. He always seemed edgy about the place. His reaction over the aerial photograph of the gorge pointed to trouble right off.

Slade revved the bike and they took off again. They bumped along and crested the next hill, and Anne craned her neck to see the main house. She couldn't wait to clean up, resolve the Canyon issue, and get to work. It was that simple.

"My grandfather's here," Slade called back to her and pointed to the open gate in the picket fence as they rattled down the backside of the hill. "Hangs his hat on the post, unless it's raining. For being a Texan, my Nan was peculiar that way. She didn't want a man's dusty hat inside her house."

Looking down at her own dust-ridden clothing, Anne replied, "I'm inclined to agree."

In about a few minutes Slade pulled up alongside the fence.

"You'd have liked Hannah."

"Probably. No matter whose they are, grandparents and I often get along well."

Slade turned off the motor. She breathed a big sigh and lifted her legs onto solid ground and stretched. Overhead, pale blue began to peek through high, thin layers of gray.

She passed through the gate and up the front path to the porch. In a way, it felt like she'd only just left the place, except so much had happened since. She slid out of her briefcase apparatus, and, once indoors, she followed her host down the corridor. As they passed the living room, she glanced at Rudy's painting. Had she just seen a ewe's ear in those brushstrokes?

"I'm eager to hear your grandfather's comments," she said, nearing the office. "How soon can we all meet?"

"At four."

"Good. I *hope* that you and I can put aside our differences and focus on the project?"

Slade slowed his pace. "You don't seem to want my apology, but I'll give you some advice, Annie. Don't ever bet on your dreams. They'll fail you. Dreams can't be trusted."

She looked up at him hard. He was dead serious. "Slade, other than prayers, my hopes and dreams are what keep me going." She stepped inside the guest bedroom and faced him.

"Your call, my warning," he said, removing his Akubra.

In spite of his embittered attitude, his vulnerability made her shudder. She forced resistance. "I believe there's a way to resolve the Canyon problem."

He cocked an eyebrow. "You really do, don't you?"

"Yes. Either through compromise or negotiation we'll make it, and I'm not giving up."

Slade shook his head. This woman had a one-track mind. Far too inflexible and too damned attractive for her own good. The unwanted shadow of her kiss flitted through his doubts and pain and lodged itself in the center of his heart. But she did give up one thing—his touch. Even though she'd put her reticence on business, he knew much more was going on with his guest. All in all, she'd revealed little about herself.

I'll peel her layer by layer, if I have to. I must know her.

He nodded at her briefcase. "My grandfather will want to read the agreement before we meet. Mind if I take it to him?"

Anne nearly choked, but she opened the case and handed the document to him. His fingers brushed hers, enough to tingle her skin all over again. She gazed into his eyes. So clear, blue, and compelling. So dangerous.

"I'm going to see this again, right?"

He stepped closer.

"You have my word."

"And it'll be in one piece?"

"I'm not signing, Annie."

The tightness behind her breastbone returned. Slade unnerved her. In almost every way he was different from any man she'd ever met. Sensual and deep, he made her stretch beyond her limitations and realize how rewards could follow. If not, at least, new adventures. Taunting ways of enriching her life.

How could she be angry about that? Perhaps he did care for her. And did that shake him up? It would explain his cryptic remark at Hannah's. But could he care that much so soon?

"You'll change your mind," she maintained. "I'll bring some other agenda items we'll need to cover. Mostly logistical stuff, like where the campers can be parked, generating power, food services, and other things for us to get started."

The more she spoke, the less Slade wanted to hear. But the lilt of her voice wouldn't release him and spread over him like the skin-softening lanolin from wool. In one instant, he couldn't wait to wash the substance off. Conversely, he wanted to wear the damned oil forever—even if it was boronia-scented.

"Oh, and another thing," she said. "Maybe we should set up a radio. Slade? You look like you're a million miles away."

He refocused on her mouth and the excitement bubbling in her eyes. Her enthusiasm, sincere and contagious, pummeled him with guilt. This woman also loved her work. In spite of everything, he still loved his work and the Red Gum. He knew how important it was to protect its privacy and beauty in an ever-shrinking world. He had no desire to advertise places like Nourombie and the Canyon. Although the publicity could help their new wool scouring plant, he still wanted to wring his grandfather's neck for making this happen now. He simply wasn't ready yet.

"No need for the radio." He rolled the agreement up into a cylinder. "And I'm making it a point to be on-site as much as possible. Remember?"

"No doubt you'll change your mind about that, too."

Anne crinkled her nose in a cute way as she closed the door. Unintentional, he was sure. He ambled away, rapping his thigh with the rolled paper.

Entering the living room, he tossed his hat onto the long table where'd he first seen his infernal guest, long-legged and leaning over. He gazed at the map where it still lay open and vulnerable, like his life. Until yesterday he felt more in control, perhaps getting some status quo back. Now he wondered.

Before he went to the office, he stopped by the kitchen to let Da-Wa know he was back and to find out how things had gone in his absence. If anything had happened, the minute Chinese man or Rose would advise him.

Slade was grateful, since as different from each other as the two house staffers could be, they worked well together and kept the place up and running. In a few things, Slade did believe he was a lucky man. This was one of them.

"Have you seen Grandad?" he asked, remembering he'd left the Esky at Hannah's hut.

"Hiya, Mr. Slade," the cook replied as he chopped fresh shallots picked from the house garden. "He go in office. He feeling sickie. He don't want Da-Wa's short soup." The corners of the man's mouth drooped under his thin, dark moustache. "I say, 'you should go bed.' He say, 'mind only cook's business.'

"I get mad as rooster. I say—"

"All right," Slade said, raising his hand. "Remember, we've a house guest, and more people will come for a few weeks." He tried to swallow his mixed feelings. "Now, *she* could use some of your soup. Tell Rose to check on her. No matter what my grandfather thinks, this is no time for the woman to be here."

The cook swept shallots into a bowl and put a lid on it. His black eyes shone. Wearing slippers, he shuffled to the refrigerator.

"No problem."

Slade left the Chinaman and turned down a short hallway that was lined with photographs of a few of the stockmen who had kept the Red Gum thriving through three generations. At the end of the row hung one of his paternal grandparents.

"Jim and Hannah McGregor, 10 September, 1946" was inscribed in faded ink on the lower right corner. That day they'd also left Melbourne for the sheep station. The older he got, Slade admired their courage and resilience even more.

He found the office door ajar and pushed it open the rest of the way and walked in. Jim McGregor sat in the leather swivel chair behind the old red cedar desk he'd brought with him so many years ago. Instead of looking up at Slade, he coughed and poured over the *Woolbuyer News* and drew circles around numbers.

"Grandad?" Slade scrutinized him as he settled in the chair opposite the desk. He noticed every tired wrinkle, white hair, and shake of his wizened hand. Except for his cold symptoms, the elderly man remained unusually quiet. That meant his mood could be ill, too. Slade shouldn't have let him go out to move those ewes in the rain.

"Da-Wa said you're sick."

"He knows too much sometimes," McGregor grumped, then sneezed. "Sit down, Slade. We have to talk."

"I reckon so." His palm warmed around Anne's agreement as he gestured toward the computer screen with its spreadsheet. "Prices changing per head, or has Neville Crane from across the canyon come up with another bright idea for the SMWA?

"Wish it was that bloody simple. Money problems can always be worked out, and the SMWA is more quiet these days. Our neighbor's decided to support the scouring operation if we take on his wool." He looked over and his eyes clouded.

"But you don't want to talk about Neville."

"You're right. It's a problem of the heart I'm wrought up over. Times like this I wish your father was still here. I'm gettin' too old for this."

Slade leaned forward and dropped the agreement on the desk. He watched the lines across the elderly man's face deepen.

"'A problem of the heart,'" Slade repeated. He'd been through plenty of problems involving the station with his grandfather, but this was a new one. "*Whose* heart? Yours?" In spite of his irritation, alarm rose. "Has someone hurt you?"

McGregor stood, circled the chair, contemplated for another second, and then sat back down.

"Not yet, but he's heading in that direction. Only a matter of time, and, dammit, it's him I'm worried about, not me."

Slade squinted as he ran over some possibilities. Being in the wool business created some fast enemies. He just needed to find out which one and take care of the situation.

"Who?"

"Someone I know who has a head on his shoulders. Man who I figured had matured and would be able to handle things and pick up the Red Gum where I leave off."

Slade stiffened as his grandfather stared directly into his eyes. "He's near and dear to my heart, and who I reckoned could meet hard things in life. Now he needs my help."

Slade averted his gaze out the window. One of the gardeners gave Dusty basic commands. If only relationships between people could be so easy.

"I've disappointed you?" he asked, incredulous. "How? I do a good job managing the Red Gum."

"Yes, on most counts."

"Then what 'hardest things in life' do you mean?"

His grandfather hunched over and another loose cough spewed into the air. "Don't give me that garbage. You know exactly what I'm talking about. But since I don't have time to beat around the bush, I'll get to the point." The old farmer pushed the newspapers aside and folded his arms. "Caroline's been gone for more than a year."

Slade's insides bent. This was the first time anyone had spoken her name around him in a long time. Anger swelled from the pit of his dark inner pain. He'd perfected clamping down on it, never letting it out. He'd become even better at making sure no one else brought up the matter in his presence. Ever.

"I know the whole situation was intolerable for you," Jim McGregor resumed, "but it's okay to move on now."

Slade looked in earnest across the desk. The bone of contention he had to pick with his grandfather about inviting the advertising agency out to the station without his knowledge went up in smoke.

"Grandad, people handle grief differently. It's my personal problem now. I'll solve it in my own way."

Burying everything that went with that day was good for him, or so he believed. Never to retread, never to reopen that heavy, black gate that he'd pulled shut forever.

Dammit to hell. He thought everyone understood what he needed. Until this moment people held their silence, at his request. Now his grandfather—his own flesh and blood—reopened the wound. His mind and emotions reeled. Caroline's face barreled through his memory.

Guilt roiled inside him, and he fought harder to control it. What a mistake he'd made. He'd married and brought her out here from Sydney, and now he paid a dear price.

He rubbed his finger over one inch on the desktop. He needed space, more time, and... to forgive himself. That would be never.

"Slade?"

He lowered his eyes. One of the metal buttons on his dirty shirt hung by a single, loose thread, the scratch on his forearm throbbed, and now his soul smoldered. He looked up angrily.

"What's going on?" he erupted.

The elderly man took a sip of brandy, the one vice he still allowed himself, save for a good fight every now and then.

"I've never known you to outright lie. Not to anyone."

Slade pushed himself up from the chair. This family conference turned worse instead of better. Apparently, *he* was on the agenda.

"And what about you?" he countered. "Since we're talking principles, I've never known you to set me up. Not once, but twice in the last month. First, you invite some citified operation out here without telling me. And now you question my honor?"

He whirled around and strode toward the locked gun cabinet. His thoughts battled as he stared through the glass pane of the door. Not a chair squeaked or papers rustled behind him.

"I thought we were family," he said over his shoulder, moving to the bookshelf. Old photographs sitting on the top came into view. There was one of his parents and the silver-framed one of his grandmother. "And I believed you and I were *partners.*"

Another moment evaporated into tension. His grandfather rose from the chair and walked over to him. Slade resisted the weight of his grandfather's gnarled hand on his shoulder. It was a strong hand, broad like his own, seeking to diffuse his frustration and pent-up sorrow. Since this kind of confrontation was so rare, Slade balled his fingers into fists.

"Now hold on," his grandfather coaxed. He moved to Slade's left side. "One step at a time." He picked up the photograph of Slade's grandmother. He traced her kind, yet strong face with his broken fingernail, then placed his most prized possession back on the shelf. "I had good reason for inviting those people out here to film."

Slade blurted, "And I have mine for not wanting them here."

"Yes, I know," he replied dryly. "But our guest is a pretty, intelligent, and gutsy woman. Don't you reckon?"

Disbelieving, Slade shook his head. "You're jumping tracks on me, Grandad." He'd noticed more and more of this lately. "Yes, she's nice with pretty eyes and all the rest, but—"

"Then cut her some slack."

"That's more than I want to deal with right now and she's not my guest. You know we're butt-deep in work."

His grandfather's white bushy eyebrows knitted over his steely eyes. Slade tried to backpedal.

"Say, what *is* this? Last night you hinted you knew her, but she says she doesn't know you."

"What's it matter? You like her, don't you? Let her film in the Canyon and go about her business. Stay away if it's too painful for you. You've been doing a damned good job of hiding out at Hannah's hut, anyway." He turned his face away and sneezed again. "It's only sixty seconds of film, not the bloody end of the world."

"Right, ignore her so she'll end up in some wild pig's gut. Annie and her crew need someone who knows the place. You, or me, or Rudy. Except he's busier than we are with the ceremony coming up."

His grandfather nodded. "You think angles like your father. I can imagine why you wouldn't want Rudy in contact with Anne. You told her there isn't another route to the Canyon when you know damned well about the old game trail. You lied to keep her away from something you haven't been able to face."

Slade's gut felt like it had just been riddled with a magazine full of bullets.

"It's still my business," he said. "Not yours."

"Nope. It's mine, because we *are* family, and we're partners. And it's unlike you to lie or hide from anything. And that's when I realized that you're in trouble. Forbidding us, who love you and care about you, from talking about that day doesn't cut it any longer. And you need something to boost you out of the past. Don't you see that?"

"No, I don't," Slade roared. "Why dig up bad dirt?"

Gazing from over top of his handkerchief, his grandfather answered, "Because every shovelful is washed by the light of day." He gave a hardy noseblow and his eyes watered. "Think about it."

"I do. Every bloody day since she rolled over the edge of that bloody canyon." Exploding felt good. It purged some of the poison he'd collected in his system since last spring.

Sadness set into his grandfather's eyes.

"Thinking's only the first step. Through your foolish guilt and anger you're losing us and your ability to dream. We've all noticed it. If you'd only open up and look. See the truth."

"I suppose the world knows something I don't."

"Might be, but how would you find out since we've all been pussyfooting around on the matter?"

Slade's heart pounded so hard he could feel his pulse in his wrists. His eyes snared his grandfather's.

"Look, with all due respect, you weren't out there. You don't get ballistic when you smell boronia, her favorite flower and perfume. You don't hear a woman's dying scream, later to find out it was your wife's." He stepped closer and snapped, "And that's truth, the one I live with every day."

His grandfather conceded, "Those are facts, but did you ever think there might be a few more?"

Slade stared at the old man. Drained, he slumped into a chair. The past year blazed in full color in his mind. He had thrown himself into running the sheep station, working relentless hours, and lending a hand in almost every task. He'd long believed in the power of work.

He leaned over and rested his elbows on his knees. He should've known better. Unresolved problems fester, and he'd tried to anticipate whatever he could to run a smooth operation. But what kind of station owner could he be if he failed at managing crises in his personal life?

He gazed up at his grandfather who looked weaker by the minute. Facing Anne now wasn't going to be easy. His mentor was correct. He'd lied to her about access to the Canyon. The trick was to not be around when she found out.

"Jesus," he murmured. Now he was turning into an ignorant, embittered coward.

"You'll make it," his grandfather wheezed. "I know you will." He glimpsed the photograph of Hannah.

Slade got up. "We've a meeting in the living room at four o'clock with your guest."

McGregor turned his head. A smile perked up the corners of his dry lips. "Anne reminds me of your grandmother."

"She's plucky, even for a Yank." His mind came up with a host of other things as well that he'd rather keep to himself. "And honest," he admitted. "I told her so up at the hut."

"Uh-huh." His grandfather's eyes twinkled. "Look, about this filming business, I should've talked to you first."

Slade didn't try to pry more out of him about his reasons. When he wanted to, his grandfather could be more closed-mouth than an echidna.

McGregor resumed. "Think about giving her permission to work in the canyon. She'll be on this project for a while, but not forever. So don't gather wool too long."

Slade frowned as his grandfather returned to the desk and asked, "Where's that agreement you were strangling when you walked in here?"

Slade handed it over. "You're signing it?"

"On the dotted line. And I'm going to approach the Bilwan elders about crossing Nourombie. All they can do is say 'no.'"

"Not true. They can get the wrong idea. The plan was to allow Rudy's people to reclaim their spiritual grounds. The Bilwan people don't want a blade of grass past Kissing Turtles disturbed, and they don't want to be put in a compromising position. And we shouldn't put them in one considering how they work for us."

"There's the game trail."

"Grandad, none of us have walked that shelf road for years.

"Annie's not talking about—"

"Annie?"

"—a morning hike. She's bringing campers and people, and enough equipment to stretch from here to Tamworth."

"I suspect Rudy can help. We might get lucky."

A sudden coughing fit left his grandfather's shoulders shaking. Slade walked over and helped him settle into the desk chair. The man got his breath, straightened, and picked up a pen.

Slade fought the urge to snatch it from his grandfather as he scratched his name on the release form.

"I'm turning in early," McGregor announced, placing the pen in its stand. "Give our guest my regards. And tell her I'll catch her next week, or so."

"Is there anything else you want added to the agenda?" Slade heard himself say as his grandfather pushed himself to his feet.

A curious smile lifted the corners of his grandfather's mouth. He repeated loudly, "Agenda?" and burst out laughing. From here his mirth would travel down the hall and carry into the living room.

Slade clenched his teeth. Unless he was mistaken, Anne would hear the laughter and be at the table ready and waiting. Disgusted, he jammed the agreement into his back pocket. She still needed his signature, and no way in Parry Shire was he going to let her change his mind.

Eight

Anne arrived early for the meeting. Wearing an ivory, pencil-skirted suit she'd found at David Jones, she approached the trestle table. There rested Slade's hat, and she touched its soft, weathered brim. Having traveled through some of the Red Gum with him, she no longer felt like such a stranger.

Now she sensed a pulse thrumming in perfect measure around her, in the people and the land. She'd missed this steady beat as she'd first driven north on Australia's version of the New England Highway.

Since then pressure mounted. She *had* to do this project more than right. It must be great, since proving herself still played a big part in her career and keeping her job with Greene.

Like anyone else who survived their first few years at G & A, she'd paid her dues. She worked extra hours and took on tasks without being asked. She stayed committed to this prestigious creative team even when offers sprang from elsewhere. But Greene could be a prick or a pussycat. Her momentum had faltered during the annulment of her marriage, but she'd bounced back. Nothing else but work kept her heart so safe.

She gazed around the room acutely aware of Slade's absence. The brim under her fingers seemed to whisper his name as she left it and walked toward the fireplace.

Again she gazed up at Rudy's painting. Its muted beiges and creams rose and fell into swells. They resembled undulating folds of soft wool and dried grasses and grains that she'd seen yesterday. Again, the artwork's magic lifted her spirits.

"People would love this," she said to herself, convinced that Rudy's work should take its place in respected art circles.

She turned to meet Slade as he entered the room at four-fifteen. His hair, slicked back from a shower, hugged the collar of his casual knit shirt. A strip of fresh white gauze trailed from the bandage on his arm.

"G'day," he said. Resentment invaded his eyes as she drew nearer, and he looked as harsh as any New England climate.

"Hello," she replied. "I'm ready to... um, trite, but you look like you've lost your best friend."

His expression carried a dark message and the deepest sorrow she'd ever seen buried in human eyes. Distraction hampered his movements, making them awkward.

"Let's get started," he said. All of his humor, gentleness, and passion had vanished. A different man stood before her now, daring her to make one wrong step.

Instinct warned her not to rush him. She could call Jack and tell him of the situation before she botched the whole deal.

"We can postpone if you—"

"Now. We'll meet now."

"Fine," she said, taking in a breath. "So where's your grandfather? We've a lot to discuss."

Slade paused. "He's not feeling well."

She tightened her hold on the gold pen she'd pulled from her pocket. Without Jim McGregor nothing could happen. She was sure he had answers and could help her with the Bilwan people.

"Let's sit over there." Slade turned sideways and gestured toward the sofas.

Eyeing the release form, Anne walked with him and sat at one end of the couch. She placed her cellular phone and notes on the coffee table, a polished primitive rock with a thick glass top. He pulled the papers from his pocket and sat in the middle of the sofa, throwing her off balance.

"Nothing serious, is it?" she asked, concern added to her jumping emotions. The elder McGregor had left a good impression on her last evening, even if he didn't stay long and had kept his face hidden. Odd, but it didn't feel like a first impression.

On the surface, he seemed direct, a straightforward man with whom you always knew where you stood. A man who'd spent decades surmounting problems. Just the kind of person she needed to help her in her quest, but her memory of him drew a blank.

"He and Rudy mustered half the night," Slade said. "But he'll manage."

He stretched out his legs and lowered his head until his chin nearly met his chest.

"Here," he said and handed her the document.

She unfolded it and flipped through to the signature block on the last page.

Her heart soared. "He signed it!" she exclaimed. "Your grandfather agreed. Oh, Slade, this is wonderful. Thank him for me, will you?"

Her eyes skimmed the next line down. As fast as her heart took flight, it dove into despair. The second signature line was blank.

"But you... still haven't signed?" Her eyes raked his. "Why?" she asked, spending her last ounce of patience.

He pulled himself forward on the sofa, splayed his fingers on his knees, and looked into her eyes.

"Because I can't do that right now," he replied evenly.

Steaming, she rose and took long steps around the coffee table and turned on him.

"Can't? What you mean is that you won't."

He ran his forefinger over his bottom lip. "Hmmm, that sounds familiar."

She placed her hands on her hips. "There must be a way to make this happen, or your grandfather wouldn't have signed."

Slade remained silent.

She charged, "You're being impossible. We're giving the Bilwan people a gift of money. We'd cross their land in any way they wish with the respect it deserves. What more can I or Greene and Associates do?" she cried. She dropped her pen onto the table, and it bounced off and hit one of Slade's boots. He leaned down and picked it up.

"Never mind," she said, not missing a beat. "I can guess what your answer is. 'Just go back home where you belong.'"

Shaking, she moved to the window. *I should have never let Jack talk me into coming out here,* she thought angrily. *I should have stuck with my decision about never doing business with graziers. They really are thickheaded.*

She bowed her head and rubbed her eyes with her right hand.

"God, I'm losing it. What am I to do?"

She bit her bottom lip. She'd forgotten an important rule of negotiation: Never let them see you sweat. She was dead in the water, and Greene would soon know.

Slade's voice sailed into the heart of her storm.

"Nothing," he said, answering her question.

She raised her chin and gazed out at the sunlight glinting through the trees. He stood behind her now. His warmth cloaked her. Ignoring him was no use.

She turned around. Concern had replaced the agitation on his face. Amidst her torment, she realized he'd been the only man who could stoke her temper, then douse her anger with his touch or reassuring glance. She needed him and resented his position at the same time.

"I—I apologize for the outburst," she said. "Frankly, I don't understand what's happening to me." Heat flooded her cheeks. "I'll get my things together and leave in the morning. Filming on the Red Gum won't work. I won't give our client second best, and without the Canyon it would be."

Slade's eyebrows shot up in surprise. She tried to pass him, but he caught her arm with his hand.

"The woman who fends off wild pigs is quitting?"

She glanced downward through moistening eyelashes.

"No, the woman who can't function like this. I'm ready to get my ideas onto tape. Now, not next month. If I don't, the inspiration and details will be lost."

She pulled away from him. She didn't owe him an explanation for anything. Greene & Associates would be out the costs of preliminary surveys, planning time, and her expenses. Because of that, she'd be skating on thin ice.

But right was right. And things felt only wrong. She went to the coffee table, picked up her belongings, then neared the archway leading to the hallway. Slade left the window and blocked her path.

"Hold on a minute," he said, rapping her pen on his palm. "Our meeting's not adjourned yet."

In vain, she tried to ignore the twinkle in his eyes.

"Don't look at me that way, and yes it has. We've nothing else to discuss. I *need* to film in Rainbow Canyon. *Fini.*"

She took another step and the cellular phone rang from her pocket, causing her to jump. She put it up to her mouth.

"Hello? Jack?"

"Hi, Anne. Just back from Brisbane. I've found us a new sound engineer."

"What happened to the one we had?"

"Twentieth Century Fox snapped him up. So I contracted a new one—within budget."

She tossed a wary glance at Slade. He wore a somewhat wounded expression on his face. It touched a part of her that begged not to listen.

"Hey, are you okay?" Jack asked.

"Actually, no. Tomorrow morning I'm coming—"

In a swift move Slade plucked the phone from Anne's hand. She widened her eyes as he pushed her backwards until the backs of her knees met the soft cushion of his big easy chair. His next effort landed her square in the middle of it. He wagged a forefinger for her to stay put.

"Hello, mate," he said into the phone. "Slade McGregor here. Nice to talk with you, too. Annie's having a seat for the moment. I reckon she's peaked."

Anne glared up at him, but he forged ahead.

"Listen, I know you're waiting to get started, but there are some things you people weren't aware of about our place. Certain arrangements will have to be made." He listened to Jack for a moment, answering, "No, I don't know how long, or even if. Until then you can get your crew and whatnot out here to begin over on our North Paddock. Sure, mate. Hold on. I'll get her for you."

Anne grimaced. Slade was incorrigible, unpredictable, and stirringly handsome. A volatile combination.

"Hey, Annie?" he called out as if she were across the room. "Are you available to finish this phone call?"

Towering over her, he pressed his hand on her shoulder and kept her seated as he relinquished the phone to her. Her knees bumped together and one of her shoes fell off.

"Jack?"

"Hey, you hate being called Annie. What's—"

"Just don't ask," she said through clenched teeth. "Please call the director, Susan Sornja and Chase Gordon, and the crew. Yes, Wednesday's good." The last part she half whispered, "The sooner we're done here the blessed better."

She clicked off the phone. If steam was generated in people, she could power a train from here to Perth.

"Cute," she hissed.

Slade sank down next to her in the chair. "So are you, love. Especially when you chuck a willy."

She stiffened. "That's disgusting. At no time since I came out here did I upchuck. Not even that pig made me throw up."

He smirked. "It means to go berserk."

She turned her head toward him. The last few minutes scrambled her thoughts. Confusion battled in her brain. Should she kick him for commandeering the phone, or she should kiss him for telling Jack maybe something could work out?

"Look, I've a lot to consider right now," she began, "but let's get one thing straight before people arrive. I'm not your 'love.' Got it?"

"Sure, but I don't want it," he replied.

"And don't call me Annie, either."

His hard, blue-jeaned thigh rested against hers. Warmth snapped like a live wire around her. His touch both calmed and alarmed her.

"But the name fits. First time I saw you, I thought, she's an Annie if there ever was one."

"You are so full of—of stuff. Do you expect me to believe that?" she said, raising her eyes to the beamed ceiling.

"Why not?"

"Uh-huh. And you immediately liked me, right?" she added, waiting for his next lie.

"Honestly?" he asked.

She nodded.

"I liked how your hair fell over your shoulders. And other things." A distinctive catch rose in his voice. He seemed to be reeling himself back in. "Now, could we finish our meeting. I've got work to do."

"Don't we all," she retorted. "I suppose I should thank you. Jack and 'the suits,' as we call them in Westport, will be happy. The SunMate Sunscreen people are eager to see what they've paid their big bucks for." That said, he still made her insides curl. "What other things?" she asked to placate her curiosity.

"I'll tell you sometime. About the Canyon, for now you'll have to accept that there's more to this than you know." He handed her pen back to her. "Can you do that much?"

She sighed. The dreaded having-to-trust-him factor reappeared. All along she'd suspected there was another unspoken angle to this. Apparently, a complex, deeply personal one. It was his business, but a part of her wanted him to share it so she could help put that charismatic smile back on his face.

Stymied, she wished she were at sea. As always, the rhythm of the waves under the boat would rock and soothe her. She needed the kind of peace that sailing gave her to live off of for another week.

Slade covered her hand with his own. His eyes told her something was making him suffer. Terribly. She'd told him she wasn't his 'love,' but now she wanted to cradle him as if she were. She wanted to be the only person in the world who could help him. Where that came from, she hadn't a clue.

Her palms moistened. She'd never made a deep difference in anyone's life, not really. Now her chances dimmed as she sat without a safety net to catch Slade as he fell into darkness.

She placed her free hand over his. His eyes burned straight into her soul, bypassing the warning veil that protected her. He didn't stay long, but he left an indelible mark. Appreciation lifted the gloom from his face. That took her breath away.

He said earnestly, "You are a remarkable woman."

She watched his eyes trail over her face, her neck, her hands. Now she understood what it meant to be reduced to Jello.

"Thank you," she whispered, then eased her voice back to a normal level. "Now could we continue with our business?"

"Lead on," he said, scooting further back into the extra-wide recliner. Without warning, he pulled her back into the crook of his arm. Pushing the button on the arm of the chair, he raised the foot support.

Though this was the most unethical, unorthodox business meeting she'd ever attended, relief surged through her. Somehow she wedged her tapestried briefcase in his front door. The light of joy sped through her, and where one beam shone another was sure to follow.

"I see," she replied, weakening. During the last half-hour, they'd somehow reached a new plateau. That realization made her glad she was sitting down, even if it was with the Devil.

"Between now and Wednesday I've got to lay out a new plan for everything else, but you said you have another agenda item?"

"Several items come to mind," he said, breathing by her ear. It nearly drove her wild. He shifted and pressed his thigh harder against her thigh. He also cleared his throat.

"Like I said, the North Paddock is open country and a good place to start until your crew gets used to the lay of the Red Gum land."

Faint enthusiasm spread into his voice.

"Deal," she said, shaking his hand. "It's not where the next episode of SunMate's series would take us, but filming in sequence isn't necessary."

Her answer must have set well with him.

"Mossman Creek will be washed out, but I've another spot on the station in mind. So do we have a date? Later next week?"

Her heart leaped, but her mind spoke.

"Depends on the weather and other factors."

His quizzical expression pressed her into explaining.

"Filming," she began, "is a painstaking process, but the crew we contracted is good and works well together. If the talent does well and we don't have equipment problems, we should have a smooth run," she said. "Then, barring any other unforeseen disasters, I can get away long enough to check out your proposed site."

A smile lifted the right corner of his mouth.

"You compromise quite well, and you might like Crystal Springs better than Rainbow Canyon." He moved his mouth near her forehead.

"Isn't that what you're hoping?"

He fell silent.

"Of course, you are," she said. So there was still the mainsail to raise. Slade's problems—personal, the Bilwan labor force, or otherwise—worked against her. "Well, like you said, don't bet on your hopes. They might let you down."

"I reckon I deserved that," he said.

Her conscience snapped to attention. Had she become completely selfish? Did her desire to gain personal acclaim in her work overide compassion?

She glanced at him. Through his tough exterior, he looked forlorn. The man needed a fix of doing what he loved most. Taking care of ranch business on that rattletrap Triumph of his.

"No, you didn't," she said softly. "I'm more task-oriented than I like to admit, and I don't compromise my standards very well."

"Why should you?"

"I guess that's why Greene and Associates keeps me. I work on making our client's corporate dreams come true, which are all about brisk sales years. Brand name recognition. Whipping the competition. Thing is, I dream big. In color and digital sound. I can't help it."

"That's a problem?"

She tilted her face towards his.

"Yes, because we both know that a person can't have everything. And even though I know that, I seem to want it all."

"Still, I admire you for trying for it." He moved his fingers to the hem of her skirt that lay in folds half way up her thigh.

"The bean counters back at headquarters report that I'm very trying," she joked. His fingers dropped fire over her sheer, summer-weight stockinged skin.

"People only want when they don't have," he said.

For once, she was speechless. His arm, still wrapped around her shoulders, cushioned her.

"My question is," he added, "what don't you have?"

She widened her eyes as he claimed hers. How can he see so much? Know my losses? My not having?

She fumbled for a face-saving response. She could tell him that she'd come from fine family stock, old New England Protestants with a strong work ethic. That she rarely wanted for much in the way of anything, and was destined to again marry wealth, thank you very much. Yet, such superficiality would vaporize in the inches that separated their faces.

He drew his fingers in serpentine fashion from her leg to her chin, then followed her jaw line up to her earlobe. The gold French loops she wore gave little protection from the thrill of once again knowing his touch.

Whatever she'd learned about mind over matter vanished as every one of her nerve endings fired. They knew what to do, regardless of how her mind tried to shut them down. This is what they lived for—to *feel.*

She parted her lips and drew in a luxurious breath and exhaled long and slowly. The warm thick air tasted better than any she'd breathed since she'd left Sydney for this mission.

"Annie?"

"Yes?" she answered, basking in yellow sunshine seeping through the window and the blue of his eyes.

"About that last agenda item for the meeting?"

She was floating again. How could he possibly be thinking about business? Her mind jumped in with reason. *Don't you know that he could accuse you of using your feminine wiles to get what you want—to film in Rainbow Canyon?* Nevertheless, her heart assured her to go ahead and humor him.

"Not now... no agenda... no meeting."

Slade whispered into her ear. "Yes now, because this is what you don't have. And you no longer have a true-blue bloke who cares enough to give it to you."

Anne's resistance crumbled like brittle celluloid film. Shifting, she bumped the arm of the chair with her hip. The remote for the TV fell into her lap. Using her free hand, she picked it up and held it loosely. Somewhere between Slade touching his lips to her forehead and the hunger exploding from the lower part of her body, she tightened her grip.

His lips roamed free and wild over her cheek as if they'd been set loose forever. He tongued the corner of her mouth and lured her lips to his. She fell into his blinding need and unwittingly showed him her own.

"Oh, Slade." Her skin clamored for more as his hand swept down her neck and effortlessly unfastened the top button of her jacket. His fingers dipped beneath the lace of her bra and inched down to her breasts. She felt her nipples harden, alert for come what may.

His kiss told her that he valued her more than anyone else on earth. She reeled from the flattery and the uncontrollable, heady sense of power that followed. His hand released the front catch of her bra under its tiny pink bow.

"Mmmmmm," gurgled from her throat.

"Hold on," whispered his moistened lips. "I've more."

She found herself lifting into him as best she could. Her body's message hit home. His fingers circled her left breast in a heated, feathery dance. Pressing forward, up the rise to its peak, he lightly brushed her left nipple. A thousand nerve endings sparked at once, weakening her, challenging her. Her right breast craved the same attention, and he gave it.

"Oh my," she muttered from helpless oblivion. She never imagined being caressed by a man could be like this. So intense, unknown, frightening. "Please don't."

The heat from his long hardness grew against her thigh and burned hotter than any Aussie sun. She squeezed the remote control so hard her hand numbed. In a far off haze, she heard it click and tossed the device aside.

"Don't what?" he asked huskily. "Do this? Or this?"

Another of her buttons eased opened, and he lowered his head. Finding her breasts with his mouth, he sucked them. She arched slightly, and a sweet, mild shattering flared from between her legs. She tried to cry out, but her voice went mute.

Parting her eyelids, she glimpsed Slade's hair and handsome profile. His eyes remained closed, and he looked as if he were lost in total, enraptured peace as blue-white light from the television wavered over them.

Nine

For this single moment, Fate had given Slade permission to begin anew. Anne responded to his fondling like a lamb chasing a butterfly. Crooking one of her knees, she laid her hand on his thigh. Her acceptance thrilled him.

"Again," she whispered.

Without doubt, she mystified him. She'd invaded not only his sheep station, but his mind as well. Her kiss sparked his senses and they popped open like bales of washed wool, ready for plying and weaving.

A lockmaster, this woman wedged open his heart's private gates. One by one, she lifted their rusted latches and entered, carrying sunlight into his maze of doubt and turmoil. He wondered if she sought his heart, or was just passing time. He listened to her touch with his own body. She revelled in the same magic that he felt. Again, it had thrown them together and bonded them.

Silently, he closed each gate behind her as she moved. Her light made him feel better, alive. Maybe he could cocoon her here in his maze forever? His thoughts paused. He no longer wasted time on dreams.

Yet his heart felt lighter with every step she took between those shaggy, green-black hedges. In a short time, she had made a definite impact on his life. Whether it was for the better or not kept him guessing.

Veering his thoughts away from her proved nearly impossible since he'd first laid eyes on her. She'd doused him with her temper and helped him thwart danger. She'd nursed his wounds, tenderly and with care. Just now she had kissed him back.

Totally moving, this woman.

Except she stayed tucked behind that veil of warning he'd seen in her eyes when he first explored them. Now he gained a glimmer of who she really was. A sheila in desperate need of healthy companionship and loyal friendship. Also, someone who'd fought deep hurts and was learning how to move on.

On the surface, she seemed sure of what she wanted, yet a part of her remained confused, afraid. Of what, he could only guess. But he was sure that taking her here and now in his big, easy chair seemed inevitable.

He applied more pressure, but his conscience backed him down a few pegs. She deserved lovemaking done well. With soft moods and music and mastering the delights of her, step by step. With all of his heart. He wondered if he'd ever reach that loft.

With considerable effort and amazement at his own sudden spontaneity, he eased up a bit. Rushing into anything wasn't his usual style. Surprisingly, it seemed that doing some things without preplanning or by committee did appeal to her. She rode with him this time, leaning into the curves, readying for the next turn they'd take together right here in his big easy chair. Part of him wanted her to be just like him. Another part pleaded for impulse. His old ways battled against new.

He wondered what was happening for Anne at this moment. Did she also fight confusion? He turned his head a trifle and glimpsed her face. The bliss he saw suggested she'd lost sight of who and where she was. Her business mission had faded into the steam rising between them.

Their chemistry meshed, formed its own entity, and pulled them closer together. He felt humbled, somewhat unworthy lying next to her. She, a queen, and he a knave.

His self-assurance took a sudden dive. First, his grandfather rattled his foundation with keen observations about his sorry attempts to patch his life back together. Now it shook with her, but for purely pleasant reasons.

She poured sheer sensual power over him like a long-awaited rain that wetted the long, dry road into the Red Gum. For the first time, receiving and giving warbled the same notes in a sweet, balanced song. He hungered for the next verse.

Through his musing, a smooth, well-modulated voice cut in and vied for his attention. He paid little mind and listened only to his thudding heartbeat and her faint sighs. Like Aboriginal clapping sticks sending a spiritual, urgent message from his heart to hers, he matched the rhythm.

He dipped his tongue into her sweet, boronia-perfumed cleavage. Smelling that fragrance caused a catch in his throat, but faded as she once again lifted herself against his hardness.

He wanted her. Bad. While kissing her supple skin, he again heard word fragments assault his ears. Clearer, the words intruded into his privately-led, rural life, into his living room, and dropped between him and Anne.

Resentment stirred. He lifted his head and again opened his eyes a slit. The magic that he'd written on Anne's face with his caresses pumped him up. His hand begged to follow the curve of her uplifted knee and cross the gully between her hips.

Yet, he held back and caught his ragged breath. He realized she was correct. He'd pushed her again, as far away from business and into the personal realm as possible. He never asked for the job, but opportunity knocked more than he'd ever admit.

Normally, he wouldn't give a bushfly about how people lived, or what they wanted to be. It seemed that some wise immortal had picked him to widen this woman's horizons. The problem was that his own horizon shifted every time he pulled her closer to him. This unexpected spin-off unnerved him. He slid his hand away.

The light from the television flickered over her as her eyelids fluttered open. He saw desire, disappointment, and reason tangle beneath them. She gazed over his shoulder and focused on the screen.

The voice he had heard grew clearer, louder, and finally won out over his intentions.

"Good evening," it said. "Phillip Cox reporting for Channel Seven. The bush fire that broke out yesterday in the New England region still burns."

Slade's muscles tensed. The outside world lured him away from the magic of the moment. Reluctantly, he shifted enough to see the screen. Anne's heartbeat slowed and softened near his ear. The taste of her moistened skin lay fresh on his lips.

Cox went on. "It is believed that sparks from lightning ignited the small blaze that was first sighted in the Corabu Forest area by visiting Boy Scouts. The wind has shifted south in the last hour.

"These dramatic clips show smoke and flames approaching the town of Wenjura near Mount Kamilaroi. Volunteer Fire Brigaders are hard at work to contain the blaze."

Anne lifted her hand away from Slade's thigh and drew her fingers across her forehead, wiping away tiny pearls of perspiration. The man created a smoldering heat in her that rivaled what she saw on the twenty-seven inch screen.

"Slade?" she said, her pulse steadying. "Is that closeby, near the Red Gum?"

He slid his arm from around her shoulders.

"It's still way on the other side of the mountain. The Bandari River should catch it. There's water flowing this year."

"Good," she stated, spying the scenes warily.

"Fire is one of our land's friends," Slade said as he reached over and kissed her forehead, then refastened her top button. "In a year the regrowth will take over. Fire reminds us of how cyclical life really is. It also controls weeds and pops seed pods that wouldn't open without the heat."

Anne slid up to the edge of the chair with him. The on-the-scene reporter again appeared. She checked his slicked brown hair and on-cue smile. His face had a rather rubbery look to it, yet was less manageable than an actor's.

"Hmmm. I remember him," she said, then caught herself from saying another word. He had been the reporter who had picked up her conversation on the night of the Olympic dinner that her agency held in the penthouse of their office building. That dreadful fight had broken out and almost caused her to miss the kick-off cocktail party completely.

As she watched, the spell Slade had cast upon her dwindled. Cox had caught her at her worst and exploited the moment for millions to see. The fact that she'd been tormented by rowdy, drinking sheep farmers had meant little.

Jack's words hit her again. "We're here to do our work, Anne," he had reminded her the next day while they cleared beverage cups from the conference room where people were invited after the penthouse party.

"Geez, give me a break," she fussed.

"I know you're somewhat of a free spirit now, but walking into trouble happens a lot to you. Ever notice?"

His words stung.

"So what if I'm out-of-sync sometimes? What gives with you today?"

"Nothing more than that we're guests in this country. We'll depend on all kinds of people to get our business done in the next year. That includes sheep ranchers, ticket takers at the Opera House, or Paul Morgan, the local C.E.O. for Jean Linden. He caught the news last night and called. He's not a happy camper. We have to keep production low-key. Our welcome sign on the lobby easel was picked up on camera."

"And Paul doesn't want to share what they're doing with the competition," Anne finished.

Jack stuffed his hands into his pockets, rocked back onto his heels and shrugged.

"All right, already," she blurted, "but this business is turning to hell on wheels, isn't it? I was thirty minutes late because of an accident, then I was caught on TV. At least, no one saw my face."

He popped a water bottle cap and drank with her.

"All in a day's work," he had quipped.

"Cheers to you, too."

The phone rang in the outer office and Jack lifted himself out of the chair.

"What was all that about being a Woolgrower Queen?" he called from the other office.

"You had to be down in the lobby."

Hearing Jack answer, "Greene and Associates," she flung her bottle cap into the trash from across the room. Sometimes, whatever she did wasn't right. She gazed out the window over the city that would host thousands of Olympic athletes and visitors.

"Well, at least I don't have to create a new world record," she had assured herself, "but I still have to go for the gold. And that's the way it is."

~ * ~

Here and now, a full month later she sat with Slade alone in his living room. He raised unfathomable desire in her. Yet, even if the Bilwan people granted her permission to cross Nourombie, she sensed strongly that Slade wouldn't sign the release. This was his home, not her film set. But, this truth was tough to take since she'd have to set aside her ultimate dream. The best in her industry was honored during the American Advertising Awards gala held in New York. She wished that her name would be engraved on one of those gold plaques this year.

Important, of course, but the mystery surrounding Slade's refusal grew and deepened her curiosity. He seemed a proud man. Slade losing his temper would be something she'd rather not witness, distantly or up close. And what she'd said about sheep ranchers that night would certainly anger him.

He nodded at the screen. "If I'm up doing paperwork, I see him on the late news. Thirsty?"

"Parched," she said, drawing her eyes away from the TV.

Slade pushed himself up and walked over to the built-in wine rack and swung open the door at its base. Behind the wood, that to Anne looked like golden pine, stood a small refrigerator.

"You're out most of the time, aren't you? Away from home?"

Slade pulled out two beers and a glass from the shelf.

"The whole of Red Gum is home," he said after popping the tops and pouring beer into a glass for her. "But the house is where our office is, clean clothes, and my bed. If not here, the hut. Quieter there."

He handed her the glass. Her skin still thrummed from his touch. The man's moves taunted her and frightened her at the same time. Being around him was all consuming. She glanced at her tapestry briefcase as she took the glass from Slade.

"I'm not home much, either. Especially during production weeks, now more than ever. When I'm gone too long, I feel like I've just moved into a new place," she said, sipping past the frothy head.

"My grandmother used to say, home is where you hang your bonnet. I'm away from the house a week or so at the most." The corners of his mouth lifted. "You'll find me out in the backyard somewhere."

She dabbed away foam from her upper lip.

"How do you know that bloke?" he asked about Phillip Cox.

His question was an honest one and deserved a forthright answer, but she thought hard about her answer. Other than the security guard, only one person made sense that night. A big elderly grazier with white hair. He'd helped her get to the elevator. There were exceptions to every rule, and he filled that role.

"Through business," she faltered. "He caught me on the air talking with some friends. That caused some trouble for my agency and embarrassed me."

"How?" Slade asked, his surprise genuine.

"Because the bottom line is that I'm in the image and impression management business. And I guess I blew it."

"You're kind of hard on yourself, love."

The term of endearment suddenly touched her heart.

"There's no room for mistakes in what I do. Many good people have had to kiss this business goodbye for a lot less," she summed up, sipping. "You Aussies make a good brew."

And better love?

~ * ~

For the next few days she tried to focus on her work. Avoiding Slade would be the only way to get things done. He still hadn't signed the release, so she tried to accomplish what she could. Even so, he still popped into her mind a lot.

Armed with a sketched map from Rudy, she drove her Land Cruiser over more of the Red Gum's dusty, rough roads. She'd gained a better feel for the North Paddock, its color, textures, and playing light. In a way, she was scouting up-close. When the director and film crew arrived she'd give them her input.

She drove by turgid Mossman Creek and observed first-hand how it had taken its own course. She recognized one of the trees from her aerial photographs. She found it amazing how quickly the ground soaked up the water, and how the cooler temperatures soared back into blazing heat.

She stopped the vehicle mid-road and opened the door and got out. She pulled out the Esky that Da-Wa had loaned her and climbed up onto the roof of the Land Cruiser. Perching between the ribs of the roof rack, she drank water, and fanned away flies with Rudy's map.

Wearing sunglasses, she gazed at the vast country that surrounded her. The diversity of the Red Gum property amazed her. Lush, green pasture gave way to waist-high grain in some places, stands of trees clustered along tributaries of Mossman Creek, then butted up against sandstone walls. Mobs of sheep grazed or cantered to the next pasture.

Earlier this afternoon she'd opened up her laptop computer and poured over schedules, sketches, storyboards, and budgets. Since she had to leave Australia early, putting this shoot on schedule became imperative.

Tomorrow was Wednesday, and the director, models, and techies would arrive. They could set up shop and be ready to begin early Friday morning. Seeing them would reduce the pressures she felt now and catapult her into action. She needed to be back on familiar ground, so to speak.

Now if only Slade would come to his senses and sign the infernal release. She had to be ready to go with the next phase, and Rainbow Canyon was it. She shot a quick prayer skyward.

Kissing Turtles loomed ahead. The road she was on veered sharply to the left of the unique rock formation, according to the map. After many miles the road would loop back to the main homestead house. Only open, tree-studded brush lay between her and the gateway to Nourombie—her unexpected nemesis.

She studied the ridge that ran on either side of the narrow pass hollowed out between. Through her binoculars, she scrutinized any interesting curve of rock, shape of tree, or anything that moved. Only rising heat altered her view, rippling the rocks and grasses and trees.

From this distance the rocks seemed not so high. Kissing Turtles did look like their namesakes. Two thick heads of rock, nearly touching noses, craned from underneath monolith-like rock shells. One would walk beneath them to enter Nourombie, the ancient people's birthplace full of songs, beginnings, endings.

In a certain way, that area seemed lifeless, foreboding, forgotten. So close, yet so far. She fought the temptation to climb back down into her vehicle, throw it into gear, and rumble across the terrain to stand beneath those sandstone turtle heads to see what lay beyond them.

She dropped the binoculars back to her chest and looked up at the sky. Cloudless, heaven's blanket reminded her of Slade's eyes. Perched up here she could take a break from her work and think. About him.

But details eluded her, only impressions swirled through her mind, skipping through her feelings, whetting them for the next time she saw him.

Hearing her name called out, she turned toward the direction from where it came.

Rudy walked up the road toward her. Dark-skinned, dusty, and wearing a headband of braided red, black, and gold, he waved at her. She waved back.

"G'day, Miss," he greeted in that rich voice of his.

"Hello, Rudy." She raised herself up on her haunches, then climbed down. "Is something wrong? Does someone need me?"

"No trouble. I am marking the trail some of my people will take on way to the ceremony." He nodded at the gateway into Nourombie. "Is your four-wheel-drive broken down?"

She shook her head. "I'm out here trying to get my bearings again before we start work."

He smiled. "Jim McGregor said that you will start at the North Paddock and want to come down here."

He seemed genuinely interested and not at all guarded.

"Slade told me that crossing Nourombie is the only way to get to the Canyon. He and his grandfather both mentioned an agreement the Red Gum has with your people. And how entering the area nullifies a major condition of that agreement."

Rudy's face reflected much of what was running through his mind. He bent over and picked up a dried-up old branch and worked the bark off the tip with his fingers. He gestured for her to go on.

"As you can guess, it causes me and my agency a big problem. I know your people and the McGregors depend on each other and have for a long time. No one could argue the importance of protecting the sacredness of the land and your heritage. And I'm not here to interfere. I'm here to do a good job."

"You do not seem a problem-causer."

She sighed. "Trouble follows me. Thing is, I'm going to have to wrap up this commercial series in an unsatisfactory way. Compromising quality nearly kills me."

Rudy gave a single nod. "I understand." He reached down and scratched into the earth and picked up a handful of earth. Loosening his fingers, he let the soil fly to the wind, then opened his palm and lifted it for her to see. Traces of red grit streaked his skin.

"For my painting, I would travel far to find the right ocher," he replied. "The best kind is the *right* ocher, and none other will do."

They stood for a quiet, appreciative moment. As his words sank in, relief swept through her. Rudy understood. He knew how one element affected the whole picture. Although he worked alone on bark or canvas, her art appeared on a television screen with the help of a carefully selected team. In creating art Rudy and she shared a common vision.

The irony of the situation struck her. The person who understood her artistry the most was a Bilwan. The very same people who could prevent her from reaching her goal to produce her artistic, professional best. Frustration pushed her into talking.

"I know that Slade is doing what's right by upholding the agreement with the Bilwans," she said. "It's just that I love what I've seen from our photographs of Rainbow Canyon. I can't seem to get the site out of my mind. It feels like an obsession. I *have* to film in that place."

Rudy looked deeper into her eyes, then walked away a few paces. After a long pause, he turned around and faced her.

"It's because you hear its song."

He gazed at her as if his answer explained everything.

"Its song?" she repeated, crinkling her forehead.

"This land speaks to us, and we can *hear* the stories it has to tell if we want to," he said. "Do you want to, Miss Kingsley?"

His question dumbfounded her. In all honesty, she couldn't *hear* anything beyond his voice, bird chatter, and the incessant flapping of a strip of canvas tarp that had loosened from the roof of her Land Cruiser.

Feeling somewhat uncomfortable she gazed down and crossed her arms, then kicked at some loose gravel by her boots. She wasn't into mysticism, magic, or ghosts, cultural or not.

"This all sounds very intriguing, but why me? I don't live here, and I don't own this land."

"Neither do we." He stretched out his arm and made a slow, wide sweep over the vista. "We are neighbors with the mountains, the trees, and the water that appeared during the Dreamtime when all you see here was created. Be happy. It is an honor to hear the song."

What Rudy said fascinated her. What he was telling her about his peoples' relationship with the earth reminded her of American Indians' beliefs. Yet, her question still burned in her mind. How could she, from a fast-track world, fit into this?

She raised a skeptical eyebrow.

"So how is it that I'm supposed to hear?"

Again, his answer was simple.

"You hear the song because the gorge has something to tell you. Something you'll need to know."

"Uh-huh. I only hope it's good news."

Rudy looked dead serious, causing her curiosity to take over. She wondered what message the canyon held for her. As they talked, Rudy had gathered up handfuls of rocks and pebbles and piled them near his feet.

He gestured for her to come closer. He crouched and dropped to his knees with a thunk onto the warm, dry ground.

She kneeled down next to him and tried to ignore the grit that roughened her skin. She watched him brush away a circle of surface debris.

While he arranged pebbles and rocks into small formations, her concerns tumbled out again in a rush.

"I can't proceed without Slade's blessing. He has definite reasons for not signing the release. Something is up with the man when it comes to that Canyon."

"You're perceptive," Rudy said, working.

"Thank you, but I've been flat out wrong, too." Her marriage had proven that, and how blind she could be, or wanted to be. "What're you making?"

He lifted his hand and followed the top of the ridge as if he were drawing in the air. He then picked up the stick and traced into the dirt what he saw in front of him. Her eyes followed his slow, deliberate movements.

"Nourombie?" she asked, pushing up her sunglasses.

He nodded and switched to constructing an overhead view of what lay behind Kissing Turtles—a blueprint of the forbidden Nourombie. The sun bore down on her and the birds chattered in the acacia nearby. Yet, she ignored her thirst and focused on Rudy's dust-encrusted hands and waited for him to explain.

He drew paths with the stick. Like meandering sheep, they wound around piles of clay and rain-washed stones. A few paths disappeared into the small rock piles he'd built. Some came out on the other side, some did not. Next, he gouged a deep serpentine trail into the soil.

"Rainbow Canyon," he told her, jabbing at the gash that lay open like a fresh, brownish red wound of sandstone.

Her pulse quickened.

He moved the stick far south outside the circle and furrowed a new line that eventually met the Canyon's edge. The path took a dip into the gorge and appeared to run along inside the Red Gum's side of the canyon wall.

Anne's heart thudded.

The trail rose up again out of Rainbow Canyon far south of the circle that represented Nourombie and stopped.

Rudy lifted the stick and tossed it aside.

"Here," he said, pressing his thumb into the dust, "is where I find my best yellow ocher. And it is the right ocher."

He looked over at Anne meaningfully.

Gratitude and honor warmed her heart. Rudy had indirectly, but definitely shown her another way to access the Canyon. In the next instant, deep disappointment chilled her soul.

Slade had lied to her.

"Thank you, Rudy," she said. "I like taking the scenic route, and it looks as though you do, too."

"Better way to see the world," he said and gave her a wink.

Why would Slade go to such lengths? she wondered. How could he kiss her one minute and lie the next? She flung her rising anger on herself. How could she be suckered in again like this? By Slade with whom she felt so comfortable. He'd raised her passions to heights she never knew existed. Had the whole male population gone nuts? A sudden outrageous thought bombarded her.

"Tell me, do you think Slade hears the Canyon's song?"

Rudy nodded. "He did. A time ago."

She stood with him. Arms akimbo on her hips, she shook stiffness from her legs, but felt as if she'd been shot by the arrow of betrayal. Though Slade and she had just met, it was if they'd known each other for a long time. His kiss breathed life into her, and she returned the favor. In a way, she felt he owed her something. Like the truth.

"Slade is a sad man," Rudy explained.

"Well, he may be sad, but I'm mad," she huffed, climbing up the short bank to the road. On the way she caught Rudy's frown.

"Be patient with him, Miss. An Aboriginal proverb says 'Those who lose dreaming are lost.' Right now, Mr. Slade, he is lost. He no longer hears the song."

Remembering Slade's cynical warning of how her dreams could only hurt, Anne was inclined to agree.

"I must go," Rudy said as they reached the road.

"Same here. I can't thank you enough."

"Until sometime soon," he added.

The breeze lifted hair from her forehead. Though her heart pumped raggedly, her feet dug deeper into the ground. A new, kind of a tough feeling came over her. Wearing this invincibility fit.

In no time, Rudy scrambled back down the bank. Before trekking the open land that stretched toward Kissing Turtles, he turned toward her. His next words bowled Anne over.

"Mr. Slade loves you," he called, resuming his foot-trek.

She released the door handle of the Land Cruiser.

"What!" Her heart almost flew out of her chest. "Hey, stop," she cried and waved wildly.

"Keep listening," Rudy urged, his image wavering in the heat. "Listen to the Canyon's song."

Ten

Anne found the long dirt road that looped west back to the ranch house. The sun lazed on the horizon while Celine Dione sang her heart out on the CD player. Passing through the open rangeland should have made her feel serene, but this was not so after meeting Rudy.

She cut around the acacias and, straight ahead on the right, arrived at an old woolshed. Parked outside its gaping door stood Slade's Triumph tilted on its kickstand. Her pulse quickened.

She slowed and took stock of herself in the rear view mirror. Her lipstick had worn off hours ago and hair escaped its clasp. She did the best she could with her fingers and a tube of Jean Linden lip moisturizer.

Her sudden uneasiness wasn't as easily fixed. A big formidable challenge walked around in that shed—in the form of a sheep rancher. On the business side of matters he blocked her entrance to the Canyon. On the personal side he'd lied to her.

With no one to blame but herself for falling for his charms, she grew angry with herself. The promise she'd made about not mixing her business and personal life went up in smoke.

Due to an inexplicable inertia she was losing control. Her priorities began to change rank. She'd let him kiss her and whet her appetite for more. Now she wanted to know everything about him, except that enduring another man's betrayal would be more than she could bear.

The washboard road coughed up dust, no answers. She yearned to confront him, make him feel responsible for her troubles and what he'd done to stir her heart. Yet that would be unwise. Business still came first. She smacked the steering wheel.

"What was supposed to be a routine work assignment— come out here, do a job, and leave—is all jumbled up," she complained out loud. "How could I do this to myself? And what for? The guy is to die for, but still a... sheep farmer!"

For whatever reason he had to block her entrance and lie to her, it jeopardized her livelihood and her heart. She couldn't let either happen. Both were the roots of her self-preservation.

Although she'd inherited a sum of money when her father died, she valued her work most. Greene held a long memory for failure and a short one for success. If she was lucky, she'd end up stuck in a cubicle copywriting forever.

She ran a forefinger over her bottom lip. Slade's blue shirt, slung over a corral post, lifted and curled in the breeze. His image flashed into her mind as it had many times during the last few days.

Suddenly she missed him and wilted under her own confusion. Things needed to be sorted out. Seeing Slade now would be risky. But certainly he'd heard her car by now.

Her mouth went dry and she uncapped a bottle of water. As she tipped it to her lips, she swerved to avoid a deep rut in the road. Evian bubbled down her neck and soaked her peach-colored shirt. She hit the brake.

Taking his time, Slade ambled outside. Tufts of fine merino wool clung to his jeans and chest hair.

"G'day, stranger," he drawled.

Hearing his voice seemed like a poem she was learning by heart, day by day. He propped one hand on top of the handle of a pushbroom. His wholesome sensuality shot a thrill through her.

"Slade," she said in a professional tone.

His eyes told her he was glad to see her. Perspiration glistened on his bronzed, muscled shoulders. Once again time slid into slow motion.

The rare solace she felt only when he was around resurfaced. She caught herself staring at him. He shifted his position and made a futile attempt to brush away some of the grey wool clip from his body.

"You need vacuuming," she quipped.

A smile eased over his lips. He hooked his thumb over his shoulder at the gaping doorway of the shed.

"Coming in?"

She stepped toward him. "Only for a short while. I should get back. I've got an early call in the morning."

He nodded. "Work. What would life be without it. I'm finishing up a job myself. But it's someone else's."

Dusty bounded out and brushed by Slade on his way to see her. The dog licked her hand and trailed along as she and Slade walked into the upper level of the cavernous shed. Dark, lanolin-stained wooden planks creaked under her boots and wool scented the thick late-afternoon air. Rich, deep hues and textures settled around her, and dust motes tumbled in a patchwork of fading amber sunlight.

Slade glanced at her soaked shirt, then into her eyes. She had no way to cover her lacey bra that showed through.

"Sticking to the roads?" he asked.

He plucked a long, dried piece of grass from between his teeth and tossed it aside. His gaze almost caused her to forget the disappointment she held about the lie he'd told her.

"Haven't run into any wild pigs," she replied.

Slade chortled. "Lucky for them."

Strolling deeper into the shed, she passed a few small wooden pens to the area where he was working. His Akubra hung on an iron spike, and a half-eaten apple sat on top of a bucket. He seemed in a reflective, but good mood.

"So what're you doing?" she asked.

He plucked up wads of wool and tossed them over his shoulder into a wire bin.

"Shedwork." His quick, easy movements revealed it wasn't the first time he'd done it. "A buyer is coming out to look over our surplus ewes."

She frowned. "Why would he care about the mess? A woolshed's just this way, isn't it?"

He shook his head from side to side. "First, he is a *she*, and buyers like to look at everything. Breeding records, pastures and facilities, and teeth. This is the Red Gum's shearing and grading site. We'll start here."

Anne peered past him. Generations of musterers and shearers had carved and scribbled their marks on the posts and wallboards, including a prayer to Bishop Blaise, the patron saint of woolcombers. She really couldn't say what the different tools and equipment were used for, or even why the place was laid out how it was. She only knew about getting ready for company.

"Hmmmm. In that case, you need two things."

"Yep. I need to see that this gets done, and that Rudy escorts you and your crew out to the North Paddock while I meet with the buyer. Have you seen him today?"

Her throat tightened. The cleaning suggestions she was about to make evaporated into the air. She wanted something to do other than wring her hands.

"Actually, yes," she answered, picking up a broom. "He helped me get my bearings. The road to the North Paddock is wider and easier than I'd expected. So the crews won't have much trouble getting out there tomorrow. And now I can lead them."

She noted Slade's silence, but went on.

"Rudy's a good man," she added, sweeping the boards.

Slade separated tools into wooden crates. Slices of sunlight backlit his hair.

"Rudy impresses almost everyone."

She nodded. "He's sincere and seems to know the Red Gum like the back of his hand. He also understands artistic endeavors."

Slade shot her a curious glance and slapped the end of a black electrical cord on the floor before coiling it up and tying it off with frayed rope.

"Not as good as my grandfather. So you should ask us if you want to get somewhere."

She held her breath. She'd said too much. Dust clouded around her knees like a surprise Mystic Seaport fog. She sneezed from it. She couldn't change the subject fast enough. She and Rudy now shared a secret.

"It's getting dark."

"No worry." He touched her chin with his forefinger and slid it down the side of her throat. "You can follow me." His eyes scanned her face. "Will you follow me? If you had good reason?"

Heat rushed into her cheeks. His question was more than a simple query.

"Time for me to go," she said, propping the broom against a post and heading for the doorway.

He caught her.

"Annie, you're jumpier than a roo looking for a lost joey."

"Am I? I always get nervous before a big shoot. Works kind of like stage fright."

Everything else aside, she had the willies. After dawn she'd be on duty. Demands would suck up all of her time and energy. Anything else would be moved to the back burner, unless it had to do with the filming. That's the way it was. Edginess went with the territory.

Slade piped up. "You hear this, Dusty? Our wild pig woman is afraid of what she does for a living."

Anne's temper let loose. He'd gone too far. "You don't understand." Placing her hands up on his bare chest, she gave him a push backwards.

"Then it's me," he said. "You're afraid of me."

She nearly choked over his conceit.

"Slade, don't be ridiculous. I'm not afraid of you. I'm trying very hard not to spoil my chances here. I *need* to get my job done. It's that simple."

But nothing was simple. How could she explain artistic purpose if he wasn't tuned in like Rudy?

He grinned unexpectedly. "Bonzer," he cheered.

She widened her eyes in awe. The first truly happy streak zoomed across his face since she'd arrived. It was priceless. The man did possess the capability for joy. But that wasn't the point.

"What?" she asked icily.

He drew nearer to her.

"Then have you missed me?"

She squinted up at him. If he threw her one more curve, she was heading back to the house. Now. She crossed her arms.

"Let me repeat. While you've been exploring about," he pressed, "and talking with top stockmen, have you missed me?"

A shock wave rippled through her. The man was an enigma. He wanted to know if she was afraid of him. He asked if she missed him. All very personal issues, not business problems. Then, except for a few certain times, it seemed that he couldn't wait to get rid of her, the crew and her ideas.

Her patience vanished.

"You know, Slade, you act like a child who can't decide whether he wants to play indoors or out."

He leaned past her and snagged his hat off the post. "Do you suggest a parental reprimand?"

Shrugging, she rolled her eyes upward to the bare rugged beams.

"I don't know. I'm not a parent."

She turned away from him and gazed blindly past the pens. Longing for children had run deep in her heart. Her ex-husband certainly didn't care. But she did. A lot.

"I reckon we have not being parents in common," Slade said.

She whirled around.

"Time out," she said, raising her hands to a T. "We don't need to have anything in common. We're supposed to be conducting business, not mapping out romantic futures."

The soft eagerness returned to his eyes.

"I'm glad you're not afraid of me."

His seriousness threw her off guard. She'd seen him in passing a few times between her trips out, and they'd exchanged a few quick words. He'd appeared busy and focused, the same as she. But now that was gone.

"Let's drop this," she said. "I find it uncomfortable."

Her thoughts chased each other round and round in a big circle. Everything started with Slade and ended with him. He caught up to her at the doorway with Dusty at his heel.

"I wanted to be a father," he continued.

He tugged her heartstrings, but she took long, decisive steps out into the twilight and open air.

"Well, then find yourself a good marrying woman," she flung, "and get busy."

He shouted, "I had, and we did. But when Caroline..."

Anne didn't know which hit her first—what he said, or the bitterness in his voice. She turned around, facing him. A wave of pain burst across his face.

Slade's housekeeper's words, *he hasn't been himself since his wife died* came to mind. Her first day at the Red Gum seemed so long ago. Whatever was going through his mind rose heavily from his heart.

She rested against the fender of the Land Cruiser and crossed her legs at her ankles. For the first time, Slade opened up to her. He seemed lost. She wanted to wrap her arms around him to guide him, but thought better of it and held back.

"Did she leave? With the child?" she asked, hoping that was the least worst of two possibilities. "You must have some paternity rights. There's visitation after couples split up."

He picked up a pebble and fired it off into the brush.

"No, we didn't split up." He drifted into some far off time and place. The muscles along his temples worked. He opened his mouth, then closed it. Nearly a half moment slipped away before he spoke.

"And our child was never born."

Anne's heart thunked.

"Oh, Slade." She stood in shock. She understood inner pain. Losing loved ones was never easy, for whatever reason. She thought she'd known the worst kind of betrayal there could be between a man and woman, and doubted she'd ever get completely over it. But the mourning one must carry over losing a child had to be unfathomable.

"There was an accident." He looked at her, then up at the darkening sky, and back again. She could feel his internal teardrops, as if they spilled from beneath her own eyelashes, leaving traces on her lips. With his every touch, she wondered if he felt the same spiritual link that she did.

"Come here," she said. "Please."

His need for relief pulsated from him. She allowed him to wrap her in his arms. It was the least she could do. She had no ready-made cures for his ton of unresolved anger and grief. Only little things.

"Are you coming in?" she asked, tilting her head at the Land Cruiser. "We can listen to some tunes until the stars come out. You know I can't see them very well in Sydney with the city lights. They're so beautiful out here."

Slade's troubled eyes searched hers. As he released her, she wondered if he'd found what he was looking for. He tightened his lips, bowed his head, and wavered.

She decided not to give grief a chance to push him to his knees. She'd been on hers, and pulling herself back up was the hardest thing she ever had to do. Thank heavens for time, blessed work and a few friends. Now it was her turn to be there for someone else.

"Okay," she said, taking charge. "Come on, whistle for your dog. I'm taking you back to the house."

He straightened up while she crossed to the fence post and returned with his shirt.

"No need. I'm fine," he said.

"Sure, you are." She tugged on the end of his belt and led him around to the passenger side and opened the door.

"Get in, please. You can get your bike later."

To her surprise, Dusty came when she whistled and he jumped into the back of the vehicle. The three of them hit the rough road home.

For the next hour, she talked with Slade mostly about the station, weather, and how the area must have looked during the Pleistocene Era. He gave her answers for almost all of her questions about the flora and fauna that the headlights skimmed over along the way.

"Pull over," Slade said abruptly.

"Here? We're not far from the house."

"Humor me," he said with an edge in his voice. He pointed out the open passenger window. "By those trees will work."

She braked. "Far be it from me to interfere with a man's needs."

"I didn't hear that," he said, giving her a wink as he left the vehicle. "Just don't insult or bash woolgrowers."

She watched Slade cross in front of the idling vehicle. Shutting her eyes for a moment, she rested her forehead on her hands still wrapped around the steering wheel. Slade's voice soon overpowered that of the pop singer's.

"Annie, come with me," he called.

She reopened her eyes, got out of the car, and set off with him. Walking revitalized her energy as they wound through some trees and spilled out at the top of a short hill.

"I want you to see something," Slade said, helping her up onto a long flat rock.

When she got up from her knees, she gasped. Her eyes feasted on the spectacular view that spread out below them. The Red Gum property looked almost surreal. Whatever appeared rough and impenetrable by day, became soft and inviting by night. The rising moon washed the land and everything on it with silver, including the roof of the unfinished wool scouring plant and the ribbon of water that curved near it. The whole place glistened right into her heart.

Slade tilted her chin upward. Clear and twinkling, millions of stars breathed life into the blue-black heavens. In a way, she felt each one shone for them alone. Truly grateful, she found Slade's hand. He was giving her most special gifts—the Milky Way, the Southern Cross, and the secrets of his heart. An unforgettable moment. The kind she could carry in her memory long after she returned to Connecticut.

"You and your grandfather own a very special corner of the world," she told him. "I'm lucky for having you share this with me."

Pride and contentment radiated from him.

She gazed back at the starry sky. "Thank you," she told him. She loved this and everything about it.

"So do I," he said, somehow knowing her thoughts.

He spoke with his soul.

She listened with her heart.

He kissed her forehead, causing mixed feelings to rumble through her again. She wanted desperately to confront him about lying. The dishonesty hurt. She stepped away from him.

"What's the matter?" he asked.

She gazed up, wishing upon a brilliant star for guidance. If she called Slade on this, he might blow up and she and her crew might be heading back to Sydney instead of the North Paddock. On the other hand, letting it fester would affect every conversation they would have from here on out.

"Tired, I guess. It's been a long, revealing day."

He squared his shoulders and looked at her knowingly.

"You don't trust me, do you?"

She gazed at the eroded sandstone beneath her feet.

"Trust doesn't come like it used to."

He paced. "You must've had a lousy marriage."

Winded from his acute perception, she felt as if she were being squeezed through a tube. She sat down a few feet away from him, pulled her knees up under her chin, and gazed at Mount Kamilaroi off in the distance.

"My marriage was fine, I thought." She focused straight ahead. A string of clouds banded in a line beyond the mountain on the right, like silvery, pinkish pearls.

"But it ended badly?"

"About as bad as it comes." She tightened her grip around her knees. "I couldn't forgive him for what he'd done."

Slade knelt next to her. She was grateful that he seemed to sense that his silence was what she needed at the moment. She could let everything flow to the top and out. Slowly.

"Finding out was terrible," she resumed. "He was a financial consultant and traveled often. To Atlanta for two weeks, back home for one week. Out to Houston for a few days, back again to Atlanta for a week, home to Westport for a few days. So it went. Until we got a call late one night from Atlanta."

Listening, Slade leaned toward her.

She took in a breath. "We'd met at a corporate holiday party. The firm he worked for contracted Greene and Associates. They were a new client for us and were included on the A List. I was introduced to Lou. He seemed to have everything, be everything. I had dated during college, but nothing ever took root the way it did with him. So we soon got married, because it seemed like a good idea at the time."

Again, she found the ease to talk to Slade. How strange to come this far to find the man who turned the key that unlocked her worst secrets.

"Then it was over. One evening we'd just come in late from a client party when the phone rang. A woman, whose voice I didn't recognize, asked for my husband. Since he was upstairs packing for his next trip, I told her that he was indisposed. She became belligerent and demanded to talk to him. When I balked, she screamed, 'Why would you want to protect the bastard? I know he's there!'"

Anne's raised voice pealed through the trees. The rest of her words spilled out. "I thought she was... well, a... girlfriend. You know?"

Tears only smarted her eyes now instead of flooding down her cheeks when she talked about it. Yet the betrayal still hurt.

"No, I don't know," Slade assured her. "Married means married." Although she had issues to resolve with him, his presence, strong and silent, stabilized her. He seemed more solid than the rock upon which they sat.

"But I was wrong about her." A full minute dragged by as she drummed her bottom lip with her fingertip. Her next words slipped out slowly. "That's when I learned that she was more... more than the other woman."

Slade raised an eyebrow.

"Who was she?"

"She was my husband's other...wife."

Eleven

Slade whistled. Amazingly, Anne seemed okay. "I don't know of any bigamists or their wives, other than of a few Aborigines. And that's rare anymore."

"It happens more often than folks think."

He figured she'd cried her eyes out and daydreamed about revenge more than once, although she appeared to be a forgiving person. His empathy burned for her. But what could he offer? Tell her that he understood what it was like to be robbed of love and strength. What good would that do? He turned his eyes to the dark, and Dusty curled up next to him.

Deep inside he still wasn't over losing his wife. He'd tried to get the ambition to recapture his dreams, but nothing released him, or gave him the peace he needed to get going again. After weeks of self-absorption, the more he analyzed, the murkier the picture grew. He would never understand why life dealt him such a nasty hand. Best thing he could do was bury the whole ordeal—nice and deep and live with the guilt for bringing her out to the Red Gum. A city girl, she was, trying to fit in. Working at driving over rough terrain to meet him at their favorite place, Boronia Point.

Ever since the tragedy things popped up that were connected to it in one way or another. The latest occurrence stood next to him. Anne Kingsley. Determined, attractive, and wearing boronia. Now she was enthralled by the starlit heavens, which was fine. But determined to use his Rainbow Canyon, which wasn't.

Confusion cornered him, and something Rudy had said flew into his mind about the song of the Canyon and its drawing power that had been born in Aboriginal beliefs.

Slade used to hear the Canyon's elusive call. Yet today was different. The only thing he heard now was a scream that ended in the crash of twisted steel and death.

His skin prickled. If he never approached the Canyon's edge again in this life, it would be too soon. That was final. Or so he'd thought—until his grandfather had first broken his silence some months back when Slade had returned home.

Long after sunset he'd found his grandfather sitting on the front porch. He knew something was up just from the way his grandfather sat in the rocker. Kind of stiff with his leg stretched to the top of the railing.

Jim McGregor handed him a blue enameled mug of coffee and asked Slade where he'd been.

"Out fixing seven-wire," Slade said, watching him.

The fence chore could have waited, but he wanted to work alone for a while. He needed to feel in control again. Nothing but the sun and wind coming at him. Keeping it simple seemed to make sense to him. No more simple than fixing fence.

Old McGregor coughed. "Mate, you got yourself locked up in a stockyard. And you need to unlatch the gate, or you're going to end up bone dry like dirt."

Slade clenched his fists at the intrusion, but he couldn't deny the concern burning in the other man's eyes.

"Grandad, I'm not up for this right now. Everyone is helping me by not talking about it. Can't you do that?"

The farmer scratched his chin and gave Slade's question some real thought.

"Nope. It's insensible, and seems downright unnatural. Been too long. The rest is my personal gripe. I don't like walking on eggs."

Slade recoiled. Grandad Jim had a way of getting to his core faster than anyone he knew. He suddenly felt like the hunted.

"And you're running," McGregor added.

"I'm still here running things. I haven't left."

The man tapped his forefinger against his white-haired temple. "I mean in here. And before you come busting at me, I know it's your business. But it's a crying shame watching you run from something that wasn't your fault. Remember, she had a choice."

It was all Slade could do to keep from walking away from his eldest relative. Maybe forever. However, fate interceded again. A calm restraint suddenly dropped over him and he was thankful. Guilt and he had gotten to be friends, but he wasn't interested in making it a party.

"You finished, Grandad?"

The man nodded and had held his peace until last week in the office when he was urging him to let Anne film in the Canyon. Nevertheless, the stockyard thing had stuck in Slade's mind. As far as he was concerned, he had no reason to come out. What's more, if he unhitched the gate, someone might barge in. Lord as his witness, he didn't want visitors. He didn't need help, either. Only calendar distance from that day.

"Look," Anne said, interrupting his musings and pointing at the Milky Way and a falling star.

Slade admired her. She'd come through her lousy situation and refused to let it ruin her life. Somehow she'd kept her sense of wonder. In the last few days she'd shown him heart, courage, brains.

She wasn't a tease and his heart wanted to know more about hers. Her body, scented and firm, and soft skin still taunted him. More than once she'd invaded his mind and held him hostage while he worked.

Yesterday, he'd gotten so hot thinking about her that he stripped and jumped into the water at Crystal Springs. To little avail. What he really needed was to finish what he'd started with her at Hannah's hut and in his big easy chair back at the house. Only then would he reap any sense of completeness. As if he were fulfilling some unknown destiny that went way beyond physical attraction. What a fine mess for a true-blue widower.

The breeze lifted strands of Anne's hair and feathered them against his arm. How her high-and-dry road crossed with his, he couldn't begin to figure.

"One of those bloody fate things," he finished his thoughts out loud.

"I don't buy fate," she stated. "But I believed in marriage. One hundred percent."

His arm touched hers and her warmth flashed through him. He fought his sudden instinctive urge to gather her up and fight off demons that may come her way from the past, present, or future.

"You didn't shoot the bastard?" he blurted.

A smile decorated her face.

"Oh, the thought crossed my mind. The court made him pay up, but he got out of doing time. What amazed me most is that he thought he could get away with it. And luck rode with him for a while. In the end, I was angrier with myself than him. I let myself get suckered in."

Slade put his arm around her shoulder.

"You're far from a fool, Annie."

"Thanks, but I should have seen it coming. I missed important signals. Friends warned me something was wrong, but I wasn't ready to see or listen."

As she gazed skyward her eyes gathered collected starry points of light. Slade wasn't a frivolous man, but he found himself wishing upon one that twinkled in her eyes.

"He used you and your trust."

"He pretty much drained the well on trust."

He squeezed her gently. For some reason she resisted cuddling into the crook of his arm, but it didn't alarm him a whole lot. He could now half understand why she ran away from him and toward him at the same time.

"Until I met him, my employer had consumed most of my time. I loved it and so did they. Now, I'm back to square one. At least I'm here."

"Do you love it now, working past dusk?"

"I guess so." She lifted one of her dark eyebrows in reproach. He was making her nervous. She added, "My ex wasn't exactly a true-blue guy, huh?"

Slade peeled his eyes away from hers.

"True blue," he repeated. Hearing a familiar expression used by an outsider was odd. His tone must have thrown her off.

"Sure," she said, "you know. As in being faithful to someone you love? Sexually and in spirit."

An opalescent fire kindled in her eyes, making them flash at him with the nod of her head.

"I'm not the enemy," he warned. "Here in Oz the expression 'true blue' means authentic. A native Aussie—like me. Or it can mean pure, like virgin wool."

She rose to her feet and dusted off the seat of her pants with her hands. He got up as she began to pace a small circle, arms folded across her chest. A frown etched her forehead. She stopped and pierced his eyes accusingly with hers.

"Will you just tell me one thing?"

He hung his thumbs through his belt loops. Answering was the least he could do.

"Shoot."

"Why do men feel it's so necessary to lie?"

Slade straightened. Her question was really a statement. Maybe she had further to go in putting things behind her than he'd guessed, but he took on the challenge and strode into the eye of her fury.

"Same reasons as women. Sometimes it's just plain easier to fib if they know it's not a life or death situation." He hoped that would suffice, but there was a lot more. Truth could hurt. Or, as in his case, the truth wasn't someone else's business. But some people never learned the value of truth, or wanted to. He didn't count himself in that lot.

"*Easier?*" she spat. "What a crock. That's not part of responsible, mature love."

"I agree with you, but it can be... hard."

"Only cowards lie."

He let her righteous opinion sink in, but only so far. Fear and guilt drove men to near anything. He could lie like a dog at midnight if needed. Like he had about the route to the Canyon. Yet, fibbing to her was tough. She looked deep into his eyes when he spoke, and he was liking her more every day.

The woman persevered and had mettle. He thought she'd have given up shooting in the Canyon by now. What drew her to Rainbow Canyon, he couldn't fathom, but she wasn't budging.

He wouldn't let his ego bask in the possibility that the reason she was still here was to have a little more of what he gave her. Or had she given it to him? Hard to tell. But he reckoned he didn't owe anybody anything. He made his own rules and chose his battles and liked where he lived.

"Slade?"

"Not every man is like your ex."

She shrugged.

He pressed his point. "Most men I know love their women and stand by them through thick and thin."

Watching skepticism contort her face reminded him of one of his Texas grandmother's sayings: You can lead a horse to water, but you can't make him drink. That seemed to fit now. If Anne chose not to believe that devotion still existed in the world, there was nothing he could do about it. She'd been deeply hurt. How could he preach something he doubted so strongly himself?

Silence took over and the moon rising over Tailem Flats told him it was about ten o'clock.

"I should get back," she said and began to retrace their steps away from the rock overhang. His stride didn't give her much of a lead. As he walked with her down the narrow path, a large bat whisked by her, clipping her shoulder.

To his amazement she just kept on moving, surefooted and stubborn as a rock wallaby. She was getting used to the critters he'd been around all his life. The amber park lights on her Land Cruiser beamed like semaphores through the shrubs.

"I'll drive," he offered. He soon gripped the steering wheel, tackling road and spewing dust.

"It's been a few more days now," she said after they drove several kilometers in silence. "Has a decision been made about our crossing Nourombie to get to the Canyon?"

"None yet." He prayed the conversation would change faster than it started. She was already riled.

"Well, I'm really hoping the Bilwans come around in their thinking," she told him.

Slade sighed. "Their decisions go through many channels."

Warm air churned over them and it was a perfect end-of-summer night. A sudden need to lighten up hit and he pointed up through the dusty windshield. "Maybe you should hang a wish for what you want on one of those stars? *Gamma Crucis* in the Southern Cross is a good one."

"Hmmm," she said, picking up on his whim. "Is that the one you'd use?"

"If I were lost."

She flung him a disappointed glance.

"This time of year," he continued, "just before dawn, the tail of that constellation hangs over Hannah's hut."

He lightened the pressure on the accelerator. His last visit to the old place, with Annie, filled his memory. Every emotionally magic moment of it. The joy he felt touching her soft, soft skin and the swell of her breasts under the thin cotton of the old shirt. The sweet yearning he'd tasted on her lips. Damn, his loins began to burn just thinking about it.

"I remember, too," she murmured.

Their eyes locked briefly, then she straightened in the passenger seat and he gripped the wheel harder. He cut the last turn too wide, and the vehicle rocked back onto the road that led up to the house. He caught her lips pursing.

She said, "Perhaps by tomorrow night we'll hear from the Bilwan."

"They're working on the ceremony," he replied. "It begins soon and will last three days."

Despite that, he was stalling. There was still a chance she'd like Crystal Springs more than the Canyon. Then the matter would be settled.

"Also, the Bilwan people," he said, "operate on different time than most."

"Guess I would also if my ancestors were around for sixty thousand years." She pulled her briefcase up from the floor and placed it on her lap. "Still I'm going to have to tell everyone tomorrow what's happening. Or, to be more precise, what's not happening."

He pulled her car up outside the picket fence. As he turned off the ignition, Anne opened the door and slid out. He dipped his hat brim, got out and opened the gate for her. As she mounted the veranda steps, he couldn't resist watching her bottom shift as she went up the steps. Tired as he was, his imagination still worked fine.

"I'll catch you tomorrow," he said, "after I'm done with the buyer. Rudy will go out with you and your crew."

"Fine. If it makes you feel better."

"You're bound to need something."

She shook her head. "You're funny."

"Just cautious." He pulled her hand away from the latch on the screen door and cradled her fingers with his own. A small voice in the back of his mind whispered to his heart, *you need her. Don't let her go.*

The message hit him like a silo full of grain. He opened his mouth to speak, but the words collided and lodged on the tip of his tongue. A change of heart rattled his complacency.

"Anne, I want to say... ahhh, never mind."

"What Slade?"

"I hope they come through, too."

Good man, he prided himself. Telling her he hoped the Bilwan would come through proved a struggle. Meaning it was even tougher. Yet, part of him really did. He had no cause to block her future or success. What's more his grandfather was correct. There was more to his frustration than not wanting any part of their property shown to the public.

Guilt veered him away from revisiting Rainbow Canyon. He simply couldn't push for a resolution that went far beyond getting permission to cross a strip of land. Not today, anyway.

Somehow he had to deal with the tragedy. If only he'd given Caroline what she wanted—to go back to Sydney—she and their child would still be alive. He should have just shut up.

Leaving the station and moving into Sydney to learn her father's petrochemical business could have saved them all. In the end, she'd won.

Anne glanced up at him, her golden hair flouncing over her shoulders as it had when he first saw her leaning over the worktable in his living room. Now he caught the last of her sarcastic words, "...hate to lose out, since there's no other way into Rainbow Canyon."

She brushed by him, opened the screen door, and entered the foyer. He stood still, watching her through the mesh as the wood framed door banged shut. The base of it bounced back out and hit the toe of his boot. He arched an eyebrow. She'd done that on purpose.

~ * ~

The next morning Anne threw her clothes on and drove out to the main road to meet everyone. Adrenaline pumped through her veins. Thank heavens she could get back into her realm.

She missed Jack now. He'd been driving since the wee hours of the morning, and would have to return right away. But a short time with him would help her feel connected again to the world she knew.

While she waited, she pulled out her video camera and filmed some raw footage of the area. She zoomed in for detail of textures. Rudy showed up in her sweep to the left.

"They're coming," he announced. His black eyes glinted with excitement. His was the first real enthusiasm she'd seen on anyone's face about her work since she'd arrived at the Red Gum.

Happier, she looked down the flat stretch of bitumen that dipped after an old narrow wooden bridge that crossed over a creek. She turned west and filmed Mount Kamilaroi. Smoke from the fire hovered near its base.

Other than the assorted vehicles approaching them, the road lay bare. Civilization as she knew it now advanced toward her and Rudy. For a mere instant, regret hit her.

Distorted by the rising heat, Jack's bright yellow van dipped from sight, then reappeared a kilometer closer. The rest did the same. She expected the crew had brought an Esky of fresh prawns. The bus brought well-paid technical talent, who held high expectations, drank Foster's Lager, and listened to lots of music that blasted louder as they neared.

"Hey, Kingsley," Jack yelled out the window, pulling up to a stop. "Good to see you. This place is way the hell *out back,* for crying out loud."

Anne grinned. "Hiya, Jack. Welcome to the Red Gum. Come meet Rudy. He'll help us get through to the first location. Rudy, this is Jack, a friend and the account manager back at our office."

Jack, bleary-eyed from travel, was wearing a blue knit shirt and khaki pants. He gave the Aborigine a quick once over, then smiled. "Hey, Rudy."

"Jack." The stockman gifted him with one of his smooth handshakes. "If you'll have your people follow Ms. Kingsley and me, we'll take a shortcut to where you can make camp and begin."

Jack gave him a thumbs-up. "You got it."

Anne looked down the road at the vehicles. The bus door swung open and various techies climbed out and stretched. Some of them waved and she threw them a thumbs-up. Jack soon pooled them all into a small huddle and more introductions followed.

"Where's Mr. McGregor?" the director, Drew, asked.

Rudy stepped forward and leaned on a fresh walking stick.

"He's with a buyer." His smile was less than full, his shake quick. "You should be careful with your smokes."

"Sure, pal," the soundman boomed. With a cache of credits, he used little personal volume control. He leaned over and snuffed out his cigar onto the bitumen surface and stuffed what was left into his shirt pocket.

"You ready, Drew?" the cameraman asked. "Let's get moving so these for-hire drivers can get back. One of their wives is expecting."

"Hold on a minute." The director gestured to Anne. "Let's meet at about four outside my trailer after we set up shop?"

"Sure," she said. "And it's more than two hour's drive to the main house from the North Paddock, so I'll stay with Marge in the make-up trailer, if she'll put me up."

"Good enough," Drew said and turned to Jack. "What's this about a location change? I thought the preliminary stuff was pinned down. Pressure's on."

Anne intervened. "We did, but it rained last week and washed out a good part of one of our site selections. Then another problem came up about using Rainbow Canyon for the final segment in the series. In my estimation, it's truly our best bet. However, the situation is still unresolved." She took in a short breath. "But Mr. McGregor says he has another place he wants to show me."

"Soon?" Drew asked.

"Yes, but I've my doubts it'll come up to my requirements. Nothing in these parts is more beautiful than that Canyon."

"That's what I like," Drew announced, tilting his head toward Jack. "Perfection personified, but without being a pain in the ass. She's good, isn't she?"

"Our best," Jack said, sliding her a wink.

She warded off a blush. "Rudy will show us the way now. Wait. I don't see Susan and Chase."

Jack answered, "They're holed up back there. Not on talking terms. She raised a ruckus over a Coke that Chase brought her when we stopped in Attunga."

"It wasn't Diet," the soundman interjected.

"Then Chase said that he hoped never to work with her again," the cameraman added.

"So she told him he could put his head up 'where the sun don't shine,'" the soundman filled in.

"It went downhill from there," Drew concluded.

Jack said, "They're still worth every plug nickel on the screen, and that's all we have to worry about."

Drew added, "Just so Susan makes her cues. Time isn't running with us this round. I heard from Jack that you have a good opportunity waiting for you back in Westport."

Back in Westport darted into Anne's mind. It prompted familiar images. Estates, office buildings, BMWs, her favorite restaurants and bookstore. Yet, the mental pictures weren't as bright and clear as they once were. For example, she couldn't remember how late Allen's Clam and Lobster House was open on weeknights.

Drew's voice pulled her back. "Is that road the shortcut you have in mind?"

Rudy nodded stoically. "Some gravel, some sand, some hills, some creeks—"

"And plenty of sheep," Anne said, half regretting that fact an hour and forty minutes later.

On their way to the main range the whole troupe waited for a mob of maiden ewes to string across one sorry excuse for a road.

"What a putrid smell," Susan exclaimed. "And this heat is about to brittle my bones. Someone please bring me a fan."

One of the prop guys brought her a little battery-operated one that she aimed toward herself. Her shiny red hair lifted away from her face, exposing high cheekbones and a perfect profile insured by Lloyd's of London.

Some of the crew started a card game on the tailgate of one of the pickups. The soundman cranked up his boombox. Pink Floyd blasted out over the moving flock. A musterer threw Rudy a hand signal, then Rudy asked the soundman to turn it down.

"Noise disturbs the sheep," Rudy explained.

The soundman obliged, muttering under his breath that his music wasn't "noise."

"Later, okay?" Anne said.

Susan whined, blotting her upper lip with a tissue, "I don't see how you've stood it out here."

"Thing called professionalism," Jack told her, handing Anne a paper cup filled with iced water from one of the yellow and red insulated barrels.

Anne wanted to set her colleague straight, but thought better of it. Professionals didn't kiss their clients. She stepped closer to Susan who appeared genuinely peaked. Anne handed the water to her.

As Susan drank, a last few stragglers of sheep cantered across the road. Rudy soon called out for everyone to pack up. Along with the others, Anne made her way to her vehicle. As she tugged on the door handle, she heard a faint, familiar buzz coming from the open pastureland behind them.

She glanced over her shoulder and saw nothing. Giving a few more seconds, she listened. Sure enough the hum reoccurred, but had moved closer.

Turning around to face the rugged terrain, she watched a trail of rising dust snake toward them. Ahead of it rode a man on a motorbike. Riding hell-bent-for-leather, he tackled the distance with fearless skill. Cutting, swerving, he lifted airborne over a gully.

Mesmerized, she leaned against the door. Only one man rode with such control and passion and spirit. Her pulse jumped. Faster, closer. Higher, deeper.

She could almost see the grin of satisfaction brighten his face. The jarring memory of the taste of his mouth made hers tingle. Suddenly she caught herself yearning and ready... to ride—with him. All the way, right into the dark core of her insecurity and, for whatever reason it existed, Slade's deception about the Canyon. God willing, they could race out again into the warm sunlight. Together.

Anne's heart fluttered in anticipation. "Maybe I should believe in fate."

Twelve

Anne strolled over to Drew and Jack.

"Who's the guy?" Drew asked.

"Jim McGregor's grandson, Slade," she said, shielding her eyes from the sun with her hand.

Slade downshifted the Triumph and skidded to a halt a few feet away. He dismounted and tapped the brim of his hat with his forefinger.

"G'day, mates."

Anne moved toward her right, making room for him in the gathering. His charisma glowed while everyone exchanged names and handshakes.

"My grandfather and I welcome you and hope your stay at the Red Gum is comfortable. You've already met Rudy, our head stockman. I trust you won't mind either of us sticking around?"

"Not at all," Drew said.

Anne regarded Slade for a moment, then mirrored his lingering smile. Despite the crew's intrusive presence and work on a project that he felt jeopardized privacy, he behaved cordially. Nor did he waste time in clearing his presence on the set. He turned his attention to Anne.

"Have you gotten rid of that headache that put you out of sorts last night?" he asked, his accent also on brilliant display.

Drew and Jack tossed her a quick glance.

"I'm fine," she replied, her smile lessening. Last evening she didn't have a headache, and he knew it.

"I reckoned we stayed up too late, love."

Everyone hushed. She avoided Jack's eyes for as long as she could. For sure he'd zero in on Slade's reference and bring it up later.

"No, no, guys," she said, waving off their host's remark. "*Love* is just one of Mr. McGregor's... charming terms. I had trouble sleeping last night. You know how I get hyped up before a shoot."

"Barely caught a wink myself," Jack said.

Anne stewed over Slade's indiscretion. He had just turned a business greeting into a revealing personal discussion, half of which was untrue. Couldn't he realize her professionalism was at stake? She swore that sometimes he epitomized the Devil himself. Why their chemistry soared together confounded her. It was a mystery, like Rudy's indiscernible painting.

Drew sped instant relief to her. "You've got quite a spread here, Mr. McGregor."

Slade beamed. "The property's been in the family for three generations. Raising superfine merinos is in our blood. It's a good life."

"Thank you for having us," Jack offered officially.

"We're happy you chose the Red Gum."

He looked at her and widened his smile.

Anne nearly choked. Although it seemed that Slade had come to his senses, she wondered if he'd slammed a few tinnies before he rode out to meet them. Lifting an eyebrow, she gave him a quick once-over. Nothing about his physical appearance supported the possibility. His clear eyes and alert manner showed enthusiasm. His speech and movements stayed smooth. All of which meant he could roll out the red carpet if he wanted to do that.

"I'd like to take the credit for deciding to come out here," Jack said, "but my boss and your grandfather put this gig together." He added, giving Anne's arm a light jab with his elbow, "So good does come out of bad, eh, Anne?"

Slade's exaggerated smile faded as he threw her a curious stare.

Not now, Jack, her mind screamed. She was still uncertain whether Slade had seen her infamous debut during the TV coverage of the SMWA brawl in Sydney. She so hoped the odds were with her.

Occasionally, she suspected that he was attempting to piece together part of his memory, the part that included her. If he ever did, she'd have to talk fast to keep him from inviting her to leave. After all, she had blasted SMWA woolgrowers pretty good for trapping her during their lobby 'negotiations.'

That night she also had reamed herself out because arriving late for such an important client kick-off event was inexcusable. Then matters worsened before she ever made it upstairs to the cocktail party. Men—scruffy types wearing dusty jeans, vests, and smelly, wooly armbands, or holding signs lashed to tree branches—had gathered and stood arguing outside the Winthrop Building.

Thick hot evening air pressed against her skin. All she wanted to do was get past them and up to the twelfth floor. So badly, she ached. No sooner did she get into the lobby when the men swarmed into the room and nearly overran her. Their voices rose and the security guard attempted to maintain order.

"The SMWA meeting's over at eight upstairs, so begone with you back to the pub."

A large man with snowy white hair had stepped in front of the group. He was wearing a grey shirt, jeans, and a shaggy wool armband. He seniored the rest of the men by twenty years.

"We'll wait here," he told the guard.

Anne spied the elevators at the back of the lobby. Before she knew it, the rowdy men's shoves turned into punches, and she stood in the middle of a brawl. Pure dumb luck helped her make it unharmed to the mirrored wall on her right. Comical and pitiful, the hullabaloo turned a mischievous eye on her.

"Look, there's a sheila," an arm-banded farmer had shouted.

A few men turned in her direction. Why they began to hold their punches to look at her, she didn't know. Perhaps they hadn't seen a dressed-up woman for a while. From the unkempt looks of them, they hadn't ever lived with one.

Anne smoothed down her short black chemise and wished for jeans and her DKNY sweatshirt. She slipped her fingers to the rhinestone clip that held her hair in a chignon at her nape. If only Merlin's magic wand would turn it into a rubber band. She would take anything that would help her get to the blasted elevator further unnoticed.

"I reckon she's a beauty queen," a stockman grunted.

"Pretty and soft as superfine wool," a sign-carrier admired, then received a shoulder thrust in his chest.

"Woolgrower Queen?" someone else picked up.

Anne cringed inwardly as more men halted their crude, hot-tempered methodology of problem solving and stared at her.

"Take a bo-peep at her legs," another hooted.

"C'mon, miss. Please baa for us. Like this, BAAAAA."

Whistles fired up and the fighting men stood shoulder-to-shoulder, gaping.

Anne's intuition rose as perspiration moistened her skin. She worried her beaded evening bag beneath her fingers. Trying to remain calm, she mustered a weak smile. Just then one of the sign-carriers lost his balance and hit the floor by her feet. Sprawling, he wrapped his right hand around her ankle.

"You want to dance?" he asked, looking up her dress.

Fuming, she yanked her high-heeled foot back, but said with all the poise and control she could dig up, "Thank you, *gentlemen,* for the invitation. Now if you'll excuse me, I'm expected upstairs."

The forty or so men gawked as her American accent floated over them. Meanwhile, she edged closer to her target.

"Ian, she's a *Yank*," someone cried. "You don't even know your own kind."

That did it. Fisticuffs erupted all around the room. Again the path to the elevator was blocked and Anne was wilting fast. She blinked away hot tears as the man with snow-white hair muscled his way through the crowd.

"Let the lady pass," he directed, facing them.

He lifted his arms as a barrier. The police had then stormed the place and ordered everyone to stay where they were. The media had picked the right time to show up. Her luck.

Now Anne's stomach fluttered to remember all this. Looking back, it seemed ironic that one of her own private moments—when she was spitting angry—was captured on national television, the most public of places. In a way, she'd been bitten by her own dog.

Her eyes met Slade's. That whole dreadful scene was best forgotten. Yet, his grandfather must have learned about it from the men there since she'd received a letter of apology with his signature and others' from the SMWA.

So Jack was correct. Something good did grow out of the annoying incident. A chance to prove her talent and ability, even if she was immersed in the sheep raisers' world. The last place she'd ever expected herself to be.

"You ranchers sure take your business seriously," Chase threw in.

"Don't we all?" Anne added.

"Not like that," Jack chirped, removing his sunglasses. "Yessir, Jim McGregor's a man of character. He personally wanted to make things better after all the ruckus."

"Ruckus," Slade repeated. The muscles at his temple began to work. "Have we met before?" he asked Jack, but locked his eyes on hers.

"Over the phone," he stated. "Last year we talked with your grandfather about filming here, but our timing was bad. He told us that there had been a death in the family. Thing is," he said, sliding the glasses back on, "my boss had flown over this place about a year and a half ago and spotted the Canyon. So he asked again, and here we are."

Nodding, Slade put his hand on her lower back. He tugged on a loop of her waistband with his thumb. She couldn't budge.

"What ruckus?" he asked hotly into her ear.

Anne nodded.

"Yes, thank you for reminding me," she said aloud for the group's benefit. "We'll do our best to keep noise away from the sheep. Won't we, guys?" They nodded in unison.

Rudy checked the sun. "We should go. You need time to set up camp."

The group began to disperse.

"Answer me." Slade gave her waistband a tug. It was unbelievable. Inspite of all this open country around them, Slade had her cornered. The suspicious glint in his eyes scared her. Had he seen and figured it out? Did he know that she was the woman on TV that night? The same woman who branded sheep farmers as undesirable, uncouth men?

"May we discuss this later?" she asked.

"Pencil me in on your appointment book."

Drew came closer.

"Excuse me, Mr. McGregor—"

"Slade, please."

The two of them seemed to gain an instant liking for one another. For that Anne was grateful. This assignment might end up better than she anticipated.

"Will you join us on the set this evening?" Drew asked.

"Sure. I want to see how all this works," Slade replied, releasing Anne's belt loop. "And you need some tips about the place."

"Like the flies?" the soundman said, swatting them away.

"Let 'em sit," Slade advised. "It can get wild out here. But then, hell, we like it that way. Right, Annie?"

Anne recoiled. She suddenly wanted to run. If he didn't shut up these people were going to get the impression they had something going other than business. Why now, of all times, was he choosing to be so forthright?

Drew gave her and Slade a curious glance and pulled a small spiral book from his shirt pocket.

"How about we meet after dinner?" the director said. "We weren't expecting a problem with using the Canyon. This kind of thing is worked out in advance, so we need to get the matter settled. Fast. In our business time—"

"Is money," Slade finished, throwing Anne a wink.

Drew sized him up. "Good man. We understand each other."

Turning on his bootheels, Slade brushed past Anne and strode to his motorcycle.

Exasperated, she returned to her Land Cruiser and climbed in. She watched Slade in the rearview mirror as he wound back up the slope, then disappeared over the ridge. She checked her watch. It read 4:10 p.m. as the caravan began to move out.

~ * ~

Lamplight lit the faces of the crew who sat around on lawn chairs outside Chase's motorhome. According to plan, Jack had left earlier with the truck drivers to go back to Sydney. Discussion turned from how Anne missed the ocean to reviewing the next day's production.

Other crewmembers began to fall into their time-off routines. About forty feet away stood portable aluminum tables where guys played cards. Music from the soundman's boombox lifted into the branches of the red gums.

Anne, however, would only rest after Slade left. She listened as the director repeated how the release agreement affected their filming schedule.

The grazier explained how the problems were based on the agreement with the Bilwan people. Of course, he left out the part about another route into the Canyon. She exchanged a quick glance with Rudy, who had remained quiet most of the evening.

For the life of her, she couldn't understand why Slade held back the information. She suspected that Rudy knew the reason, but he'd kept it to himself out of loyalty to his employer.

"You must understand that our people might not deny your request to cross Nourombie," Rudy said. "The elders will give us audience about this matter, but only after our ceremony is over."

Drew's expression turned grim.

"Point is," he said, "we may get two sites done here, but not Rainbow Canyon. That leaves us with a major production hole. And, my friend, that's serious trouble."

"Not to mention the Canyon's the main reason we wanted this property at all," Anne added, taking in Slade's stiff look.

A shock of his streaked hair escaped from beneath the brim of his hat. Again, she wished his grandfather was here. Days had passed since that rainy night in Hannah's hut. He seemed to be running the place with a silent hand.

"We're prepared to offer the Bilwan a handsome sum. But Mr. McGregor thinks it'll get us nowhere."

"Correction," Slade spoke up. "I said some things can't be fixed with money. And the Bilwans are not materialistic people."

"We're not stupid, either." Rudy put up his hands to end the quibbling. His eyes looked strained and Anne wondered if he was getting enough rest. The soundman dropped the volume on Los Del Rios by a few decibels.

"Maybe someone should pull some strings," Drew suggested. He leaned back in his director's chair and steepled his fingers.

Anne looked deeper into Slade's eyes, and for a moment that was all that mattered. A simple, unspoken plea swirled beneath the surface. She heard only quickening beats of her heart.

Help me, his eyes cried into hers.

Anne shivered. This was big, strong, and authoritative Slade McGregor wanting her to save him?

"I-I-I w-w-will," she stammered out loud.

Peace rose in Slade's eyes. Undeniably, she'd been the elixir he needed. Extracting her gaze from his, she fell back into the business conversation at hand.

"You'll pull the strings?" Drew asked her, scrunching his eyebrows together. "Anne, I'm sure you mean well, but you shouldn't make rash promises. And, frankly, your firm is already on the brink of that with this no-go Canyon situation. Nor is it the best way to keep your paying clients happy."

"Drew, we sell them and contract you to film them," she said sharply. "Remember that."

Slade pushed himself up from his chair and walked over behind her. He laid a calming hand on her shoulder.

"I reckon Anne knows exactly how to make someone happy."

She lowered her lashes and clasped her palms together. She couldn't figure him out. One minute he pulled the rug out from under her, the next minute he massaged praise into her every pore. Such a curious sort this Aussie.

"Drew is right," she said. "I can't fix this. I was just wishing out loud."

She then stood and took a deep breath.

"What time's breakfast call?"

"Five thirty," the cameraman said.

She set the alarm on her wristwatch.

"You'll keep us posted about the Canyon decision?" Drew asked Slade.

"You'll be among the first to know, mate."

Anne wished everyone a good night and headed toward the small motor home parked out under the jacaranda tree.

"Wait up," Slade called after her.

Knowing he wanted answers, she took long, purposeful steps. She needed to keep up a good rapport with him and his grandfather during these next few weeks. For now, it was better to skirt the issue. Success of her project still depended on a smooth, professional relationship.

Besides, she wanted to take a shower before crawling into the extra cot in Marge's trailer. Roughing it on location got easier each time. She could say that for almost everyone, except for Susan Sornja. She was beautiful and could be difficult.

Anne could only take being around the super model in small doses. It wasn't because of jealousy. She simply expected more maturity and less complaints from a woman who had made it so far into six-digits at her age of twenty-three.

As she reached the trailer steps, she glanced over her shoulder. Her breath caught. There was no way to prevent what was about to happen, but she cried out, "Watch out, Slade!"

As he barreled around the corner of a stack of equipment crates, Susan plowed into him, chest-first. She stood nearly as tall as he. Her mouth glanced off his chin. The model squealed. Quickly, Slade steadied her.

Anne winced. For a few seconds, a strange feeling pumped into her veins. She wanted to walk over there and separate the Slade and the model.

"I—I'm sorry," Slade offered. "Are you okay?"

Susan, doe-eyed and curvaceous, whimpered, "Yes. Oh no. My lip is hurt. Now it's swelling up." She touched her mouth with her perfectly manicured fingertips. "Ow, I'm bruised."

"Here, let me see."

"This can't be true," she cried, pushing him away. "Not the night before a shoot."

Anne called for Marge, but got no answer. She pulled open the aluminum door, fumbled for the light, and found the small refrigerator by the sink. She wrapped up ice cubes in a clean tea towel and hurried back outdoors.

Slade met her half way across the lot. It amazed her to see him look so muddled.

"I've caused a mess," he said, taking the ice pack from her.

His smooth moves turned awkward as he began to make his way back to the super model. She sat down about twenty yards away on a toppled crate. She held a wad of tissue against her mouth.

"Calm down, she'll live," Anne said. She barely matched his pace. "It was only an accident."

He disappeared around the side of a red gum, and she passed around the other side to meet up with him.

"There's no such thing as accidents," he said.

"Oh, come on, Slade," she huffed. "You can't believe that."

His intensity nearly bowled her over.

"Your star model's face is damaged."

Anne said, "Yes, and we'll deal with it. Everyone has accidents."

"But not everyone causes them."

Why was he being so hard on himself? she wondered.

"Look, this may cause a delay in close-up shots, but it's not the end of the world. I mean, Susan's not about to jump off a cliff," she quipped mindlessly.

Slade halted mid-step. Turning his head toward Anne, he stepped in front of her and roughly pulled her to him. A tornado brewed in his eyes. This unexpected fury stole her next breath.

"That was *not* funny," he snapped.

Anne stood dumbfounded. His reaction, swift and strong, had burst straight from his heart. Her curiosity needed answers, but she pushed looking for them to the back burner.

"I apologize," she said. "I certainly didn't mean anything by it."

Slade towered over her. He shook his head and let her go as if she were a hot poker. He glanced in Susan's direction and the storm that raged across his face began to fade.

"No, I'm the one who's sorry," he said quietly.

Anne struggled for the right words to say and the right thing to do. She could feel his pain in her own heart. How could she help him over the wall? For now the only answer she could come up with seemed too simple, but it was worth a shot.

"Slade, I don't know what's wrong—" He began to walk past her and she put her hand out to stop him. "But I've been around the block a few times, you know? And I can listen."

He switched the ice pack from one hand to the other. Her efforts didn't erase the frown that wrinkled his forehead. She could nearly read the battle that broke out in his mind. She'd bet her next box of Godiva chocolates that it was one so very familiar to her: to trust or not to trust?

"Anne, I…" he stalled out.

"Please, Slade, let me help."

She held her breath. He seemed desperate and ran his hand through his hair. Doubt rang clearly in his voice.

"What is it you think you can do?"

She took a step towards him and he stayed put. With her feet spread slightly apart, she looked him square in the eyes.

"Don't shut me out. It's part of my business to hear what people want, remember? So talk to me."

She understood his confusion while he regarded her for a moment. Slowly, he lifted his free hand and rested his thumb on her chin. His breath warmed her forehead.

"What's done is done," he said bitterly.

Their noses nearly met. At any other time, she would be sure he was going to kiss her and wrap her up in his magic all over again. Lord, she yearned for that other time.

"Wait here," he instructed.

Slade crossed the short distance to Susan. He helped her with the ice pack and talked briefly with Chase and Drew who now fussed over her. The model burst into tears and blamed Slade for not watching where he was going.

Slade returned with his hat in hand.

"You know you're the most changeable woman I've ever met. You slam my screendoor in my face, then you can't stand to see me suffer."

She had to hand it to him. At the moment, she sounded as confused as he looked. She sighed, wishing she'd come further than this. Reentering the singles world took every drop of her courage and saavy. The fact was she liked being married.

But she'd made a big mistake and said 'yes' to the wrong man. She took some comfort in knowing she wasn't alone. After all, his other wife had also made a wrong choice.

Until the last few weeks that rationale worked smoothly. Now it seemed as if she were pushed over a new threshold. An uneasy feeling haunted her. Much more was at stake here than geography.

Slade put out his hand and she took it.

"Let's go. I talk better when I walk."

He began to guide her away from the glow of the makeshift camp. Walking into the shadows, he quickly bent over and broke off a stalk of dried grass.

She said. "What was that all about? Somehow I put my foot in my mouth."

For a while the only sound that came from him was the crunch of his boots on the ground.

"Not your fault," he finally said. "A big part of my life ended last year. Suddenly. And if I had been more careful, it wouldn't have. Nothing, absolutely nothing, has felt right since... except meeting you."

Thirteen

Anne held that in her mind as if it were precious gold. Slade was opening up to her and it pleased her no end. She held her silence, giving him time to think while they walked beneath the red gums. She felt even less like an outsider in this beautiful and wild place.

Slowing, Slade dipped his shoulder against hers.

"Are you listening?"

Anne nodded and ambled with him to the fringe of camp. The early night hummed with nocturnal life. Ready to go until dawn, crickets sawed and cicadas droned in the shrubs.

"Happened faster than a flood," he told her. "I was here. She was here. We were married for only three months. Then in one afternoon the roof blew off."

"Oh my. Roofs blowing off are very serious."

He stopped moving and gazed at her, his eyes growing lackluster. To her surprise he pulled her against his chest. She slid her hands up his back, hugged him, and lifted her chin. His sigh resembled a shudder.

She'd pushed the envelope, but her intentions were good. She wanted him to talk his problems out. For his benefit, not hers. In all the good things that Slade had out here a void remained in his eyes. Undoubtedly, he'd paid her a compliment when he sent her his silent appeal for help.

He lowered his head and rested his chin on the top of her shoulder. At the moment, the man needed a little emotional support. That was what mattered now. Piecing the remnants of a crises into understandable sense took more courage than most average people had on their best day. Dealing with them took even more.

The realization hit her that little about Slade McGregor seemed average. He was a diamond in the emotional rough, needing the right conditions to sparkle again. In some ways, he was bigger than life. For once, her heart and mind agreed. She was lucky to have met him.

He eased his hold on her, and the night air passed between them. Watching her intently, he gave it to her straight.

"My wife wanted us to move to the city," he began, "and for me to learn her father's business. A good one, at that."

The creases in his forehead deepened.

"And when you fought about it," Anne guessed, "you held your ground."

He paced a circle, then faced her.

"Damn, look at me," he said, muscular arms outstretched, palms up. "You think I'd leave the Red Gum for a petrochemical company? How long would that last?"

"Maybe a week." She smiled wryly. "Then she accused you of thinking only of yourself."

"Yes, and not of our child's future." He threw her a skeptical look about how she would know. Responding, she lifted her right shoulder into a slight shrug.

"And when you said she was asking too much, she got so hurt and angry she left you standing in the dust."

Slade cut her off. "Stop. Right there. My grandfather's been talking to you, hasn't he?"

She shook her head back and forth. "He hasn't betrayed your trust. The only words we've shared were those when he stopped by that night at Hannah's hut when you and I..."

She let her voice trail off and looked up. A low-flying aircraft approached and sputtered discord in its wake. Its presence didn't fit—the moment or the place.

Waiting for her to finish, Slade watched her. She could only imagine what was going on behind those mystified eyes. Whatever emotions he'd managed to cast aside, appreciation softened the strain on his face.

She added, "I don't think you should feel guilty. You laid it on the line and told her the fair-dinkum truth."

Anne sucked in a quick breath. *Fair-dinkum?* Slade didn't bat a dark eyelash at her use of Aussie lingo. Yet, hearing herself say it sent a charge through her.

"Honesty costs," he said. "I thought she understood. This station is my life's blood. Damned if I know how she missed that. She wanted someone I'm not."

Anne tucked her fingers into her pockets, and Slade trained his eyes on the aircraft as it zoomed overhead.

"Then it happened, and she was gone."

"Gone?"

"Over the edge," he shouted above the noise.

Crows, flying foxes, and kookaburras flapped from the trees.

"You mean... she went crazy?"

His answer drowned in the roar, and the plane's silver belly skimmed low. He lifted his hand and waved.

"That's Lindsay Sanders," Slade yelled into her ear. "He's a Flying Doctor and is our neighbor on the north. Flies his own plane. I wonder why he's coming this way?"

Anne nodded and noticed the beam of a flashlight bobbed this way and that in the bushes. Squinting, she realized that it was Rudy coming toward them. Every part of his body seemed in motion, and his eyes were opened wide in concern.

"We've been looking about for you," he reported.

"What happened?" Slade asked.

"You must go. It's your grandfather. His heart." Rudy gestured at the plane. "Lindsay is transporting him to Newcastle."

"What the hell? His heart? When, how?"

Rudy filled him in how Da-Wa had radioed for help when Jim McGregor collapsed in the kitchen.

The expression on Slade's face looked worse than fearful.

Anne felt helpless, except in one way.

"Here, take my car." She dug the keys from her pocket and tossed them to Slade. "Better for night driving than your bike." The gratitude flooding his eyes overwhelmed her.

"Right. Rudy, look after Annie. Keep her safe until I get back."

"You have my word, boss."

Slade touched her shoulder, turned away, and broke into a run back to camp. In a few moments Anne heard her Land Cruiser charge off into the night.

~ * ~

Two days later Anne observed the filming. She couldn't help but be impressed. The team spent every ounce of their creative hearts and souls, and more than their share of hours to do it.

They also argued.

"If you can't give me the best angle, how do you expect the model to look good?" Drew complained. "And if she doesn't look good, why the hell would anybody buy SunMate Sunscreen?"

"Keep your shirt on," the cameraman said. "Marge did her best make-up job on that lousy swelled-up bruise. It's either this angle, or wait until it goes away."

Anne closed her eyes. She loved her business, but all these painstaking efforts boiled down to work for the sake of one thing. That was profit. She wondered if things were going any better on Slade's end. An eternity seemed to have passed since he'd left.

Rudy had kept his word, and he often radioed Rose. When he received news about Jim McGregor's condition, he passed it along to Anne first.

The most recent call was about an hour ago. The news was good. Jim McGregor had stabilized and angioplasty surgery was scheduled for this afternoon. According to Rudy, if all went well, Slade would return to the Red Gum tomorrow or the next day.

Rudy also said, "I've brought news."

She felt her muscles constrict on the back of her neck. Lately, news was usually bad. What she wouldn't give now for one of Slade's back rubs. She tried to sweep that wish away and looked at the Aborigine and half-listened to him. In a domino effect one problem flared up after another since Slade and Susan smacked into one another.

"I must be at the ceremonies that begin tomorrow night. So you and your people will come with me."

Anne widened her eyes.

"Us? In Nourombie?" She ducked as two grips carrying sun reflectors narrowly missed her as they swung around and dropped the aluminum supports in a pile in the dust.

"You'll be my guests."

Now she felt like a burden.

"Rudy, just go. Nothing will happen to me here. Your people's ceremonies are private, sacred affairs."

"Some parts are public."

"Maybe so, but I wouldn't think of crashing something so—"

Rudy silenced her with a reassuring smile.

"I gave Slade my word to keep you in my watch," he said with resolve. "My people have gatherings for as many reasons as your families do. Our first ceremony in Nourombie will be a happy one. Women will sing songs of our origin and men will dance. And my cousin will receive his new bride."

Anne's spirits lifted. The prospect of being included in something this special and being so near Rainbow Canyon made her heart pound. She glimpsed Drew who still ranted about making Susan's fat, bruised bottom lip look better than good on the necessary close-up.

"Drew, shut down," she called decisively. "We're going to Nourombie for a couple of days. Now we can see the place first-hand. We'll pick up here when we get back."

Drew needed no urging, nor did anyone else as the word spread. It was a prime opportunity. Anne's call, however, was not as easy as it sounded. Naturally, she'd have to justify the shutdown. No matter, she looked at going as an investment. She asked Rudy if they could possibly film the area.

"Your chances will be limited, and it could never be like this." He gestured the paraphernalia scattered about. "None of you must walk outside the boundaries. They have been set by our elders to protect our dreamtime. I will show you."

"Of course. Please tell them that we'll comply."

Satisfied, he nodded. "This is good. We leave after the breakfast call tomorrow."

"Thank you," she said, shaking his hand. Although toughened by bush life, he seemed rather shy about his art. In the little spare time she had, she'd given his need to get his work "out there" more thought. But, lately, he hedged from any further discussion about his creations.

175

"May I get you something?" she asked, wanting to repay some of his favor.

Rudy grinned and lifted his brown forefinger as if he had concocted a brilliant, new idea. "A Bud Light," he said wistfully. "I have wanted a Bud Light. Those lizards and bullfrogs make me laugh."

Anne smiled. The power of American brand-name advertising had struck again.

~ * ~

Anne marveled at her up-front view of Kissing Turtles, the gateway to Nourombie. With Rudy's permission she turned on her video camera as Drew drove beneath the arch formed by the rock creature's thick, short necks.

Ahead, the narrow, flat road, running between the mound-like sandstone shells, serpentined toward the west and disappeared beyond stands of flat-topped trees. Outcroppings of grey rocks, greened with splotchy lichen, hemmed the land in far on their right to the north and left to the south.

Traveling this deep into the Red Gum heightened her sense of adventure. The switch to her senses flipped on. Although sight and sound were the mainstay senses used in her trade, she often tried to entice viewers to use all of those senses while watching her clients' commercials.

Sunmate Sunscreen emphasized touch, along with sight since it protected natural beauty. Other than sight, touch remained Anne's favorite, and no one she could remember had ever touched her like Slade.

"Will Slade come here to Nourombie?" she asked Rudy who sat between her and Drew.

He pointed to the small, gleaming white aeroplane parked on the crest of a long grassy slope.

"Dr. Sanders is checking children during our gathering. It would be my guess that he brought the boss back here with him."

She decided to bring up the concern that nagged her all the way here.

"Won't he be surprised... I mean, when he finds us here?"

Rudy tossed her a knowing glance while Drew swerved out of the path of three wallabies napping in the road.

"No worries. He'll not be angry. As he wished, you are under the safety of my watch."

Looking about, Anne spotted many vehicles parked beneath trees, under rock overhangs, and baking in the sun in the middle of open country. Yet, she saw no sign of Slade.

During the afternoon, the Bilwan ceremonial manager busied himself with preparing the ground while others visited and traded goods. Anne worked at a makeshift table that Rudy and Drew set up for her under a sprawling flame tree.

It didn't take her or the others long to get their bearings. As Rudy had said, they were instructed about where they could go and where not. The space was limited.

Performances and celebrations would take place in a large circle. Its west parameter almost edged Rainbow Canyon, but they were not to go any farther than the trade area of ground.

"Rainbow Canyon," she murmured. "So close, yet so far."

Pulling papers from her briefcase, she did necessary tasks. Yet each gave her little satisfaction. She opened her trip journal and, in a rare moment, released her feelings to go as they may and wrote:

> *PASSAGE TO NOUROMBIE*
> *I have never been in any forbidden, sacred place,*
> *Meant to protect and stay forever in grace.*
> *My footprints whisper to this red dust,*
> *Make room for my heart, his dreams—*
> *And eternally for US?*

Finished, Anne gazed at her words. Dressed in blue ink, they'd flowed from her heart onto the page. She sighed. She added the date and reread the last line.

> *And eternally for US?*

A sudden wish for time to move forward rushed over her. If only it were next year. For then she might know the answer to her burning question. Would she ever find a trustworthy, life-long mate? If so, who would he be?

She took in the activity that bustled about, kicking up dust and brewing excitement. Many Aboriginal men, women, and children, carrying bark bags and baskets and ceremonial spears, had already arrived, but some still streamed in on foot.

Setting down her pen, she glimpsed the hill and the gleaming white Cessna on top. She began to doubt Rudy's guess that Slade had come in with the doctor.

Disappointed, she closed her journal. An intermittent breeze puffed her blue chambray overshirt away from her sides. The branches rustled behind her.

Windswept, her papers fluttered and the gold pen began to roll. She jumped up from the folding chair to catch the pen as it reached the end of the plank. Except the movement from behind her was faster. A familiar hand reached down and snatched the pen up quicker than she could say "Slade McGregor."

"G'day, Annie," he said over her shoulder.

She spun around a half-turn to face him. "Slade, you're here," she said, then, "Don't you ever come in the front door?"

"I did, and it looks like in the nick of time." He pulled her pen out of reach. "What're you writing?"

She stowed the journal behind her back.

"Some notes," she said. "How's your grandad?"

Slade looked somewhat different. Maybe it was the new flicker in his eyes.

"We're damned lucky he pulled through. It was a close call, and he's not completely safe yet."

A certain amount of heaviness lifted from her. She hated to think what would happen if Slade lost his grandfather now. "I'm happy for you both."

He rubbed his stubbled jaw with his hand.

"He's tougher than... you and me put together. He'll be home soon."

He touched her hand. The chemistry between her and Slade was undeniable. But he seemed to be holding something back like he was taking a chance by going any further.

"What is it?"

"My grandfather and I had a good talk."

Anne sighed. "That's great. Good."

"He was more than direct this go around. He said he's not sure about time. He wants to see us... together."

"Together? As in... Slade, tell me he was coming out from under anesthesia."

Slade's blue eyes glimmered into hers. Her stomach flipped. He leaned forward and kissed her, not caring who saw him do it. She tried to pull back.

"Thank you for listening the other evening," he said, releasing her lips.

Anne's senses basked in newfound delirium. Her heart nearly soared from her chest as his eyes beckoned her soul to come forth. They spoke too frankly and told her too much. They said he wanted her. Completely.

She looked away. Although the prose she'd written spoke of her need, this was the worst time for someone to enter her life in a serious way. Not here, fifteen time zones away from home. Not with her heart still muddled with distrust and her having to leave in a few weeks.

Her expression must have revealed her mixed feelings.

"I don't understand much of this myself," Slade added quietly. "But I never met a woman like you, Annie."

She wanted to believe that he was lying again as he did about the route into the Canyon. Her instinct told her otherwise. His words rang clear and honest.

"Slade. Please stop. I... I don't know what to say."

"That may be a first," he said.

Anne swiped her pen from his hand.

"You're impossible."

He shrugged. "Whatever you say, my friend."

She regarded him for a second. *Friend.* Whew, she relaxed. Putting their relationship in that light seemed reasonable, comfortable, and brought less responsibility than lover, or wife.

It also rang up as quite inadequate.

Slade had kissed her, and she'd kissed him back. He'd once fondled her, and after he started she had trouble keeping her hands off him. His body promised more, and so had hers.

"Fine, I'm a friend," she said, swallowing hard.

She looked past his shoulder. The world continued to turn, even though it felt like she'd left for a short while. Across the way, an elderly Bilwan waved at Slade.

"I'm going back to Newcastle tomorrow to check on him." He strode toward the man with yellowed, crooked teeth who held a spear and a log drum.

She looked around for signs of her own reality. Drew and the cameraman sat under a tree. Legs outstretched, the two men tried to blow through the long, hollow didjeridus, which they supported with their feet. The soundman had turned off his boom box and waited for a turn at the instrument, while Susan and Chase reclined under blue striped beach umbrellas and sipped chilled lemon water.

The Bilwan men, who'd shown up in shirts and shorts or jeans, went into a long, hastily-built stick hut. Reappearing, they wore little more than body ornamentation of white and yellow ocher, beads, and bark woven pubic bands or longer printed loincloths. They'd taken their leave of the present, carrying all those who watched with them. The women unpacked and prepared food and readied for their place in the performance circle.

Slade stopped by only once before dusk after she'd freshened up from the nap she'd taken. When she returned to her worktable, she found him stretched out on top of it. Legs crossed, arms folded under his head, he lifted his hat from his face. The plank bowed under his weight.

She raised an eyebrow.

"You're in for an interesting evening," he said. "The Bilwan blokes get into it, give a good show."

She fiddled with the string of her straw hat. "None like I'd ever see in Westport." Excitement riddled her voice. The movement, earth-dye colors, and textures pulled her into the scene further. She turned back to him, wondering. "Will they do anything gross? I'm not one for watching people eat grubs."

Slade stretched his mouth into a half-smile, pulled himself up, and swung his legs over the edge.

"They might. Each person will express the heritage they know and has the inherited job of keeping alive and passing to others. Only elders really understand the layers of the music and dance, but we know their ancient songs reveal their ancestor's journey. Many are vocal or musical maps about places or events that happened along the way."

Anne fanned herself with an emu feather given to her by a spindly-legged child who carried a bouquet of the grey plumes.

"On their way where?"

"To here, where we are now. In this time and place. It will get fully spirited after the moon rises over the Canyon."

Shadows lengthened as the sun's amber rays fingered the horizon. Anne was thrilled when the ceremonial manager trumpeted the opening of the performances. She and everyone else in her crew sat cross-legged around the perimeter of the two large Bilwan circles. Men sat on the inner, women on the outer. The center had been brushed clear of debris for the ocher-painted dancers who now held everyone's rapt attention.

Crouched, the dancers huddled, charged, then ducked again as if they were stalking prey. The women sat side-by-side, singing in unison. Aboriginal men played didjeridus. Simultaneously taking in air through their nose and blowing into the instruments that were fashioned from thick hollow eucalyptus branches and painted in bright colors, the players voiced guttural sounds in a rhythmic drone. Clapsticks added variety.

Slade was correct. Little of it meant anything to her. But the feelings she derived as she watched the rituals were what she imagined the Bilwan peoples shared: fellowship, joy, and spiritual renewal.

She glanced across the way where Slade leaned against a tree and talked with Dr. Sanders. They were enjoying themselves, but hardly as much as she. She reveled with being in touch with life, the earth, and all that made it go around. They glanced in her direction, and Slade's friend handed him something, which he pocketed.

The bonfire flicked sparks up into the darkening sky as Slade strode toward her now. His features and ready-for-whatever-anybody-dares-give-me body caught the flames' gilding light. Once again he appeared larger than life. Less of a brooding mystery, more healthy every day.

His stance, comfortable and sexy, moved her. No sooner did he kneel down beside her than Rudy and his family brought forth his cousin, the groom. The tone of the music changed and the middle-aged man took the hand of his very young new bride.

According to Slade, the girl had been promised to Rudy's kinship not long after her birth. The two of them soon moved out of the circle and sat with other Bilwan people.

"They're her parents," Slade explained. "They all gain from this arrangement."

"Arrangement," she repeated. "Does she love him and he love her?"

Slade answered her kindly, inspite of her naivety.

"It can happen that way and they have European style weddings in town, but it's not a factor this time." Slade asked, "See those two women with children singing near the groom?"

She squinted past the blaze, then nodded.

"They're his other wives. He must be from where some groups still practice this, probably the Northern Territory."

Dumbfounded, she fired off a mere squeak. "You know," she said, "you could have gone all night without telling me that."

He pursed his lips.

Memories of the pain and unfairness of her own brush with bigamy roiled in her mind. The worst experience she could have lived through left a legacy of caution in its wake.

"Calm down, Annie," he said. "These people live with old customs. It's all legal and simple."

Nothing appeared simple anymore to her. Appalled, she checked the bride more closely.

"That girl doesn't look a day over fourteen," she said. "How can she know about marriage?"

Slade looked fully at Anne now.

"You're killing the translator."

"She's being exploited," she retorted.

He reached over, took her hand, and gave it a firm squeeze.

"Not now," he warned. "Remember where you are and why you're here. This isn't the time to judge others or project your own hurt or values onto them."

Anne recoiled. "Is that what you think I'm doing?"

Fourteen

Anne took a tissue from her pocket and blotted perspiration from her hairline. The sun had barely set, yet she felt very warm. The colorful gauzy skirt and blouse she'd changed into after her nap clung to her hips and legs.

"Lucky guess," Slade replied, wearing a resolute expression. "The bride and her family are carrying on tradition."

Anne drummed her fingers on her knee. "In effect, she's been traded for custom's sake. That's terrible and unfair."

"Not to them. She knows she's not the only wife."

Anne straightened her spine. This whole scenario of multiple spouses got too close for comfort. Resentment flashed through her as she was pushed into the past where she no longer cared to go. She lashed out.

"So what's your point?"

Slade leaned over and flicked a firefly from her hair as the next group of dancers took their places in the circle.

"That you weren't supposed to know."

As much as Anne wanted to, she couldn't look away from him. Although she'd been over it a hundred times, what Slade said made sudden, perfect sense.

Even though Jack and other colleagues had done their best to convince her of that, she'd half-believed that she somehow chased her husband away. In her crumbling self-image, she'd never given herself permission to think otherwise. She believed in cause and effect, so now fear attached itself to her sense of judgment.

Slade read her face. "You can let it go now."

This was the closest she'd come to believing the maverick Aussie station owner since she'd met him. A pristine calmness rippled through her. She could use a little safety in her life.

"I wish I could," she said, gazing ahead.

A young Bilwan boy played a whistle and another stretched a tanned animal skin over his knees, then tapped it with black, nimble fingers. Women, singing, moved into the circle. They knelt and lifted their faces and hands to the bright, rising moon and fluttered their fingers like falling rain.

"What are they praying for?"

"Abundance," he answered, his features softening.

Anne sensed there was more.

"And fertility?"

He smiled. "You're getting more out of this than most Yanks. As anywhere, children are the future."

On his mention of children, she watched the shadow that rode through his eyes steal his peace. Instinct told her not to chase the shadow. Instead, she immersed herself along with the crew in the magic of the once-in-a-lifetime evening.

After everyone shared a festive and sumptuous meal, the celebration spread out and broke up into smaller groups to socialize away the rest of the evening.

Rudy and some of his friends, decorated with ocher, feathers and seedpods, stopped by and mingled with Anne's production people. The soundman, wearing shorts and a Jerry Garcia shirt, had turned on his portable compact disk player.

Before long Marge and the script girl began dancing the almost-forgotten Macarena. Its rhythm and their happy mood lured two of Rudy's cousins to join in. The soundman cranked up the music, and a few others picked up the dance, then more people took part.

Anne could hardly believe her eyes. Beneath the Southern Cross and in front of fading bonfires, the current century danced with the carryovers of ancient, primitive ages. Right arm out, left arm out, right palm up, left palm up, shoulder, shoulder, head, head, hip hip, rear, rear, turn dissolved the barriers of time and culture.

Yes, she thought while being pulled into the corraboree by a cameraman, *they certainly know how to party Down Under.*

Fascinated by her ability to fit in, Slade watched Anne. Her face brightened with every passing minute. Her long legs tempted him. She circled her hips, and heat speared him where it counted most. Her hair—long undone from its tortoise shell clasp—rippled and shimmered over her shoulders.

He'd never met a princess, but she seemed one. He wondered if Fate had changed its course and brought him royalty.

Along with the others, she laughed at her mistakes. He liked that. She seemed at home, always part of the place.

When he'd called her "friend," he meant it. She'd helped him delve into his darkest hour. Once he'd taken the first step, he discovered talking with her was easy. So much so that he began to doubt the wisdom of his plan to quash that part of his life: never to speak of it and demand others around him do the same. He not only had shut out their words, he denied their chance to share his grief and help lighten it.

Stronger, he wanted to tell her more, tell her everything. He wanted to shed his pain—all of it—in full daylight. But how well would Anne take hearing about the death of his child? *Hell,* he thought, *that answer was simple.* She would have expected him to do more. Like save his baby.

He dragged his palm over the back of his neck and decided silence was best. Why should he spoil something that, in spite of certain problems, was pleasing the hell out of him? That being, having Annie around.

~ * ~

Just before eleven o'clock Anne said her goodnights and headed back toward the make-up artist's caravan. The music faded and the light grew dimmer as she approached the worktable where she'd spent time earlier in the day. Her steps spry, she felt like she was glowing from the inside out. She'd had *fun*. Pure, simple fun. The kind she used to know before life got so tough. Before she needed to put her career first. Before she'd decided never to marry again.

Savoring this carefree feeling, she glanced over her shoulder and spotted Slade striding behind her.

"Wait," he called.

She turned around and leaned against the table. Lifting her hair from her neck with both hands, she let the air cool her skin. Moisture clung to her cleavage and the back of her knees.

He lankered toward her.

"It's been a delightful evening," she began.

"That it has. Tired?"

She shook her head. Sleep would elude her for hours. Her senses hummed from overstimulation.

"Good." He pulled a set of keys from his pocket, tossed them into the air, and caught them. "Let's cruise."

She gaped. Slade never ceased to surprise her. He lived halfway around the world, but managed to sound as if he lived up the block.

"Now where'd you hear that?"

"An old movie on satellite." Grinning, he shrugged and put out his hand. "Trust me, you'll like where we go."

She lifted her right hand to take his, then hesitated.

Without doubt, she would like wherever he had in mind. She admired his taste, except for his Triumph. As it was, his smile nearly stopped her heart. Still, the trusting part tensed her up.

She gazed at him and he at her. The moonlight haloed his ruffled hair and broad shoulders. She tried to resist him, yet her defenses left her stranded. *Lighten up,* chided her inner voice. The man was not placing a ring on her finger, he was asking her on a ride. She slowly took his hand. Together they walked to Drew's rented vehicle. Her curiosity brewed.

"Where *are* we going?"

"About ten kilometers south, to Crystal Springs."

"Now? Wouldn't it be better to see it in the daylight. At least then I could see if the area is lensworthy."

He tugged her on. "The Springs has two personalities, one by day and one by night. Either way, you won't regret going. You can return later with your people all you want."

He opened the car door for her, and she slid into the seat.

"Okay, but I can't write off the Canyon," she said, rolling down the window after he shut the door. "You know that."

Slade winced and rounded the front of the vehicle. Hopping in beside her, he adjusted the rearview mirror, and started the engine. On the way back toward Kissing Turtles the headlights doused the narrow pasture road formed by the hoofs of thousands of merinos over the decades.

She slipped into silence.

"I'm only asking you to give Crystal Springs a chance."

"Deal," she said.

Light conversation ate up the next twenty minutes, and Anne now stood with Slade in a moon-washed paradise. Never could she have imagined the lustrous, wild enchantment that surrounded them, nor his obvious pleasure at showing the oasis to her. She sensed he knew every inch with his heart.

"Do you come here often?" she asked, walking with him into a small tropical-like clearing. Sounds of water falling and birds punctuated their small talk.

"Yep. Ever since I was a kid."

Two sandy shoals hugged clear water where moonlight rippled on the surface. Moss and velvet-like grass carpeted patches of ground beneath her feet as she made her way to the bank. Veils of water cascaded into a pool at their left, having fallen from the two pools above.

"You're right. This place is one step from paradise."

He responded with a peaceful sigh as foliage brushed her arm. He pointed out things as they went along: the bulbous trunk of a twisted tree, moonbeams cutting through high rounded rock crevices, and an occasional bird taking wing. He helped her down a steep bank to the silt-edged pool.

"From here on we go barefoot," he instructed, situating himself on a log and pulling off his boots.

She settled next to him. Their thighs nearly touched as she lifted her skirt to her knees and removed her Capezios. She glanced at the ground. Her shoes—light and stylish woven leather sandals—lay unbuckled against his tough, scuffed, practical footgear. Different, but cradled together.

"Now follow me," he said, pulling her to her feet. The power of his muscular arms sent all kinds of signals through her. It was all she could do to keep from wilting against him.

The moon rested overhead while Anne's senses pulsed. Every one of them readied to take off like a rocket, land in unknown turf, and collect valuable samples to take back home.

"Ms. Kingsley, have you ever been creek walking?"

She remembered summers spent at Camp Starr on Lake Dove, but came up empty-handed.

"I'll have a go at it, Mr. McGregor."

She tied the folds of her skirt into a loose knot below her left hip, leaving enough of the gauzy fabric to fall mid-thigh. She picked her way over pebbles of all sizes. She nearly lost her balance as a leafy stick jutted up between her toes. She cried out, in surprise rather than in pain.

In a swift move, Slade turned and gathered her up into his arms. Being so close to him unnerved and thrilled her. Yet, she stiffened. She'd already let him get way too far, and she liked it way too much when he did.

"Relax," he said as he began to carry her down the short bank and into the water. With the ease that he handled her, she felt lighter. At the mercy of the bounce of his stride, she pressed her temple against his shoulder.

His leatherwood scent aroused her and mingled with the night air. His hand, supporting her under her arm, came dangerously close to her breast. The hardness of his chest muscles gave her cause to twitch. So close, she heard his heart thumping strongly.

"Hold on," he coaxed. "We're almost there."

She was sure she must have said something back, but wouldn't take a bet on what it was. He chortled and drew to a halt near the middle of the shallow water. Loosening his arms from under her legs, he set her down.

Refreshing coolness wet her skin as the water swirled up to her calves. He moved his hands to her waist, keeping her close. Their eyes had little choice but to meet. The sweetness of the moment was so fragile she feared to move lest she lose it forever.

Her heart pounded now. She'd never been or could be a good-time girl. Yet, one by one, she discarded her ten best reasons not to go any further. Leaning into him, she lifted her chin.

Slade thought it would take the Australian Defense Force to hold him back. Setting her down took all of his willpower. Now this. Whenever she was so near, his blood rushed through his veins, and somehow his common sense checked out on holiday.

He set his jaw. He needed to control the passion that churned through him. But when he gazed upon the yearning that lit up Anne's face and was reminded that his touch put it there, he swallowed hard. Her lips moist and poised, she wanted his kiss. She invited him to return and explore the wonder of her.

Save for innocuous flora and fauna, they were alone. He closed his eyes, feeling her hips under the thin cloth. Damn, his palms itched to travel. Up and down her thighs, eventually to find the hot comforts between them.

Anne teetered on the edge of completely losing it. She tremored as her senses pleaded *touch me now.*

Slade reopened his eyes. Only by the grace of God, he summoned inner strength. Who knew how long it would last? He took a short step backwards, then another, and let his hands fall away.

"You're lovely," he said.

Dazed, she frowned. Disappointment tangled with relief. That was too close, she decided. He took her hand and they began to walk, saying nothing. The sloshing sounds their feet made faded into the splashing noise from a waterfall on the other side of the bank.

"Down that way," he said, giving her a moment to get her bearings. "I'll show you why this is called Crystal Springs."

Her feet hugged the smooth, solid bedrock. She took quick stock of herself. It was near midnight, and she stood in the middle of a moonlit spring with an Aussie who, up until a short while back, she'd never known. Or ever dreamed of meeting. If someone had told her on her last birthday that she'd be doing this before her next, she'd have laughed them out of her chic Westport condo.

"Who named it?" she asked, catching up with him.

"My grandfather did. Back in the spring of 1958 when he came through that cave during a heavy rain."

She glimpsed the dark, craggy slit in the rocks that hemmed in what could easily be monikered God's Country. After turning a short bend that was nearly hidden by shaggy trees, they exited onto a sand bar.

"You okay?" Slade asked without touching her.

"So far so good," she said, readjusting her soaked skirt.

He made his way across the sand and dove into a deeper, silvery surfaced pool. Coming up again, he shook water from his hair that glistened in the moonlight. His shirt molded itself to his shoulders and pectorals. God had done a very nice job on him, indeed. He called for her to come in.

Anne splashed into the water. As she trod toward him, the water changed in temperature. Tepid, cool, and warm again around her legs and it surpassed her waist. She looked down and saw her blouse puff away from her chest like a filmy cloud.

"You once said you like sapphires," he said over his shoulder.

"Yes. They're beautiful and the gem of truth."

"You'll like this."

He disappeared behind a thin sheet of water overflowing from the pool above. By the time she swam through the falls, he'd gotten out of the water and removed his shirt.

"Over here," he called as she surfaced and spied him through soaked eyelashes. He met her at the water's edge and helped her onto a level, powder dry rock shelf. She wiped water from her face and wrung out the ends of her hair. In her opinion, she couldn't have looked worse.

"We've certainly taken the scenic route."

She glimpsed down at herself and felt the heat of a blush coming on. Every inch of her loose-fitting outfit found a place to cling, nestle, and reveal secrets about her figure. She crossed her arms to cover her breasts and the knot she'd tied over her hip had long unraveled.

Slade made an exaggerated effort to look away.

"You don't like roughing it?" he asked, crossing a short distance to a barrel stored in an eroded rock hollow. "No worry. We do have some comforts here."

He bent over and worked off the lid. Watching in mild amusement and curiosity, she trained her eyes on his muscular back. Once they had their fill, she let them wander down to his narrow waist, then over his pants. Seeing him half-naked and water-soaked was more than a healthy woman could take.

He stood and replaced the lid on the barrel. She averted her eyes to the pocked rock ceiling, evidence that at one time the whole place had been under water. Carrying a large plastic bag, he returned to her side.

"Here. Compliments of Bondi Beach."

She took the bag, dumped out a jumbo-sized beach towel, and swagged the terry over herself in sari fashion.

"Better?" he asked, seemingly impatient.

"Now what?"

He cocked an eyebrow and lifted the corner of his mouth. His bare chest disconcerted her so badly, she pretended that sand bothered her feet and bent over to brush it off.

He turned and his eyes, burning with mysterious excitement, dove into hers.

"Only my grandfather and I know of this."

She fidgeted. "I don't keep secrets well," she said. "I have a low tolerance for pain under torture."

"Could have fooled me."

"Okay, you want to talk weaknesses, there's one. And for what it's worth, here's another. Smoke messes up my sinuses. For days."

"So noted," he quipped and headed for a low rock overhang. He dropped to his knees in the sand. Crawling between two large round rocks, he sat with his back against one and pushed against the other with his bare feet. The rock slowly moved aside, letting moonlight escape from behind it. He got back up and his silhouette, darkened against gleaming dust motes.

"Drop that ridiculous towel and follow me. If we don't go now, you'll miss it."

Anne's curiosity overrode all else. She discarded the terrycloth and tried to fluff her skirt away from her body. It worked somewhat as she crossed the distance to drop on her knees beside him.

"Couple of things here," he said, lowering his voice.

"At no time do you scream, it'll shoo any bats that're still here. You don't put so much of a toe in the water, your skin will yellow. And you don't snitch samples. Got it?"

Anne widened her eyes. Her curiosity backed down a few pegs. The willies set in the same manner as when Slade had coaxed her onto the back of his Triumph. Untravelled turf simply made her nervous. Another weakness.

"Annie, are you with me?"

"Uh-huh," she croaked, casting her fate once again to Slade McGregor who took off in front of her.

"Stay close, Love. We've little room."

When he turned his back to her she shortened her skirt by tucking it up into the elastic waistband and crept behind him through the passageway. The ground texture changed from soft and dry to harder, cool and dank under her palms.

"Watch, on your left," he warned.

Paying attention, she veered to her right and avoided the yellowy ribbon of water trickling past her.

"Now we duck."

She did so and the closer they came to the end, the brighter the moonlight. The surface under her hands and knees took on a gritty kind of feel.

"Slade, what's this we're crawling on?"

"Basic ground and limestone and sulphur—and a little bat guano."

Anne sprang upright on her knees. "What?" she rasped. Her hair scraped the rock ceiling and she lowered herself again, placing hands on her thighs.

"Nothing to get excited about. It's about six or eight thousand years old."

She stopped in her tracks. This took the ever-loving cake. "You've got me crawling on *bat* crap?" Her stomach warned mutiny. "I swear I'll never forgive you for this. I don't care how old it is." Giddiness lightened her head.

Slade whispered, "Minable guano makes good fertilizer."

"Whatever, but so help me, this had better be worth it."

Slade stopped. "If you're not up to this we'll turn around. I'm not forcing you to go on."

"Tell you what," she began, struggling to keep her voice down. "I'm going, but the next time you invite me on a little escapade, how about you fill me in on the all implications? Then I'll make a decision whether or not to put it on my agenda."

Water dripping filled the silence that followed.

"You know, you can be one *difficult*, even bitchy woman."

"Hey, maybe so, but that's helped me."

He began to move again toward the light.

"You know what your problem is?" he flung over his back.

"Nothing some fresh air won't solve."

"You need a hobby."

Anne saw red in the half-dark. Of all the audacious remarks for Slade to make. But, then again, she should have expected it.

"Right, all I need is another husband," she fired back. "A good man is a good man, but having one doesn't guarantee my problems will be forever gone. What is it with you guys, anyway? Always thinking you're the answer to our problems?"

Slade sat up and faced her. The end of the tunnel gaped behind him. Still on her hands and knees, she gazed up at him. Mixed emotions warred on his face.

"I said *hobby*," he stated. "Like painting or playing the piano."

Anne skipped her next breath. Embarrassment rushed through her now for other reasons—the foolworthy kind.

"You mumbled. And God forbid, we disturb the bats."

He leaned toward her. "Could we go on now? Because I'm this far away from giving you what you really need."

Suddenly transfixed, she tried to unravel his meaning.

Whatever it might be, he'd laid a trap and she couldn't pretend she didn't notice. She couldn't let him get away with that inch.

"Is that a threat?"

"Nope, a promise." His eyes sparked. "Now come up here beside me and close your eyes."

She sighed. She'd irritated him enough and resolved herself to do as he asked. He was still her guide.

He helped her to her feet. "I'm going to lead you." He tugged and she took a few steps, then froze. She could see light brightening behind her closed eyelids. The ground under feet again changed to gritty soil scattered over bubbled rock.

"Annie, relax. My intentions are good."

She exhaled. He was obviously trying to do her a favor. He was about to share again from his world. Shame tinged her conscience, but her curiosity nearly smothered her.

"Why do you show me your favorite places?"

He paused, which told her that she'd caught him off-guard. She'd asked the question because she really wanted to know the answer.

"Because part of me wants you to know," he said. "The part that knows someone like you won't be coming to the Red Gum again. You're the most responsive woman I've ever met." Then he added, as if he were thinking aloud, "Seems like I'm on some kind of a roll here, but I never shifted into gear."

Anne tightened her eyes. She wanted to flee. He was serious, more serious than she wanted to know. For that matter, she felt more serious about him than she ever wanted to be for someone again. Slade constantly challenged her. He'd spin her into fine wool and would reweave part of her into something new. She felt it in her heart and soul. She seemed to understand more about herself each day that she spent at the Red Gum.

How could she deny such a wonder? What man ever cared before like Slade appeared to? Resolute, she kept her eyes closed and took a step, then another. Surely, something new would shine from her eyes the next time she looked in the mirror. Slade squeezed her hand.

"Only a few more steps. And you'll see this at its best."

Almost giving in, she followed him.

"When I say so," he said casually, "you leap."

Fifteen

Anne shriveled inside. "Leap?"

"Yes. A giant step, with some push behind it."

She stood stock-still. Slade didn't understand. Walking these few feet represented a major exercise in trust. He wanted her to depend on him. Actually have faith in him enough to *jump*? Her eyelids quivered. Only he could see what needed to be done. "Slade, I... I can't."

"Relax. I'll go first, then I'll pull you to me. It's less than two meters, and the rest you don't worry about."

"What's the rest?"

"Never mind."

Her pulse fluttered and panic pitted her stomach. The way their voices echoed off the cave walls made her feel there was limitless space around them.

"No. This is more than I can do."

"You've come this far."

She had to admit that he had a point. Her knees weakened and first steps were the worst. Although she was a woman of her word, it didn't mean that she couldn't ask questions.

"What if we—"

"Stop thinking. Be over faster than tailing a jumbuck."

"Oh, goodie. Now I feel much better."

Her palms moistened, and she fired a quick prayer to heaven. Other than woolgrowers, only He knew what tailing a jumbuck was or how fast it happened.

Slade withdrew his arm from around her waist and stepped away. She now saw with her ears. Next, she heard his feet thud a very short distance away. In seconds he gripped both her hands and stabilized her. She sucked in a deep breath, then zipped her lips together.

"Ready? Go," he said.

In miraculous, blind faith and with heart pounding, Anne leaped across the unknown space and landed against him and on solid ground. Relief gushed through her as he wrapped his arms around her and reminded her to keep her eyes closed. Turning her half way around, he said, "Go ahead. Look."

Anne opened her eyes and first blinked at the ground. Milky light swathed her feet and beneath them the taffy-colored stone surface that most likely had been water-washed on and off for a million plus years. She raised her eyes and found his. Shifting to the right, he allowed her a better view of the natural wonder. She gasped. Their timing proved perfect. Beaming through a hole in the cavern ceiling, lunar light shimmered onto a waist-high pinnacle of opalescent and crystal clear rock.

He nodded. "Mother Nature's gift to the Red Gum."

She bent over at the waist, catching a better look.

"It's magnificent."

He stood with his hands splayed at his waist.

"And rare. There's no fit price."

"May I?" she asked, entering the cone of soft moonlight. Pinpoints and streaks of fiery aqua and tangerine and gold flickered under the watery surface. She reached out and touched its side. Slade went to her as the light slowly eased upward from the base of eroded formation.

"How did it become so polished?" she asked.

"Mostly rainwater and silt running over it year after year during wet season, and we helped it along."

She glanced at him quickly. He wore an amused, somewhat smug look on his face. He seemed more impressed with her than the natural wonder they admired. He pushed a strand of hair behind her ear.

Together they stood in surreal luminescence. He moved behind her again, then touched her arms. She tingled all over from what being so close to him promised.

"Thank you for showing me this," she said. "And for proving me wrong about jumping." She'd risked her safety and he'd proven that he could be trusted—at least in some matters.

"My pleasure," he said, while she tilted her head back against his shoulder.

Water droplets plinked into a nearby puddle. The downward breeze fanned her face. As he turned her toward him, his masculinity mesmerized her. Any past wish she'd ever had dimmed in comparison to what she wished for now.

"I know what you want," he said. A frown formed across his forehead, as if he were engaged in some frantic inner battle.

Was she so transparent? Did she have 'you turn me on so much I can hardly stand it' stamped on her forehead? Lord, she hoped not. How had she ever stumbled into such a personal, high-stakes game? One that taxed her heart and career plans and made her insides quiver for another of his gentle touches.

"Really? And what do *you* want?"

He breathed into her ear. "The same as you."

She hoped for the best. Of him.

"And what's that?"

The light streaming in the hole brightened around them. Slade placed his thumb against her chin. For a mere second she yearned in vain for the good old days when she could dissuade a man's charm with the flick of an eye.

"This," he said, his voice deepening.

Slade moved his mouth onto hers. She'd hoped for the best, and he began to give it. Making her heart throb, he feathered her lips with his tongue. Heeding their call, she parted them.

He surged into her imploringly. Her wits took flight, but her heart roosted in delight. Pull, push, rise and fall in uncontrollable heat, her mouth danced with his. Each wave crashed deeper into her need. Need for what a man and woman shared. For him. For how he did it and for who he was.

"Heavens, Slade," she panted between rounds.

Like that night in Hannah's hut, the more he had done with her the less she had cared about lousy breaks in life and Greene & Associates. Her breasts pressed against his lean hard muscles, lifted and ached for their due. The wet warmth returned between her thighs.

She was passing the point of no return. She'd never made love underground. Creative lovemaking only happened in her imagination and was fed by her old friend, curiosity.

"Hold on," Slade whispered, drawing away his palm from her right breast and lifting his face from hers. "I can give you better than this, Annie."

She nearly fell apart at the seams.

"Better?" she croaked. "It couldn't get any better. The way you hold me, touch me."

His face, inching away from hers, was covered with desire, embarrassment, and a plea. His eyes glittered in what was left of the light.

"I'm sorry. We need to leave. Now."

Her senses still ping-ponged off one another, and her mind drifted back. Her heart now pounded with exasperation.

He pulled his arms away from her shoulders.

"How... d'you do that?" she stammered.

"Do what? The light is going. We have to get back through the tunnel."

Anne followed his lead to the edge of the deep crevasse over which they'd again have to jump. Only this time her eyes were wide open. Yet, her fear was overcome by a rush of anger.

"You're playing with my head. You get the cameras rolling, then yell 'cut' at your convenience. Well, never again." Her voice shook. "You're insensitive, and a tease, and a... a big quitter."

He whirled around and faced her. Thunder stormed across his face and that old hard glint returned to his eyes.

"I was watching you, not the light, Your Highness." Giving her a firm pull, he got her across the chasm with him. "And don't tell me you haven't put the brakes on yourself whenever we touch. We're in this together. Damned deep."

She exhaled in frustration. Their short outburst of passion could have cost them dearly. They were unprepared to make love. Of course, he was the cause for this to escalate as it had, which she was sure he wouldn't want to hear.

"Well, I move we table this discussion. Indefinitely."

He nodded sharply. "Now who's quitting?"

She refused to take the bait. "There are two things you should know. One, I'm not a wimpy crier. And two, when something is really important to me, I don't quit."

He threw his head back and chuckled.

She clamped her mouth shut. The meaning of what she'd spouted off in frustration hit her like a stray arrow. She admitted what they were doing was *important* to her. Very important. That was a bigger jump than across the chasm and carried with it far-reaching consequences.

"I need to clarify that," she backpedaled.

He moved ahead of her.

"No you don't. Save what you have to say for the boardroom. See you on the other side."

He dropped to his knees at the tunnel entrance and scrambled into it. By the time she'd hiked up her skirt and reentered the near darkness, he was way ahead of her. The light faded behind her, but she could see some from the other end as it splayed around his shifting silhouette. Her hands and knees cooled on the petrified surface.

Her thoughts centered on Slade. No matter the reason, the fact was he left her wanting. The man possessed more self-control than an Indian guru. Or was he afraid?

She ducked under a low rock and a sudden, terrible doubt flashed through her head. She remembered that he had more he wanted to tell her. Some part of his past. His expression revealed that it couldn't be at all pleasant and sensed it was something extremely personal. A weakness? She paused. *Oh, my gosh. What if Slade was damaged in some way?*

As fast as that possibility hit, it flew away. From what she'd seen and felt, he had no trouble getting aroused. As it looked now, she'd probably never know for sure whether it lasted.

That bold thought made Anne cringe at herself.

Exiting the tunnel, she found Slade lighting a lantern. The glow warmed his face and threw his shadow against the boulders as he strode back to the barrel. Rifling through it, he collected supplies he'd apparently stowed on previous trips to Crystal Springs. He returned and dropped the assortment on the ground.

She asked, "We're not going back?"

"Ahem," he coughed and gestured toward her front. "That's hardly proper business attire for a meeting."

She looked down at her clothing. Her skirt, still hiked up nearly to her waist, revealed bare thighs and higher.

"Oh, geesh." She turned around and dropped the crinkled cloth like a blind. Through all of this she was completely mussed. Her skin felt tacky in some places and dust dry in others, and she had only four decent fingernails left. She figured she resembled the Wreck of the Hesperus and eyed the spring water. Walking through it would take care of some of the problems on their way back.

"Here, you should have some of this."

She turned around again, and he tossed her a can of apple cider. She opened the top and drank heartily while he unfurled a long rectangular piece of canvas. Laying it down near the lantern, he secured the four corners with rocks he'd gathered.

"What're you doing?" she asked. "We have to get going."

"Sun won't be up for hours. We've plenty of time."

He dragged the lantern over and set it on the wrinkled, tan tarp. His smile and assured movements made her squeamish.

"For what?"

He gave her a signal to wait with his forefinger. He then broke a stick off a vine and wrote 'Greene & Associates' in the sandy soil and flipped the stick over his shoulder into the water. Next, he pulled out tins of food and crackers from a small duffle, and a couple of sheafs of paper that he laid in a stack in the center of the cloth.

"Our meeting. An urgent meeting of the minds. Please, take your seat."

Slade dropped on his butt on the other side of the tarp and gestured for her to sit down across from him. She glared at him. The name of the agency scrawled in the sand did it. He was mocking her world.

"You're playing games."

"What? You don't like your conference room? Look. There's the entrance," he said, pointing toward the bank on the other side of the pool. "We've indirect lighting, plants, and a big water cooler." He raised his open hand and slapped the tarp. "And this, Annie, is the conference table."

"You're crazy."

"And you're late." His eyes twinkled. "Let's pick up the discussion you started about my quitting and bad timing."

Shaking from anger, she fisted her hands.

"No."

Her verbal resistance appeared to fall on deaf ears.

"You said we'd table our discussion 'indefinitely,' but that motion wasn't seconded. And since I'm the only other member of this Ways and Means Committee, I get equal say. So let's get down to business, Annie, since that's what you seem to like best. Nine to five and all that."

He twisted the top off an Australian Army canteen, threw his head back and allowed the water to gurgle down his throat, then tossed it toward the lantern.

"This is an outrage." Refusing to tolerate his charade another second, she turned and sloshed off into the water. Ripples slid over her skin like cool satin. She needed to wash away the dust and her frustration, but mostly Slade's arrogance.

In the moonlight she could see the pebbled bottom, sparkling like brilliant crystals. She dove and began to cool down as the water flowed through her hair. Resurfacing, she got her bearings as a loud, heavy splash followed her. Choked up by dread and desire, she glanced over her shoulder. Slade swam headlong toward her with powerful armstrokes and solid kicks.

She twisted around in the water, faced the bank where she'd find her shoes, and resumed her breaststroke. In less than two arm pulls, she felt Slade's hand wrap around her right ankle, then her left. She wriggled fiercely. Like a barnacle attached to the bottom of a boat, there was no shaking him.

"Let me go," she gurgled.

Slade released her, swam alongside her, and clutched the elastic waistband of her skirt. In a desperate lunge, she pushed ahead with all her might—without her skirt—leaving him in her wake. When she realized her predicament, she popped up in the water and paddled around. Grinning, he waved the sopping wet garment at her. A dare rested on his lips.

If only Slade wasn't having so much fun, or wasn't such a good kisser. Her heart skipped its next beat. Now was the perfect time to use her negotiation skills, but she couldn't remember the first rule—or the last.

Furious, she treaded water as he back-pushed and widened the gap between them.

"My skirt," she demanded.

She couldn't hear his reply over the rush of the waterfall. There was no way she could return to camp alone half-dressed. Disgust ran rampant through her and she reset her course for Slade who now made his way back. The man was dead meat.

As she reached the more shallow water, she found Slade waiting for her, barechested, in waist-deep water. Again she felt the alternating waves of warm and cool. If she were in a better way, she could enjoy its sensual quality. As it was, she closed the distance on a scoundrel. She waded toward him as fast as the water would allow.

"I see you're a woman of sense," he said, openly enjoying the sorry sight of her.

Closer, she bit back her salty reply and the urge to drown him. She merely stuck out her hand, palm up, and snapped her fingers for him to give her the skirt.

"Not so fast," he said. "We've some business to finish." He gestured toward the trees where birds still chirped and insects buzzed. "My night crew said they'd leave the door open to the conference room until we were finished."

Anne rolled her eyes skyward. "We've nothing to finish. You need to drop this. Now." The stars still flickered and the moon had dipped behind the treetops. She couldn't move another foot without rising above the water line. She crossed her arms, covering her breasts.

"I don't agree, Madam Chairman. You complained about my quitting. That interests me greatly."

Of course, the topic and what started it interested her beyond words. If they didn't get this issue resolved soon, they'd be looking dawn in the face.

"Fine. We'll reopen the matter for discussion. Now give me my skirt."

He reached over and dropped it over her hand.

"Thank you," she said. "Turn around, please."

Slade the Terrible, crossed his arms and looked at her. "Not on your life."

"Very well." She found the waistband, stretched it over her head, then pulled the rest down over her blouse, to her waist. When she looked up at him again, the twinkle had returned to his eyes.

"All right," she said resignedly. "Let's get this over with. I need to get back to Nourombie—in this lifetime."

She gave him an insolent push, sloshed back out of the water and stood by the lantern setting on the newly dubbed, so-called conference table. She had to give the point to him. He was resourceful and knew how to push her buttons.

He splashed out behind her.

She plopped herself down on her side of the canvas sheet. A chill was beginning to set into her bones, and she pulled her legs up against her soaked chest.

Slade was standing over her now, and she sensed his bare legs near her shoulder blades.

"Annie, you're cut." He pointed at her foot.

She looked down. It was minor scratch, and she couldn't remember how she'd earned it.

"It's nothing. Sit down, please."

"And you're shivering."

"I am not."

"You know, you make yourself a bitch nicely," he said and crossed back to the barrel.

She shook her head. What could he know about bitchiness? "Maybe, but I also make a good cup of coffee. And right about now we could use one."

She watched him pull out a rolled up shearling and a small white cloth bag. A simple red cross and "Community Hygiene Pack" was stenciled on the front. Coming back, he unrolled the shearling and turned it over her shoulders.

"You're cold," he repeated.

"Only maybe," she echoed, tugging the silky lambskin around her. She reached for the tin of crackers and opened it.

"You're also stubborn. Some tea tree salve will help that cut heal faster."

He fumbled with the string on the bag and rummaged through what looked like an assortment of standard hygiene or first-aid supplies. She pulled her foot in tighter toward her body.

"Tell you what. When I think it's a problem, I'll call your friend the Flying Doctor. He seems a nice enough man."

She began to munch on a handful of crackers.

"And he prefers nice patients," Slade returned.

She sighed. He could be so taciturn. "You belong on the other side of the table, and let's keep focused on the agenda."

"No worry. If I remember adequately, the topic is about how you've decided I'm a quitter and a tease."

Blast him. He was putting her on the spot, trying to make her regret her remark. One that she'd made with little thought, but a lot of frustration. She gazed evenly at him.

"I did say that, yes."

A wild kind of smoldering erupted deep in his eyes, enough to make her nerves jangle. She leaned back a bit from their heat.

"Here's something else *you* need to know about *me*," he said with resolve. "I postpone, never quit."

With that he swept her onto her back, spewing papers and tins from the tarp. In an equally swift move, he gently pressed her against the soft shearling cloak. Its edges fell away from her shoulders, and her soaked blouse offered no chance for modesty.

"What're you doing?" she managed to ask, breathless. Truth be known, the desire gleaming in his eyes pleased her to the hilt.

"What we've wanted since we first met in my living room."

For a moment, she struggled. But how could she argue? Their instant chemistry *had* knocked her socks off. He seemed supercharged, relentless, a man on an overdue mission. He lowered his body closer to hers.

"But we can't," she huffed, caught breathless between desire and sense.

"Why not? You've never done it on a conference table?"

His feigned surprised tone hit her funny bone, and she giggled.

"That's not what I meant. Think, Slade."

He lifted his leg over and straddled her. She accepted his weight with anticipation. He not only could be trusted in certain situations, he also was turning out to be a man of his word, a fulfiller of promises.

"Annie, honey. Hush. We're done thinking and talking." He gathered her hands and pressed them above her head. "Do we have a consensus of opinon on that?"

He was so close she could hardly breath, let alone laugh. There was no mistaking his heart-claiming intentions. She knew deep in her heart that in another few seconds her will would match his. She suddenly felt cornered by her own feelings. Too fast, they were both moving too fast. They weren't prepared.

"Maybe, yes," she murmured in a rush. Somewhere from the back of the haze of desire, a lingering thought groped to the forefront. It'd be her last coherent one, she was sure of it. Complete logic meltdown was imminent. "But not without protection."

Slade moved his hands up alongside her head and let his eyes dive into hers. "I have what we need in the kit. We won't have to quit again. I promise."

She shuddered inside. He pressed his lips onto her forehead, down her nose, and found her mouth. He brimmed with a new level of confidence with her.

Anne kissed him back, deeply, fully. Opening herself up with all she had. How this moment could feel so right, she'd never know. He ravaged her mouth. She reveled in the joy of his eroticism and that he wanted to know all of her.

Likewise, she couldn't wait to explore him. She moved her hands around his neck and spread her fingers over his shoulder muscles. He pushed his hands beneath her head and slid one hand down behind her shoulders, lifting her chin, curving her neck, and exposing her skin for whatever he wished.

His lips left hers swollen and hot, and then dipped into the dimple in her chin. Leaving a drop of moisture with his tongue, he skipped lightly over and down near her earlobe, and hovered over her pulse point. Her heartbeat flashed, and she heard a smile shine through his sigh. He trailed his tongue down to the base of her throat, where he played and kissed.

Anne dug her heels into the soft canvas. His heat fanned her own. Her breathing sped up, growing audible with every exhalation she managed.

"Slade, please..." she protested in a dying whisper as he trailed his tongue down to the top of her cleavage where he again paused, allowing the effect to take hold.

"Ohhhhh, my... more. Okay, just a little... more."

Still raised on his knees, he pulled one of his hands free from beneath her and tugged her blouse out of the waistband. She lifted herself to make it easier for him. With his other hand he pushed his fingers up between her back and the fabric, and, in a quick move, unfastened her bra. With his hands bracing her from beneath, her chest arched higher. He ran his other fingers along the top of her blouse, and pushed it down further to make way for his tongue.

His every move carried her to a higher plateau of ecstasy. *More, I need more* plowed through what was left of her mind. His moves exceeded foreplay. This was discovering him, and his ways more than thrilled her. They settled her. Made her happy.

Her soft moans signalled him to continue. She unwrapped her arms from his shoulders and laid them back with her palms up near her head against her own hair.

"Lie back, enjoy," he said.

She gazed at him from beneath her eyelashes. The promise on his face melted her. He was still raised on his knees, and she pulled hers slightly up to meet his firm rear. He began to rock.

He bent his head and hunted his next erogenous target—her breasts. Her nipples hardened so intensely a feather could almost make her come. She wriggled under him, her leg muscles tensing. His male scent drove her wild.

Closer he inched, proving he was a practiced hunter. He knew the territory well, and he'd arrived. His tongue drawn for action, he licked and sucked heartily in soul-burning hunger.

Her breath wrangled with a deep gurgle of pleasure.

He pressed his lips around her nipple and worked them left to right and right to left, rubbing with moist stubborness. Then, ever so lightly, he brushed his stubble over its primed sensory center.

Her muscles strained, and starting at the very core of her, a deep, earth-shaking shudder raced through her. Barely coherent, she tried to turn over on her side. He flipped her back, slipping aside the other side of her bra, and repeated his skillful ways on her other breast. She fell further into oblivion, willing only to rise for the next wave of his passion.

Slade shifted his position over her. The lantern light made him appear to be a golden god. He lifted her hips with both hands, and she pushed the waistband down enough for him to pull the skirt off the rest of the way. His hands made hurried movements, eagerness burned in his eyes.

Anne reached up and ran her fingers through his chest hair, then separated her fingers into a vee, catching his nipples between them and squeezing.

He took in air and undid his belt. Next he reached for the white bag with the red cross on it. She followed his hands with her eyes as he pulled from it a condom and tore off the top of the packet and settled squarely over her again.

Taking a breath of her own, she sat up and pulled her blouse completely over her head and tossed it aside. Only her underpants remained. She began to slip out of those.

Slade pulled her hand away.

Desire ripped through her. No man had ever helped her undress. Raised on his knees, he opened his zipper that was nearly at eye level. The bulge behind the khaki cloth grew considerably since she'd sat up. Near nude, she initially felt vulnerable. But by the way he looked at her now, completely enamored, she dropped her hands from her breasts.

He popped the top snap above the zipper, and his shorts began to give way, exposing white cotton briefs. The realization hit her. Hard. This man had removed her defenses little by little and was about to tenderly ride her senseless. In turn, she was about to ride the life out of him.

The tuft hair just above his shorts now formed a light mat, and led to a deeper forest of it. Turned hunter, he pushed himself up to his feet and let his shorts drop to the ground. She watched in awe and anticipation. His thighs were lightly haired, thick with muscles.

She looked up at him slowly. All the dreams she ever had about a man's physique stood before her in the real, live, hardened flesh. Her eyes locked on his. He knelt in front of her, and she helped him snug the condom on his erection.

Shifting his position, Slade lifted her hips. He fluttered his tongue downward over her stomach and lower. He paused direct center. Anne gazed at him and readied herself to give him some of her own. No way would he have the last say in this. It simply wouldn't be a fair deal.

Sixteen

Slade's heart thundered. Anne, willing and lying under him, humbled him. The serenity and eagerness dancing over her face fueled him as he cupped her bottom with his hands. Slipping her panties down, he moved his hands around front to finish the job.

Their eyes melded, and happiness soared through him. Being with her made him feel worthy and half-willing to risk dreaming again. Of sharing his life with a wonderful woman and reaching his goals.

The best thrill was yet to come as he pressed his knee between her thighs, spreading her open. He shifted positions and followed with his fingers. Her plentiful, moist heat coated his skin. Her patch of honey hair lured him like a bee to a flower, and he lowered his head.

Parting her soft curls with a breath, he rested the side of his head against her thigh and tasted her. Swirling his tongue over her center, he slid his hands up over her torso to her breasts to nip and cajole her senses.

She lifted and rocked and sank, and he only heard her throaty cries as he lashed her gently. Increasing the pace, he closed his eyes. A sudden realization dawned. He wanted to have more impact on her life than sharing pleasure in sex. He wanted for her to depend and build on what he could provide. The possible meaning and intensity of that insight shocked him as he tasted her essence. How had this displaced, determined, and delicious woman gotten so far with him?

She had no right. No, she had every right. Never had he tangled with such feelings, nor had anyone responded the way she did to his touch. The whole heart-boggling thing was enough to give an iron man the shakes. He reopened his eyes.

Anne thought she'd burst out of her skin when Slade pulled his hands away from her breasts. Her whole body had tuned itself to his moves, scent, and intentions as he eased his fingers inside her. Feeling him discover her was more than she could bear. Delight turned into deep need.

"Now, Slade, please... now."

He twisted his fingers inside her, and she arched her back and sank again against the silky fleece. It was the sweetest, hottest gesture she'd ever felt. Shudders shook her, leaving her poised for him to enter her.

"I'm only beginning," he breathed huskily into her ear.

"Me too." She ravaged his hair with her fingers, then pulled at his shoulders, urging him up and over her. He pushed himself back onto his knees and lowered his hardness against the very center of her lust.

She gripped his hips with her thighs as he pushed his amply girthed and long erection into her, gently at first, then further in as she expanded. He was a perfect fit. She accepted him deeply, and together they lifted and fell. Souls entwining. Skin pleasuring skin. Faster and deeper, harder. Her whole being centered on what was happening inside her. Perspiring, she matched his thrusts, and her heart raced beyond control. The magic they created escalated into something beyond words.

One more demanding, hungry, happy drive was all it would take now. He pulled back slightly, then with perfect timing, prod his hardness home. Claiming him, she panted as her insides shattered into pure, unbridled ripples of pleasure. The thrill rushed through her, up and down, again and again.

Barely holding back his own climax, he'd let her have first go, but the boiling pressure in his groin begged for release. He slowed his rhythm and gave her a chance to collect her breath, but not escape his tenderness. He kissed her, then reentered the joyful dance, not missing a step, a nuance, or pleasurable groan that escaped.

"You're wonderful," he whispered. "I need you, Annie."

She sought his lips and kissed him back heartily. Rising and lowering, he pulsed. Gently, then firmly, slow and fast. Surer of the route, he soon vibrated her back into a fervored, wild pitch. Reeling from another round of her thousand quivers, he couldn't hold back another instant and burst into his own explosion. From the way she writhed and hugged him he knew he'd gotten his wish. For now, at least, he'd made her happy. And for the first time making love with a woman he felt as though they'd become one.

Weakened and wet, Anne opened her eyes. Gazing onto Slade's face, she gathered his peaceful smile and tucked it forever into her soul. He removed his protection for discarding. He reached for the canteen as she rolled over on her stomach, stretched, and sighed. Every muscle was spent. Every desire satiated, and every bit of her subconscious hoped for a repeat visit to Crystal Springs.

"Cheers," he said, handing her a drink of water.

Anne propped herself up on one elbow as he resituated himself behind her.

"Thank you." Whatever edge her voice had carried drifted away. The warm water from the flask washed away the dryness in her throat the same as Slade had diluted her fears. She'd given herself to him and felt no regrets. She found his interest in her amazing.

Their union of spirit and body intrigued him. As they engaged in smalltalk, he stroked her wavy hair and pulled strands up and away from her bare shoulders and back. Her crowning glory felt like spun gold between his fingers. He neatened and tied it off with a piece of leafy vine lying on the sand next to the rumpled tarp.

Slade gazed with wonder from her neck over to her shoulder blade, then abruptly stopped. He stiffened and stared. There was no mistake. A beauty mark shaped like a butterfly rested near her spine. Now he remembered. This woman was *her*!

Blonde hair pulled back into a knot. Bare shoulders. Sparkling hairclip. Strapless black dress. Sydney? Yes! The night of that confounded, blasted brawl his grandfather had gotten himself into.

His memory brought back bits of the TV news report he'd watched from his big easy chair. The mess in the lobby. His fellow graziers all battered. Her cutting words and acid tone. "Remind me never to do business with *sheep ranchers*," she'd said.

His stomach knotted. Although her snobby insults had been waged at sheep farmers in general, he'd bristled all the way into the city. He never understood why it bothered him so much. They were only a stranger's words. He'd certainly heard bloody worse.

Slade jerked his hand away from her luring, supple skin.

Congratulations, chum, you've made love with a Yank who hates who you are and what you do! ripped through his mind.

Other doubts sprang. There *had* to be a connection between her and his grandfather. They were in the same lobby when the SMWA hullabaloo broke out, weren't they? Apparently, she didn't think the late night news reached his remote house. Well, ya bloody hoo surprise!

Damn her and his grandfather. He'd wait until his grandfather recovered to confront him about his role in this little charade.

"We better go now," he said and thought about his options. "I'll be flying back to Newcastle after dawn."

Still basking, Anne turned her head and glanced over her shoulder at Slade. He'd pulled back and sat up and was raking her with a confused, reticent look. The open pathway between their spirits seemed suddenly blocked.

"I suppose so." She pushed herself up to her knees. When he gave her a hand up the rest of the way, she could have sworn she saw resentment tinge his eyes. She wondered if somehow an unhappy memory had been triggered. Whatever it was, she was glad he didn't go there. She wanted to walk around on this cloud as long as she could.

She studied him as he gathered his clothes and she hers. He whisked his khaki shorts and shirt back on, and took to repacking everything up with few words while she dressed.

Puzzled, she couldn't imagine why he'd become so quick to leave the paradise he'd taken so much trouble to show her. For a blip in time in this ancient land their souls meshed into one. He'd shown her the stars, and she showed him the moon, but hadn't really done her best. As he'd asked, she let him show her what he could do with her, for her, and to her, then left her with barely a breath to her name. Above all, she was compelled to tell him how she felt.

"I want you to know," she said and laid her hand on his arm, "it's never, ever been like that for me."

He gave her a mixed glance, finished rolling up the tarp, slung it over his shoulder, and slapped it with his palm. The noise cracked off the rocks behind them and dust motes sparked into the lantern light.

"For me either, wa-a-jumkai. You ready to go?"

She raised her eyebrow, but he ignored it and went to the old wooden barrel, stuffed everything back inside, and hauled the lid over it.

Mercy. Now she felt nervous. Perhaps it was her fault, but he'd unlocked her inhibitions. While under his spell she'd shamelessly hungered for more and the chance to reciprocate. Passion like theirs went far. It was the kind based on mutual understanding, a hallmark of a good relationship that could turn into commitment. Did Slade sense such a possibility and feel threatened? Or was this how it was with Aussie men? Seduce and ravage a woman stark silly, then get the hell out?

That registered too painful for her to accept.

Fighting to fan the fire that he'd lit in her heart, she at least owed him the benefit of the doubt. And despite the fact that he'd taken her to Crystal Springs to keep her away from Rainbow Canyon, surely Slade would explain himself.

To Anne's relief the make-up woman wasn't in her trailer when she and Slade returned to Nourombie about a half-hour before dawn. Only a few lit lanterns dotted the montage of tents, parked cars, and motorhomes, giving the place the appearance of a sleepout the night before the Olympic Grand Final tickets went on sale.

Now holding a mug with rock art etchings, Anne finished her tea and gathered up some of her equipment. Slade had left with Dr. Sanders, and what she'd seen of anyone associated with the project was practically nil, except for Drew who said she could again use his car until Slade brought hers back from Newcastle where he left it the night of his grandfather's heart attack. The whole afternoon would be hers to use as she wished.

The sunlight, ducking in and out behind the clouds, offered contrasting illumination over the landscape. Videotaping raw footage beckoned her, something she hadn't done in a long while.

Rudy came around the sound crew's van with its faded bumper sticker that read SUPPORT WILDLIFE, THROW A PARTY. He veered toward her as she snapped shut a camera case and her briefcase.

"G'morning. Where are we going?" he asked.

"I'm going south on the road for a while. Alone."

He eyed her keenly.

She patted the camera case. "I'll be all right. There's no need to watch over me while Slade's gone. He's quite aware of my capabilities."

Rudy grinned and that made her uneasy. "You will be back by sunset?"

"Sure, I wouldn't miss tonight's ceremony and meal." She tapped her temple. "I still have the map up here that you drew on the ground for me about where to find the best ocher." Poker-faced, she looked at him as if this little photography trip was the only thing on her mind. Little good it did. She hedged a bit as Rudy gave her a closer look. He seemed to see all, know all. So much so she half expected he could see photosynthesis taking place in the leaves of the river gum trees.

"Do you like him?" he asked simply.

"Who?" she feigned ignorance.

His teeth flashed in the light, and the breeze lifted the long garment away from around his bare calves.

"Ahhh, you *love* him."

His ebony eyes looked for confirmation in hers. Miffed, she bulked. Rudy had no right to pump her about something this personal. Had Slade put him up to it? They all were kind of an extended family around here.

She fired off, aiming her indignance at him. "You're full of questions today."

He raised his chin.

"My apologies. I speak too much of what I see." He picked up her briefcase, and together they walked back to Drew's vehicle. "You should stop and take pictures of the banksia tree," he suggested. "It's the oldest in New South Wales. A tall cross stands nearby."

She turned her eyes toward him. Rudy suggested nothing lightly. He was a deeply textured man, possessing self-control and ancestral secrets along with those as recent as last year.

"Sounds interesting. Thanks for the tip."

"I await your return," he said quietly and handed her the briefcase. "Is there something you need from the cupboard?"

She climbed in the car, dropped her paraphanelia on the passenger seat, shut the door and rolled down the window. Her irritation began to wane. She knew he only meant well. He'd shown the highest regard for the McGregors.

"Thank you, I have supplies in the Esky. But I do have a question. Tell me what is wa-a-jumkai?"

Rudy bent down to her and draped his hands on the door with fingers folded under his hefty knuckles. They were a worker's hands, capable of fixing fence and producing fine art.

"In Bilwan it means 'butterfly.'"

His deep-voiced explanation pleased her, and she turned on the ignition. She smiled inwardly. Slade really had his moments of endearment. A butterfly, how nice.

Still, Slade had turned rather taciturn as they left Crystal Springs, and he had little to say on the way back. Suspicion drove a taproot into her chest.

"Have you seen one?" Rudy asked.

She shook her head. "Not here."

"When you do, you will not forget as they are beautiful."

He lifted his hands from the car door, crossed them, and fluttered his fingers like wings.

She forced a smile and released the emergency brake.

"Travel left at the fork to find the banksia tree," he told her. "Enjoy your day, Miss Kingsley." Although he didn't realize it, he'd made her feel less accusatory toward Slade. Maybe the sheep farmer had really paid her a compliment. But why had his mood changed?

She gripped the wheel. Was he the kind of man who wanted absolute perfection in a woman? If so, he must've been disappointed. The purple-blue birthmark that had run through three generations of women blossomed by her shoulder blade. A silent marring that she'd rarely given thought to once she'd passed her teen years. She couldn't believe Slade would be so put off about it. He was strong and far from shallow, so why would something like that matter?

She pulled away and drove past Kissing Turtles, negotiated a left turn southward onto the same old dirt and gravel road Slade had taken the night before to Crystal Springs.

Being with him still had her senses humming. The colors around her shone brighter. The chattering of lorikeets resounded clearly. Except for the odor of wood burning, she sighed and wished every detail and feeling could stay indelible in her memory. Slade's gentleness, virility, and skill had set her head spinning and her heart free.

By three o'clock the sky grayed. Anne parked and walked the last fifty yards to the remarkable banksia tree about which Rudy had spoken. Sure enough a weathered cross stood halfway between a wooded area and a rugged, rock-piled rise not far from the Canyon's edge.

The tree was old all right, and she used up some film on it, but the cross interested her more. Fashioned with braided branches, the memorial reached her shoulders. A wreath of vines, decorated with dried boronia and other wildflowers, hung over its arms. She had no idea whose grave this was, but she felt compelled to snap a shot of it anyway.

The breeze picked up a bit and rustled the scant bushes and trees around her. She gazed ahead unable yet to see the Canyon's edge. She stood much further south than where she'd chosen to film and was about where Rudy had indicated the other route would begin. Her curiosity took backseat to her hunger, however.

Going back to Drew's vehicle, she dug out some food and her briefcase that contained a few aerial photos of the Red Gum. Ten minutes later she'd settled atop a large rounded rock and ate. Keeping Rudy's dirt map in mind, she checked the photos and had little trouble orienting herself.

She was correct. No more than the length of Slade's front yard away lay the old game trail that led down into Rainbow Canyon. She burned to explore that less traveled road. She was closer than ever to getting a close-up view at what the Canyon had to offer. She hungered for the challenge. Yet, common sense told her not to venture alone. Up here, at least, she wasn't too far from the fork in the road and, if need be, someone could find her.

In a wink, temptation got the better of her. She packed up and scrambled down off the rock. She'd only go as far as the edge of the Canyon. There, she could see how steep the trail angled along the rock wall and its condition.

A frilled lizard skittered across her path and she remembered her first encounter with one. She'd come a long way since then, and tomorrow they'd all head back to the North Paddock to finish the segment over the next few days. Susan Sornja's mouth had healed to its natural, beautiful condition.

Withstanding the model's temperament, everyone would have to push, work longer, and keep focused to recover lost time. Anne hoped the weather would continue to cooperate, for only it could throw them an unexpected loop.

She also half-expected to hear from the elders about crossing Nourombie after the ceremonies. Rudy and Slade had introduced her to one of them. He seemed pensive, his mind on many things, but kindness softened the planes of his broad face.

Abiding by the elders' wishes, she hoped her crew was making a favorable impression. Enough so that the Bilwan would trust the whole troupe to make the short journey through Nourombie for easier access to the Canyon. Her desire to film there grew more acute every day.

As she hiked farther over some rough ground and took a narrow gully in stride, her eyes began to water. She wasn't surprised, since she walked amidst foreign pollen-producing plants and trees and the odor of smoke.

Rounding a sizable rock hill, she halted to catch her breath. She faced north and the Canyon fell away at her right. It lay jagged, open and ripe for adventure. She sneezed. Again, and a third time for luck. Blinking through her moistened eyelashes, she gazed across the Canyon to the other side. It looked much the same as from where she now stood. Spacious brush country, shades of tan and green and dotted with mobs of grazing sheep and some cattle.

The only thing that was different was the grey and black smoke that rose in the distance against the clouded sky. With her video camera she zoomed in on the area across the Canyon. A rim of red-orange flames licked the ground as far north and south as she could see. But it seemed miles away, like Slade was now, and he'd traveled east in the opposite direction. She stood for a moment longer, missing him, then sighed in frustration.

Such an impossible situation. She really needed to cool her jets with this man. What chance would they really have to make anything more meaningful than some nights in the hay? None. She knew her limitations, and her conscience couldn't handle that kind of assault on her desire to do right. She had to get back to her reasons for being here at the Red Gum.

She gazed longingly farther into the Canyon and tried to satisfy her curiosity by taking closeup shots of the flora and fauna. Absorbed in the spectrum of variety and detail, she lost herself in concentration for two hours on making each frame a work of art.

In the meantime, the wind changed direction, but it didn't bother her much. Kneeling, she photographed pebbles against the red dirt and black beetles on their way home. Stiff-legged, she stood. One thing was true about the scenery. As she walked or drove it, the view changed every five minutes, giving a new perspective for yet another great photograph.

Her nose plugged up from the smoke and she searched her pocket for a tissue. Warily, she gazed over to the neighbor's ranch on the other side. She froze. A wall of black smoke engulfed it completely.

"Good heavens," she murmured.

A fringe of orange leaped to the left, then the right and back again. Certain danger to all things living, and the exploding gum trees blasted her senses. Gusts of wind escorted the bush fire and gave it its own head. Only Rainbow Canyon lay between it and her.

She gathered up her belongings and noticed the birds had stopped singing. She bit her lip and removed the camera strap from around her neck and placed her camera back inside its case. She began to cough hard. Roiling across the Canyon, the haze instantly enveloped her. As best she could, she began to retrace her steps around the rock hill, much farther from the trail head than she remembered.

"Please, let me get to the car."

Her eyes burned, and she lifted her shirttail to her face and tried to breathe less. Her heart raced as she slid on the loose gravel, her camera case bouncing on the ground. She got up, but couldn't see more than three feet in front of her, much less find the car.

Panic erased her sense of direction. Where to go? Nothing around her offered safety. No shelter. No deep creek. No way to fly up and away. Her tears weren't only from smoke. They fell from terror that wrung her insides out.

"No," she cried, needing fresh air. She turned about-face. Blinking wildly, she hunched her shoulders and forced her way through the smoke that shrouded the rugged landscape. *Move* her intuition told her. *Keep moving.*

She tripped and landed on her knees and began to crawl. Faster, faster. The earth and stones sanded skin from her palms and knees, and she reached out clutching for guidance in the haze. She uttered a cry of relief as she found her attaché case that she'd left behind. Holding it suddenly meant everything— security, familiarity, and safety—and she couldn't let go.

She knew the head of the old game trail lay only a few more feet away. Her only hope for escape was to go *down*, down under. She would follow the path that would take her beneath the deadly smoke. Spiraling embers urged her on as she summoned her will. She stood and began her descent.

Rutted and steep, the trail shelf took a steep dive. Only a horse would make this, never a car. Rocks and boulders edged out half the width and trees and brush overhung it making it unrecognizable as an entry to the forested Canyon bottom.

As she trekked downward, the smoke thinned. Her lungs seemed only capable of shallow breaths. She popped open her briefcase and pulled out a foil of sinus capsules, put them in her mouth and swallowed with hardly a drop of saliva left to her name.

Quickly, she closed everything up again and edged farther downhill. At least she could see fifteen feet in front of her now. But not up, where she'd never seen such a swarthy, unnatural cloud in her life.

Sucking in a deep breath, she ached for Slade. She'd done the best she could and she wanted him so badly. She needed him. Surely, he'd get over what was bothering him and comfort her. Lord knew she needed that and him.

Seventeen

For good measure, Anne went deeper into the Canyon. Growing more worried, she checked her watch. The Bilwan ceremony should've started a half-hour ago. People would wonder where she was and Rudy should come looking for her, if that were possible.

Worse, the flames might've jumped the canyon to the Red Gum. Since the gorge was about a quarter-mile wide, the wind could easily carry embers to Nourombie and far into the station. The natural destruction of the pastures and trees would sadden her. She'd grown much fonder of the place.

Her lips were parched, and it was difficult to move them in prayer. The smoke brought early dusk and soon she'd have to stop moving. Her tapestried briefcase grew heavier, yet, she carried her sole possession closer. Inside lay order, predictability and her identity—at least as it had been before coming to Australia.

Frustration bolstered her temper.

"SunMate Sunscreen sucks," she complained, climbing over a log. Her heart pounded and her body ached. Without the trail she'd be hopelessly lost.

Thickly vined brush lay ahead, all knotted and dark. She rubbed her eyes with her free hand. The overgrowth had form and size. And man-made parts? Hard to believe, but she was staring at charred and twisted metal. Tilted on its battered side lay an open-top Jeep, with a history.

She drew closer and skirted the wreckage. Dropping her camera case and briefcase by a bent wheel, she pulled away some of the brush and ran grimy fingers over the dented doorframe. Dread knotted her stomach. No one could have survived a horrible crash like this.

Quickly, she gazed straight up the side of the canyon wall. The four-wheeler had to have come from way up, beyond the overlying smoky ceiling. Many questions popped into her head. To whom had this vehicle belonged? When had the accident happened? Did anyone even know about it?

Apparently so, since she found no human remains. The wreckage had been left here to corrode, far away from life and notice. Conveniently buried and forgotten.

She stood stock-still and made a vague, far-fetched connection. Answers to more of her questions pooled. The lump in her throat turned heavier. Unlike the upbeat, romantic and classy commercials she created, the song of Rainbow Canyon handed her a raw, gruesome reality.

Why was she called upon to witness such an unhappy scene that had ended someone's life? It had to be the workings of Fate, the same that had brought her here to the Red Gum. Now destiny gave her this front row seat to tragedy.

Aching and fatigue zapped her. She could almost breathe normally again, but had few options about what to do. Waiting for dawn seemed daunting, but best. Everything else would seem clearer in the morning. Also, by then the smoke should let up enough for her to make it back out on her own.

Darkness thickened by the minute, sharpening her growing uneasiness, bringing with it pain in her ribs and left ankle. She bent over to relieve a sudden case of giddiness and noticed a faint glimmer of gold in the red dust. She knelt for a closer look. Brushing away the dirt revealed a prize of sorts, and she picked it up.

Three large, dull beads formed a cluster, which she rubbed cleaner with her shirttail. To her surprise, she found pearls—large ones, bound with gold drops—that shone up at her.

An eerie feeling shrouded her. Unquestionably, she stood in a death zone. So had the earring belonged to the victim? She swallowed and pocketed her find for now. As she turned toward the rock hollow behind her, a distant voice reached her. It came from far up the game trail, way beyond sight.

"Miss K-i-n-g-s-l-e-e-e." Then a drawn out, sharp and high-pitched call followed. "COOOO-EEEE."

"Rudy!" she cried, hoping her ears weren't playing tricks.

"Are—you—below?"

Joy flashed through Anne and she cupped her hands on either side of her mouth and shouted, "Yes! Yes, I'm here."

She got up and limped to her briefcase, opened it, and pulled out a penlight. Leaning against the crumbled fender of the Jeep, she pushed on its switch and waved the tiny light over her head in a wide arc.

"Give me good news," he answered.

"I'm alive!" Tears smarted her eyes. She so needed someone with whom to share that amazing fact, despite that each breath jerked pain from her rib cage and her lungs burned and she never felt so tired in her life.

"Coming—down. Keep—talking."

For once, she didn't have a clue what to say. So she started spouting off whatever came into her head. Nonsense, and otherwise, she raised her voice into the haze above.

"Hurry. It's getting darker. I'm alone. I'm by the Jeep. Can you hear me now?"

Muffled voices followed, and she kept going.

"Did you know I was once a Girl Scout? In situations like this we were taught to STOP. That's short for sit, think, observe, and plan. Rudy? Have you ever had smores? I bet not. I'll make them for you if you get me *out of here*."

Chills set in and she fought weakness in her knees. She knew what she really wanted. Slade. She felt as if she were breaking apart like a doll. She'd do anything to see him right now. She needed his warm strength wrapped around her. Only then would everything be all right.

"Again," Rudy called. "We need to hear you."

"No more than I need to see you."

She turned toward the direction of the voices and strained to see people emerging from the smoke. Thank the Lord. A rescuer couldn't be far now. Very soon she'd be out of this dreadful predicament. Yet, she fully expected to plunge into another. Slade would have a thunderous fit when he heard about this fiasco.

She lifted her chin. No way could she handle him being angry. Not now. That would take strength, and she had nothing left to fight with. Trying to boost her spirits, she remembered his caresses and how tightly he had held her in the wee hours of this very morning. The world could have fallen apart around them, but they would have lasted like a rock. That seemed like eons ago.

"Ms. K-i-n-g-s-l-e-y. Call out."

She threw her head back and cared less about what she said.

"Out!" she yelled back. "Three strikes and you're out. In the old Outback. Get it?" Words were all Rudy and the others needed, and noise. She banged the penlight against the fender. "You like baseball? My dad did, too. He was in a league that played on Friday nights at Marina Field. He was the catcher for the Full Mast team. They'd hardly lost a game. Mom and I were so proud."

Anne's throat clutched, leaving her breathless. "He hardly ever lost a regatta, either. He loved boats, you know."

She closed her eyes, tears flowing freely. Was this how it was for her father? Pitching about in the fog, unable to see anything past the bow of that ill-fated boat. She wiped her cheeks. It was still difficult to believe he was gone. He was so strong and a real winner, in many ways.

She always admired that about him. She wanted to win just like him. *Be the best, never settle for less.* Suddenly, a shower of dirt and loose pebbles rained over her from above the rock hollow. She shielded her head with her arms. *Be strong*, she willed herself. She couldn't crumple yet.

The last place she wanted to spend the night was down here. Fear of dingoes, wild pigs, and deadly snakes or spiders would keep her awake all night.

"Rudy?" she cried back, hanging on with hope.

Nothing.

"Don't leave me," she cried and clutched the roll bar. "I'm over here!"

Spent and sobbing, she shook the debris from her hair and rested her forehead on her hands. Her head ached and the corkscrewed steering wheel that jammed into the seat blurred. Everything began to spin.

"Lord, please help me. I don't deserve this."

Fading fast, she heard the thunk of boots behind her.

"That's bloody debatable," stated a familiar male voice.

She hardly had a second to refute that before the man's strong arms pulled her away from the Jeep and whirled her around into his chest. She flung open her eyes.

"Slade!" she wheezed.

His strained expression both frightened and comforted her. He gathered up her limp body.

"You're okay now." His tone was laced with worry.

She could barely wrap her arms around his neck, "I've never been so alone, so afraid. How did you know I was down here? Where's Rudy? I heard him and some—"

He cut her off. "Rudy, I've got her!"

"Good news, boss," came directly after.

Anne closed her eyes. She was safe, but thoroughly disoriented. She fought for coherency.

"The fire. Did it jump the Canyon?"

"No, the wind changed direction."

"Then the Red Gum is safe?"

He pulled her closer, causing new jabs of pain to knock the breath from her.

"Yes, and I'm taking you home. Where you belong. Rose is waiting to help."

His voice cradled her heart and soothed her senses. She collapsed into rambling chatter. "I couldn't stand the smoke. Why did you call me a butterfly? Is the crew safe? We have to leave in the morning. We're already off schedule."

"Hush, Annie. Quit pushing yourself."

"Oooh no, put me down. I'm going to throw up. Nothing feels right, not at all," she said, wishing her vision would straighten. "Slade, what happened here? Something awful. Can you hear me?" she murmured, falling into delirium. "I... love you. I'm down here in Rainbow Can—"

As if God's own hand reached down and pulled a plug, she slipped into sleep.

~ * ~

The third time Anne awakened Australian wildflowers were scattered across pale yellow wallpaper and met her opening eyes. Slowly, she turned her head against a pillow cased in white, crisp cotton.

Thirst cornered her, and foggy memories lifted into her mind. Slowly they cleared as the clock ticked on the nightstand.

She gazed down at the length of herself. Her feet tented the pale blue coverlet. Beneath it, her right foot rested on a pillow. Gauze encircled her right arm and a ribbon of head bandaging trailed onto her cheek.

She ached all over. Yet, she felt calm and safe. This was the guest room where she'd stayed when she'd first arrived at the Red Gum. Except now it looked somewhat like a hospital room with an IV stand, the shade drawn, and a chair at the side of the bed. The door stood ajar. Varied voices traveled up and down the hallway, but no one walked by.

She lifted her right arm and reached for the water glass on the nightstand. Next to the pitcher sat a small brass bell. As she wrapped her fingers around the glass, it slipped and hit the bell, which dropped to the floor.

"I'm worthless," she moaned.

A bare second passed before Slade ambled into the room.

"So you're awake again." He wore a black knit shirt and well-cut gray pants. He stopped at the bottom of the bed and rested his forearm against the tall bedpost. She caught his eyes wandering over her from head-to-toe. The relief on his face was unmistakable.

"G'morning," she replied sleepily. "Or is it afternoon?" A flood of thoughts rushed into her head. She didn't know where to start. "Slade, I, I must—"

He raised a hand for her to stop. "Lindsay Sanders will stop by again this afternoon. Until he says different, there are no 'musts' for you. You're only to get well." He moved to the side of the bed and picked up the bell and put it back on the nightstand. "And I'm here to make sure that happens. Use this when you want something."

She gazed up at him. Determination lit his eyes.

"Fine, so be it," she whispered, her throat still sore. "What's wrong with me, anyway?"

A smile tagged one corner of his mouth as he refilled the water glass from the pitcher.

"Shock, smoke inhalation, exhaustion, allergic reactions, abrasions, strained ankle and ribs, and a knack to put yourself at the wrong place at the wrong time. Here, try to sip this."

He slid his other hand under her head, lifted gently, and touched the rim to her lips. The cool water tasted like nectar. The warmth of his fingers comforted her. She finished drinking, and he eased her head back down onto the pillow. Aside from her broken physical condition, she felt terrible. She'd caused him a lot of trouble, and now for other people.

"You have a right to be angry with me," she sputtered.

He bent over her and neatened the cover under her arms. His chest and shoulders were only inches from her body and aroused newfound yearning through her.

"Later. We'll discuss such matters then. All you have is the right to rest." He slid his fingers down her cheek and tucked the gauze back into the bandage that wound around her head. She needed his tenderness, but was sure it only temporarily overshadowed brewing dismay. He rested his hands on his hips.

"Slade, where's my crew?"

He lifted his hand to his chin and rubbed his forefinger back and forth.

"You sure can… talk."

The strange nervousness in his eyes added to her discomfort.

"Talk? Oh, no. What'd I say?"

"Mumbo-jumbo." He paused, then went on. "Your friends are back up at the North Paddock, doing their jobs, I reckon. Jack's been here and doesn't want you to worry. He's contacted the home office, and your stay has been extended. He'll call with details when you're better. And your camera and briefcase are locked up in my office. Figured I'd rid you of temptation."

He stepped away from the bed. "I'm going now to check on my grandfather."

She turned her thoughts away from herself.

"He's home and better?"

"Yes and yes." She noticed that Slade looked rather tired. "Rose will bring you some tucker. Eat it, or I'll embarrass you." He stopped in the doorway and made a half turn.

She was certain he wanted to say more about the situation. Instead, he held back and said softly, "You took a pounding, Annie, but you're okay. You look... pretty."

She gazed at him. Although she felt half-dead, she was never more alive. She owed him and dearly wanted him to know that.

Her mind fumbled for something to say so he would really understand. The perfect reply spilled from her lips.

"Bonzer," she murmured.

~ * ~

Six days of recuperation passed for Anne, and by the end they seemed like months. Much stronger and growing more restless by the hour, she wanted something to do.

Slade had checked in on her every morning and various other times throughout the day, but as she recovered his visits shortened and grew further apart. When she did see him, he seemed preoccupied and some of his surliness had cropped up again. This morning he hadn't come at all.

Dressed in an oversized lime green shirt, white pedal pushers and U.S. Keds, she went to the kitchen and drank a cuppa with Rose, Da-Wa, and Rudy. The windows were open, and she could see Dusty romping the yard.

"Giving him the day off," Rudy said about the dog.

"More than I happen to get," Rose slipped under her breath.

"What is 'day off?'" Da-Wa chimed, making a joke.

Anne looked at all three of them. Guilt pangs hit her. Taking care of two recovering people, in addition to the staff's usual house and garden chores, had to have taxed them while they performed above and beyond the call of duty. For her benefit.

"I wish you could all leave for a while and do something for fun."

Wistfulness traveled from one face to another.

"Perhaps after everything settles down around here again," Rose said, folding napkins.

The Chinese cook shook his head and concurred. "Much stir-fry to make."

Rudy sat stoically on a tall stool, taking it all in.

Rose added, "Keeping up with laundry is important, especially with Slade's grandfather home. I am most happy, though. Jim has nearly recovered. We are fortunate."

The two house staffers gazed out the open window. The breeze puffed the curtains. Anne rested her chin on her hand, and Rudy eased himself from the stool and pulled the truck key off the hook by the cupboard.

"I am driving to Tamworth for supplies," he said, picking up on everyone's thoughts. "In five minutes."

"Perfect," Anne said. "I can prepare Jim's meal and take it to him. Then I'll tidy up around here. No, please let me. I want to repay you for the favor of your care. You both go on with Rudy." She grinned and shrugged. "Doing your work will keep me busy for a while."

Rudy raised his eyes to the ceiling fan. She suspected it was in prayer. Rose smiled pertly. "You're a fine lady. I gathered that from the minute I saw you. I passed along my thoughts to Slade about the matter. I'll get my bag."

Meanwhile, Da-Wa opened the vegetable bins, cupboard, and refrigerator. He sped from one to the other and uttered in Chinese what she thought to be a grocery list. Slamming everything shut, he went out to the veranda, leaving Rudy and her to follow. The cook pulled off his slippers and tugged on a pair of beat-up boots and a bush hat that sat on the outside shelf by the screen door.

Rose returned, carrying a floppy straw hat with a scarf attached and a small purse with a gold chain. She'd added a dash of color to her lips and crossed the porch to the top step as Rudy and Da-Wa left to get the truck.

"Mr. Jim McGregor takes tea in his office now," she told Anne. "He's fond of ginger jam on his damper. You'll find it all in the cupboard by the potato bin. Lamb stew is in the fridge, so you and Slade and he will have plenty. Perhaps, you'd water the plants and dust the front room tables? Cloths are in the third kitchen drawer next to the stove."

"Okay, got it."

"Then don't do another thing. I couldn't bear knowing you've overexerted yourself. May I ask what's that you have there?"

Anne had been worrying the pearl earring in her pocket. This morning, while she prepared things for laundering, the earring fell out onto the bed. Half-expecting a visit from Slade, she quickly stashed it away. But she'd pulled it out into the sunlight as Rose waited for her ride.

"I found this by the Jeep in Rainbow Canyon."

Rose's eyes riveted to the glistening gold and pearls.

"My word," she whispered, lifting her fingertips to her lips. "You've found the other one." She glanced over her shoulder and opened her palm for Anne to pass it to her.

Anne hesitated.

Rose asked, "Does Slade know you've found this?"

She shook her head to the negative. Around the corner of the house, the pickup backfired, soon to turn around by the sheep pen.

"Best he doesn't," the housekeeper said. "Caroline was wearing those when... He'll not tolerate you trespassing, you know. You've walked into his past, and he still won't let us talk about it. He's kept mum this long, and so have we."

"Why?"

"That's the way he wanted it."

"I'm sure you've done the best you could under the circumstances, but shouldn't someone have pointed out to him what he was doing to himself?"

"We tried, but he's the boss." Rose turned her face away as Rudy pulled the truck up alongside the porch steps. "I can tell you, Miss, for him to go down that gorge took the will of God. You must mean the world to him."

Anne pulled her eyes away from the woman and gazed at the earring. Images of the wrecked Jeep rushed into her mind.

"She died down there last year," Rose added, her voice turned rugged. "The police came out and the incident was declared an accident, of course. Too much trouble to remove the car, so there it'll stay. Out of the way."

Anne's palm moistened around the earring. She should have left the jewelry behind. After all, it was *his* past, not hers.

"To crown it all," the housekeeper said, placing her hat on her head and tying the scarf beneath her chin, "the word was she was pregnant."

"Slade told me he'd lost his wife... and child."

Rose eyed her with eager relief.

"Good. That means he's opening up and he'll learn some things he ought to know."

"Like what?"

"Then again, maybe its better that he doesn't ever find out. If he does, it won't be from me, Miss. He's seen enough sorrow."

Anne took a step toward her. "Rose, what do you mean?"

Rudy revved the engine and called for Rose, but the two women didn't budge.

"I'm saying that things aren't as they appear sometimes. Now, if you find it in your heart to give me that earring when we return from town, I'd be grateful. You see, I own the mate. They were once Slade's mother's. Years after she died Jim gave them to me. They seemed a good gift for Caroline as they'd be kept in the family that way."

"Of course," Anne said, truly puzzled. "I'll keep it right here for you."

Rose straightened her shoulders and went down the wooden steps. She got into the truck, without looking back.

Despite Anne's torment over Slade and what had happened in Rainbow Canyon, she walked back into the kitchen and busied herself. The room, cheery and warm, boasted windowpanes that cranked outward under iron awnings. She found the necessary items for preparing a meal for Jim McGregor. She was excited about spending some time with him. She'd not seen him since that rainy night when he stopped in at Hannah's hut. A slicker had hid his features well, and he didn't stay long.

It occurred to her that she had to find the office. So after she'd watered the plants, she indulged in a brief, self-guided tour. The office door stood ajar and she peeked in past it. The desk lamp wasn't lit, and Slade's grandfather wasn't in. But it was early, and she had more to do.

She hummed "Kokomo" by the Beach Boys as she worked. Who would believe that dusting the living room furniture would soothe her? But she felt useful and taking big swipes with the dust rag across the trestle table felt good. Her mother wouldn't have believed it, nor would Jack.

Done, she sat down on the edge of Slade's big, easy chair and settled back. She gazed up at Rudy's painting over the fireplace. Those brushstrokes, long and short, did form a field of grass. She was sure of it now. The rest still remained hidden in soft, overlapping colors.

"Someday, I may figure you out," she said, and got back up at the sound of Slade's step. She turned to face him. He looked somewhat strained, even distant.

"Hi, Annie. Resting in the living room?" he asked, strolling into the room with a tin map cylinder under his arm.

"Actually, I was dusting."

He dropped the item onto the coffee table.

"Why are you dusting?"

She slapped the cloth against a side table. "It's great for creative thinking. I missed you this morning."

"Where's Rose? And Da-Wa?"

"They've gone to Tamworth with Rudy. They needed an afternoon off, so they went along."

It was good that much of her strength had returned, because his scowl was enough to weaken ironwood. He scratched behind his right ear.

"My grandfather let all of them go? At one time?"

She cleared her throat. "Actually, it was me. I gave them the rest of the day off. They've done so much for me. Taking care of the sick isn't easy, Slade."

His eyes darkened. She really didn't give a flip. As far as she was concerned, she'd been to hell and back and survived. Facing a miffed McGregor paled in comparison.

"They could've asked me."

"You're right, but this is only a simple payback. I'm doing them a favor."

"What do I have to do, rope you to the bed?" Exasperated, he moved to the worktable. "You're still under doctor's orders."

Anne's anger flared. "Those people needed to get away for a while. You know, like go have some fun? Not cater to the McGregors, or my care—and put up with your censorship."

She bit her tongue. He may have some issues with her, but a lot had come to light in the past week here in this house. Now she had some with him.

"They do housework and gardening and cook meals. That's all I ask of them. Do their jobs, not meddle into family affairs."

She paused. "It would hurt Rose terribly to hear that. After all these years, she's very much family."

His eyes flashed.

"What? I don't take care of the people who work for us? Is that what you're worried about?"

"Of course not," she said. "I'm more worried about you."

"Yeah? Don't."

"And how you don't take care of yourself. Frankly, I don't get it. You pull sheep from brambles and protect the rights of the Bilwan. You've saved me. But you can't seem to get square with yourself. Not completely, anyhow. Until you do, you'll be forever tied up in misery. And generally angry about things."

She steeled herself for trouble that she'd probably never seen the likes of, but he surprised her.

"You think that I'm pissed off?" he asked.

Now it was her turn. She was pulling him over the line into the personal zone. She wanted him to release himself from forever torment.

"Yes, I do. Angry and running," she confirmed, "and don't you think it's time to stop?" She took a step toward him.

Slade drew up like a dragon ready to spit fire. The planes of his face hardened. He opened his mouth, then closed it. Turning away from her, he stalked to the hutch, and pulled out a bottle of sauvignon. Filling a glass, he faced her.

"Cheers," he said and took a swig.

She frowned and dropped the cloth onto the worktable.

"I don't think this is the time to—"

"And you don't bloody mix business with pleasure. You don't take second best, except you won't forget Crystal Springs in a hurry. And you don't know good true-blue men when you see them." He sneered. "No wonder you hitched up with that loser."

Anne nearly doubled over from his caustic blow. She'd put him on the defensive, but she was trying to help. Instead of thanking her, he mocked her. He was smart, and one helluva lover. He continued to build a good wool business. But the man didn't get it. He had to deal with unresolved issues.

Exasperation swelled and she wanted to throw something. She fisted her hands and chided herself for expecting more from a man carrying a grudge against life.

"Okay. Fine," she heard herself exclaim. Her insides rumbled. "Anything else, Your Lordship?"

He crossed the distance between them in three quick strides. Wrapping his hands around her arms, he spun her around so her back was to him. His breath heated her right ear. He loosened the robe away from her nape and pulled the terrycloth down over her shoulder. He rapped his finger against her skin.

"Yes," he snapped. "As a matter of fact there is. You have a butterfly on your back."

Eighteen

Anne wriggled free, swung around and stared at him.

"Are you bonkers?" she demanded, her voice rising with each word. "I'm talking about something important, and you want to discuss birthmarks?" She jammed her hands into her pockets causing the earring to nearly bounce out.

Slade regarded her for a moment, his facial lines deepening.

"No, I'm referring to how you must know my grandfather."

Growing furious, she raised her chin in defiance.

"I'm curious as to how you think so."

"Now *that* I'm sure of," he stated.

She withdrew her hands from her pockets and slapped them emphatically against her legs. She had all she could handle and turned on her Isotoner-slippered heels. "I repeat, I don't know him. Arrangements for me to come out here were all made above me. The aerial photographs were turned over to me for this job, and silly me, I thought I could turn a piece of your back country into a great flight of commercials, since that's what I do best. Find the good and enhance it."

Fires of opal raced through Slade's eyes, and he reached out and swept her to him. He zeroed in on her mouth with his own. Her emotions somersaulted. She widened her eyes, then closed them as she fell into the sincerity of his kiss.

Weakening, she leaned into him. The moment she did he lifted his mouth from hers. She struggled for composure and ran the back of her hand across her warming lips.

"Annie, you do a couple of things 'best'," he reminded her, then firmly pushed her back a step. "But, I saw you on TV at the same place he was."

Anger and a good deal of anxiety prevented her from moving. How devilish and demeaning, she ranted. Especially when she knew she didn't know his grandfather.

Slade's hair caught a band of sunlight from the window, burnishing it into a rich halo. Halo, hell, she muttered inside. The man, wearing black, was badgering her. She heaved a deep breath and let it go. "Slade, I don't like being goaded into agreeing with you."

Cocking his head to one side, he levelled his eyes on her. Something else smoldered in him. Unflinching, she challenged his gaze. There didn't seem to be anything else to say. Because she cared, she desperately wanted him to face his demon. He could, at least, try harder at getting over Caroline's death. But she'd learned weeks ago that he was a proud man. Especially, about what he did for a living.

The clock ticked off indifferent seconds, and a door shut somewhere down the hallway behind her. Slade's eyes flickered with uncertainty and unstated regrets as he watched her. She looked like she was about ready to pack up.

He said simply. "You can't leave." Releasing her from his eye's embrace, he made a half-turn and looked out the window.

She raised her hand to her throat.

He went on, "You don't have a clean bill of health."

She looked down at herself. She was trembling and pulled her robe back into place over her shoulder. Disagreeing with him would have given her great satisfaction, but the energy she'd stored up was fading. He was correct. She didn't feel the worth of a plug nickel.

"I guess I don't understand," she said, fingering the pearl earring in her pocket. "For some reason you're shutting me out."

"I reckon I have."

Her mouth went dry. She could hardly believe this was the same man who had made her feel tuned into life again and helped her regain her trust. Now he couldn't trust her. He'd seen her in the news.

"Why?" she asked.

"Two reasons. You don't like sheep farmers, and I don't like blokes talking behind my back."

Heavy footsteps and movement caught Anne's attention. She felt saved by them. In tandem with Slade, she turned her head toward the source. A tall, elderly man entered the living room under the arch and gazed at Slade.

"Then let them talk to your face," he suggested, bringing the chill of autumn with him.

Stunned, Anne stared at him. His big frame and snowy white hair struck her memory bells. They bonged loud and clear. Dread hit her stomach with a thud. So *this* was Slade's grandfather? How could she have known that the one man in the crowd who helped her the night of the brawl was Slade's relation? She fought to keep recognition off her face. She desperately needed time to think.

Slade stood with his feet shoulder-width apart and raised his eyes ceilingward. Irritation ran rampant over his features. Gazing back down, he shot her a quick glance, then moved on.

"Grandad, you're up." His expression softened a bit as he helped him to a sidechair at the worktable where the dull aluminum canister now rested.

"No other way to be around here with all the commotion you two raise. Hello, Anne. Nice to see you," McGregor said, and nodded in her direction. "Where's Rose? I want some good billy tea, none of that weak stuff Lindsay's got me on."

Slade explained the staff's whereabouts, and his version excluded how Anne had released the staff for the rest of the afternoon.

"How's the film project going?" McGregor asked. "Call me Jim, by the way. By now, you must feel like family."

She blinked. Even though everything seemed topsy-turvy with these people, *family* had a nice ring to it.

Slade glowered at her.

She scrambled for *savoir faire*. She'd walked into a can of worms labeled Unresolved McGregor Family Matters. A situation more threatening than any fire.

Slade began to answer for her. "She's not—"

"Thank you, Jim. The crew is proceeding according to plan in my absence. In another few days I'll be back on the job."

That seemed to satisfy the elder McGregor. His grey eyes twinkled under his shaggy white eyebrows.

"Heard how you ducked the fire and ended up in the Canyon."

She nodded, but held her peace.

He turned toward Slade and said, "Good sheila here. Told you she was smart and pretty."

"She's smart all right," Slade said. "Let's see if she gives the right answer to a question."

Slade faced her now.

The elderly woolgrower laughed and slapped his thigh. "I'll wager she does. Then could I ask you to boil me some tea, Anne?"

"Sure, but it'll have to be the bagged stuff."

Disappointment took a turn in his eyes.

"You don't cook?"

She smiled at him. "Actually, I do cook."

"But it's not what she does best," Slade slid in.

"I fix good hot New England clam chowder," she countered, trying to ignore him.

"Now that's fair dinkum," Slade agreed with gusto. "She can make things *hot*."

An awkward beat followed as she darted her eyes over the two McGregors. Slade wore his grandfather's likeness handsomely. They even had the same body build, except Jim's mouth turned down at the corners and his hands were bigger than Slade's. She tried to picture Slade in white hair, but it just wouldn't form. Right now all black clothes with a cape seemed to fit.

"You're not cooking anything, Annie," Slade said. "I will. But not before I ask my question." He pulled a chair away from the trestle table. Turning the seat around, he squared himself over it, sat down, and folded his arms over the back.

"Okay. I'll play," she said with resolve, quickly sitting across from him. "But may I ask one first?"

"Depends," Slade fired back.

Jim put up his hands.

"What in the bloody hell is going on here between you two?" He razored Slade with reproach. "Anne's our guest." He turned to her. "Go ahead, sweetness. Ask your question first."

She smiled. "Well, it's actually for you, Jim. I'm wondering if the Bilwans have given us permission to cross Nourombie yet? As far as I know, our crews have honored the Bilwan people's requests during the ceremonies. We, of course, would go only with their guidance. And we'd like to make that offering of funds I spoke of. It would be the only way." She eyed Slade uneasily. "Since I've been part way down the other route into the Canyon, I doubt we could make it down and back out with our equipment, or without someone getting hurt."

Jim gazed at her for the longest time. So long, in fact, she reached over and touched his arm.

"Jim?"

"Don't shake him," Slade said calmly. "He's taking a short walkabout. This is how and why he ends up in Sydney, or Tamworth, or Leura at the drop of a bush hat. And if he can't travel in the ute, he does it up here." Slade tapped his temple. "It's also how he ends up in fights."

Jim stirred. "I only go for what's right. Last I heard a bloke up north got something else mixed in with merinos, just like I warned would happen. Muddy up the lines, then what'll we have? Nothing pure, cloning, and hell to pay, that's what!"

Anne laid her moistening palms against the wood while Slade leaned back in his chair and crossed his arms. Jim reached over and patted the top of her hand.

"In answer to your question, Anne, I'll make another call on your behalf. Now that the ceremonies are over, there may be some news and we'll have a better chance."

Slade blurted. "*We'll* have a better chance?"

Jim spun around and faced his grandson. "Still fighting reality, mate? It's not fair to deprive this young woman here of her chances because you'd rather be a martyr. Seems puny reasoning to me, so listen up. I meant that *you'd* be going with her, that's why I said 'we.' Because, like I told you, 'we' is 'us' in the McGregor family." He turned back to Anne and said kindly, "We've built a reputation of how good we treat people out here, and as long as I'm around we'll keep that in motion."

Anne's heart swelled with gratitude. She slid a glance over in Slade's direction who stared daggers at her. She gloated.

"Thank you very much," she said. "I'll bring you some good herbal tea before I turn in."

Slade's sigh erupted so loudly it sounded as if steam rose from the floor. He wrapped his hands around the top of the chairback and pushed himself up and out of the seat. The chair clattered to the wood floor. Leaning over the table, he glared at his grandfather, then at her at eye level.

"My turn to ask a question, Butterfly," he said, conviction hardening his features.

She ignored his sarcasm and clasped her hands together in a neat fold in front of her on the table. *He is amazing, so electric,* she thought. His muscles taut, his eyes alive with passion and wanting her. She was learning to read that look. Although fleeting, his desire showed its glorious presence. She wondered what he'd do if she shot up out of the chair and kissed him.

"I'm ready," she said, her elbow touching Jim's arm. After such a wild thought, she needed an anchor.

Slade pointed at his grandfather.

"Now look at him," Slade said evenly. "And look closely."

She took in the features of the elderly man who sat next to her. Afterwards, she looked back at Slade, ready as she'd ever be, particularly since she already figured out what he was going to ask.

"My question is simple. Do you know him?"

Bingo. She was correct, but she still cringed inside. Her answer was anything but clear. Both men waited.

"Yes and no," she responded, doing some quick thinking.

Jim McGregor threw his head back and roared. "Ha! Told you she had brains."

"Quiet, you old codger. What kind of answer's that?"

Anne pushed herself up from the chair.

"The only one I'm going to give you." She walked behind Slade's grandfather and rounded the end of the table before Slade planted himself in her path. She brushed past him.

"Why didn't you ask me?" McGregor piped up. "I remember her real well."

"Excuse me," Anne said. "I'm going to the kitchen, then to rest for a while." Disgusted, she scooted out the archway into the hall.

"Hold it." Slade firmly guided her to the kitchen as her Keds squeaked across the floor tiles.

Jim's voice trailed after them, "I'm going to my office. After you're done, don't forget my bloody tea."

"Coming right up," Anne called cheerfully.

Reaching the kitchen, she whirled on Slade.

"Let go of me, silly, and tell me where the tea's kept."

"Not yet, on both counts."

"Slade, you're being—"

He picked her up and sat her on the counter. With a furnace burning in his eyes he dazzled her.

"I'll make the tea," he said, then released her. "He'd have you making it white with evaporated milk before he's done."

"Fine. I want sugar in mine."

He filled the teakettle with hot water and lit the stove, then gave her a sly wink.

"You're not up to sugar."

She rolled her eyes. "You know, you have a one-track mind." Slade opened a red tin of tea bags and set it aside. "You like what I do with it, don't you?"

Heat rushed through her. Their lovemaking would never be forgotten. "Sure, except you talk too much."

He moved between Anne's legs and put his hands on her waist. "Don't fire me up."

She pushed them away. "Apparently someone has to since you've cut your friends and family off."

A fast, serious glint appeared in his eyes.

"I really don't want help."

"I think you do, so include them. It would make them feel better, and you never know what may come of it."

For some reason, that hit home with him. He suddenly looked forlorn and lost. If only he could let all his guilt go, then he'd be free. Free as she was, working on her dreams. Above all, she wanted him to be able to love again. She gazed into his blue eyes. Somewhere along the line the sign over her heart had fallen down.

He'd locked his gaze into hers, but this time with genuine interest. The storm in them began to quell. Urgently, he pulled her closer to the edge of the counter and she placed a soft, nurturing kiss on his forehead. The water in the teakettle on the stove began to simmer and emitted pops.

"I'll make a deal with you," she whispered.

He sighed, and lifted his head. Her serious tone produced its desired effects. She knew a thousand reasons to save him.

"What kind?" he said speculatively.

She slid her arms around his neck. Being so close to him was driving her up the wall. She yearned for his touch.

"Let me take your grandfather his tea."

He looked down his nose at her.

She slid her hand and traced the top of his black shirt pocket. Her heart fluttered. He plucked her fingers from his shirt and put them in his mouth and sucked.

"Are we discussing a merger, Ms. Kingsley?" he asked around them. She leaned into his ear and nibbled on his lobe.

"Affirmative, Mr. McGregor."

She'd grown unable to hold back.

"Fair enough," he said, wrapping his arms around her waist.

The teakettle shrilled. She jumped and Slade stiffened and pulled his fingers away from her lips.

"Damn," he exclaimed over the high-pitched whistle. Leaving the warm niche between her legs, he crossed to the stove and removed the kettle, then proceeded to make the tea while she looked on. "Cups, please," he said.

She slid off the countertop and found clean ones on the drain board. He fixed two small trays with tea and some damper with ginger jam. He then handed her the tray and said, "I'll wait at the guest room door for you."

With that she left the kitchen and headed down the hall to the office. Upon reaching it, she knocked lightly on the door with one hand and supported the tray with the other.

"Good, it's you," Jim said, pushing aside piles of papers on the desk. "I'll not keep you long, but I want you to know some things. Some difficult things." He waited for her to sit down. "I'm very concerned about Slade and have been for a long while. He won't talk to us or Lindsay Sanders about it, but we believe Slade's blamed himself for his wife's death."

She raised a wary eyebrow. "Why?"

"He's the kind of man who makes things happen around here. He likes the responsibility. The only reason that woman was out here was to be his wife." His tone grew grave and Anne's curiosity grew.

"I understand. How'd they meet?"

"His enjoyment of music took him to the Sydney Opera House to hear the symphony. There was a mix-up on tickets, which put them next to each other. He came back to the station excited about her. Couple months later they got married. She was pretty enough and rather rich, but out here, a lionfish out of water."

"Oh," Anne said quietly. "Guilt can consume a person."

"I agree, but Slade can't see that." McGregor pulled out a desk drawer and propped one of his legs up onto it. "My grandson is stubborn, but a good man. Have you noticed?"

"Yes," she said, crossing her legs. "I see a lot of good in him."

He peered at her. "He needs a push."

"A push?"

"From someone strong and level-headed."

She looked steadily at him across the desk.

"Like you, Anne."

She couldn't believe she was hearing this. If there were two things she wasn't feeling these days, it was strong or levelheaded.

"Why, thank you, Jim. I can see you mean that. But you place more faith in me than you should. In the end Slade will have to face his own problems. And time does heal."

"True, and he's almost there," he said, preening his fingers over his cup. "He just needs a nudge." He paused. "I know living out here takes a... a special kind of woman."

Incredulous, she leaned forward. From this point on things sank in. One thing connected to another. She had to know for sure where he was coming from.

"Is that why you invited Greene & Associates to come out here after initially turning us down? Because you saw me that wretched night and figured Slade needed to meet me?"

He shrugged in mock innocence with his hands, then poured his tea. "Don't worry about the TV thing. In your boots I'da been unhappy, too. Bad first impression. Can you get me some canned milk?"

"No," she said blankly. "Too much fat."

He smiled, then sipped a half-cup of the tea. The satisfied look on his face told her that she'd passed some kind of test.

"I'll make that call to the Bilwan elders after I finish with this."

"Thank you," she replied, somewhat at a loss.

"No worry. I want to see people happy, especially my grandson. Not so many years left for me." He set down his cup and picked up a wooden-framed photograph and turned it toward her so she could see the woman's face under the glass.

"Slade's grandmother, Hannah." He coasted off in thought for a moment. "You remind me of her," he added as she stood. "Like her, you're not afraid of your own shadow. And you've got class. You should get some more rest. I didn't mean to keep you."

She ran her tongue over her lips.

"Oh, yes you did, Jim."

Delighted, he smiled, and she couldn't help returning it. But a frown soon wrinkled his forehead. "Wait a minute. There's something else." The elderly farmer leaned forward and whispered one last piece of vital news to her. One she wished she'd never heard. So heartrendering, it half-sickened her.

Anne left the office and found Slade waiting as he had promised, leaning against the wall outside the door of the guestroom. She was beginning to feel as if it were her own.

"How'd it go?" he asked.

She pursed her lips. "How'd what go?"

"You're being coy. That doesn't fit you."

He held the door for her with his free hand, then laid the tray on the small round table by the windows. She poured some tea for them both and gestured for him to sit with her.

"Listen, I know you've—"

"Wait, Annie. I'm up first, and what I'm going to tell you will shock you. Real bad." He picked up the butter knife and tapped it nervously against the serving plate.

"Try me," she said, lifting a cup from the tray.

"I didn't... know she'd get so upset. Reckon I should have. No excuse, though. The fact is..."

Tap, tippity, tap.

"The fact is, Anne, I as good as... killed Caroline and our baby." He blurted out the words as if his mouth would lock up forever before he finished, and he deserved it if it did. His face twisted with guilt as he looked away. "Now it's out."

Anne took all of him in as if Fate had given her the most precious gift. Hardly the appropriate response, but she smiled. She stood and took his face in her hands and turned it toward her own.

"Good for you," she said softly. "Now let's eat."

Slade's face wrinkled in perplexed horror.

She sat back down and folded a napkin over her lap.

He dropped the butter knife, she snagged it on the rebound, and he caught her wrist.

"Annie, did you hear me?"

She pulled her hand away and began buttering a select slice of damper. "I'm sitting right here, am I not? Of course I heard you. I just don't believe it. I know that you two argued—because you've told me that much—and there was a horrible accident—and I saw the wreckage, so I believe that part, but not the rest." She nibbled and swallowed. He sat transfixed as she went on. "I feel very sorry you had to go through such a tragedy. God, Slade, that would be unimaginable for me—losing a spouse and baby. Please understand. I'm no shrink, but I guess it's natural for you to feel somewhat responsible. And I'm honored that you've chosen me to turn to, and I'll do whatever I can. Except you ought to also let your grandfather, Rose, and Rudy help. They're your family."

Slade slowly rose. For a moment she thought he was going to reach over and shake her by the shoulders. Make her live his pain. Or make her run away while the getting was good.

"My grandfather discussed her death with you?" he asked in disbelief.

"He did."

He rubbed the back of his neck. "Damn. Now he's putting ideas into *your* head."

She rose from her chair and laid her hand on his shoulder. Her throat tightened and tears blurred her vision. Remembering what Jim had shared with her, she simply didn't have it in her to say another word.

Anne replayed the scenario in her mind, it was Slade's distrust that'd hurt the most. When Rudy had returned from Tamworth last evening, she was sure that the stockman encountered a fitful boss. But Rudy owned the wisdom of a spirit god, and she suspected earlier that he'd welcome the chance to set Slade straight.

As for her and Slade, she wasn't sure what to expect next. He'd left the guest room in torment, but not before she'd pulled her hand from her pocket and mistakenly dropped Caroline's earring on the floor.

Slade had watched it bounce and come to rest on the rug beside the bed. He gazed at the earring with vague interest at first, then recognized the piece of jewelry.

Quickly, she scooped it up and fisted it.

"Is that what I think it is?" he asked.

Her heart had flown into her throat.

"Yes."

Perspiration now beaded on his forehead.

"Open your hand," he said.

"That's probably not a good—"

"Please?"

He took the earring and rubbed his thumb over the pearls. His eyes misted. Her timing could have been totally off, but she decided to risk it.

"Think back, Slade," she said gently. "You argued and she said she couldn't live without you. Right?"

He nodded slowly and his voice wavered.

"What're you getting at, Annie?"

She collected a myriad of thoughts. "Oh, something that Rose had told me this morning. She said things weren't as they seemed."

Slade suddenly drew up. "You and my grandfather are alike. Damn, never mind. Don't say another word. Look at you. You're pale again." He tucked her in under the coverlet and ran his finger down her cheek, then strode from the room.

Pale? she wondered. More like scared stiff. He'd taken a much deeper place in her heart than any man. So deep, his problems seemed like hers. She tossed and turned, praying that a certain truth be sped to him, or else die forever hidden.

Only God could decide which was better.

Nineteen

Anne expected a telephone call from Dr. Sanders after breakfast. She looked forward to getting back to work. Restless and sitting at the table in the living room, she gazed at Rudy's newly drawn map of the Red Gum. She located Hannah's hut and could almost hear the welcome swallows flit about under the eaves. Finding Crystal Springs was easy also, and she could nearly see sparkles scattered through the clear waters. Then came Nourombie with its warm, dry dust.

Running her fingers along the wide etched line of Rainbow Canyon, she spied the old game trail where she'd found the wreckage. It wasn't on the first map. She turned her thoughts to Slade. He still troubled her. She had to let him work things out, and she believed he would.

Jim McGregor's footsteps drew her attention to him.

"You ready for some good news?" he asked, wearing a pleased expression.

Hope sprang. "About Slade?"

Jim ambled over to the sideboard and plucked an apple from the cedar bowl. Chomping into the fruit, he nodded and came back to the table.

"Some of it is. Late last night I heard Rudy and him talking out on the porch," he said. "Got pretty heated. Guess you've noticed that when my grandson thinks he has things straight, it's hard for him to reckon otherwise."

She returned his keen gaze. "Well, he's stubborn, but it was my fault. I encouraged your staff to leave for a while. They've done so much for me, I wanted to return the favor."

"No worry. That's not what the ruckus was about," he said. "It's up to him now. What I needed you for was that the Bilwan elders have made a decision."

"Really?"

"You're in," he said, eyes twinkling. "You and your crew can cross Nourombie to do your work in the Canyon."

Ecstatic, she clapped her hands and raised them over her head in victory. Containing herself seemed pointless. She left the chair and gave him a hug. "Finally, a break. A real break. Wait'll the rest hear. Jack's been trying to bide time, but they're all probably ready to pack up."

McGregor grinned and tossed the apple core into the fireplace. "Rudy will lead you over a specific route."

As she thanked him the telephone rang in the hallway. Rose bustled into the room and nodded at her.

"It's the doctor, for you."

Anne took the call and Dr. Sanders asked a few questions and indicated he was satisfied with her recovery. "Cheers and see you about," he said. "By the way, you're doing a good job with Slade. Goes to show how well meds from the heart work best."

~ * ~

The next day crossing Nourombie proved uneventful and Anne and the whole troupe made good time. However, their descent into the gorge caused them a few problems. At the onset the dirt shelf road appeared in better shape than the old game trail. But its one-and-a-half-mile surface soon looped and steepened. Moving and reassembling the equipment and setting up a makeshift tent camp took almost a day longer than she anticipated.

"But it's worth the effort," she reminded Jack.

"Got that right. We just need to get this project in the can and fly it back to Westport. Actually, you being laid up bought us some time. Gave the crew a little break."

"Glad to oblige."

"So how'd you like the footage from Crystal Springs?"

A thrill ran through her. The magic of the night she'd spent with Slade still made her skin tingle. Together they'd christened that site in a very private and personal way.

She sighed and crossed her arms. For a fleeting moment, she understood Slade's wish to keep parts of the Red Gum away from the public eye.

"Hello, Anne?"

Her memories wavered. "Sorry. Yes, I looked at the takes this morning and made the picks. And, you're right, that location is lovely... but nothing outdoes this."

The autumn sun warmed her shoulders as she stood by the Rainbow River. The water cut through the most rugged and beautiful country God had created on Earth. Ever-changing light played over wide-leafed temperate foliage quivering about branches that were dotted with sulphur-crested cockatoos. Ancient rock strata and glistening eddies swirled mid-stream. All hummed in unforgettable ecological harmony.

So her hunch proved correct. Rainbow Canyon would be unsurpassed as a natural backdrop for the wrap-up of the SunMate Sunscreen series. She smiled as Jack laid his hand on her shoulder.

"This one's your baby, Anne. We'll be ready to begin in the morning. We've got a helluva good director. The talent is primed. The crew's ready to go." He lifted his chin and took in a deep breath. "Just a kind of sizzle in the air, you know? Like we're really on the edge of something big. I can feel it."

"Me too," she murmured.

Meetings with the producer and director, and standing in front of the monitors kept her busy for the next three days. All the while a relentless curiosity about Slade haunted her. He was to have come with her and the crew, but he'd bowed out at the last minute. She fretted over what his absence meant.

If he didn't show up soon, she'd wonder if he was angry with her. Perhaps he had the right since she'd made his personal business hers. On the other hand, they'd shared the most personal of experiences.

Busy as she stayed, she missed him. His touch, his eyes, and his voice laced with that smooth Aussie accent that could charm the bitter out of bitterroot. So when Dusty bounded up to her while the sun teetered on the line of night, her spirits soared. She leaned down and stroked the dog's head and glimpsed Slade as he rounded the last hairpin turn of the road. Bush hat pushed back on his head and a swag slung over his shoulder, he whistled a tune as he walked with his hands in his pockets.

He disappeared and reappeared from behind thick brush that lined the road. Sunglasses protected his eyes, and he wore a wheat-colored shirt. His jeans snugged his hips and legs. He moved onto the set with resolution in his stride and found her.

"You got a minute?"

Her heart stoked her senses as he removed the glasses and hung them in the vee of his shirt. His eyes carried purpose, but some of their characteristic twinkle remained unreadable.

"Certainly," she answered. She pulled the pencil away from behind her ear and tossed it with her clipboard onto the folding chair. Wending their way around the tents and mosquito-netted hammocks, she fell into easy step with him. Tunes from the boombox faded away as they turned upstream and covered some distance and stopped under the spread of a gum tree. Fading sunlight graced its elongated leaves and curvy branches that stretched up and over the rippled skin of the river.

"Sorry to duck out on you," he said, removing his hat and holding it in his hand. "But it was important, and—"

"This is a big place. I imagine you've been busy."

"Yep, flat out like a lizard drinking." He faced her now. "Busy mucking things up."

Her sympathy welled. She sensed a major difference in him. Apparently, Rudy had taken matters into his own hands after returning from Tamworth. Even though it must have hurt, Slade was better off knowing the truth and moving on.

"It's tough," she began, "handling deceit."

Surprise lifted his eyebrows.

"So you knew what really happened?"

"Yes."

Back pressed against the bark, Slade bent his right knee and hung his boot heel on a knob that protruded from the trunk.

"Then you heard Caroline wasn't pregnant? There was no child. She lied to persuade me to leave the station for the sake of our child." His voice shifted into a hollow monotone.

"I—I couldn't bear to tell you," she said.

"It wasn't your place, and I didn't believe Rudy until he showed the letter he'd found that Caroline wrote to her sister. Seems my refusal to live in the city really bugged her. She planned everything out well enough, I'll give her that much. Next thing that was to happen was another visit to her sister's." He paused to shake his head. "My late wife went often to see her family. In the city. Did I mention that?"

Anne swallowed. "No, Slade, you hadn't."

"Hmmm. While she was there she was to have had a so-called miscarriage. And the same Sydney family doctor who said she was six weeks pregnant would confirm we'd lost our baby."

"What doctor would do that?"

"None. No such doctor as Dr. Shrike," he added dryly. "So she had dreamed up a condition to get her own way. Whether I agreed to leave the Red Gum or not, the pregnancy would have ended. Phony pregnancy and miscarriage. But she didn't get that far. God only knew what else she'd reckoned to do."

Anne squeezed his hand. "If it helps, I know how you feel."

"So many answers," he said. "But I never asked the right questions, because I trusted her. And I figured no one else could help."

"Yes, you trusted her. She was your wife."

He reached out and folded her hands into his own. His touch fired through her. Only this time she noticed a difference. His palms carried a new and tender, slow-motion message. He spread her fingers apart and slid his in between. The connection seemed so natural, solid and right.

"I've caused you some problems," he said. He lowered his hands, entwined with hers, to his sides causing her to step closer to him. His masculinity wafted over her, and her feminity drank him in. She doubted she could ever get enough of this man—certainly not enough to last forever. Yet, she'd have to learn how. Her time here at the Red Gum grew shorter with every passing sunset. Life back in Westport waited for her, and her future with Greene & Associates needed serious honing.

She smiled up at him. "This is true. But that's water under the bridge. C'mon, let's—"

He shook his head. "Please, hear me out. I should hate her," he said matter-of-factly. "Truth is, I don't feel anything. It's like she was never here." He pointed to his heart with his thumb.

Anne sighed. He confirmed what Jim McGregor had told her. He released her hands. Slade had faced his worst demon.

Relief and happiness swelled inside her, but for some reason failed to flow into joy. Her amazement over his honesty choked her. She'd longed for this kind of inclusion from her ex-husband, but it was always absent.

Slade resumed, "Rudy was out there at Boronia Point hunting for ocher. I heard her scream, but he saw everything. He told me that after I left she'd sped around the tree..." His voice trailed off, but came back quickly. "A dozen roos with their joeys laid about in her path. To avoid hitting them, Caroline cut the wheels too tight to the left, and the Jeep rolled three times. She was too close to the edge and... it was all over."

"How horrible," Anne whispered.

"Weeks passed into oblivion, most of it spent under the stars and out at Hannah's. Lindsay Sanders diagnosed me not talking about it as denial and depression. Of course, he was right, but I called it something else. Survival. I stayed away from Boronia Point. At least until you ended up on the old game trail. Then it took—"

"Courage," she interjected.

In a swift move, he pulled her to him. Regret riddled his voice. "I'm very sorry."

"No, you don't need to apologize," she said, laying her finger on his lips.

Her pulse increased. She pushed her arms beneath his and nestled into his warmth. Her worry for him unraveled as she rested her cheek against his chest. He laid his chin on the top of her head. She could have stayed cocooned in his arms like this for the rest of the night. His voice drifted down over her like a cashmere shawl.

"No way to treat a special woman."

She gazed up at him.

"Yes, I mean you," he said, lifting a corner of his mouth.

Life suddenly blazed around her. Crickets sawed in the high grass, leaves rustled overhead, and water burbled along the bank. The unspoken, loving message in his eyes was all she needed.

"I'm glad," she said, wondering what to do next. Slade lived in this wild and beautiful place with the whole of his heart, and the heart of this place lived in him. As sure as she was standing here, she realized that anyone who tried to lure him away simply didn't understand him.

"How glad?" he probed, hiking an eyebrow.

"Immeasurably so."

He fell quiet, yet from his eyes spilled lovelight ready for her to catch. "I can tell you this," he whispered. "I'll miss you, Anne Kingsley from Connecticut."

Choking back tears, she closed her eyes and tried to escape the inevitable prospect of leaving.

"And me you." She swallowed. "We're from such different worlds, Slade."

His fingers kneaded her back with urgency and he lowered his hands onto her hips and pulled her to him. "Tell me again. Like you did in my arms after I found you in the Canyon. Show me what you feel, Annie, only like this."

He covered her mouth with his and kissed her deeply, as if it were for the first time. She stretched up on her tiptoes and returned his tenderest kiss. Finished, she let her arms fall to her sides and took a step back.

She wanted this moment to never end and needed to capture his image forever in whatever way she could. Handsome and earthy, vulnerable and worthy, he still stood in the middle of his world, not hers. Therein lay the problem.

She tried to lock him in her memory, heart, and soul with every intention of throwing away the key. Yet the details were certain to fade into faint impressions as days passed. Like the fine lines at the corners of his eyes, the curl of his sun-streaked hair, his sexy gait. The pressure of his tongue on hers, his breath in her ear, and the renewed spark in his eyes.

Her idea from a few weeks ago flashed forward. The way to visually remember him better and a decided means to improve her SunMate project. One could call it a marriage of personal and business interests.

"There's something I'd like, if you're up for it," she ventured.

"What's on your mind, sweet Annie?"

She explained her idea and answered all his questions. She could understand how he'd have to think about the plan so didn't press him for an answer. It'd be a challenge for him. But his face relaxed into a proud smile as he agreed.

The shoot segments would take some spontaneous arranging with the producer, and Drew had only one afternoon and sunset to do the job before they packed up shop and returned to Sydney.

"You sure about this?" he asked, opening his palms.

"Absolutely," she assured him. "You're perfect."

"Hell, you know that's not fair dinkum."

He wrapped his arms around her and she reveled in his virility. He kissed her again, picked up his bedroll, and pulled her along with him beneath a rock overhang.

Together they undid the swag and peeled off their clothing. Surrendering to his soul wrenching passion, she took him up on the offer his body now gave hers. For it could be her last chance for her spirit to entwine with his. She needed his kisses and to sigh away the night. Every fiber of her needed to know him just once more.

~ * ~

Next day at noon all four men—Jack, Drew, the producer, and cameraman—looked at her in disbelief. But she held her ground as she ran her idea by them.

"You heard me. I said I want a change in the script," she repeated and stirred her coffee in slow, careful circles. "An addition, actually. A simple cameo shot, it'll be a perfect touch. Slade McGregor's so charismatic, don't you think?"

The others exchanged mixed glances.

"He may know about sheep and wool," Drew said, "but he doesn't know jackshit about acting."

Jack slung him an evil glance. He made no bones about his dislike of that expression.

"Hold on," the producer said. "Anne may be onto something. If he stands still—wearing what he wears, looking how he looks with that collie of his, and a couple of sheep meandering about—the three-second bit could highlight the realistic aspects."

Pleased he took her suggestion seriously, Anne propped her feet up on a folding stool. Pride hit her heart.

"He's the real McCoy. But no helicopters. Just a long-range shot of the gorge, tighten up with him looking out over the gorge from higher up on the shelf road before we zoom down to the actors in the raft."

The cameraman confirmed, "Got it. He's nothing more than part of the scenery."

Anne nearly choked on her coffee. Slade was a helluva lot more than part of the scenery. The man *moved* her, altered the rhythm of her life. He challenged her passion for loving and living. He tempted her to make major life changes.

"For our purposes that's about it," she said, finding her best business tone and wiping her dripping chin.

"What's his fee?" the producer asked.

269

She scribbled the amount on a piece of paper and handed it to him. He didn't blink an eye as she continued, "He's asked us to add it to the sum we've offered the Bilwan people in exchange for our passage across Nourombie. Many Aboriginal kids suffer from trachoma and go blind. They're raising funds for a special children's clinic nearby, which I'll be personally contributing to, and you might want to give it some thought."

"Indeed. We'll factor it in," he said.

"How about you, Jack?" she asked.

He appeared to have something niggling at him.

"I think you know exactly what you're doing." He turned his head so she could catch his wink, but she wished she hadn't.

Drew pulled his cap off, ran his hand over his head, and resettled the hat.

"Inspired maybe, but a guy like him won't take direction worth a hoot. He owns this place. He's not used to someone telling him what he should do next."

"Or ever," the cameraman thought aloud.

Anne gripped the pencil and pressed its point onto the shooting notes. Everyone was talking about the man who pushed and pulled her into the future as if he were merely a means to an end. One that they'd have to tolerate to get the job done. Guilt struck her. Since that was just what she'd decided to do. Get past Slade in order to do her work. But all that had changed, and now the crassness of it turned her insides out.

"Drew," she said, "I suggest you ask him to do something, not tell him. Besides, he knows what to expect."

"Good. That'll save time," the producer put in.

Drew leaned forward. "Okay, but then you add a mongrel and a coupla' sheep? I don't have to tell you how all hell can break loose when you work with animals."

"Lotta retakes," another cameraman put in.

The pencil point broke. She raised her chin and forced her voice into a natural timbre.

"Dusty is trained and will do anything Slade signals or whistles for him to do. And the merinos will just graze. If they do move, Dusty'll take over."

"No problem," the producer said. "As I see it, Slade's an extra, just like any other we've hired."

Something snapped. Anne pushed herself out of her chair, sending coffee and notes flying.

"No he isn't!" she cried, shocking even herself.

Four mouths shut simultaneously. Heat fired into her cheeks. Only kookaburras would have dared to laugh, and for once no one had anything to say.

She exhaled and sat back down. "I mean, trust me on this, okay? Remember whose property we're on and how damned lucky we are to be here. This segment is a winner."

The producer applauded in the silence.

The director raised his palms to surrender.

Jack grinned and said, "I've been working with you long enough to know your inspirations are on the money." He said to the others, "And for *our* purposes her idea works. So let's go with it."

"Thanks," she said, eyeing him tentatively. After the men wandered off Jack sidled over next to her.

"Although, I'm not sure of *your* purposes," he said, shaking away a few persistent flies.

Still somewhat disconcerted at her own outburst and having heard enough, she swung around.

"Call it creative intuition. You know I get an idea, and something clicks, and I go with it. In this case, a cameo of Slade will give the piece local flavor and the realism it needs."

"Yeah. Local flavor."

Another flare of temper beseiged her. He wanted to hear about how deeply they were involved.

"You're pushing it, you know that?" she said.

"Actually, Anne, I think you're the one who's pushed the envelope." His tone turned cryptic. "Rumor is that the two of you have something serious going."

She raised an eyebrow.

"Whether that be true or untrue, it's personal, Jack."

"My point exactly," he said, "And personal and business don't mix. And no one should have to remind you of that."

She looked away and sighed. No doubt her life was changing again. It felt as if she were riding on a mystery train. Where and when it would stop was anybody's guess. This time the ride was long and the door slid open at the Red Gum.

She gazed again at Jack. Amazing how far she'd come. She'd taken his advice and emotional support after the last stop when Lou nearly derailed her forever. No, she couldn't be too annoyed with Jack. He'd seen her talent before she knew she had any.

Ever loyal to Greene & Associates and empathetic, he'd helped keep her on her career track when she was coming apart at the seams. Even so, she still wanted to tell him to take his business vs. personal philosophy and shove it.

"Listen, Jack. We work hard on the creative end of this business because we hit the market with new angles and do it well. Otherwise, we are just another bean-counter-run agency." He nodded, but her voice began to rise.

"I'd like to see our ads up on those big screens winning the competition in New York." Like steam in a whistle kettle, her voice hiked up another notch. "So whatever I can bring to the table to make that happen, I'm doing. Okay?" she shouted. "Is *that* okay?"

Her words ricocheted off the rocks. She pressed her fingers together over the bridge of her nose.

Jack's solitude drew her out.

She looked up. "I'm not sure I want to leave."

He rubbed the back of his neck with his hand. "That's what I thought, and it's ridiculous. You have to go back."

She fought off frustration. "Of course, that's true. But what I have to do and want to do aren't the same any more."

He slapped his notes onto the folding table. "Shit! You're in deeper with McGregor than I suspected. What're you thinking? You know that getting involved destroys your chances."

Slade's image slammed into her mind.

"How could I not?" she asked thickly, lost in a haze of warm, fuzzy confusion. But one thing shone through clearly. "I need you to let me work this out. It's my personal business affair."

Jack nodded. "Well, it is that, isn't it?" He picked up his belongings. "I'll see you later this afternoon on the job. The one that pays us."

Her stomach knotted. She'd come to know that if Jack sent out a warning signal there was good reason. Yet had she sought his advice too often?

"Right," she said. "We'll run through it, see how it goes today, and I'll pick the additional takes in the morning. That's still part of my job."

"Convenient, at least for now."

"Aren't you exaggerating a little?"

He humphed. "You know what's expected of us. Be at constant beck and call. Forget you have kids and a wife. Or, in your case, an Aussie lover. To Greene they all translate into one thing: Interference."

She wanted to lapse into idle listen, the mode she saved for bores and gossips. Except what he said was true.

"But don't worry," he went on. "I'll not divulge. You *do* get inspiration hitting, and when it does, which is damned near every day, we put out the best work in the industry. Bar none. Why? Because of you and your emerging, fresh style. And I'm not bullshitting you on this."

She shook her head. If he were anyone else, she'd have shut him up. But he had more to say.

"So if you want McGregor's image appearing on the SunMate Sunscreen billboard along I-95 outside Westport, I'm not objecting. I just hope you don't quit."

So that was the issue. Jack was afraid she'd leave. Although the temptation thickened, taking all into consideration, she wouldn't. She couldn't do something so irrational and brash.

"I'm not about to."

His quick once-over annoyed her. "Look, I know you're standing with your feet in two camps right now. But you belong in Westport, Anne, not here in the goddamned bush. Not to be some woolgrower's woman, barefoot and pregnant!"

She snapped her head up.

"Points taken," she retorted. Her muscles tightened beyond breathing. She resented his crass reference, brotherly advice and logic. "But from now on it's *my* concern."

As she spoke, Slade's old Triumph buzzed under the trees. She caught his movement through the corner of her eye as he leaned into the last hairpin turn with grace and power. A shiver shook her to the core.

"Mine and his," she murmured and shifted her weight, making the curve with him.

Twenty

Slade coasted the motorbike to a stop and eased himself off. Turning around, he faced uphill and curled his forefinger and thumb between his lips. Dusty heard Slade's whistle and leaped from behind five merinos. He charged to the front and slowed them to a halt. Slade turned to Anne and tapped his hat.

"Fancy meeting you down here."

"Hey, I'm down here every morning," she joked. The place was so wonderful she wished that were true.

"I'll remember that next time I want to kiss you."

"Oh, get out."

She waved him off and he nudged her arm with his elbow. For a moment she eyed Slade wistfully. Other than American slang, there was so much she wanted to tell him. Like how her spirits soared when he paid attention to her and how his warmth lingered.

If he ever spoke those three words of commitment of the heart, she would be in eternal Heaven. But she caught herself before indulging in any further fantasies surrounding her host. Today, she *had* to devote her energy to work.

"Thank you for coming," she told him. "I promise it'll be painless. All you have to do is stand up on that rock and look down over this river. We'll do the rest."

"You sure you want me for this job?" Sincerity shone in his eyes. He really cared about her reaching her best-project-to-date goal. He'd even set aside his work and privacy to make her happy. Handsome, sensitive and tough, Slade McGregor was proving to be a treasure for her heart and the camera.

"Very... very sure," she answered. "You're everything a woman... Rather, you have all the qualities... that I need. Er, that we require for this shoot. So relax and be yourself."

"Be yourself," he repeated softly and hooked his thumbs into his jeans' pockets. "Fact is, I'd lost sight of who I was until I met you. When I first saw you, something popped. And I know you felt the same. I didn't want to believe it then, but I saw in your eyes what happened in here." He reached over and tapped his fingers over her heart. A slow smile eased across his mouth. "And my grandfather may be right."

She swallowed, pushed up the bill of her cool white Tennis Club of Westport sunvisor, and raised her chin. Every word Slade had just spoken chased away bits of the world around her. Only him meeting her on equal ground filled her field of vision.

She cherished his voice. The meaning of what he said nestled into her busy mind and stroked her soul, giving rise to a sweet calmness for her spirit to love.

"Right about what?"

Slade took her hands in his and gazed down at her. He hesitated, seeming to work everything out before he went on.

"Lately he tells me anything that's on his mind." He paused, looking further into her eyes. "But what's he know, right? About us being perfect mates."

Her heart surely stopped. It was one thing to hear from Jim McGregor that he'd worked it so that she could come out to the Red Gum to meet his grandson, but having Slade bring it up nearly did her in.

"You mean, he means what I think he means?"

Slade nodded. Tense as he seemed, his eyes still sparkled in the shade of his dusty, sweat-stained bush hat.

"As in... for each other?" she asked.

"That was my take on the matter." He was watching her every move now, measuring her reactions. "And he often sees things first. Or he arranges for them to happen, as we've learned."

"My, my," she said, lifting a brow. "So he's 'fessed up.'"

"Comes time when a man should."

"Which? Matchmake or 'fess up?'"

He ran his hand along his jaw. "He has a point. In spite of that hardball business front you pull out faster than the snap of a croc, and your temper when you're throwing a mental, you're compassionate. Easy on the eye, too, and have the sweetest kiss this side of the Dividing Range." He let that perk for a second or two and went on. "Above all that, you *move* me, Annie. Every day. You keep up with me. You're all I could want in a woman."

"I-I don't know what to say," rushed out of her mouth.

He took another step toward her, moved his hands to her upper arms and drew her closer. "So I reckon... you ought to think about being my wife."

Anne's mouth parched.

"Your wife?"

"No worries. I'm not asking right now, you understand." Darn, he was smooth, causing her head and heart to reel. She realized he was serious and it appeared that teasing her wasn't his motive. Although he was tough enough to bash a comfortable life out of the bush, she couldn't blame him for being unsure about what she'd say. Proposing was risky, heady stuff even on a good day.

"Okay," she said. "I'll... I'll give the matter some consideration."

Deep inside her, joy tangoed with dread. Destiny delivered her the ultimate dream of love and fulfillment all right. But why did it come on the eve of her return to Sydney and then on to Westport next week? Marrying him would turn her career upside down. She had worked so hard, she could never throw it all aside. In her position, what woman would?

His mouth hovered over hers.

"I know I'm asking a lot. But I decided to take the risk. I think you're halfway with me already. You just need some time to get used to the idea—before I ask you, that is."

Frantic and mesmerized, she gulped.

He said tenderly, "I'm sure this isn't how you imagined settling down. But there are answers. We'll find them. Together."

Before she could respond he kissed her fully and deeply and a thousand fairy dust sparkles rained over her. After he finished, she opened her eyes. The hustle and bustle of the temporary film camp rushed back into focus. In a flash, it all transformed into a horrible interference.

Quickly, her mind sorted her impressions into discernible, manageable facts. Slade intended to ask her to marry him. Part of her wanted to scream "Yes!" with elation. Yet, another part demanded she say, "Are you nuts?"

And for good reason. He'd forgotten something so important she wondered how he missed it. He hadn't told her that he loved her. His best intentions were meaningless without it.

Like any other woman, she welcomed being needed by a man. She prayed for the completeness that being loved and loving back brought. She needed to hear Slade say those golden words. Again and again. Simple and clear. From his heart.

In all fairness, she sensed he was on the edge of telling her. But when? Her hours at the Red gum were numbered. He had very little time left.

"We'd better get going," she said, trying to get her knees to cooperate. "I need some time to think, Slade."

"Of course," he said. "So what happens now?"

Relief sped through her, and they began to walk through the maze of tents. "First you'll see Marge at the make-up table, then maybe a quick stop at Reggie's chair. He's the hair guy."

Slade cocked a wary eyebrow. "Whoa, hold it." He gestured toward his face with his thumb. "This is as good as it gets."

She said, grinning, "In your case it's a formality, believe me. Now come on. Slow as this process appears, we are on a schedule. The director will go over blocking with you. Then, you'll hike up there and wait for him to give you a cue."

"Right."

"At that point all you'll do is put your foot up on the rock and turn your head and be cool. Easy. Yes?"

He threw his head back and chuckled.

"That's what my father said about shearing sheep and shaving my face. Fact is, my first ewe looked like a goat chewed it, and my first shave took me near all morning."

"Wish I could've seen that," she said. "Did you like growing up here?"

"It had its rough spots, but after I'd gone through the uni and Army Reserve I knew I had the best that life offered waiting for me right here." He tossed her a wink. "At least, almost."

As they approached a food tent, the aroma of coffee wafted around them.

"You want a cuppa?" she asked. "You can take it with you."

"I'll pass," he said, turning pensive.

"Something else on your mind?"

"You. Always you."

Another thrill spiraled through her. But the voice of experience pointed its rigid finger at her. *Focus on your job.*

"Our wardrobe guy needs to brush you up a bit. Could we hold this thought until later?"

"And how close we've become and what we've done together."

She hungered for his touch. Uneasiness replaced the thrill as techies passed by within easy hearing range. She had enough to do without becoming even hotter gossip material.

"Which do you like better?" he asked flat out. "You on top, or me?"

Anne did a double take.

"Shhh!" She wanted to strangle him despite how his uninhibited spontaneity accounted, in part, for what attracted her to him. He didn't need a planner to get through his day. He was fresh and wonderful and appealing, but very hazardous on a film set.

"No, I really want to know," he pressed.

Mental images of both ways of making love with him flashed and warmed her. "We're at work," she reminded him, attempting to shut off the valves he opened. "And look, here comes the director. He's a terror today. Just do what he asks, and you'll be done by sunset." She moved from his side. "Welcome aboard. You're on company time now."

The man, looking preoccupied, approached them. "You two been going over things?"

Anne shot Slade a warning glance.

"We've been discussing strategies," the grazier replied, "and I'd like your opinion."

She widened her eyes against the mischievous flicker in his. No telling what the Aussie king of his castle would do at the drop of a bush hat.

"What strategies?"

Slade nodded toward the place Anne had indicated. "Would it be better for me to be up on top of that rock, or on the bottom of that crevice?" He kept a stoic, straight face.

May the Devil be proud, Anne scathed.

The director surprised her and tolerated the intrusion into his professional arena rather well. He actually squinted up at the sites. Meanwhile, Slade threw her a sly grin. Blast him! She wanted to wring his neck for making her squirm.

Drew stretched the moment out to an eternity and finally said, "Up top is better, don't you think, Anne?"

Slade cut in, "She didn't have a preference."

The director threw her a quick, curious glance.

"It depends," she blurted. "I mean sticking to the plan makes better sense. We're ready to go with it and we should."

Drew nodded. "Agreed." Turning away from them, he called over his shoulder, "Have Marge ruddy up Mr. McGregor's face and forearms with some number five. We roll in half an hour."

As the director walked away, relief swept over Anne. "That wasn't funny. You forget my position here."

He laughed. "Forgive me, wasn't that what you and I were discussing?"

She rolled her eyes and caught the big, deep blue sky.

"Please. This is my *living* you're toying with."

His smile faded, but she grew more annoyed. Not with him, but with herself. Now she even wondered if she were taking her job too seriously. Yet, she knew Greene & Associates wouldn't take anything for granted, and the longer she worked for them, the more she adopted their way of thinking. Big billings were serious, and tomorrow morning her fantastic job would have her pulling up stakes and hitting the long road back to Westport.

Torn, she avoided Slade's eyes. She'd loved the creative end of the ad agency business. Finishing a project and moving onto the next always inspired and energized her. The kind of work she did kept her plugged into life and her spirits buoyed. But she'd begun to appreciate the slower, laid-back, cyclical pace of sheep station life.

~ * ~

The settling of evening in Rainbow Canyon couldn't have been more beautiful. Anne hiked up to the rock where Slade and Dusty had made their film debut two hours ago. Except for a few minor altercations, the session had finished smoothly.

During the last few takes she found herself praying for a downpour or equipment failure, even another fire. Anything to prevent hearing Drew yell, "Cut," into the bullhorn for the last time. A cheer went up from the crew when he did.

Now it was all over. She'd packed her heart and soul and most of what she knew into this series. The raw film work was good and unique. She looked forward to working on the edits and wished she could see the faces of the paying executives of SunMate Sunscreen at what would be a blowout party in Sydney in a month or so. Jack would cover that base.

Tomorrow she'd travel back to Sydney with the others. By the end of next week, she'd be back on the other side of the world, resuming her routine life without Slade. That fact jolted her.

Glum, Anne breathed deeply and awaited the rising of the Southern Cross. Alone. Slade, his Border collie, and the sheep had already gone back up the canyon road. Before he left he said, "I'll catch you in the morning. You're all invited to the house for a Sunday barbie, one of our traditions. And, I'll have something important to ask you."

Then he kissed her and left. She marveled over the remarkable change in Slade. He'd swung from isolating himself to involvement. He moved from dark and brooding and cynical to bright, friendly and uplifted. But again just in time for her leave. Shortchanged is how she felt. Go figure why Fate decided this ill timing was good. She mentally stood back from her life for a moment. All in all, she looked forward to taking on the challenges the new project that Jean Linden Products would give her. It was being without Slade that would knock the wind out of her sails.

That would be scarier than facing any brush fire, hanging on for dear life on the back of Slade's motorbike, or more undesirable than crawling over petrified bat guano. She shuddered from indecision.

~ * ~

The windshield of Anne's Land Cruiser captured the late Sunday morning sunlight and bounced bright rays into Slade's living room. Lingering, Anne gazed up at Rudy's painting. She now could see all that the painting offered in fine detail. Under dry grasses, lay a ewe with her creamy ears and soft golden eyes imbedded in ivory brush strokes showing thick, shaggy wool. She was nursing her lamb.

Simple, basic and natural.

A mother and her child.

Anne loved it. Unexpected tears stung her eyes and she bent her head. "Pull it together," she urged herself. Fitful emotions had popped up more and more during the last few days. At the moment, sadness created a tight lump in her throat. Leaving the Red Gum was turning out to be a bigger challenge than leaving Sydney. Much harder than she'd imagined.

She set down her things, pulled a tissue from her pocket, and dabbed away her tears. The house brimmed with chatter, and she heard the kitchen screen door bang often. The station house was the crew's last stop. Assorted vehicles were parked willy-nilly around the place.

Except for Slade's motorbike.

Surprised not to find him at home when they returned this morning, she diverted her disappointment into packing up the rest of her belongings and joined the crowd.

On the surface she celebrated, but longed to see him. She'd spent the night tossing and turning, steeped in reality. Loving Slade wasn't a problem. Loving a man so far away from all she knew was what pulled her chain now.

How could she stay here? Far away from favorite lunches at The Moorings, smelling saltwater air. Hearing the cry of gulls and drone of boats. Sweating in the conference room where Greene & Associates' high-ticket deals gave her the opportunity to do what she loved. This leap required a lot more than trust.

She sniffled. The situation boiled down to making a soul-wrenching choice. Either way, she'd lose a vital piece of her life. Mainly, her heart, or the career that she'd worked so hard for. She let her briefcase drop to the floor and paced between Slade's big easy chair and the fireplace.

"This is ridiculous," she fretted aloud. "None of my friends have ever been forced to do this. 'Course they had sense enough to fall in love with local men. But when I went that route, it ended up in disaster. So why do I have to be the different one?"

Instead of Slade finding her talking to herself, Jack did.

"Hey, partner, you've gotta try some of this. It's barbecued bird of some sort."

"You should ask Da-Wa. He'll know what it is."

He balanced a plate with one hand and licked his fingers on the other. "One thing for sure, these Aussies eat well. You're having some, aren't you?"

She glanced at the plate of food.

"Thanks, but no thanks. I'm not very hungry."

He downed a forkful of potato salad and gave the room a quick glance and stopped at the painting over the mantel.

"Lovely, isn't it?" Anne said, dabbing her eyes.

Jack ambled to her side. "So what's going on with you on this bright and sunny morning, as if I didn't know?"

"Meaningful beauty gets me." She waved a finger at Rudy's art.

He studied it for a few seconds. "Uh-huh, interesting. Kind of shifts and pulls. What is it?"

The longer she looked at Rudy's painting, the more peace fell over her. "Magical," she answered.

Jack stepped closer. "It's sand blowing around, that's what. No, wait. There's something, right under the surface." He took another bite of food. "Damned if I can make out what it is, though."

Anne smiled. For once she could see things Jack couldn't. A milestone in its own right. Rudy ambled into the room.

"Hi. I was admiring your work," Jack said.

Amusement flickered in the Aborigine's eyes.

"Rudy has more," Anne hinted. "For sale."

Before further discussion Rudy turned and told her, "Slade just radioed in. He's out at the main road, fixing the mailbox."

"Thanks."

Her heart sank and her temper rose. She'd eagerly been waiting for him for hours. She now had an answer to his important question. Yet, finding out that fixing a mailbox preempted sealing their future was more than her heart or ego could handle. What kind of prioritizing was that?

"Look at this," Rudy added with widened eyes. "The boss didn't put on his hat." Slade's Akruba rested in its place on the trestle table. "Never once saw him do that, Ms. Kingsley. He must have something big on his mind."

"Sure, he does," Anne said cynically. "The Red Gum."

After the two men headed to the office to talk about more of Rudy's artwork, she glanced over at the hat. Anger and hurt sped through her. It soon surfaced as pure energy, ready to hurt him back.

She stalked over and picked up his hat. *You ought to think about being my wife.* Ha!

She took it over to his big easy chair and dropped it with little regard onto the deep cushion. She turned and walked to the sideboard and picked up the decanter of wine and returned to the chair. Removing the stopper, she doused his Akubra. A small, but sweet revenge.

The memory of his persuasive kiss she'd tasted right here faded on the spot. He'd used her. Took her to untread heights, taunted her with the promise of love and marriage, then he stood her up. To fix a mailbox?

She threw her head back, lifted the bottle, and swigged the last drops of cabernet sauvignon to wash him out of her life.

~ * ~

Slade dropped the paintbrush into the bucket. He crossed his arms and eyed his handiwork on the big, tin mailbox.

"Perfect. Annie's going to love it."

He looked up and judged it to be almost noon from the sun's position. Damn. Time had flit. He'd headed out here early from the house to do this job, but one of his stockmen was found half-dead from a fall, so he took a detour and got the man to Hannah's. All the while, he practiced in his mind how he'd ask Anne to marry him.

He opened the mailbox and pulled out the small tissue-wrapped box he'd temporarily stored inside. In it lay a gold ring crowned with three perfectly matched sapphires with diamonds tucked between, a family heirloom.

If she were of the same mind, they'd have a big country bash and have a minister he knew perform the ceremony. He rarely attended services, but held strong, simple religious beliefs. Even though he'd lost sight of the Golden Rule for a while, it still made good sense to him.

He intended to treat Annie with the respect she deserved. Of course, he hadn't told her he loved her, but he would today—as soon as he saw her back at the house. And if that went well enough, he'd fall to one knee, pop the question and give her the ring. If she said yes to his proposal, he'd bring her out here and show her the mailbox. Then she could snuggle in his arms all she wanted and they'd work out differences as they came. Forever, side-by-side.

He reached for his shirt hanging on the handlebar of his bike and, amazed at even himself, he shook his head. He'd actually devised a plan, something that Annie did with ease. In his livelihood, he looked ahead from season to season about increasing, selling, or changing stock, and what plantings to rotate. This was as tight as his planning got.

He'd rather let things happen as they may. In their own time and way. For example, finding the right woman and marrying her. Now, he was on the brink of doing just that. They were right for each other, and with any luck, she'd agree to be his wife.

He glanced back at the mailbox. *Anne.* A beautiful name for an incredible woman. She'd taught him to love and dream again. He could now finish the wool scouring plant. He cared now. He'd sure be giving up some of his independence, but Annie being the woman she was, she'd breathed life into him. He was bouncing back, better than ever.

Annie made him want to get up in the morning and to hear her ecstasy at night. She fed his varied passions, whether they be for riding hell-bent-for-leather, repairing fence, or just loving her. She could miraculously keep up with him when those yearnings flared. A real mate.

So to his way of thinking the matter was settled. He harbored no doubt that he needed Annie Kingsley. Without her, he was doomed to be only half a man. He'd never love anyone like her again.

~ * ~

Time ticked away Anne's patience. Picking up her briefcase, she took one last look at the living room. Remorse tugging at her, she left the house.

"Let's go," she said to Jack, opening the car door.

"You sure you're ready?"

"Yes, you bet I am."

She snugged on her sunglasses with shaking hands and climbed inside the Cruiser. Jack caught the door handle, preventing her from slamming it shut. He leaned toward her.

"You're really pissed."

She buckled up.

"Drive safely, Jack," she said, looking out the dusty windshield. "I'll see you back at the office in the morning for our ten o'clock meeting."

He furrowed his eyebrows. "There's no meeting in the morning. None of us will get back to Sydney until way after dinner. We're done for a couple of weeks."

She winced. Jack didn't understand. She desperately needed routine. She needed life as she knew it before she ever stepped onto Red Gum soil. Everything shook beneath her right now, falling apart. Slade hadn't returned and the fact remained that fixing a mailbox was more important than proposing. She swallowed hard. Only work would calm her. It always had and it wouldn't fail her now.

"Well, I just called one." Fighting another round of tears, she pulled the door shut and dumped the clutch.

Taking to the dirt road with a vengeance, she jostled over the ruts, into the dips, and around blind curves. River gums, birds, and kangaroos skimmed by. She could barely stand the sight of any of it now. This place no longer held intrigue and charm. It only reeked of Slade.

So she wanted out. Far out. Back on the asphalt of Route 95 that would take her through Tamworth, then onto the New England Highway, and finally to Sydney.

She sighed. Soon she'd take the last leg of her journey back home. But not fast enough. The end of the dirt road lay just ahead. Slade, hatless, straddled his Triumph that was parked near the mailbox. He pulled his leg back over and strode to the middle of the road and waved for her to stop.

"No way, buddy," she said. She pressed the pedal to the metal, and gripped the wheel. Closer. To him. His beat-up motorbike. And a stupid metal mailbox.

In the nick of time she swerved. Her rearview mirror picked up his reflection. Dust churned and gravel sprayed up his khaki-shorted legs and waist, and adhered to his perspiration soaked shirt.

The shock on his face was priceless as he vanished into dusty oblivion. Forever—she sincerely hoped.

"Where are you going? Come back here!" faded in her ears.

It only took one hill and dip before she slammed on the brakes. Her last two months flashed before her. Suddenly, things felt wrong. Terribly wrong. Her heart had just turned inside out from frustration. Slade should hear how she felt.

If she didn't tell him, it'd be a cop out, and she'd chew on it forever. But a deeper issue hit her. Had she become so fearful of another big hurt that she'd turned completely unforgiving?

Slade was the man she loved, like no other. She needed one last look. But, she mostly wanted something to reassure herself that not seeing him again was the right choice.

Making a hard U-turn, she changed gears and coasted back down the hill and up to its crest.

"Damn." Half-smirking, half-sick, she gripped the steering wheel. Coming at her car, full-blast, sped Slade. Hair flying, shirt flapping, he stood on the pegs. Looking steamed.

She turned off the ignition and stared.

Slade skidded to a full stop an inch from her front bumper. For a full ten seconds, he didn't move, and neither did she.

Finally, Anne lowered the window.

He dismounted.

She opened the door and got out. The heat blasted her air-conditioner-cooled skin. Her temperature rose.

Now he stood right in front of her, glaring.

"What the hell was that all about?"

"You should know." She could feel her bottom lip quiver as he stepped toward her.

"Annie, be reasonable."

"Me?" she yelled.

He put up his hands. "Hold on. Just in the span of one sunrise, I've lost all credibility with you. You must've figured something came up is why I didn't get back to the house."

Anne cocked an eyebrow.

He didn't flinch.

She drove right to the heart of the matter. Her insides churned, but she held him to the line. "You certainly know how to keep a girl waiting."

"I put it on hold," he answered, his jaw muscles working. "There was business to handle. You should know all about that. Time got away from me."

Anne took a step back. A certain fact took sudden, deep root in her. So strong it nearly sickened her. Her doubts were confirmed.

"Never mind," she said, shaking her head. "This simply won't work. If it's not fly-strikes, it'll be fires. If it's not that, it'll be floods. Or something else. Like mailboxes."

A glimmer of joy skipped across his frown.

"I'll show it to you if you have a minute."

Anne stood motionless. Slade simply didn't get it. She gazed down at the road and back up at him. A great sadness began to well up in her. *Over.* Their time together was over. Once again, she failed in love.

"No, I don't," she said resignedly, and turned away to get back into the Land Cruiser. "I really, really don't."

His hands on her shoulders made her draw up as he roughly turned her around to face him.

"You know what?" His eyes burned into hers. "When you told me you couldn't settle for second best, that it would be compromising your standards?" He gave her a shake. "You remember that?"

She looked skyward and nodded.

"What you really meant was that *you* don't ever want to be in second place. It's a real thing for you, isn't it, to be first in my attention every minute. Damned spoiled for a grown woman."

"That's not true," she flung back. "I'm talking about our chances of being together. Truly together, got it? Not me here and you out on the North Paddock or Tailem Flats for days on end."

"Mate, you've got it wrong. We'd be in this—together."

"Oh, whatever. You set me up for a fall this morning. And it hurt when you didn't show up, Slade. Now, *please* let me go."

He slowly withdrew his hands from her arms.

"Only if you're sure that's what you want."

"Yes... I am. I... had to be sure, and now I am."

He gazed down at her, working at controlling the emotions that must be exploding in him. He remained quiet for a moment and then spoke.

"You taught me an important lesson, Annie. You showed me how to let go. Set myself free from pain. Now I *can* let go of you—if it's what it takes to move on."

"Good," she said, choking back tears. "Then our time together wasn't a total waste."

She climbed into her Land Cruiser. Slade unfolded his arms and said with disgust, "Go, then, Butterfly. Fly home."

Passing through Attunga, Anne exhaled freely at last.

Conceited as it seemed, she could never tolerate being stood up, especially by a man to whom she had given herself. She popped the top of a bottled water and drank thirstily after traveling south on the hot, smoother road.

Along the way, it occurred to her that Jim McGregor was mistaken. Opposites did attract, but there was a limit. She and Slade were too far apart. She'd never understand him, or his priorities. He was all too far Down Under.

Twenty-one

Winter in Westport didn't want to leave. Anne shook late April snowflakes from her coat and hung it up. She switched on the halogen lamp on her desk and exchanged her boots for a new pair of Evan Picones. Her Daytimer showed her first appointment for today.

9:00 a.m. SunMate Project Review.

She sighed. It was do or die time. All of her ideas, travel, and efforts were on the line. Without obtaining the necessary sign-offs she could forget working on the Jean Linden account, or much else at Greene & Associates.

She'd awakened in the middle of the night, again unable to turn off her mind, then finally dozed off. Now needing coffee, she gathered the videotape and notes, the decanter from her Krups, and left for the kitchen.

The smart room with its indirect lighting snapped on when she walked in. Skirting the acrylic table and ice blue chairs, she walked across the marble floor to the white counter. It dared crumbs to exist. She set everything down on it anyway, except the decanter. Next, she tapped a code into a keypad.

"Good morning," replied the programmable electronic kitchen assistant. "How may I be of service?"

Dipping the decanter under the spigot, Anne commanded, "Cold water."

As water bubbled into the glass pot, she glanced around and let her thoughts stray. How different the McGregors' kitchen was from this one. There, people lingered for a while. Here, not at all, even at lunch.

But no loss, really. Who had time to come and linger over a microwave lunch? Who cared about wallpaper or cinnamon baked apples or breeze-puffed curtains? Who would ever dare? The answer punched her. She did.

Suddenly nostalgic, she found herself missing the jar of golden everlastings with mint bush nipped from the garden by a stockman's boy who dreamed of mustering. Under open beams, that kitchen abounded with life.

Honest, unsuperficial life, Red Gum style. Luring her back to ride again rough-and-ready over the timeworn land. To know Slade's fingers on her skin. Sleep beneath the Southern Cross. Hear his accent and the call of a kookaburro. Refuse vegemite. And watch the merinos *linger.*

"Slade..."

A soft ding chimed. "Your request is unavailable," replied the electronic voice in a monotone. "Please try again."

Anne blinked. As she retracted the overflowing decanter icy water spilled over the scar she'd gotten in Rainbow Canyon. Numb, permanent evidence of the struggle between wanting career successes and needing contentedness of the heart that only a man could give her. Had she gained one and lost the other?

Of course, she had. She'd come back with spectacular footage of Rainbow Canyon, but at the same time she lost her head about what counted more. Falling in love with Slade McGregor. And she knew she was. Deeply so. With her here in the snow and him there in the sun. Two people unable to get it right.

Only her love affair with her work lasted and she wasn't about to pull up stakes any time soon. Even if Greene hated what she'd produced, she'd still love creating good ads.

Anne sucked in a breath and let it out fast. Lord, she hated inner battles. They drained her. At least she took consolation in knowing that it wasn't only her ambition that had caused problems. Slade's sheep interfered, too. If not them, then walkabouts did, or fires and broken mailboxes—elements of a true blue woolgrower's life shouldered some of the blame.

"Water, off!" she commanded, getting back to business.

As ever, work would reliably save her. Funny, but that was where she and Slade operated alike. Each found satisfaction and solace in doing their work. He matched her commitment to excellence. She matched his respect for the talents they were given. God knew they were both task-oriented.

But *she* knew when to ease up. Slade sure didn't. His crazy, endless passion just wouldn't quit. Admittedly, great for sex. Necessary for riding the Triumph. Ideal for living in the bush and woolgrowing. Yet passion was also the driving force behind, "Love and I love you," she murmured aloud to a man across the International Dateline. "Go ahead, say it."

"Your request is not—"

"Oh, stuff it," she said. "Towel. Towel!"

A crisp, white paper square popped up from its chrome dispenser. She tugged it free, dried her hands, and stashed it in the vacuum trash removal tube.

"Thank you," piped the kitchen assistant. "The temperature outside is thirty-one. Have a good day."

Anne caught herself from answering, gathered her stuff, and left the kitchen to its own devices. Passing through dim corridors, she tried to force her thoughts to deal with what had to be accomplished this morning—a great job of knocking Greene and his suits on their asses, as Jack would say.

But it wouldn't come easily. Two days ago she and a few techies had finished the edits and voice-overs at an off-site production house. She believed the team had crafted, from what seemed like miles of videotape, a sizzling collection of fifteen, thirty, and sixty-second commercial spots for SunMate Sunscreen. After the last edit and splice was completed, she packed up the videotape and hadn't looked at it since.

Professionally, that was unadvisable. She could have practiced with the tape again. On the personal side, avoidance seemed justified. In order to recover from another false start in her love life, she needed to forget Australia. Just let it all go.

Sudden envy hit her. She'd just bet that Slade wasn't going through this. With her help, he'd learned to let go. But now she couldn't. Not one hundred percent, or even ninety.

The taste of his kiss stayed with her—way too close at hand. Their lovemaking was too easy to relive. How he gazed at her when he didn't think she noticed still tickled her too much.

But it's over, Anne sternly reminded herself. *Get back to this world and stay here.*

She sighed with new resolve. After this morning, things would be easier. Until then, she'd have to look once again at the wild and rolling beauty of the Red Gum and Slade, larger-than-life on a big screen. That would be tough.

Moreover, she'd have to do it in front of three men who each shepherded his own flock by covering his ass. Any of them could decide her work didn't measure up, for whatever reason. Then, good-bye to Anne's involvement with this client. Decisive and devastating, it all came with the territory.

For now, though, the office agency jungle slept. No ad veterans slammed doors on the fourth floor of River Plaza III, pushed deadlines, crunched numbers, or highlighted printouts.

No one answered two phones at once and sold creativity by the second.

She reached the conference room and the jitters crowded her insides. She set the decanter on the floor for her return to her office, then straightened up. She next slid the videotape and notes under her right arm. Pressing down on the handles, she pulled open the doors and stepped inside. 'The Devil's Lair' some people called it.

Thick burgundy carpet cushioned the soles of her shoes as she stood in the cool hush. She first gazed at the tinted ceiling-to-floor windows across from her, then left at the bar that had been extracted from a 1930's passenger liner. On her right, a built-in state-of-the-art sound and screen system would usher her SunMate Sunscreen series to the agency's tribunal.

But the twenty-two-foot boat-shaped conference table still dominated the scene with its black leather chairs. She reached the head of the table and put down her tape and notes, then touched the polished wood.

Major account campaigns were hashed out here, a keystone in a mecca of expensive ideas and strategies. Many careers soared or died over this bird's-eye maple and black lacquer. In an hour and a half, her work would be up for scrutiny.

She knew in her heart that the series turned out solid and competitive. But, frankly, her opinion mattered little. Greene and his associates decided what did. If her boss and the other two men liked what they saw, then Greene would probably approve the final product. It would set off a final phase of preparation before the presentation to Jean Linden Products.

Still, first things must come first. She said a prayer while setting things up and headed back to her office for that cup of coffee. Not even it washed away the niggling secret wish that Slade was by her side while she sweated this out. His priorities might be screwed up, but his quiet strength stood like Ayres Rock.

Forty-five minutes later she smoothed her Bloomies' navy and pale yellow dress with its soft-cut jacket and returned to the conference room to wait for the suits to arrive. They didn't keep her waiting. Only Slade had kept her waiting. She clamped her mind shut on the issue.

"Good morning," greeted Tom, her boss and VP of Creative. "You're going to do fine." A tall, bulky man dressed in grey tweed with a riotous tie, he shook her hand. From earlier conversations she believed she had his vote of confidence, but he'd been known to change his mind.

The next suit, VP of Finance, brushed past her and told Tom, "Let's meet at three, instead of two."

"Good to have you join us, Dick," she said to his back. His dark pinstriped threads complimented his thin face and round wire glasses, from behind which he squinted most of the time. To date, he'd withheld approval of the over-budget expenditures attached to the project.

"Hello, Anne," Harry said. He was Brooks Brothers' favorite customer and wore polished Italian shoes. He could be trouble since he'd expressed concern earlier about how the last storyboard had been changed and how talent was added on-site—soley by her, not committee. JLP headed his account list.

"Let's get started," Tom said and walked to the far end of the table. The VP of Finance removed his coat, exposing a white shirt and snappy dark suspenders. He chose a chair away from the other two men.

She walked calmly as possible to the head of the table. As she sat down, they also did—simultaneously.

She cleared her throat. "To begin, we are all aware of various aspects of the JLP project. So the purpose of this meeting is to brief you on its finalization and show you what's been produced. Any questions before I go on?"

Silence and poker-faced expressions were given.

"Fine. The intro is one that we could use for the preview session for the Jean Linden team."

She got up from her chair, stepped a few feet away, and tapped the rubbery buttons of the remote control. Recessed lighting and the wall sconces dimmed while the cherry-veneered vertical blinds slid from either end and crossed in the middle.

One-hundred-twenty inches of video screen descended into view as a projector tilted down from the ceiling. Another click on the illuminated pad brought up the agency's logo on the huge screen behind her on the right.

"G'day, mates," pealed an Aussie voice-over from six built-in speakers. "Greene and Associates welcomes you to Australia, the home of the Sydney 2000 Olympics. What you are about to see are fifteen, thirty, and sixty-second spots to be aired during the Games. All filmed down under, in SunMate Sunscreen country."

Anne let the video roll. The initial camera angles were grabbers and appeared fresh and captivating. The music and sounds distinctively Australian. All blended into a moving collage designed to sell a product.

So far no one had uttered a peep or signaled Anne to stop.

"Segment three," she said as it illuminated behind her. The North Paddock, wild, open and free covered in tufts of blonde grass, and the big sky dipping down behind the river gums. Susan and Brad did a great job. But seeing the landscape again took her breath away.

"Segment two," she announced, her voice wavering.

Crystal Springs. Her heart began to pound harder. The camera panned over the creek as the falls tumbled into the outer pool where the spokesperson models continued their adventures. Anne lowered her eyes as penetrating sensations washed over her.

Water, cool and warm, wetting her skin. Skirtless, shameless. Kissing Slade, taking and giving and unable to get enough, causing her mind to temporarily recall every touch.

"Ohhh, yesss!" burst from her mouth.

Anne's blood curdled. She opened her eyes and stared ahead—at the mural of the Titanic. Everything slammed to a halt.

Tom leaned forward. "I beg your pardon?"

Unable to breathe, she squeezed the remote and caught a button with her thumb. Fast forward. Right into the middle of segment one, the finale of the SunMates for Life series. God must've helped her quickly press the Pause button. Or the Devil?

Slade, larger-than-life, covered the screen. Dusty leaned against the rancher's leg. Slade gazed out over Rainbow Canyon. Mortalizing heat shot up her neck, and she fisted her fingers so hard they hurt.

"Gentlemen," she said, forcing herself to look at them. "Excuse me, it's nothing, really. A slip. I just remembered something that I... wanted to bring up at the conclusion of the showing. I'll move on now." Again, she aimed the remote at the electronics panel.

"Hold it, Anne," Harry said. He pointed his pen up at the screen. "Is this the talent you had added at the last minute?"

"Yes, that's Mr. McGregor. He and his grandfather own the sheep station."

Harry rolled the pen between his palms and looked across the table at Tom. "Inviting him to the client showing in Sydney next week would be a good move wouldn't it?"

Her boss nodded. "You bet. Jack's already working on it, and the McGregors have accepted. Of course, Anne, we want you to attend. Everything's been set up for you to go back this coming Saturday."

Whoa. Hold it. She lifted her chin. How could she put her best foot forward for the client with Slade melting her with just one look? Only that's all it could ever be now. A look. They had no more to say to each other.

"Thank you. I'd be honored to go," she lied.

"Nobody's going anywhere," the VP of Finance interjected, pulling his glasses down onto his nose and gazing over the rims. She looked directly into his eyes. After her road-trip auditor ex-husband, she distrusted agency pencil necks. Aside from power trips, their penny-wise, pound-foolish rationale stifled creativity. Except, ironic as it was, this accountant might save her from disaster.

"Look, Dick," Tom began, "you know the extra expenditures get charged back to JLP. So what's your beef? And, sure, as you've stated many times that Palo Dura, Texas would have been cheaper. But this client *wanted* Australia for their series, and that's what we're giving them."

"As contracted," Harry put in.

Undeterred, Dick replied, "Mr. Greene requires justification for the extra time, people, and expenses. So come up with it. He wants to know why Anne took almost a month longer to get the job done. Time is money—all the way around." He leaned back and preened his fingers.

Harry jabbed a thumb toward the screen. "You're looking at the justification," he snapped.

Dick glared at him. Nobody moved, but someone knocked on the door from outside. Anne turned to answer it and stopped when Tom's voice thundered past her.

"Go away! We're in a meeting here!"

His abruptness cut through her, and she faced the group.

Tom resumed, "We're pulling out the stops and doing a first-class pre-preview in Sydney. Now, please, zoom that up, Anne. Thank you. Rugged-looking guy, your Mr. McGregor."

"He's... not mine."

"Of course not, but is he the real thing?"

"Hmm-hmm. He's true-blue all right," she confirmed.

"I can see why you wanted to bring him in. And, in all fairness, you finished the addition fast."

"Sure did," she said and nodded. "Flat out like a lizard drinking." Again, she tried to swallow her stupidity.

Amusement flickered in Tom's eyes, but she wanted to set him straight. "It's just an expression. Yes, we pulled it together quickly. We had a great crew Down Under and got the job done better than most, I feel."

Tom poured himself a glass of water and drank.

"Go ahead, give us the rest."

She rewound the tape and hit play. The next sixty seconds turned into the longest of her life. The three men's faces reflected in the conference table. At this point, it was impossible to guess what they thought.

She clutched the remote to her chest and looked back up at her work. To her, the whole series served intelligence and heart. She hoped against hope that these men recognized this as her best and that Greene would concur. Now she wanted to lead the new JLP project. She was ready to sink her teeth into the challenge and some real money, for that matter.

The last three seconds faded and the screen returned to the bright blue Greene & Associates logo. Pressing rewind, she slowly turned around and faced the group. All three men pushed back their chairs and stood. She met their stalwart gazes and felt completely alone. Would she make it out of here alive like she had in Rainbow Canyon?

Tom looked at Dick and he looked at Harry, who looked back at Tom. In tandem, they nodded at her.

Applause erupted. Enthusiastic and loud, their approval slammed into her heart. Instead of wilting from relief, she stood taller. She'd done it. Her work had hit home!

"Great job," Tom said, striding toward her as the other two men repeated similar accolades.

"Thank you," she said, accepting his handshake. Inadvertently, she tapped the remote twice before letting it clatter to the table. She glanced over at the screen. Once again Slade filled it in a close-up.

Her voice shook. "I truly appreciated the opportunity."

The knock returned on the door, more loudly this time.

Tom's expression soured and he crossed the distance and flung open the doors. A new intern from the Traffic Department lifted a large carton from the floor.

"I'm sorry, sir," he blurted. "This is a rush delivery for Ms. Kingsley. I was told she was in here. And we deliver—"

"Immediately, yes, yes," Tom gruffed and lugged it over to the conference table. The dinged-up cardboard box, tied with a piece of hemp rope, landed with a thud in front of her.

"Heavier than it looks," he complained.

Dick eyed the postmark. "From Attunga, Australia."

"But there's no real return address," Harry noted.

Anne ran her fingers over her name printed in large black letters. "It's the art work that Jack ordered. But I don't know why they'd rush it."

Harry said, "I collect art. How about we have a look now?"

"Sure, why not," she conceded.

The men crowded around one end of the conference table where the package was situated. As Dick and Tom worked on the rope, her heart began to flutter. The box emitted aromas she'd doubted she'd ever smell again. Wool and boronia. And leatherwood?

"I'll get it," Dick said and slit open the lid with a gold-plated knife he pulled from his pocket.

Several uncomfortable beats passed as Anne turned away to leave. She needed out of here to call her mother. Despite how Eleanor Kingsley wouldn't know her, since that's how it'd been the last dozen visits since she'd come back home, Anne still wanted to tell someone in the family her good news. She'd celebrate with a couple of friends after she got back.

"What's this?" Tom asked. The other two men dipped their hands inside the box and pulled out wads of springy, clean superfine Merino wool.

"Packing?" she guessed. "May I catch you later? I have a phone call to make. Oh, the artwork was done by Slade McGregor's right-hand stockman, Rudy. Jack said he'd ordered a lot of it."

Reaching the doors, she heard another thud from behind her and Harry's voice slowed her steps.

"Not like any Aboriginal artwork I've ever seen."

"Must be folk art," Dick commented. "Or is this some Aussie's idea of a bad joke?"

"Beats me," Tom said. "Anne, what's this all about?"

She turned and glimpsed a pile of washed wool clip, glowing warmly under the soft lights. But what rested on the table in the middle of the fluff caused her eyes to widen. The three executives leveled critical gazes on her.

"What's wrong?" she ventured, arriving at the table's edge.

Tom turned the object toward her. Stepping aside so she could see it better, he quipped, "More than native art, I'd say."

Anne's mouth flew open. She was looking at a galvanized mailbox, wrenched from its post. A big dent, fist-size, interfered with the large hand-painted words resided on its side. She read them aloud.

"SLADE & ANNE MCGREGOR, RED GUM STATION."

In effect, Anne died on the spot.

So this was how Slade was 'fixing the mailbox' the morning she left him standing in the dust. He'd painted their names on the station mailbox—linked together—as if they were a married couple.

Blast him. Why did he send this to her? Worse, why did it have to turn up now? She turned toward the screen and looked up at Slade's image. Full of passions, strong and confident, he'd really intended to marry her. Damn his lovable, imaginative soul. But where were the words she needed to hear?

"Anne? Are you with us?" came from over her shoulder.

Dick scorned, "Tch. Tch. Hanky panky on company time?"

"Knock it off," Harry said, opening the mailbox. "The work is done and Anne did a great job. So what if she got married?"

"You're not thinking," Dick corrected. "We don't send people out to screw around, have affairs and embarrass us. Almost a month longer in production because of a site dispute and an accident? Ha, that's a joke. You're done, Anne."

He whipped his jacket from the back of the chair, slipped it on, buttoned the buttons, and gave the front a snappy tug down into perfect place. "Greene's going to be... disappointed, I guarantee you. And you know what that means."

Heat scorched Anne's cheeks. She struggled to keep her voice level.

"I did not, repeat, *did not* get married."

Meanwhile, Harry pulled out a bouquet of dried boronia from inside the box.

"Then this *is* only a joke?" her boss asked.

She faltered. "Not exactly."

Dick smiled smugly and strode for the door as she took the bouquet away from Harry. The raffia tied around the stems also held fast a fold of brown paper. Her nerves and heart rumbled in roller-coaster chaos. She tossed the flowers down on the tufts of ivory wool, but kept the note. Somehow holding it in her palm gave her unhallowed, much-needed strength.

Her boss said, "Harry, if you'll excuse us?"

"Certainly." From the doorway the account executive gave her a fast once-over. "Good-bye, Anne." His tone carried finality.

"Don't bet on it, Harry."

Tom rounded the end of the table.

"Look, forget all *this* for a minute," he said, gesturing at the mailbox. "You've done an exceptional job on the series. That's what counts. I still want you to go back to Sydney and do the preview for SunMate."

"You do?"

"Yes. Then take a week off to disengage yourself from this personal mess, okay? In other words, get rid of it. I'll take care of things here."

She tightened her fingers around the note.

"*Personal* mess?"

Tom's frown deepened under fringes of graying hair.

"Exactly. Dick's right." He stuffed his hand in his pocket and softened his tone. "Look, I know it's tough. We pay our dues longer than others in the industry."

"What you mean is that we forget life outside G & A."

His face hardened. "You're missing the point." He spread his arms wide to encompass the room. "*This is life*. And we believed you understood that when we brought you on board."

"I did understand."

"Then I strongly suggest you get back on track for your own good."

She stood motionless. Tom had never coached her with such graveness, and she'd never given him reason to. He'd been tolerant, even helpful, during her marital breakup. But she'd attributed his patience to the fact that during those rough days she'd worked long and hard like she had right after she started here. Losing herself in this office saved her. And she proved she was good, which was why she was asked to do the Sydney assignment with Jack.

But now she faced a new problem. She'd fallen in love with a man fifteen time zones away, and he wanted her. Worrying the note, she gazed back up at Slade's image, then back again coming to rest on the conference table.

"You know what, Tom?"

He looked at her with disdain and half shrugged.

"I do need to get on track," she said.

Tom's face beamed with relief. "Good for you. You're a smart woman. I'll talk to Greene." He moved toward the door. "He can't deny the caliber of this series, that's for damned sure. Good luck with your admirer." He gave her a curt nod and left her standing alone in the room.

Anne tugged on a chair and sank into it. Crossing her arms on the table, she pressed her forehead against them for a moment. Her head spun. As she saw it, there were two tracks. One ran along this New England coast and the other into the heart of that New England region. She lifted her head, uncrumpled the note, and read. *Annie, I love you and miss you. Come home. S.*

So there it all was. Short and sweet. Written with a somewhat uneven hand, but it took emotional courage to write it. She bit her bottom lip to still it. Mere seconds passed before she burst into tears, blurring the sensibility of her life.

Twenty-two

Anne greeted JLP executives and the guests of SunMate Sunscreen as the gala preview kicked off to a smooth start in the Koala Room of the Winthrop Building. Mingling and chatting, she kept a watchful eye on the door. Slade would arrive soon and she wasn't quite sure what to expect. No messages had come through from him.

What she did know was that she had to get through this last leg of the JLP project. Little could be finalized until these executives accepted it. Unlike other Greene & Associates' clients, this firm implemented an all-or-nothing policy. That meant that a one-hundred-percent in-house agreement needed to be reached before the SunMate Sunscreen commercial series project earned done-deal status.

Anne wasn't about to take any bets on the outcome. She'd seen it happen before when G & A had made it to the wire and the client would request changes. So another round of ads were created from square one with the hope they would fly.

She lifted her chin and moved deeper into the crowd to schmooze with the dressed up men and women. Although being with people, including her friends, didn't offset the loneliness that had stirred in her for weeks. Worse, part of her now was only going through the motions. She didn't laugh as much or sleep as well since she'd made the presentation to the agency executives.

Tom had stipulated what part of this return mission was to be about. Namely, ditch Slade for good. He'd repeated himself when he dropped her off at the airport a few days later.

"Thank you for that advice," she'd said in earnst. "It *really* helps me keep on track."

Sanctimonious pride glutted his face. "I knew we could count on you. You're a trooper. Good luck."

She avoided his handshake and hurried to Gate 15. Frankly, the jetway never looked better.

Nor had a man's handwriting.

Tucked in her evening bag, Slade's note now rested by her lipstick. A sharp bump from behind nearly knocked the strap from her shoulder. Making a half turn, Anne stood face-to-face with Jack. Dressed in a tuxedo, he dripped in high spirits.

"Kingsley, if you're not celebrating yet," he raised his voice over the chatter, "you should be." He signaled the waiter and helped himself to caviar served on abalone shells.

"I'm not counting any chickens. This is a tough sell."

He dabbed his mouth with a napkin. "You're worrying for nothing. You've done great." More caviar and dabs followed. "So gloat. You're entitled."

Anne smiled. "Without you to fill in while I recovered we'd have been even more delayed."

"And without you we'd be up the creek."

She let that comment ride and gazed across the roomful of people at Jim McGregor. In a gregarious mood, he fit in well with the corporate crowd. "Looks like he's enjoying himself."

"Yeah, he jumped on our invitation when I called. Wouldn't hang up until I promised him you'd be here." He thought for a moment, then said, "Nice of him, huh?"

"Yes, nice."

His eyes flickered. "Other than this was mainly your project, any other reason why he'd want you here?"

Lifting a glass of blush from a waiter's tray, Anne ventured, "I imagine it's because Jim feels he has a vested family interest."

Jack kept talking. "Stands to reason since his property was used. Like the Bilwans, he'll also get a check."

Anne glanced at the door and back at him. "Maybe more. I think his grandson wants to marry me."

Jack's euphoria visibly dropped.

"Will you?"

The smile in her heart warmed her cheeks. "I'm considering the possibility."

She stepped away from Jack with his mouth agape.

Wending her way around candlelit, écru-clothed buffet tables adorned with warratah and eucalyptus, she again caught sight of Slade's grandfather. His white hair glistened, but he appeared to be thinner than she remembered. When he arrived at the party, he'd given her hand an extra squeeze.

"You're missed out at the station."

"I've missed you too. Very much, Jim." If they were anywhere else, she'd give him a hug, but she needed to maintain what professionalism she could muster.

McGregor must have sensed that. "Some fancy indoor barbie you've got here." She explained that this one was rather low-key. Then he asked, "You been taking care of yourself?"

She replied wryly, "Just myself. Mother was moved into full care at the hospice while I was here earlier. How about you?"

Jim chuckled. "With help these days. But I wouldn't miss tonight. Not even for triple wool prices."

Anne smiled. Her time away from the Red Gum had been packed with many mixed emotions and issues. Some still clouded the picture. Yet, for the most part, they'd been diluted with the excitement bubbling in her to see Slade again. Almost more than she could tolerate at the moment.

"My grandson will be up here straight away," Jim continued, "He's downstairs yammering with the security guard. The man didn't want to see woolgrowers again in his lobby. Hell, the SMWA half owns it now."

Anne laughed. "You can be a wild and unpredictable lot."

McGregor winked and snared two hors d'oeuvres from the next waiter's tray. "Tucker's good. What're these?"

"Shrimp Olé. Sort of Cajun goes Tex-Mex."

He knocked them down like popcorn and glanced at the door. "I'm making this quick," he said. "You and Slade are like Hannah and me. Different, but alike. She had bales of spunk and some education. I had the God-given will to make the Red Gum work. Being together made each of us better." He reached for some grapes from another tray. "Thought I'd throw that in, while it was on my mind."

Anne's heart had leaped as he moved toward the windows to talk with some other guests. She couldn't argue with what was fair dinkum. Now if she made eye contact with Jim, he smiled like the cat that ate the canary.

"Hey, where's your Romeo?" Jack asked, sidling up to her.

She winced and set her wineglass on a return tray.

"Isn't it time to usher everyone across the hall?"

"Nope, we still have twenty minutes." He looked like a bewildered parent wondering where he went wrong. "Anne, what's happening with you? You're not the same."

"Nothing's happening that shouldn't be. Is the equipment working properly?"

"The techs checked it twice." He paused. "All I'm suggesting is that you think ahead. You worked hard for this."

Anne swept the room with her eyes. "Yes, I did. And your advice is good. I have been thinking."

311

Suddenly the penthouse room seemed small and so did the reason everyone had gathered here. In essence, for very big money on a very grand scale. AKA advanced economics. The challenge it once held for her had diminished.

She glanced again at the door. The cocktail hour was near end and moist wisps of hair hugged her nape. She wanted to tidy up before the preview.

"Excuse me. I'll meet you in the ballroom."

He stuck out his hand. "Good luck."

She gave it a firm shake and many memories flared up. All in all, she'd been lucky to run into Jack. On the business side, he was a good mentor. And while her personal life was falling apart, he'd helped by involving her in smaller projects that gave her more experience.

"Whether JLP accepts the series or not," she said, "we do good work, don't we?"

A smile rebrightened Jack's face. "Only the best."

Anne left him and walked into the hush of the corridor and turned right. Her buzzing senses welcomed the change. She passed the ballroom on her left. Inside, a mini-theatre had been set up with plush chairs. A podium stood on one side. Banks of screens that formed a huge one ate up the whole front wall of the room. Jack would take over once everyone was seated.

As she approached the brass elevator doors at the end of the hall, she checked her reflection. Not bad, really. She'd found the perfect dress, the next size down.

A ding chimed and the doors parted.

For none other than Slade McGregor.

Anne's heart thumped louder as their eyes met. Now she understood what was meant by 'seeing stars.' It didn't take a knock to the head, and her ability to move took a sudden dive.

Slade strode forward. His well-cut jeans, white shirt, and new boots and fawn Akubra finished off God's best work. A smile teased his mouth.

"G'day, Annie."

She stepped toward him, then pulled back. *Professionalism rules.* For a while longer, anyway. She struggled not to put in too much emotion. She couldn't afford the risk of tears.

"Hello, Slade. I'm... glad you could come."

He arched a cool eyebrow.

"You—look—beautiful."

His tone hung flat, like hers, with the feeling half-sucked out. A mirroring ploy to warm her up, she was sure. It worked.

"My grandfather said you'd called," he said, dropping it.

She crinkled her eyebrows. "Jim said that?"

Slade raised his right hand. "He did."

Curious, indeed. Jack had called Jim McGregor, not her.

"So how's life in the big city?" Slade's eyes hinted mischief. Even that appealed to her now.

"Hectic as ever. Charming as Westport can be, and..." She looked away. How she'd made it for the past month without the special connection they shared, she didn't know. Stronger than ever, it enveloped her.

But she'd grown fearless. She proved she could exist without Slade. She also learned about the vast difference between existing and living. They were miles apart, just like she and Slade had been.

"And?" he prompted.

Anne lifted her face to him. "Dry, very dry." Returning to headquarters had dropped her into materialistic, shifting sands. Unsuitable ground for building true and lasting happiness.

"You don't say?" Slade said, his accent smooth as ever. "With all that ocean water close by?"

She unclasped her hands. "Stormy waters. The kind that throw you about and... show you where you went wrong."

Transfixed, he gazed at her.

Time and all the worry of the gala ground to a halt.

"Your flight was good?" he finally said.

She nodded. "Long, but satisfactory. I call it 'forced relaxation.'"

The journey back here had given her time to think, nap, eat and read. At the end, she'd pressed her forehead against the window and looked down at the Sydney Opera House. Rising against a field of blue, its arched roofs reminded her of wind-puffed sails. White and beautiful, they withstood everything the elements dished out. Invincible, with dignity.

As she'd snapped a mental picture, the inevitable question popped up again. If Slade loved her and she loved him, why not let the chips fall again as they may? From this point on she should be strong, like those sails.

Now standing here, with G & A business pushing at her back and longing for Slade to pull her to him, more questions charged through her. She looked up into his eyes.

Along the way it occurred to her that love was a two-way street. For a while Slade was headed in one direction and she in the other. Yet this street also had a beginning and an end. Where they stood now on it Anne didn't know. When she'd left him, she was sure they'd reached the end. Then, after she'd read his note, she saw only the beginning.

Slade's eyes, immersed in hers, weren't saying either way. At the moment, making small talk apparently satisfied him. So she would have to wait it out to know whether he still wanted her, or not. But he was worth the wait.

Removing his hat, Slade took in the spectacular whole of Anne. He already felt better. Being with her brought him stimulation and peace. If she only understood her effect on him.

Their time apart served a good purpose, he'd decided as he drove into Sydney. It gave him time to be sure. He liked her determination and natural beauty. But more so, she held the power to seduce his heart, soul and mind. He'd missed the surrender.

Tonight, though, was *her* night. In every sense. Each move she made in the midnight-blue cocktail dress fueled his need to hold her. Her eyes drew him in. Unwavering, she sent him the most powerful of feminine signals—a simple, sweet smile.

Slade twitched his mouth. Why play games and pretend he didn't need her? Hell, he loved her—for who she was, and for who she wasn't. Weeks without Annie had nearly done him in. Night and day blended into one long void. He'd resumed work on the wool scouring plant, but that didn't fulfill him.

Seeing her now eased everything back into place. He wanted to make the Red Gum a success for reasons other than watching numbers grow in a tally log. He wanted it for her and some little McGregors. That is, if she'd have him and wanted it that way. She loved her work, but he'd be willing to settle for one little part of what was left over. What she gave him was that rich.

"Annie?" He stepped forward and breathed deeply. Boronia fragrance wreathed her. She speared him with hope and fire.

Couldn't she feel it?

"Yes, Slade?" Anne never wanted to forget the way he was looking at her right now, enamored and accepting.

"You've cut your hair," he said, still waiting for a signal. He wasn't going to embarrass her in the middle of important business. If she wanted more from him, she'd have to show it was okay for him to give it.

Anne lifted her fingers to the wavy tips.

"You like it?"

He nodded and the wholesome maleness of him rendered Anne weak-kneed. His next step brought him close enough to encircle her with his arms. She longed for his kiss.

Slade ran his hand down his jaw. No, he wasn't going to cover her mouth with the tornadic kiss he'd stored up. She needed to pay attention to what she'd come here to finish. But hadn't her invitation for him to attend this counted for something? If only he'd caught her call instead of his grandfather. Hearing her voice would have helped a heap.

Anne's resolve dwindled by the second. The chemistry they once shared still cooked. Slade was the finest specimen of a "personal mess" she'd ever seen, or would want to. It pleased her beyond belief as he reached over and touched her cheek.

Slade gave out a faint whistle. This was as far as he was going to go. He swore he wasn't going to push her to the fancy-papered wall and rekindle what he was sure he'd lost. His heart rattled his breastbone, but logic towed him back in line.

Which worked fine until she slid her fingers along his cheek. Then his unselfish intentions skidded into the billabong.

"I'm going to kiss you," he stated. Lowering his head, he centered his lips on hers. Tasting them again rumbled from his head through his groin and down to his toes.

He absorbed her tremble as she opened her eyes.

"Slade, I—"

"Hush." The softness and yearning in them brought out his best intentions. Yet, he was unsure she'd have him. It was true that they'd hailed from different lives and places, but something else was also true. She'd confounded him and loved him with such sweet intensity it neutralized any doubt that loving her would be a mistake. He let loose what was locked up in his heart.

"I've missed you," he said, stroking her face with his thumbs. "Annie... I love you."

Her eyes widened and she leaned into him.

There, he'd done it. He finally said what he'd realized long ago, but was never able to say until now. He repeated his words. "I love you."

Anne returned his kiss with joy. After she finished, she rushed to say, "I never should've left you. I was angry, hurt, and confused. I needed to understand."

He released her. "We both did."

"The boronia you put in the mailbox was the icing on the cake," she murmured. "You wouldn't have sent the flowers if you weren't over the tragedy. I had to know it'd just be us. Only you and me." He tried to pull her to him again. "Wait, let me finish. I've never been in love like this, or ever could be again. Nothing else matters. And your note made all the difference. It was beautiful."

Slade raised an eyebrow and opened his mouth, then closed it again as Jack burst out into the corridor. Slade stepped back a few respectable paces. "Damn, I wanted—"

"Wanted to what?"

"Hey, Anne," Jack called as guests began to follow him across the hall. "Hi, Slade. See you made it."

Slade smiled and waved back.

Jack gestured for her to join him. "It's time."

She flashed him a one-minute signal.

Slade resolved not to waste it. Quickly, he pulled Anne past the powder room and made a hard right near the elevator. In another swift move he yanked open a door marked CLEANING. He led her into the small closet and shut the door.

Dark covered them. In it Slade pulled her to him and asked, "When?"

Anne's heart beat wildly. "When what?"

The excitement in her voice turned him on so much he wanted to marry and seduce her right here. He'd been too long without her. Nights at Casey's Pub amounted to hell.

It was there that he got the idea to have Rudy send her the mailbox after he'd knocked the bloody thing off its post. He'd wanted to say to her, "See, what I was doing the morning you left? Something for *us*." She didn't want to listen, so he was going to show her.

But damned if he could stay angry at her, especially with their bodies pressed together exchanging heartbeats.

"When can I kidnap you?"

The heat of his lips guided her. His scent triggered memories and signaled the promise of a next time, and a next, for years to come.

"Midnight," she said. "Then I'm yours for a whole week."

His breath raced along her neck as he slid his hands down onto her bottom and pulled her tighter against him.

"Don't count on it for just a week." His voice turned husky. "I want it to be forever. We'll go back to Westport if that's what you need. All I want out of the deal is you. Marry me, Annie."

She felt his hand slide between them into his jeans pocket and out again. He fumbled for her left hand and slid a ring on her finger. It felt heavy and warm and for all she cared it could have been the key ring from his old beat-up Triumph.

Ecstatic, she kissed him with her first answer.

"Say it, Annie," he urged. "Tell me."

She could, because she was sure of it now. They were ready to go on a lifelong walkabout—as Slade and Anne McGregor— just like he'd painted on the mailbox.

"Yes, I'll marry you. Only take me home to the Red Gum. That's where we met and where we belong."

He kissed her again, parting her lips. "You sure?"

"Hmm hmm. Give me a little while, though. This won't be like moving up the road to Boston."

A mass of voices erupted from beyond the door. Anne slipped from Slade's hold. Her other life called. The one she wasn't at all sure about what she'd do with.

"We have to go."

She found the doorknob and turned it. A wedge of light cracked the dark and she gasped at the sparkling diamond and sapphire ring on her finger. The pride on Slade's face outshone the heirloom.

"I'll do better when we can shop together."

"There is no better. It's lovely."

Moments later, she led Slade to their seats. As Jack finished up his introductory remarks, the lights dimmed and the logo for Greene & Associates flashed up on the bank of floor-to-ceiling screens.

Perfect. Five beats passed and the soundtrack kicked in as the debut of the ten-part series took flight.

"Australia. Down Under. Where the sun kisses your dreams. And you can take your SunMate everywhere."

Anne sighed. With Slade at her side, some of the stress she'd built up dissolved. Their arms touched and he shifted a couple of times in his seat. Something else was on his mind. What, she couldn't imagine. The worst had passed for him. Now she wore the worry cap. The outcome of this preview was still pending, and the crowd had grown critically quiet.

Slade spilled into her ear, "I didn't send you a note."

Anne scrutinized his face. His expression proved he wasn't joking. "I sent you flowers, not words."

She half rose from the chair before Slade caught her with a restraining hand. Confusion bolted through her. She opened her mouth to speak, but what would she say?

Slade told her in person he loved her and now she was wearing his engagement ring. Even so, her curiosity churned. If Slade hadn't written the love note and signed his initial to it, who had?

Instantly, their eyes and minds locked on the same wavelength. The telepathic answer bounced from her to him and him to her. In tandem, they leaned forward enough to catch the culprit across the aisle from them. Jim McGregor.

The wise old rancher wore a satisfied smile and kept his eyes straight ahead. She wanted to believe it was because he enjoyed seeing the series that featured a place he loved as much as Slade. But intuition told her that wasn't the only reason. He was hiding out in the middle of the crowd.

"He's roo meat," Slade growled.

"Maybe, but he's still great and we owe him."

Slade peeled his stony stare away from his grandfather and gazed at her. Immediately, his eyes embraced her with love.

"You're right. Again."

Slade wrapped his hand around hers. He settled back and when he first saw himself up on the big screen he let out a surprised hoot. No matter. By then the crowd had already cheered twice.

Jack threw her a thumbs-up and Slade gave her a congratulatory kiss. Hours later as she and Slade headed to her room, Anne mused over how things had turned out. Completely and absolutely... bonzer.

~ * ~

On a bracing, rainy August night, Slade walked into the kitchen of the Red Gum. His hair damp from showering, he poured two teas and set them down on the table.

"What's all that in the mail? Looks important."

Anne slit open the large Global Priority Mail envelope from Greene & Associates. Today being Wednesday she'd picked it up from the box on her way back to the house from her bi-weekly trip to Tamworth.

"A check, a very nice plaque, and a photograph of Tom accepting our award in New York for the series."

Proud of her, Slade nipped at her right earlobe.

"Congratulations, Mrs. McGregor."

She loved it when he did that.

"Thank you for letting me use your canyon."

"Our canyon," he corrected.

Anne ran her fingers over the engraving and fell silent. He straightened and laid his hand on her shoulder. "Maybe you should've gone to New York for the awards."

She shrugged. It was difficult to explain how she felt at the moment, although his quietness was asking for her to do that. A minute or so passed and he asked, "Are you sure you're okay with this?"

She knew what *this* meant.

"Slade, you know I'm happy here with you."

He read her face. "In case you change your mind, just say the word and I'll buy a place in New England for us." She laid her hand on top of his. "There's no reason now with mother gone. Her heart stopped. I should've been in the room. I needed to go, it'd been a long day." She bit her bottom lip.

"You did the best you could," he told her. "So did the doctors."

"Thank you. I love you so much it hurts."

He kissed the top of her head and turned to his tea.

Anne opened another letter. "Well, look at this. It's from one of my college sorority sisters. She's coming here next year to visit the Blue Mountains. She'd like to come see us and our digs."

He set down his mug. "We certainly have room. I know a couple of forestry blokes who'd help her see some back country."

"Good." She finished reading. "She wants to know how I'm doing."

Slade's eyes flickered. "What're you going to tell her?"

Growing more relaxed, she sipped and leaned back. "About how I'm still adjusting to being here, and some days are easier than others. That I'm learning the wool business and more of my way around. Also, with starting up a new field office, there's much to do. And who would have ever dreamed Greene and Associates would offer a limited partnership for me to set up shop in Tamworth?"

"I would. He knows what he has in you."

"Thanks, but more likely he smells untapped business."

Slade eased his fingers under her bathrobe and cupped her breast. "You done with the mail? We can talk some more in bed."

She dropped the letter as he leaned over her shoulder and tugged on her earlobe with his lips. She scooted half way around in the chair. Looking up at him, she tugged on the cord of his robe. "Good, because I never quite know what to expect next."

He pulled her up onto her feet and let his mouth open up its passion on her lips. "It's all a cycle, love. Lambing season's coming up soon."

Anne clutched the pockets of his robe and held onto them. Trying to steady her heart, she knew exactly where he was headed with this. His robe slipped open at the waist.

"Really?" she said. "Lambs are so cute."

"They're more than that, Annie. They're next year's promise for the Red Gum."

Seeing the affirmation rise in his eyes, she resumed her visual journey down onto his hard, flat stomach muscles and beyond to the dark cap of hair that partially hid his hardness.

"So will be our children, for us," he vowed, picking her up.

Anne wrapped her arms around his neck and they soon passed by the arch leading into the living room.

"Wait," she said, catching something different about Rudy's painting over the fireplace. Slade slowed, giving her a moment.

The more she'd come to understand Slade and the Red Gum, the more the subjects in Rudy's painting revealed themselves. The last piece of the puzzle fell into place.

"Look at the ewe," she said, pointing. "She has *two* lambs."

"Sure enough. Rudy can sure paint the future, can't he?"

Reaching the bedroom, Slade kicked the door closed behind them, and set her on the edge of the massive four-poster bed. Her robe slipped from her shoulders and he held her face in his hands for a moment.

"I'm one lucky bloke."

"Yeah, you are," she teased, turning over and scrambling to the middle of the bed. He stripped off his robe and dove in. She squealed as he flipped her over and straddled her.

Firelit from the hearth, her husband hovered over her and said, "I'll show you what we can do on a sheep farm on winter nights." Slade untied the ribbon of her robe. "Lie back and enjoy, my true-blue Annie."

Sighing with contentment, Anne melted under his touch as they set free their love that could easily fulfill next year's promise. Because Jim McGregor was right. She and Slade were perfect mates.

Meet Karen Hudgins

Karen Hudgins loves good stories and writes what she likes to read—warm, entertaining books with happy endings. Enrolling in a university continuing education novel writing program about ten years ago started Karen's journey into learning how to create fiction. "But I can now see that I was preparing for this since I was little." She has studied art, business, and obtained a degree in behavioral science. (Disciplines rooted in real life, but also how it *could* be.) The author is a mom and lives in the Midwest with her husband, a newspaper businessman. She enjoys travel, gardening, and the family pets.

Look For These Other Titles

From

Wings ePress, Inc.

Romance Novels
Amaryllis by Tricia McGill
Next Year's Promise by Karen Hudgins
Rachel's Journey by Mary McGuire
Shadows Of The Eclipse by Bonnie Napoli
The Fixer-Uppers by Cynthianna Appel

Coming In December
Baltimore Beauty by Sue Thornton
Flight Of Angels by Marilyn Gardiner
Phoenix Farm by Olga V. Button
Rory's Prince Charming by Patricia S. Otto
Scent Of Diamonds by Dorothy Skarles
Sex, Lies And Rodeo Games by Diana Kirk
The Prince In The Flower Bed by Roberta Olsen Major
Through All Time by Judi Phillips

General Fiction Novels
Return To Madrona by Marilyn Nichols Kapp

Be sure to visit us at http://www.wing-press.com
for a complete listing of our available and upcoming titles.

Anne Kingsley, determined to boost her advertising career, promised herself never again to mix business and pleasure. Easy--until she arrives on assignment in Australia and confronts the handsome sheep station owner, who mysteriously blocks her plans and tests her pledge. What widower Slade McGregor wants --routine days at the Red Gum--collides with what he needs, when the film job of his beguiling Yankee "guest" leads Slade back to Rainbow Canyon where he must face tragic truths. Her kisses sear his soul and he soon finds himself wanting her to stay forever Down Under. But will she?

Next Year's Promise
Karen Hudgins

4 1/2 stars from Affaire de Coeur. "...incomplete romance this romance, while virtual characters deal with true problems. The beauty of the Aussie Outback.. The symbolism of the dry, fiery bush and the seductive dialect tempt the reader to travel deep into this well researched romance."

Wings Press, Inc.

ISBN 1-59088-985-1

9 781590 889855